Inspector Maigret
Omnibus 1

GEORGES SIMENON

Inspector Maigret Omnibus 1

PENGUIN BOOKS

PENGUIN CLASSICS

Published by the Penguin Group
Penguin Books Ltd, 80 Strand, London WC2R 0RL, England
Penguin Group (USA) Inc., 375 Hudson Street, New York, New York 10014, USA
Penguin Group (Canada), 90 Eglinton Avenue East, Suite 700, Toronto, Ontario, Canada M4P 2Y3
(a division of Pearson Penguin Canada Inc.)
Penguin Ireland, 25 St Stephen's Green, Dublin 2, Ireland (a division of Penguin Books Ltd)
Penguin Group (Australia), 707 Collins Street, Melbourne, Victoria 3008, Australia
(a division of Pearson Australia Group Pty Ltd)
Penguin Books India Pvt Ltd, 11 Community Centre, Panchsheel Park, New Delhi – 110 017, India
Penguin Group (NZ), 67 Apollo Drive, Rosedale, Auckland 0632, New Zealand
(a division of Pearson New Zealand Ltd)
Penguin Books (South Africa) (Pty) Ltd, Block D, Rosebank Office Park, 181 Jan Smuts Avenue,
Parktown North, Gauteng 2193, South Africa

Penguin Books Ltd, Registered Offices: 80 Strand, London WC2R 0RL, England

www.penguin.com

Pietr the Latvian first published, in serial, as *Pietr-le-Letton*, in *Ric et Rac* 1930
This translation first published in Penguin Classics 2013
The Carter of La Providence first published as *Le Charretier de La Providence* by Fayard 1931
This translation first published in Penguin Classics 2014
The Grand Banks Café first published as *Au Rendez-Vous des Terre-Neuvas* by Fayard 1931
This translation first published in Penguin Classics 2014
The Hanged Man of Saint-Pholien first published as *Le Pendue de Saint-Pholien* by Fayard 1931
This translation first published in Penguin Classics 2014
006

Set in 13/15.5 pt Dante MT Std
Typeset by Palimpsest Book Production Ltd, Falkirk, Stirlingshire

Printed and bound in Great Britain by Clays Ltd, Elcograf S.p.A.

A CIP catalogue record for this book is available from the British Library

ISBN: 978–0–141–39688–0

Contents

Pietr the Latvian

Translated by DAVID BELLOS

PIETR-LE-LETTON

ROMAN
PAR
GEORGES SIMENON

A. FAYARD & Cie - PARIS

PRIX : 6 Fr.

1. *Apparent age 32, height 169 . . .*

ICPC to PJ Paris Xvzust Krakow vimontra m ghks triv psot uv Pietr-le-Letton Bremen vs tyz btolem.

Detective Chief Inspector Maigret of the Flying Squad raised his eyes. It seemed to him that the cast-iron stove in the middle of his office with its chimney tube rising to the ceiling wasn't roaring properly. He pushed the telegram away, rose ponderously to his feet, adjusted the flue and thrust three shovels of coal into the firebox.

Then he stood with his back to the stove, filled his pipe and adjusted his stud collar, which was irritating his neck even though it wasn't set very high.

He glanced at his watch. Four p.m. His jacket was hanging on a hook on the back of the door.

Slowly he returned to his desk, mouthing a translation as he went:

> International Criminal Police Commission to Police Judiciaire in Paris: Krakow police report sighting Pietr the Latvian en route to Bremen.

The International Criminal Police Commission, or ICPC, is based in Vienna. Broadly speaking, it oversees the struggle against organized crime in Europe, with a particular responsibility for liaison between the various national police forces on the Continent.

Maigret pulled up another telegram that was similarly written in IPC, the secret international police code used for communication between all the world's police forces. He translated at sight:

Polizei-Präsidium Bremen to PJ Paris: Pietr the Latvian reported en route Amsterdam and Brussels.

Another telegram from the Nederlandsche Centrale in Zake Internationale Misdadigers, the Dutch police HQ, reported:

At 11 a.m. Pietr the Latvian boarded Étoile du Nord, compartment G. 263, car 5, destination Paris.

The final message in IPC had been sent from Brussels and said:

Confirm Pietr the Latvian on board Étoile du Nord via Brussels 2 a.m. in compartment reported by Amsterdam.

Behind Maigret's desk there was a huge map pinned to the wall. The inspector was a broad and heavy man. He stood staring at the map with his hands in his pockets and his pipe sticking out the side of his mouth.

His eyes travelled from the dot representing Krakow to the other dot showing the port of Bremen and from there to Amsterdam and Paris.

He checked the time once again. Four-twenty. The Étoile du Nord should now be hurtling along at sixty miles an hour between Saint-Quentin and Compiègne.

It wouldn't stop at the border. It wouldn't be slowing down.

In car 5, compartment G. 263, Pietr the Latvian was presumably spending his time reading or looking at the scenery.

Maigret went over to a door that opened onto a closet, washed his hands in an enamel basin, ran a comb through thick dark-brown hair flecked with only a few silver strands around the temple, and did his best to straighten out his tie – he'd never learned how to do a proper knot.

It was November and it was getting dark. Through the window he could see a branch of the Seine, Place Saint-Michel, and a floating wash-house, all in a blue shroud speckled by gas lamps lighting up one after the other.

He opened a drawer and glanced at a dispatch from the International Identification Bureau in Copenhagen.

> Paris PJ Pietr-le-Letton 32 169 01512 0224 0255 02732 03116 03233 03243 03325 03415 03522 04115 04144 04147 05221 . . .

This time he made an effort to speak the translation aloud and even went over it several times, like a schoolchild reciting a lesson:

> Description Pietr the Latvian: apparent age 32 years, height 169 cm, sinus top straight line, bottom flat, extension large max, special feature septum not visible, ear unmarked rim, lobe large, max cross and dimension small max, protuberant antitragus, vex edge lower fold, edge shape straight line edge feature separate lines, orthognathous upper, long face, biconcave, eyebrows thin fair light, lower lip jutting max thick lower droop, light.

This 'word-picture' of Pietr was as clear as a photograph to Inspector Maigret. The principal features were the first to emerge: the man was short, slim, young and fair-haired, with sparse blond eyebrows, greenish eyes and a long neck.

Maigret now also knew the shape of his ear in the minutest detail. This would enable him to make a positive identification in a milling crowd even if the suspect was in disguise.

He took his jacket off the hook and slipped his arms into it, then put on a heavy black overcoat and a bowler hat.

One last glance at the stove, which seemed on the verge of exploding.

At the end of the corridor, on the stair landing that was used as a waiting room, he reminded Jean:

'You won't forget to keep my stove going, will you?'

The wind swirling up the stairs took him by surprise, and he had to shelter from the draught in a corner to get his pipe to light.

Wind and rain blew in squalls over the platforms of Gare du Nord despite the monumental glass canopy overhead. Several panes had blown out and lay in shards on the railway tracks. The lighting wasn't working properly. People huddled up inside their clothes.

Outside one of the ticket windows an alarming travel notice had been posted:

Channel forecast: gale-force winds.

One woman, whose son was to catch the Folkestone boat train, looked upset; her eyes were red. She kept on telling the boy what he should do, right up to the last minute. In his embarrassment he had no choice but to promise not to go out on deck.

Maigret stood near platform 11 where people were awaiting the arrival of the Étoile du Nord. All the leading hotels, as well as Thomas Cook, had their agents standing by.

He stood still. Other people were agitated. A young woman clad in mink yet wearing only sheer silk stockings walked up and down, stamping her heels.

He just stood there: a hulk of a man, with shoulders so broad as to cast a wide shadow. When people bumped into him he stayed as firm as a brick wall.

The yellow speck of the train's headlamp appeared in the distance. Then came the usual hubbub, with porters shouting and passengers tramping and jostling their way towards the station exit.

A couple of hundred passengers paraded past Maigret before he picked out in the crowd a short man wearing a broad-checked green travelling cape of a distinctly Nordic cut and colour.

The man wasn't in a hurry. He had three porters behind him.

Bowing and scraping, an agent from one of the grand hotels on the Champs-Élysées cleared the way in front of him.

Apparent age 32, height 169 . . . sinus top . . .

Maigret kept calm. He looked hard at the man's ear. That was all he needed.

The man in green passed close by. One of his porters bumped Maigret with one of the suitcases.

At exactly the same moment a railway employee began to run, shouting out something to his colleague standing at the station end of the platform, next to the barrier.

The chain was drawn closed. Protests erupted.

The man in the travelling cape was already out of the station.

Maigret puffed away at his pipe in quick short bursts. He went up to the official who had closed the barrier.

'Police! What's happened?'

'A crime . . . They've just found . . .'

'Carriage 5? . . .'

'I think so . . .'

The station went about its regular business; only platform 11 looked abnormal. There were fifty passengers still waiting to get out, but their path was blocked. They were getting excited.

'Let them go . . .' Maigret said.

'But . . .'

'Let them go . . .'

He watched the last cluster move away. The station loudspeaker announced the departure of a local train. Somebody was running somewhere. Beside one of the carriages of the Étoile du Nord there was a small group waiting for something. Three of them, in railway company livery.

The stationmaster got to them first. He was a large man and had a worried look on his face. Then a hospital stretcher was wheeled through the main hall, past clumps of people who looked at it uneasily, especially those about to depart.

Maigret walked up the side of the train with his usual heavy tread, smoking as he went. Carriage 1, carriage 2 . . . He came to carriage 5.

That's where the group was standing at the door. The stretcher came to a halt. The stationmaster tried to listen to the three men, who were all speaking at the same time.

'Police! Where is he?'

Maigret's presence provided obvious relief. He propelled his placid mass towards the centre of the frantic group. The other men instantly became his satellites.

'In the toilet . . .'

Maigret hauled himself up onto the train and saw that the toilet door on his right was open. On the floor, in a heap, was a body, bent double in a strangely contorted posture.

The conductor was giving orders from the platform.

'Shunt the carriage to the yard . . . Hang on! . . . Track 62 . . . Let the railway police know . . .'

At first he could only see the back of the man's neck. But when he tipped his cap off its oblique angle, he could see the man's left ear. Maigret mumbled to himself: *lobe large, max cross and dimension small max, protuberant antitragus* . . .

There were a few drops of blood on the linoleum. Maigret looked around. The railway staff were standing on the platform or on the running board. The stationmaster was still talking.

So Maigret clenched his pipe between his teeth even harder and turned the man's head over.

If he hadn't seen the traveller in the green cloak leave the station, if he hadn't seen him taken to a car by an interpreter from the Majestic, he could have had doubts.

It was the same physiognomy. The same fair toothbrush moustache under a sharply defined nose. The same sparse blond eyebrows. The same grey-green eyes.

In other words: Pietr the Latvian!

Maigret could hardly turn around in the tiny washroom, where the tap was still running and a jet of steam was seeping from some poorly sealed joint.

He was standing right next to the corpse. He pulled the man's upper body upright and saw on his chest, on his jacket and shirt, the burn-marks made by gunshot from point-blank range.

It was a big blackish stain tinged with the dark red of coagulating blood.

One detail struck the inspector. He happened to notice one of the man's feet. It was twisted on its side, as was the whole body, which must have been squashed into a corner so as to allow the door to close.

The shoe was black and happened to be of a very cheap and common kind. Apparently it had been re-soled. The heel was worn on one side, and a coin-shaped gap had opened up in the middle of the sole.

The local chief of the railway police had now reached the carriage and was calling up from the platform. He was a self-confident man wearing a uniform with epaulettes.

'So what is it, then? Murder? Suicide? Don't touch anything until the law gets here, OK? Be careful! I'm the one who's in charge. OK?'

Maigret had a tough time disentangling his own feet from the dead man's legs to extricate himself from the toilet. With swift, professional movements he patted the man's pockets. Clean as a whistle. Nothing in them at all.

He got out of the carriage, His pipe had gone out, his hat was askew and he had a bloodstain on his cuff.

'Well, if it isn't Maigret! . . . What do you make of it, then?'

'Not much. Go have a look yourself . . .'

'It's suicide, right?'

'If you say so . . . Did you call the prosecutor's office?'

'As soon as I heard . . .'

The loudspeaker crackled with some message or other. A few

people had noticed there was something unusual going on and stood in the distance, watching the empty train and the group of people standing next to the running board of carriage 5.

Maigret strode off without saying a word. He left the station and hailed a cab.

'Hôtel Majestic! . . .'

The storm had got even worse. Gusts swept down the streets and made pedestrians totter about like drunks. A roof tile smashed onto the pavement. Buses, and more buses.

The Champs-Élysées was almost entirely deserted. Drops of rain had begun to fall. The porter at the Majestic dashed out to the taxi with a huge red umbrella.

'Police! . . . Has someone from the Étoile du Nord just checked in?'

That prompted the porter to fold his umbrella.

'Yes, sir, that true.'

'Green cape . . . Fair moustache . . .'

'That right. Sir go reception.'

People were scrambling to shelter from the rain. Maigret got inside the hotel just in time to avoid drops as big as walnuts and cold as ice.

Despite this, the receptionists and interpreters behind the polished wood counter were as elegant and efficient as ever.

'Police . . . A guest in a green cape . . . Small fair mousta—'

'Room 17, sir. His bags are on their way up right now . . .'

2. *Mixing with Millionaires*

Inevitably Maigret was a hostile presence in the Majestic. He constituted a kind of foreign body that the hotel's atmosphere could not assimilate.

Not that he looked like a cartoon policeman. He didn't have a moustache and he didn't wear heavy boots. His clothes were well cut and made of fairly light worsted. He shaved every day and looked after his hands.

But his frame was proletarian. He was a big, bony man. Iron muscles shaped his jacket sleeves and quickly wore through new trousers.

He had a way of imposing himself just by standing there. His assertive presence had often irked many of his own colleagues.

It was something more than self-confidence but less than pride. He would turn up and stand like a rock with his feet wide apart. On that rock all would shatter, whether Maigret moved forward or stayed exactly where he was.

His pipe was nailed to his jawbone. He wasn't going to remove it just because he was in the lobby of the Majestic.

Could it be that Maigret simply preferred to be common and self-assertive?

You just couldn't miss the man wearing a big black velvet-collared overcoat in that brightly lit lobby, where excitable society ladies scattered trails of perfume, tinkling laughter and loud whispers amidst the unctuous compliments of impeccable flunkeys.

He paid no attention. He wasn't part of the flow. He was impervious to the sound of jazz floating up from the dance-floor in the basement.

The inspector started to go up one of the stairs. A liftboy called out and asked if he wanted to take the lift, but Maigret didn't even turn round.

At the first landing someone asked him:

'Are you looking for . . . ?'

It was as if the sound waves hadn't reached him. He glanced at the corridors with their red carpets stretching out so far that they almost made you sick. He went on up.

On the second floor he read the numbers on the bronze plaques. The door of no. 17 was open. Valets with striped waistcoats were bringing in the luggage.

The traveller had taken off his cloak and looked very slender and elegant in his pinstripe suit. He was smoking a papirosa and giving instructions at the same time.

No. 17 wasn't a room, but a whole suite: lounge, study, bedroom and bathroom. The doors opened onto two intersecting corridors, and at the corner, like a bench placed by a crossroads, there was a huge, curved sofa.

That's where Maigret sat himself down, right opposite the open door. He stretched out his legs and unbuttoned his overcoat.

Pietr saw him and, showing neither surprise nor disquiet, he carried on giving instructions. When the valets had finished placing his trunks and cases on stands, he came to the door, held it open for an instant to inspect the detective, then closed it himself.

Maigret sat there for as long as it took to smoke three pipes, and to dismiss two room-service waiters and one chambermaid who came up to inquire what he was waiting for.

On the stroke of eight Pietr the Latvian came out of his room, looking even slimmer and smarter than before, in a classically tailored dinner jacket that must have come from Savile Row.

He was hatless. His short, ash-blond hair was already thinning. His hairline was set far back and his forehead not especially high; you could glimpse a streak of pink scalp along the parting.

He had long, pale hands. On the fourth finger of his left hand he wore a chunky platinum signet ring set with a yellow diamond.

He was smoking again – another papirosa. He walked right up to Maigret, stopped for a moment, looked at him as if he felt like saying something, then walked on towards the lift as if lost in thought.

Ten minutes later he took his seat in the dining room at the table of Mr and Mrs Mortimer-Levingston. The latter was the centre of attention: she had pearls worth a cool million on her neck.

The previous day her husband had come to the rescue of one of France's biggest automobile manufacturers, with the result that he was now its majority shareholder.

The three of them were chatting merrily. Pietr talked a lot, but discreetly, with his head leaning forwards. He was completely at ease, natural and casual, despite being able to see the detective's dark outline through the glazed partition.

Inspector Maigret asked reception to show him the guest list. He wasn't surprised to see that Pietr had signed in under the name of Oswald Oppenheim, ship-owner, from Bremen.

It was a foregone conclusion that he had a genuine passport and full identity papers in that name, just as he no doubt did in several others.

It was equally obvious that he'd met the Mortimer-Levingstons previously, whether in Berlin, Warsaw, London or New York.

Was the sole purpose of his presence in Paris to rendezvous with them and to get away with another one of the colossal scams that were his trademark?

Maigret had the Latvian's file card in his jacket pocket. It said:

> Extremely clever and dangerous. Nationality uncertain, from Baltic area. Reckoned to be either Latvian or Estonian. Fluent in Russian, French, English and German. High level of education. Thought to be capo of major international ring mainly involved in fraud. The ring has been spotted successively in Paris, Amsterdam (Van Heuvel case), Berne (United Shipowners affair), Warsaw (Lipmann

case) and in various other European cities where identification of its methods and procedures was less clear.

Pietr the Latvian's associates seem to be mainly British and American. One who has been seen most often with him and who was identified when he presented a forged cheque for cash at the Federal Bank in Berne was killed during arrest. His alias was Major Howard of the American Legion, but it has been established that he was actually a former New York bootlegger known in the USA as Fat Fred.

Pietr the Latvian has been arrested twice. First, in Wiesbaden, for swindling a Munich trader out of half a million marks; second, in Madrid, for a similar offence involving a leading figure at the Spanish royal court.

On both occasions he used the same ploy. He met his victims and presumably told them that the stolen sums were safely hidden and that having him arrested would not reveal where they were. Both times the complaint was withdrawn, and the plaintiffs were probably paid off.

Since then has never been caught red-handed.

Is probably in cahoots with the Maronnetti gang (counterfeit money and forged documents) and the Cologne gang (the 'wall-busters').

There was another rumour doing the rounds of European police departments: Pietr, as the ring-leader and money-launderer of one or more gangs, was said to be sitting on several million that had been split up under different names in different banks and even invested in legitimate industries.

The man smiled subtly at the story Mrs Mortimer-Levingston was telling, while with his ivory hand he plucked luscious grapes from the bunch on his plate.

'Excuse me, sir. Could I please have a word with you?'

Maigret was speaking to Mortimer-Levingston in the lobby of

the Majestic after Pietr and Mortimer's wife had both gone back up to their rooms.

Mortimer didn't have the athletic look of a Yank. He was more of the Mediterranean type.

He was tall and thin. His very small head was topped with black hair parted down the middle.

He looked permanently tired. His eyelids were weary and blue. In any case he led an exhausting life, somehow managing to turn up in Deauville, Miami, Venice, Paris, Cannes and Berlin before getting back to his yacht and then dashing off to do a deal in some European capital or to referee a major boxing match in New York or California.

He looked Maigret up and down in lordly fashion.

'And you are . . . ?'

'Detective Chief Inspector Maigret of the Flying Squad . . .'

Mortimer barely frowned and stood there leaning forwards as if he had decided to grant just one second of his time.

'Are you aware you have just dined with Pietr the Latvian?'

'Is that all you have to say?'

Maigret didn't budge an inch. It was pretty much what he'd expected.

He put his pipe back in his mouth – he'd allowed himself to remove it in order to speak to the millionaire – and muttered:

'That's all.'

He looked pleased with himself. Levingston moved off icily and got into the lift.

It was just after 9.30. The symphony orchestra that had been playing during dinner yielded the stage to a jazz band. People were coming in from outside.

Maigret hadn't eaten. He was standing calmly and patiently in the middle of the lobby. The manager repeatedly gave him worried and disapproving looks from a distance. Even the lowliest members of staff scowled as they passed by, when they didn't manage to jostle him.

The Majestic could not stomach him. Maigret persisted in being a big black unmoving stain amidst the gilding, the chandeliers, the comings and goings of silk evening gowns, fur coats and perfumed, sparkling silhouettes.

Mrs Levingston was the first to come back down in the lift. She had changed, and now wore a lamé cape lined with ermine that left her shoulders bare.

She seemed astonished not to find anyone waiting for her and began to walk up and down, drumming the floor with her gold-lacquered high heels.

She suddenly stopped at the polished wooden counter where the receptionists and interpreters stood and said a few words. One of the staff pushed a red button and picked up a handset.

He looked surprised and called a bellboy, who rushed to the lift.

Mrs Mortimer-Levingston was visibly anxious. Through the glass door you could see the sleek shape of an American-made limousine standing at the kerb.

The bellboy reappeared, spoke to the member of staff, who in his turn said something to Mrs Mortimer. She protested. She must have been saying:

'But that's impossible!'

Maigret then went up the staircase, stopped outside suite 17, knocked on the door. As he'd expected after the circus he'd just watched, there was no answer.

He opened the door and found the lounge deserted. Pietr's dinner jacket was lying casually on the bed in the bedroom. One trunk was open. A pair of patent-leather shoes had been left at opposite ends of the carpet.

The manager came in and grunted:

'You're already here, are you?'

'So? . . . Vanished, has he? Levingston as well! Is that right?'

'Now there's no need to go overboard. Neither of them is in his room, but we'll probably find them somewhere else in the hotel.'

'How many exits are there?'

'Three. The main entrance on the Champs-Élysées . . . Then there's the entrance in the covered mall, and the service entrance on Rue de Ponthieu . . .'

'Is there a security guard? Call him . . .'

The telephone worked. The manager was in a temper. He took it out on an operator who couldn't understand him. He kept his gaze fixed on Maigret, and it was not kind.

'What does all this mean?' he asked as he waited for the guard to come up from the glass-walled box where he was on duty beside the service entrance.

'Nothing, or almost, as you said . . .'

'I hope there's not been a . . . a . . .'

The word *crime*, dreaded like the plague by hoteliers the world over from the humblest lodging-house landlord to the manager of a luxury resort, just would not pass his lips.

'We'll find out.'

Mrs Mortimer-Levingston appeared.

'Well? . . .' she inquired.

The manager bowed and muttered something. A figure appeared at the far end of the corridor – an old man with a straggly beard and ill-cut clothes at odds with the luxurious appearance of the hotel. He was obviously meant to stay in the back, otherwise he too would have been given a fine uniform and been sent to the barber every day.

'Did you see anyone go out?'

'When?'

'In the last few minutes . . .'

'A guy from the kitchen, I think . . . I wasn't paying attention . . . A guy with a cap . . .'

'Was he short? Fair?' Maigret interrupted.

'Yes . . . I think so . . . I wasn't watching . . . He was quick . . .'

'Nobody else?'

'I dunno . . . I went round the corner to buy the paper . . .'

Mrs Mortimer-Levingston began to lose her temper.

'Well now! Is that how you conduct a manhunt?' she said to Maigret. 'I've just been told you're a policeman . . . My husband might have been killed . . . What are you waiting for?'

The look that then fell upon her was Maigret through and through! Completely calm! Completely unruffled! It was as if he'd just noticed the buzzing of a bee. As if what he had before him was something quite ordinary.

She was not accustomed to being looked at in that way. She bit her lip, blushed crimson beneath her make-up and stamped her heel with impatience.

He was still staring at her.

Because he was pushing her to the limit, or perhaps because she didn't know what else to do, Mrs Mortimer-Levingston threw a fit.

3. The Strand of Hair

It was nearly midnight when Maigret got back to his office on Quai des Orfèvres. The storm was at its peak. The trees on the riverbank were rattling back and forth and the wash-house barge was tossing about in the waves.

The building was almost empty. At least Jean was still at his post in the lobby at the entrance to a corridor of empty offices.

Voices could be heard coming from the duty room. Then, further down, there was light streaking out from beneath a door – a detective or an inspector working on some case. One of the official cars in the courtyard below was running its engine.

'Is Torrence back?' Maigret asked.

'He's just come in.'

'My stove?'

'It was so hot in your office I had to open the window. There was condensation running down your wall!'

'Get me some beers and sandwiches. None of that soft white bread, mind you.'

He pushed a door and called out:

'Torrence!'

Detective Torrence followed his chief to his office. Before he'd left Gare du Nord Maigret had called Torrence on the telephone and told him to keep going on the case on his own.

Inspector Maigret was forty-five and his junior was barely thirty years old. Even so, there was something solid and bulky about Torrence that made him an almost full-scale model of his boss.

They'd conducted many cases together without ever saying an unnecessary word.

Maigret took off his overcoat and his jacket and loosened his tie. He stood for a while with his back to the stove to let the heat seep in. Then he asked:

'So?'

'The Prosecution Service had an emergency meeting. Forensics took photographs but couldn't find any fingerprints – except the dead man's, of course. They don't match any we have on record.'

'If I remember correctly, don't they have a file on our friend from the Baltic?'

'Just the 'word-picture'. No fingerprints, no anthropometric data.'

'So we can't be sure that the dead man is someone other than Pietr.'

'But there's no guarantee that it *is* him, either!'

Maigret had taken out his pipe and a pouch that had only a sprinkling of brown dust left in it. Mechanically Torrence handed him an opened packet of shag.

There was a pause. Tobacco crackled in Maigret's pipe. Then came a sound of footsteps and tinkling glassware on the other side of the door, which Torrence opened.

The waiter from Brasserie Dauphine brought in six glasses of beer and four thick-stuffed sandwiches on a tray, which he laid on the table.

'Are you sure that'll be enough?' he asked, seeing that Maigret had company.

'That's fine.'

Maigret started drinking and munching without putting his pipe out, though he did push a glass over to his assistant's side of the desk.

'Well?'

'I questioned all the staff who were on the train. There's definite proof that someone was on board without a ticket. Could be the victim, could be the culprit! We're assuming he got on at Brussels, on the track side. It's easier to hide in a Pullman car than in any other because each carriage has a lot of luggage space. Pietr had tea in the restaurant car between Brussels and the French border and spent his time flicking through a pile of French and English newspapers, including the financial dailies. He went to the toilet between Maubeuge and Saint-Quentin. The head waiter remembers that because as he went past him Pietr said, "Take a whisky to my seat".'

'And he went back to his seat later on?'

'Fifteen minutes later, he was back at his regular place with a whisky in front of him. But the head waiter didn't see Pietr again, since he didn't go back by way of the restaurant car.'

'Did anybody try to use the toilet after him?'

'Sure! A lady traveller tried to get in, but the lock was jammed. It wasn't until the train got to Paris that a staff member managed to force it open. The mechanism had been clogged with iron filings.'

'Up to that point, had anybody set eyes on the second Pietr?'

'Absolutely not. He would have been very noticeable. He was wearing shoddy clothes and would have stood out a mile on a de luxe express.'

'What about the bullet?'

'Shot at point-blank range. Automatic revolver, 6 mm. The shot caused such burning of the skin that according to the doctor the victim would have died from the heat shock alone.'

'Any sign of a struggle?'

'None at all. The pockets were empty.'

'I know that . . .'

'Sorry! However, I did find this in a small button-down pocket on the inside of his waistcoat.'

Torrence then extracted from his wallet a folded piece of transparent paper inside which you could see a strand of brown hair.

'Hand it over . . .'

Maigret hadn't stopped eating and drinking all the while.

'A woman's hair? Or a child's?'

'Forensics says it's a woman's hair. I left him a few strands that he's promised to examine closely.'

'And the autopsy?'

'All done by 10 a.m. Probable age: thirty-two. Height 1 m 68 cm. No hereditary abnormalities. One of his kidneys was in poor shape, which could mean he was a boozer. Stomach contained tea and other digested matter that couldn't be identified straight away. They'll work on the analysis tomorrow. Now the examination is over the body is being kept on ice at the morgue.'

Maigret wiped his mouth, stationed himself in his favourite position in front of the stove and held out his hand, which Torrence mechanically supplied with a packet of tobacco.

'For my part,' Maigret said eventually, 'I saw Pietr, or whoever has taken over his role, check in at Hôtel Majestic and have dinner with the Mortimer-Levingstons, which seems to have been arranged in advance.'

'The millionaires?'

'Yes, that's right. After the meal, Pietr went back to his suite. I warned the American. Mortimer then went to his room. They were obviously planning to go out as a threesome, since Mrs Mortimer came down straight after, in full evening gear. Ten minutes later, both men had vanished. Our Latvian had switched his evening wear for less swanky clothes. He'd put on a cap, and the guard just assumed he was a kitchen worker. But Levingston left as he was, in formal attire.'

Torrence said nothing. In the long pause that ensued, you could hear the fire roaring in the stove and the window panes rattling in the storm.

Torrence finally broke the silence.

'Luggage?' he asked.

'Done. Nothing there! Just clothes and underwear . . . The usual accoutrements of a first-class traveller. Not a scrap of paper. The Mortimer woman is certain that her husband has been murdered.'

Somewhere a bell rang. Maigret opened the drawer in his desk where that afternoon he'd put all the telegrams about Pietr the Latvian.

Then he looked at the map. He drew a line with his finger from Krakow to Bremen, then to Amsterdam, Brussels and Paris.

Somewhere near Saint-Quentin, a brief halt: a man died.

In Paris, the line came to a full stop. Two men vanish from the middle of the Champs-Élysées.

All that's left are suitcases in a suite and Mrs Mortimer-Levingston, whose mind is as empty as Pietr's travelling chest.

The gurgle from Maigret's pipe was getting so annoying that the inspector took a swatch of chicken feathers from another drawer, cleaned the shaft, then opened the stove door and flung the soiled feathers in the fire.

Four of the beer glasses were empty but for sticky froth marks on the rim. Somebody came out of one of the offices on the corridor, locked his door and went away.

'Who's a lucky man!' Torrence observed. 'That's Lucas. Tonight he got a tip-off from some moneyed brat and arrested a pair of drug dealers.'

Maigret was poking the fire, and when he stood up his face was crimson. In routine fashion he picked up the translucent paper, extracted the strand of hair and turned it over in the light. Then he went back to the map and studied the invisible track of Pietr's journey. It made a sweeping arc of almost 180 degrees.

If he had started out from Krakow, then why had he gone all the way north to Bremen before swerving back down to Paris?

He was still holding the slip of paper. He muttered:

'There must have been a picture inside this once.'

In fact, the tissue was a glassine envelope, a slipcover of the kind photographers use to protect customers' orders. But it was an obsolete size known as 'album format' that could only now be found in provincial backwaters. The photo that this cover must have protected would have been about half the size of a standard postcard, printed on off-white glacé paper on cardboard backing.

'Is anyone still there at the lab?' Maigret suddenly asked.

'I guess so. They must still be processing the photos of the Étoile du Nord affair.'

There was only one full glass left on the table. Maigret gulped it down and put on his jacket.

'You'll come along? . . . Those kinds of portrait photos usually have the name and address of the photographer printed or embossed on them . . .'

Torrence got the point. They set off through a labyrinth of passageways and stairs up into the attic floors of the Law Courts and finally found the forensics lab.

An expert took the slipcover, ran it through his fingers, almost sniffed at it. Then he sat at an arc lamp and wheeled over a carriage-mounted multiplying glass.

The principle is straightforward: blank paper that has been in protracted contact with another sheet that has been printed or written on eventually acquires an imprint of the letters on that other sheet. The imprint cannot be seen by the naked eye, but photography can reveal it.

The fact that there was a stove in the lab meant that Maigret was destined to end up there. He stood watch for the best part of an hour, smoking pipe after pipe, while Torrence trailed the photographer as he came and went.

At long last the darkroom door opened. A voice cried out:

'We've got it!'

'Yes?'

'The photo credit is: *Léon Moutet, Art Photography, Quai des Belges, Fécamp*.'

Only a real expert could decipher the plate. Torrence, for instance, could only see a blur.

'Do you want to see the post-mortem photos?' the expert asked cheerfully. 'They're first-rate! But it was a tight fit inside that railway toilet! Would you believe it, we had to hang the camera from the ceiling . . .'

'Have you got an outside line?' Maigret asked, gesturing towards the phone.

'Yes . . . the switchboard shuts down at nine, so before she goes off the operator connects me to the outside.'

Maigret called the Majestic and spoke to one of the desk interpreters.

'Has Mr Mortimer-Levingston come back in?'

'I'll find out for you, sir. To whom do I have the honour of . . .'

'Police!'

'No, sir, he's not back.'

'What about Mr Oswald Oppenheim?'

'Not back either, sir.'

'What is Mrs Mortimer up to?'

A pause.

'I asked you what Mrs Mortimer is doing.'

'She is . . . I think she is in the bar . . .'

'Do you mean she's drunk?'

'She has had a few cocktails, sir. She said she would not go up to her suite until her husband comes back . . . Do you . . . ?'

'What's that?'

'Hello? . . . This is the manager speaking,' another voice broke in. 'Any progress? Do you think this will get into the papers? . . .'

Cruelly, Maigret hung up. To please the photographer he took a look at the first proof photos laid out in the drying trays, still gleaming wet. While doing that he was talking to Torrence.

'You're going to settle in at the Majestic, old pal. The main thing is to take no notice whatsoever of the manager.'

'What about you, *patron*?'

'I'm going back to the office. There's a train to Fécamp at 5.30, It's not worth going home and waking up Mme Maigret. Hang on . . . The Dauphine should still be open. On your way, order me up a beer . . .'

'Just one . . . ?' Torrence inquired, with a deadpan expression on his face.

'As you like, old pal! The waiter's smart enough to know it means three or four. Have him throw in a few sandwiches as well.'

They traipsed down an unending spiral staircase in single file.

The black-gowned photographer was left on his own to admire the prints he'd just made. He still had to number them.

The two detectives parted company in the freezing courtyard.

'If you leave the Majestic for any reason, make sure one of our men holds the fort,' Maigret instructed. 'I'll telephone the front desk if I need to get in touch . . .'

He went back to his office and stoked the fire so vigorously he could have snapped the grate.

4. *The* Seeteufel*'s First Mate*

The station at La Bréauté, on the main line to Le Havre, where Maigret had to change trains at 7.30 a.m., gave him a foretaste of Fécamp.

The ill-lit station buffet had grimy walls and a counter offering only a few mouldy pieces of cake alongside a miserable fruit stack made of three bananas and five oranges.

The foul weather had even more impact here than in Paris. Rain was coming down in buckets. Crossing from one track to the other meant wading through knee-deep mud.

The branch-line train was a rickety affair made up of carriages on their way to scrap. In the pale half-light of dawn you could hardly make out the fuzzy shapes of farmhouses through the pelting rain.

Fécamp! The air was laden with the smell of herring and cod. Mountains of casks. Ships' masts peering over the locomotive. Somewhere a siren blared.

'Quai des Belges?'

Straight ahead. All he had to do was walk through slimy puddles gleaming with fish scales and rotting innards.

The photographer was also a shopkeeper and a newspaper vendor. He stocked oilskins, sailcloth pea-jackets and hempen rope alongside New Year's greeting cards.

A weakling with very pale skin: as soon as he heard the word 'police' he called his wife to the rescue.

'Can you tell me what photo was in this slipcover?'

It dragged on. Maigret had to squeeze words out of him one by one and do his thinking for him.

In the first place, the technician hadn't used that format for eight years, ever since he'd acquired new equipment to do postcard-sized portraits.

Who might have had his or her photograph taken eight or more years ago? Monsieur Moutet took a whole fifteen minutes to remember that he'd got an album with archive copies of all the portraits done in his establishment.

His wife went to get it. Sailors came and went. Kids came in to buy a penny's worth of sweets. Outside, ships' tackle scraped on the dock. You could hear the waves shifting shingle along the breakwater.

Maigret thumbed through the archive album, then specified what he was looking for:

'A young woman with extremely fine brown hair . . .'

That did it.

'Mademoiselle Swaan!' the photographer exclaimed. He turned up the snapshot straight away. It was the only time he'd had a decent subject to photograph.

She was a pretty woman. She looked twenty. The photo fitted the slipcover exactly.

'Who is she?'

'She's still living in Fécamp. But now she's got a clifftop villa five minutes from the Casino . . .'

'Is she married?'

'She wasn't then. She was the cashier at the Railway Hotel.'

'Opposite the station, I suppose?'

'Yes, you must have seen it on your way here. She was an orphan from some small place around here . . . Les Loges . . . Do you know where I mean? . . . Anyway, that's how she got to meet a traveller staying at the hotel . . . They got married . . . At the moment she's living in the villa with her two children and a maid . . .'

'Mr Swaan doesn't live in Fécamp?'

There was a pause. The photographer and his wife exchanged glances. The woman answered:

'Since you're from the police, I suppose we'd better tell you everything. Anyway you'd find it all out in the end, but . . . They're only rumours, but . . . Mr Swaan almost never stays in Fécamp. When he does come he stops for a few days at the most . . . Sometimes it's just a flying visit . . . He first came not long after the war . . . The Grand Banks were being reorganized, after five years' interruption. He wanted to look into it properly, so he said, and to make investments in businesses that were being started up again. He claimed to be Norwegian . . . His first name is Olaf . . . The herring fishermen who sometimes go as far as Norway say there are plenty of people over there who have that name . . . Nonetheless, people said he was really a German spy. That's why, when he got married, his wife was kept at arm's length. Then we discovered he really was a sailor and was first mate on a German merchantman, and that was why he didn't show up very often . . . Eventually people stopped bothering about him, but we're still wary . . .'

'You said they had children?'

'Two . . . A little girl of three and a baby a few months old . . .'

Maigret took the photograph out of the album and got directions to the villa. It was a bit too early to turn up. He waited in a harbour café for two hours, listening to fishermen talking about the herring catch, which was at its height. Five trawlers were tied up at the quay. Fish was being unloaded by the barrelful. Despite the wind and rain, the air stank.

To get to the villa he walked along the deserted breakwater and around the shuttered Casino still plastered with last summer's posters. At last he got to a steep climb that began at the foot of the cliff. As he plodded up he got occasional glimpses of iron railings in front of villas. The one he was looking for turned out to be a comfortable-looking red-brick structure, neither large nor small. He guessed that the garden with its white-gravel paths was well tended in season. The windows must have had a good view into the far distance.

*

Maigret rang the bell. A great Dane came to sniff at him through the railings, and its lack of bark made it seem all the more ferocious. At the second ring, a maid appeared. First she took the dog back to his kennel, and then asked:

'What is it about?'

She spoke with the local accent.

'I would like to see Mr Swaan, please.'

She seemed hesitant.

'I don't know if sir is in . . . I'll go and ask.'

She hadn't opened the gate. Rain was still pouring down, and Maigret was soaked through. He watched the maid go up the steps and vanish inside the house. Then a curtain shifted at a window. A few moments later the maid reappeared.

'Sir will not be back for several weeks. He is in Bremen . . .'

'In that case I would like to have a word with Madame Swaan . . .'

The maid hesitated again, but ended up opening the gate.

'Madame isn't dressed. You will have to wait . . .'

The dripping detective was shown into a neat lounge with white curtains and a waxed floor. The furniture was brand new, but just the same as you would find in any lower-middle-class home. They were good-quality pieces, in a style that would have been called modern around 1900.

Light oak. Flowers in an 'artistic' stone vase in the middle of the table. Crochet-work place-mats. On the other hand, there was a magnificent sculpted silver samovar on a side-table. It must have been worth more than the rest of the room's contents put together.

Maigret heard noises coming from the first floor. A baby could be heard crying through one of the ground-floor walls; someone else was mumbling something in a soft and even voice, as if to comfort it. At last, the sound of slippered feet gliding along the corridor. The door opened. Maigret found himself facing a young woman who had dressed in a hurry so as to meet him.

She was of medium height, more plump than slim, with a pretty and serious face that betrayed a pang of anxiety. She smiled nonetheless and said:

'Why didn't you take a seat?'

Rivulets of rainwater flowed from Maigret's overcoat, trousers and shoes into little puddles on the polished floor. In that state he could not have sat down on the light-green velvet of the armchairs in the lounge.

'Madame Swaan, I presume? . . .'

'Yes, monsieur . . .'

She looked at him quizzically.

'I'm sorry to disturb you like this . . . It's just a formality . . . I'm with the Immigration Service . . . We're conducting a survey . . .'

She said nothing. She didn't seem any more or less anxious than before.

'I understand Mr Swaan is a Swede. Is that correct?'

'Oh no, he's Norwegian . . . But for the French I guess it's the same thing . . . To begin with, I myself . . .'

'He is a ship's officer?'

'He's first mate on the *Seeteufel*, out of Bremen . . .'

'As I thought . . . So he is in the employ of a German company?'

She blushed.

'The ship-owner is German, yes . . . At least, on paper . . .'

'Meaning? . . .'

'I don't think I need to keep it from you . . . You must be aware that the merchant fleet has been in crisis since the war . . . Even here you can find ocean-going captains who've been unable to find commissions and who have to take positions as first or even second mates . . . Others have joined the Newfoundland or the North Sea fishing fleets.'

She spoke quite fast, but in a gentle and even tone.

'My husband didn't want to take on a commission in the Pacific, where there's more work, because he wouldn't have been able to come back to Europe more than once every two years . . . Shortly after we got married, some Americans bought the *Seeteufel* in the name of a German shipping firm . . . Olaf first came to Fécamp looking specifically for more schooners to buy . . . Now you must see . . . The aim was to run booze to the USA . . . Substantial firms were set up with American money . . . They have offices in France, Holland, or Germany . . . The truth is that my husband works for one of these companies. The *Seeteufel* sails what's called *Rum Alley*. It doesn't really have anything to do with Germany.'

'Is he at sea at the moment?' Maigret asked, keeping his eyes on that pretty face, which struck him as an honest and even at times a touching one.

'I don't think so. You must realize that the sailings aren't as regular as those of a liner. But I always try to keep abreast of the *Seeteufel*'s position. At the moment he ought to be in Bremen, or very nearly there.'

'Have you ever been to Norway?'

'Never! I've actually never left Normandy, so to speak. Just a couple of times, for short stays in Paris.'

'With your husband?'

'Yes . . . On our honeymoon, as well.'

'He's got fair hair, hasn't he?'

'Yes . . . Why do you ask?'

'And a thin, close-cropped blond moustache?'

'Yes . . . I can show you a picture of him if you like.'

She opened a door and went out. Maigret could hear her moving about in the bedroom next door.

She was out for longer than made sense, and the noises of doors opening and closing and of comings and goings around the house were just as illogical.

At last she came back, looking somewhat perplexed and apologetic.

'Please excuse me . . .' she said. 'I can't manage to put my hand on that photo . . . A house with children is always upside down . . .'

'One more question . . . To how many people did you give a copy of this photograph of yourself?'

Maigret showed her the archive print he'd been given by the photographer. Madame Swaan went bright red and stuttered:

'I don't understand . . .'

'Your husband presumably has one?'

'Yes . . . We were engaged when . . .'

'Does any other man have a print?'

She was on the verge of tears. The quiver of her lips gave away her distress.

'No, nobody.'

'Thank you, madame. That will be all.'

As he was leaving a little girl slipped into the hallway. Maigret had no need to memorize her features. She was the spitting image of Pietr the Latvian!

'Olga! . . .' her mother scolded, as she hustled her back through a half-open door.

Maigret was back outside in the rain and the wind.

'Goodbye, madame . . .'

He caught a final glimpse of her through the closing door. He was aware that he had left her at a loss, after bursting in on her in the warmth of her own home. He picked up a trace in her eyes of something uncertain but undoubtedly akin to anxiety as she shut her front door.

5. *The Russian Drunkard*

You don't boast about these kinds of things, they would raise a laugh if they were mentioned out loud, but all the same, they call for a kind of heroism.

Maigret hadn't slept. From 5.30 to 8 a.m. he'd been shaken about in draughty railway carriages. Ever since he'd changed trains at La Bréauté he'd been soaked through. Now his shoes squelched out dirty water at every step and his bowler was a shapeless mess. His overcoat and trousers were sopping wet.

The wind was slapping him with more rain. The alleyway was deserted. It was no more than a steep path between garden walls. The middle of it had turned into a raging torrent.

He stood still for quite a while. Even his pipe had got wet in his pocket. There was no way of hiding near the villa. All he could do was stick as close as possible to a wall and wait.

Anyone coming by would catch sight of him and look round. He might have to stay there for hours on end. There was no definite proof that there was a man in the house. And even if he were there, why should he come out?

Grumpy as he was, Maigret filled his wet pipe with tobacco all the same, and wedged himself as best he could into a cranny in the wall . . .

This was no place for a detective chief inspector of the Police Judiciaire. At most it was a job for a new recruit. Between the age of twenty-two and thirty he'd stood this sort of watch a hundred times over.

He had a terrible time getting a match to light. The emery board on the side of the box was coming off in strips. If one of the sticks hadn't finally ignited, maybe even Maigret would have given up and gone home.

He couldn't see anything from where he was standing except a low wall and the green-painted railing of the villa. He had brambles at his ankles and a draught all down his neck.

Fécamp was laid out beneath him, but he could not see the town. He could only hear the roar of the sea and now and again a siren or the sound of a car.

After half an hour on watch he saw a woman with a shopping basket, who looked like a cook, making her way up the steep slope. She only saw Maigret when she passed close by him. His huge, unmoving shape standing next to the wall in a wind-swept alley so scared her that she started to run.

Perhaps she worked for one of the villas at the top of the rise? A few minutes later a man appeared at the bend and stared at Maigret from afar. Then a woman joined him, and both went back inside.

It was a ridiculous situation. The inspector knew there wasn't one chance in ten that his surveillance would be of any use.

Yet he stuck it out – just because of a vague feeling that didn't even deserve to be called an intuition. In fact it was a pet theory of his that he'd never worked out in full and remained vague in his mind, but which he dubbed for his own use *the theory of the crack in the wall.*

Inside every wrong-doer and crook there lives a human being. In addition, of course, there is an opponent in a game, and it's the player that the police are inclined to see. As a rule, that's what they go after.

Some crime or offence is committed. The match starts on the basis of more or less objective facts. It's a problem with one or more unknowns that a rational mind tries to solve.

Maigret worked like any other policeman. Like everyone else, he used the amazing tools that men like Bertillon, Reiss and Locard have given the police – anthropometry, the principle of the trace, and so forth – and that have turned detection into forensic science. But what he sought, what he waited and watched out for, was the *crack in the wall*. In other words, the instant when the human being comes out from behind the opponent.

At the Majestic he'd seen the player. But here, he had a premonition of something else. The tidy, quiet villa wasn't one of the props that Pietr used to play his hand. Especially the wife and the children he'd seen and heard: they belonged to a different physical and moral order.

That's why he was waiting, albeit in a foul mood, for he was too fond of his big cast-iron stove and his office with glasses of frothy beer on the table not to be miserable in such awful weather.

He'd started his watch a little after 10.30. At half past noon he heard footsteps scrunching the gravel and swift, practised movements opening the gate, which brought a figure to within three metres of the inspector. The lie of the land made it impossible for Maigret to retreat. So he stood his ground unwaveringly, or, to be more precise, inertly, standing on two legs that could be seen in the round through the sopping wet trousers that clung to them.

The man leaving the villa was wearing a poor-quality belted trenchcoat, with its worn-out collar upturned. He was also wearing a grey cap. The get-up made him look very young. He went down the hill with his hands in his pockets, all hunched up and shivering because of the contrast in temperature.

He was obliged to pass within a metre of the Detective Chief Inspector. He chose that moment to slow down, take a packet of cigarettes out of his pocket and light up. It was as if he'd positively tried to get his face into the light so as to allow the detective to study it in detail!

Maigret let him go on a few paces, then set off on his tail, with a frown on his face. His pipe had gone out. His whole being exuded a sense of displeasure as well as an ardent desire to understand.

The man in the trenchcoat looked like the Latvian and yet did not resemble him! Same height: about 1 m 68cm. At a pinch he could be the same age, though in the outfit he was wearing he looked closer to twenty-six than thirty-two. There was nothing to determine that this man was not the original of the *'word-picture'* that Maigret knew by heart and also had on a piece of paper in his pocket.

And yet . . . it was not the same man! For one thing, his eyes had a vaguer, more sentimental expression. They were a lighter shade of grey, as if the rain had scrubbed them. Nor did he have a blond toothbrush moustache. But that wasn't the only thing that made him different.

Maigret was struck by other details. His outfit was nothing like that of an officer of the merchant fleet. It didn't even fit the villa, given the comfortable middle-class style of living that it implied.

His shoes were worn and the heels had been redone. Because of the mud, the man hitched up his trouser legs, showing faded grey cotton socks that had been clumsily darned.

There were lots of stains on the trenchcoat. Overall, the man fitted a type that Maigret knew well: the migrant low-lifer, predominantly of Eastern European origin, who slept in squalid lodging houses and sometimes in railway stations. A type not often seen outside Paris, but accustomed to travelling in third-class carriages when not riding the footboards or hopping freight trains.

He got proof of his insight a few minutes later. Fécamp doesn't have any genuine low dives, but behind the harbour there are two or three squalid bars favoured by dockhands and seamen. Ten metres before these places there's a regular café kept clean and bright. The man in the trenchcoat walked right past it and straight into the least prepossessing of the bars, where he put his elbow on the counter in a way that Maigret saw right through.

It was the straightforwardly vulgar body-language of a guttersnipe. Even if he'd tried, Maigret couldn't have imitated it. The inspector followed the man into the bar. He'd ordered an absinthe substitute and was just standing there, wordless, with a blank stare on his face. He didn't register Maigret's presence, though the inspector was now right next to him.

Through a gap in the man's jacket Maigret could see that his linen was dirty. That's not something that can be simulated, either! His shirt and collar – now not much more than a ribbon – had been worn for days, maybe for weeks on end. They'd been slept in – God knows where! They'd been sweated in and rained on.

The man's suit was not unstylish, but it bore the same signs and told the same miserable story of a vagrant life.

'Same again!'

The glass was empty, and the barman refilled it, serving Maigret a measure of spirits at the same time.

'So you're back in these parts again? . . .'

The man didn't answer. He downed his drink in one gulp and gestured for a refill straight away.

'Anything to eat? . . . I've got some pickled herring . . .'

Maigret had sidled up to a small stove, and stood in front of it to warm his back, now as shiny as an umbrella.

'Come to think of it . . . I had a man in here last week from your part of the world . . . Russian he was, from Archangelsk . . . Sailing a Swedish three-master that had to put in to port because of the bad weather . . . Hardly had time to drink his fill, I can tell you! . . . Had a devil of a job on his hands . . . Torn sails, snapped yards, you name it . . .'

The man, now on his fourth imitation absinthe, was drinking steadily. The barman filled his glass every time it was empty, glancing at Maigret with a conniving wink.

'As for Captain Swaan, I ain't seen him since you was here last.'

Maigret shuddered. The man in the trenchcoat who'd now downed his fifth neat ersatz absinthe staggered towards the stove, bumped into the detective and held out his hands towards the warmth.

'I'll have a herring, all the same . . .' he said.

He had a quite strong accent – a Russian accent, as far as the detective could judge.

There they were, next to each other, shoulder to shoulder, so to speak. The man wiped his face with his hand several times, and his eyes grew ever more murky.

'Where's my glass? . . .' he inquired testily.

It had to be put in his hand. As he drank he stared at Maigret and pouted with disgust.

There was no mistaking that expression! As if to assert his opinion all the more clearly, he threw his glass to the ground, leaned on the back of a chair and muttered something in a foreign tongue.

The barman, somewhat concerned, found a way of getting close to Maigret and whispering quietly in a way that was nonetheless audible to the Russian:

'Don't take any notice of him. He's always like that . . .'

The man gave a drunkard's strangled laugh. He slumped into the chair, put his head in both his hands and stayed like that until a plate of herring was pushed over the table between his elbows. The barman shook his shoulder.

'Eat up! . . . It'll do you good . . .'

The man laughed again. It was more like a bitter cough. He turned round so he could see Maigret and stare at him aggressively, then he pushed the plate of herring off the table.

'More drink! . . .'

The barman raised his arms and grunted as if it was an excuse:

'Russians, I ask you!'

Then he put his finger to his head and turned it, as if he was tightening a loose screw.

Maigret had pushed his bowler to the back of his head. His clothes were steaming, giving off a grey haze. He was only up to his second glass of spirits.

'I'll have some herring!' he said.

He was still eating it with a slice of bread when the Russian got up on unsteady legs, looked around as if he didn't know what to do and grinned for the third time when he set eyes on Maigret.

Then he slumped down at the bar, took a glass from the shelf and a bottle from the enamel sink where it was being kept cool in water. He helped himself without watching how much he was taking and smacked his tongue as he drank.

Eventually he took a 100 franc note out of his pocket.

'Is that enough, you swine?' he asked the waiter.

He threw the banknote up in the air. The barman had to fish it out of the sink.

The Russian struggled with the door handle, which wouldn't open. There was almost a fight because the barman tried to help his customer, who kept elbowing him away.

At long last the trenchcoat faded away into the mist and rain along the harbour-side, going towards the station.

'That's an odd 'un,' the barman sighed, intending to be heard by Maigret, who was paying his bill.

'Is he often in?'

'Now and again . . . Once he spent the whole night here, on the bench where you're sitting . . . He's a real Russian! . . . Some Russian sailors who were here in Fécamp at the same time as he was told me so . . . Apparently he's quite educated . . . Did you look at his hands? . . .'

'Don't you think he's got the same looks as Captain Swaan? . . .'

'Oh! So you know him . . . Well, of course he does! But not so much as you'd mistake one for the other . . . All the same . . . For ages I thought it was his brother.'

The beige silhouette vanished round a corner. Maigret started to walk faster. He caught up with the Russian just as he was going into the third-class waiting room at the station. The man slumped onto a bench and once again put his head in his hands.

An hour later they were in the same railway compartment with a cattle trader from Yvetot who launched into shaggy-dog stories in Norman dialect. Now and again he nudged Maigret to draw his attention to the other passenger.

The Russian slipped down little by little and ended up in a crumpled heap on the bench. His face was pale, his chin was on his chest, and his half-open mouth stank of cheap spirits.

6. Au Roi de Sicile

The Russian woke up at La Bréauté and stayed awake from then on. It has to be said that the express from Le Havre to Paris was completely packed. Maigret and his travelling companion had to stand in the corridor, stuck near a door, watching random scenery fly by as the darkness swallowed it bit by bit.

The man in the trenchcoat seemed entirely unflustered at having a detective by his side. On arrival at Gare Saint-Lazare, he didn't try to use the milling crowd to throw Maigret off his tail. On the contrary: he went down the great staircase in leisurely fashion, realized that his packet of cigarettes was wet through, bought another one at a station stall and was on the verge of going into a bar. Then he changed his mind and began to loiter along the pavement. He made a sorry sight: a man so absent from the world and in such low spirits that he was no longer capable of reacting to anything.

It's a long way from Gare Saint-Lazare to Hôtel de Ville, there's the whole city centre to get through. Between six and seven in the evening, pedestrians flood the pavements in ocean waves, and traffic pulses along the streets like blood pumping down an artery.

With his mud- and grease-stained coat belted at the waist and his recycled heels, the narrow-shouldered pauper waded on through the bright lights and the bustle. People elbowed and bumped into him, but he never stopped or looked over his shoulder.

He took the shortest route, by way of Rue du 4-Septembre and then through Les Halles, which proved he'd gone this way before.

He reached the ghetto of Paris, that's to say, the area around Rue des Rosiers, in the Marais. He sidled past shop fronts with signs in Yiddish, kosher butchers and window displays of *matzot*. At one corner, giving on to a passageway so dark and deep it looked like a tunnel, a woman tried to take him by the arm, but let go without his saying a word. Presumably he had made a strong impression on her.

At last he ended up in Rue du Roi-de-Sicile, a winding street giving on to dead-end alleys, narrow lanes and overpopulated courtyards – a half-Jewish, half-Polish colony. Two hundred metres along, he dived into a hotel entrance.

The hotel's name, Au Roi de Sicile, was written out on ceramic tiles. Underneath the nameplate were notices in Yiddish, Polish, maybe also Russian and other suchlike languages that Maigret didn't know.

There was a building site next door where the remains of a house that had needed buttressing to keep it standing were still visible. It was still raining, but in this rat-trap there was no wind.

Maigret heard a window closing with a sharp clack on the third floor of the hotel. No less resolutely than the Russian, he went inside.

There was no door in the entrance hall, just a staircase . . . At the mezzanine level there was a kind of glass box where a Jewish family was having dinner.

Inspector Maigret knocked, but instead of opening the door the concierge raised a hatch, like at a ticket counter. A rancid smell wafted from it. The man was wearing a skullcap. His overweight wife carried on with her meal.

'What is it?'

'Police! Give me the name of the tenant who just came in.'

The man grunted something in his own language, then went to a drawer and brought out a grimy ledger that he shoved through the hatch without a word.

At the same instant Maigret sensed he was being watched from the unlit stairwell. He turned round quickly and saw an eye shining from about ten stairs above.

'Room number?'

'Thirty-two . . .'

He thumbed through the ledger and read:

Fyodor Yurevich, age 28, born Vilna, labourer, and Anna Gorskin, age 25, born Odessa, no occupation.

The Jew had gone back to the table to continue eating his meal like a man without a worry. Maigret drummed on the window. The hotel-keeper stood up slowly and reluctantly.

'How long has he been staying here?'

'About three years.'

'What about Anna Gorskin?'

'She's been here longer than he has . . . Maybe four and a half years . . .'

'What do they live on?'

'You've read the book . . . He's a labourer.'

'Don't try that on me!' Maigret riposted in a voice that sufficed to change the hotelier's attitude.

'It's not for me to stick my nose in where it's not wanted, is it?' he now said in an oilier tone. 'He pays up on time. He comes and he goes and it's not my job to follow him around . . .'

'Does anybody come to see him?'

'Sometimes . . . I've got over sixty tenants in here and I can't keep an eye on all of them at once . . . As long as they're doing no harm! . . . Anyway, as you're from the police you should know all about this establishment . . . I make proper returns . . . Officer Vermouillet can confirm that . . . He's the one who comes every week . . .'

Maigret turned around on an impulse and called out:

'Anna Gorskin, come down now!'

There was a ruffling noise in the stairway, then the sound of footsteps, and finally a woman stepped out into a patch of light.

She looked older than the ledger's claim of twenty-five. That was probably hereditary. Like many Jewish women of her age, she had put on weight, but she was still quite good-looking. She had remarkable eyes: very dark pupils set in amazingly white and shining corneas. But the rest of her was so sloppy as to spoil that first impression. Her black, greasy and uncombed hair fell in thick bunches onto her neck. She was wearing a worn-out dressing gown, loosely tied and allowing a glimpse of her underwear. Her stockings were rolled down above her thick knees.

'What were you doing in the stairwell?'

'I live here, don't I? . . .'

Maigret sensed straight away what kind of a woman he was dealing with. Excitable, irreverent, hammer and tongs. At the drop of a hat she could throw a fit, rouse the entire building, give an ear-splitting scream and probably accuse him of outlandish offences. Did she perhaps know she was unassailable? In any case, she looked at her enemy with defiance.

'You'd be better advised to go look after your man . . .'

'None of your business . . .'

The hotelier stayed behind his window, rocking his head from left to right, from right to left, with a morose and reproving look on his face; but there was laughter in his eyes.

'When did Fyodor leave?'

'Yesterday evening . . . At eleven . . .'

She was lying! Plain as day! But there was no point coming at her head-on – unless he wanted to pin back her arms and march her down to the station.

'Where does he work?'

'Wherever he chooses . . .'

You could see her breasts heave under her ill-fitting dressing gown. There was a hostile, haughty sneer on her face.

'What've the police got against Fyodor, anyway?'

Maigret decided to say rather quietly:

'Get upstairs . . .'

'I'll go when I feel like it! You ain't got no right to order me about.'

What was the point of answering back and risking creating an ugly incident that would only hold things up? Maigret shut the ledger and handed it back to the hotel-keeper.

'All above board and hunky-dory, right?' the latter said, after gesturing at the young woman to keep quiet. But she stood her ground with her fists on her hips, one side of her lit by the light from the hotelier's office, the other in darkness.

Maigret looked at her again. She met his gaze straight on and felt the need to mutter:

'You don't scare me one bit . . .'

He just shrugged and then made his way down a staircase so narrow his shoulders touched both of its squalid walls.

In the corridor he ran into two bare-necked Poles who turned away as soon as they saw him. The street was wet, making the cobblestones glint. In every corner, in the smallest pools of shadow, in the back alleys and passageways you could sense a swarm of humiliated and rebellious humanity. Shadowy figures flitted past. Shopkeepers sold products whose very names were unknown in France.

Less than 100 metres away was Rue de Rivoli and Rue Saint-Antoine – broad, well-lit streets with trams, market stalls and the city police . . . Maigret caught a passing street urchin with a cauliflower ear by the shoulder:

'Go fetch me a policeman from Place Saint-Paul . . .'

But the lad just looked at him with fear in his eyes, then answered in some incomprehensible tongue. He didn't know a word of French!

The inspector then spied a beggar.

'Here's a five franc coin . . . Take this note to the cop at Place Saint-Paul.'

The tramp understood. Ten minutes later a uniformed sergeant turned up.

'Call the Police Judiciaire and tell them to send me an officer straight away . . . Dufour, if he's free . . .'

Maigret cooled his heels for at least another half-hour. People went into the hotel. Others came out. But the light stayed on at the third-floor window, second from the left.

Anna Gorskin appeared at the doorway. She'd put on a greenish overcoat over her dressing gown. She was hatless and despite the rain she was wearing red satin sandals. She splashed her way across the street. Maigret kept out of sight, in the shadows.

She went into a store and came out a few minutes later laden with a host of small white packets, plus two bottles. She vanished back into the hotel.

At long last Inspector Dufour showed up. He was thirty-five and spoke three languages quite fluently, which made him a precious asset. But he had a habit of making the simplest things sound complicated. He could turn a common burglary or a banal snatch-and-grab case into a dramatic mystery, tying himself up in knots of his own making. But as he was also uncommonly persistent, he was highly suitable for a well-defined job like staking out or tailing a suspect.

Maigret gave him a description of Fyodor Yurevich and his girl-friend.

'I'll send you a back-up. If one of those two comes out, stay on their tail. But one of you has to stay behind to man the stake-out . . . Got that?'

'Are we still on the Étoile du Nord case? . . . It's a mafia hit, right?'

Maigret went off without answering. He got to his office at Quai des Orfèvres fifteen minutes later, dispatched an officer to back up Dufour, leaned over his stove and swore at Jean for not stoking it up to a red-hot glow. He hung his sopping greatcoat on the back of the door. It had gone so stiff that the shape of his shoulders could still be made out in it.

'Did my wife call?'

'This morning . . . She was told you were out on a case . . .'

She was used to that. He knew that if he went home she would just give him a kiss, stir the pot on the stove and serve him a delicious plate of stew. The most she would dare – but only when he'd sat down to eat – would be to put her chin on her hand and ask:

'Everything OK? . . .'

The meal would always be ready for him, whether he turned up at noon or at five.

'Torrence?' he asked Jean.

'He called at 7 a.m.'

'From the Majestic?'

'I don't know. He asked if you'd left.'

'What else?'

'He called again at ten past five this afternoon. He asked for you to be told he was waiting for you.'

Maigret had only had a herring to eat since the morning. He stayed upright in front of his stove for a while. It was beginning to roar, for Maigret had an unrivalled knack for getting even the least combustible coal to catch. Then he plodded his way to the cupboard, where there was an enamel sink, a towel, a mirror and a suitcase. He dragged the case into the middle of his office, undressed and put on clean underwear and dry clothes. He rubbed his unshaven chin.

'It'll have to do . . .'

He looked lovingly at the fire, which was now burning grandly, placed two chairs next to it and carefully laid out his wet clothes on them. There was one sandwich left over from the previous night on his desk, and he wolfed it down, still standing, ready to depart. Only there wasn't any beer. He was more than a little parched.

'If anything at all comes in for me, I'm at the Majestic,' he said to Jean. 'Get them to call me.'

And at long last he slumped into the back seat of a taxi.

7. The Third Interval

Torrence wasn't to be found in the lobby, but in a first-floor room in front of a top-notch dinner. He explained with a broad wink:

'It's all the manager's fault! . . . He practically went down on bended knee to get me to accept this room and the gourmet meals he sends up . . .'

He was speaking in a whisper. He pointed to a door.

'The Mortimers are next door . . .'

'Mortimer came back?'

'Around six this morning. In a foul mood. Wet, dirty, with chalk or lime all over his clothes . . .'

'What did he say?'

'Nothing . . . He tried to get back to his room without being noticed. But they told him his wife had waited up for him in the bar. And she had! . . . She'd ended up befriending a Brazilian couple . . . They had to keep the bar open all night just for them . . . She was atrociously drunk . . .'

'And then?'

'He went as white as a ghost. His mouth went all twisted. He said a curt hello to the Brazilians, then took his wife by the armpits and dragged her off without another word . . . I reckon she slept it off until four this afternoon . . . There wasn't a sound from their suite until then . . . Then I heard whispering . . . Mortimer rang the front desk to have the newspapers brought up . . .'

'Nothing about the case in the papers, I hope?'

'Not a word. They've respected the embargo. Just a two-liner saying that a corpse had been found on the Étoile du Nord and that the police were treating it as suicide.'

'Next?'

'Room service brought them up some lemon juice. Mortimer took a stroll around the lobby, went straight past me two or three times, looking worried. He sent coded wires to his New York bank and to his secretary, who's been in London these past few days . . .'

'That's it?'

'At the moment they're just finishing dinner. Oysters, cold chicken, salad. The hotel keeps me abreast of everything. The manager is so delighted to have me shut away up here that he'll sweat blood to do me any favour I ask. That's why he came up just now to tell me that the Mortimers have got tickets to see *The Epic* at the Gymnase Theatre tonight. A four-acter by someone or other . . .'

'Pietr's suite?'

'Quiet as the grave! Nobody has been in it. I locked the door and put a blob of wax on the keyhole, so nobody can get in without my knowing . . .'

Maigret had picked up a chicken leg and was chewing at it quite shamelessly while looking round for a stove that wasn't there. In the end he sat on the radiator and asked:

'Isn't there anything to drink?'

Torrence poured him a glass of a superb Mâcon blanc, which his chief drank thirstily. Then there was a scratching at the door and a valet entered in a conspiratorial manner.

'The manager requests me to inform you that Mr and Mrs Mortimer's car has been brought to the front.'

Maigret glanced at the table still laden with food with the same sorrow he had expressed in his eyes on leaving the stove in his office.

'I'll go,' he said regretfully. 'You stay here.'

He tidied himself up in front of the mirror, wiping his mouth and his chin. A moment later he was in a taxi waiting for the Mortimer-Levingstons to get into their limousine.

*

They weren't long in coming. Mortimer was wearing a black overcoat that hid his dinner jacket; she was swaddled in furs, as on the previous night.

She must have still been tired, because her husband was discreetly propping her up with one hand. The limousine set off without a whisper.

Maigret hadn't known that this was an opening night at the Gymnase, and he was almost refused entry. City police formed a guard of honour beneath the canopy. In spite of the rain passers-by stopped to watch the guests alight from their cars. Inspector Maigret had to ask to see the manager and wait his turn in corridors, where he stuck out as the only person not wearing formal attire. The manager was at his wits' end, waving his arms about.

'There's nothing I'd like better than to oblige! But you're the twentieth person to ask me for a "spare seat"! There aren't any spare seats! There aren't any seats! . . . And you're not even properly dressed! . . .'

He was being assailed from all quarters.

'Can't you see? Put yourself in my shoes . . .'

In the end Maigret had to stay standing up next to a door with the usherettes and the programme-sellers.

The Mortimer-Levingstons had a box. There were six people in it, of whom one was a princess and another a government minister. People came and went. Hands were kissed, smiles exchanged.

The curtain rose on a sunlit garden. Shushes, murmurs, footsteps. Finally the actor's voice could be heard, wobbly at first but then more confident, creating an atmosphere.

Latecomers were still taking their seats. More shushing. Somewhere a woman giggled.

Mortimer was more lord of the manor than ever. Evening dress suited him to a tee. The white shirt-front brought out the ivory hue of his skin.

Did he see Maigret? Did he not? An usherette brought the

inspector a stool to sit on, but he had to share it with a portly lady in black silk, the mother of one of the actresses.

First interval, second interval. Comings and goings in the boxes. Artificial enthusiasm. Greetings exchanged between the parterre and the circle. The foyer, the corridors and even the front steps buzzed like a hive in high summer. Names were dropped in a whisper – names of maharajahs, ministers, statesmen and artists.

Mortimer left his box on three occasions, reappearing in a stage-box and then in the pit, and finally to have a chat with a former prime minister, whose hearty laugh could be heard twenty rows away.

End of Act Three. Flowers on the stage. A skinny actress was given an ovation. Seats flapping up made a racket and shuffling feet sounded like the swell of the sea. When Maigret turned to look up at the Americans' box, Mortimer-Levingston had vanished.

Now for the fourth and last act. That was when anybody who had an excuse got into the wings and the actors' and actresses' dressing-rooms. Others besieged the cloakrooms. There was much fussing over cars and taxis.

Maigret lost at least ten minutes looking around inside the theatre. Then, without hat or coat, he had to quiz the doorman and the policemen on duty outside to find out what he needed to know.

He learned eventually that the Mortimers' olive-green limousine had just driven off. He was shown where it had been parked, outside a bar often frequented by traders in cloakroom receipts. The car had gone towards Porte Saint-Martin. The American plutocrat hadn't retrieved his overcoat.

Outside, clumps of theatre-goers huddled wherever they could get out of the rain.

Maigret smoked a pipe with his hands in his pockets and a grumpy look on his face. The bell rang. People flocked inside. Even the municipal police went in to watch the last act.

The Grands Boulevards looked as scruffy as they always did at

11 p.m. The shafts of rain lit by the streetlamps were thinning out. The audience spewed out of a cinema which then switched off its lighting, brought in its billboards, and shut its doors. People stood in line at a bus stop, beneath a green-striped lamp-post. When the bus came there was an argument, because there were no number-tags left in the ticket machine. A policeman got involved. Long after the bus had left he remained in contentious discussion with an indignant fat man.

At last a limousine came to a gliding halt on the tarmac. The door opened even before it was at a standstill. Mortimer-Levingston, in tails but without a hat, bounded up the stairs and went into the warm and brightly lit lobby. Maigret took a look at the chauffeur. He was 100 per cent American: he had a hard face with a jutting chin, and he sat stock still in his seat as if he'd been turned to stone by his uniform.

The inspector opened one of the padded doors barely an inch or two. Mortimer was standing at the back of his box. A sarcastic actor was speaking his lines in staccato. Curtain. Flowers. Thunderous applause.

People rushing for the exits. More shushing. The lead actor uttered the name of the author and went to fetch him from a box to bring him centre stage. Mortimer kissed some hands and shook others, gave a 100 franc tip to the usherette who brought him their coats. His wife was pale-faced, with blue rings under her eyes. When they had got back into their car there was a moment of indecision.

The couple were having an argument. Mrs Levingston was agitated. Her husband lit a cigarette and put out his lighter with an angry swipe of his hand. Eventually, he said something to the chauffeur through the intercom tube, and the car set off, with Maigret in a taxi following behind.

It was half past midnight. Rue La Fayette. The white colonnade of La Trinité was sheathed in scaffolding. Rue de Clichy.

The limousine stopped in Rue Fontaine, outside Pickwick's Bar. A concierge in a blue and gold uniform. Coat check. A red curtain lifted and a snatch of tango emerged.

Maigret went in behind the couple and sat at a table near the door, which must have always stayed empty because it caught every draught.

The Mortimers had been seated near to the jazz band. The American read the menu and chose what he would have for supper. A professional dancer bowed to his wife. She went on the floor. Levingston watched her with remarkable intensity. She exchanged a few remarks with her dancing partner but never once turned towards the corner where Maigret was sitting.

Most people here were in formal attire, but there were also a few foreigners in lounge suits. Maigret waved away a hostess who tried to sit at his table. A bottle of champagne was put in front of him, automatically. There were streamers all about. Puffer balls flew through the air. One landed on Maigret's nose, and he glowered at the old lady who'd aimed it at him.

Mrs Mortimer had gone back to her table. The dancer wandered around the floor for a moment then went towards the exit and lit a cigarette. Suddenly he lifted the red plush curtain and vanished. It took three minutes for Maigret to think of going to see what was happening outside.

The dancer had gone.

The rest of the night dragged on drearily. The Mortimers ate copiously – caviar and truffles *au champagne*, then lobster *à l'américaine*, followed by cheese.

Mrs Mortimer didn't go back to the dance-floor.

Maigret didn't like champagne, but he sipped at it to slake his thirst. He made the mistake of nibbling the roasted almonds on the table, and that made him even thirstier.

He checked the time on his wristwatch: 2 a.m.

People began leaving the nightspot. Nobody took the slightest notice of a dancer performing her routine. A drunk foreigner with three women at his table was making more noise than all the other customers put together. The professional dancer, who had stayed outside for only fifteen minutes, had taken some other ladies round the dance-floor. But it was all over. Weariness had set in.

Mrs Mortimer looked worn out; her eyelids were dark blue.

Her husband signalled to an attendant. Fur coat, overcoat and top hat were brought.

Maigret sensed that the dancer, who was talking to the sax player, was watching him nervously.

He summoned the manager, who kept him waiting. He lost a few minutes.

When he finally got outside, the Americans' limousine was just going round the corner into Rue Notre-Dame-de-Lorette. There were half a dozen taxis waiting at the rank opposite. Maigret began crossing the road.

A gunshot rang out. Maigret put his hand to his chest, looked around, could not see anything, but heard the footsteps of someone running away down Rue Pigalle.

He staggered on for a few metres, propelled by his own inertia. The concierge ran up to him and held him upright. People came out of Pickwick's Bar to see what was going on. Among them Maigret noticed the tense figure of the professional dancer.

8. *Maigret Gets Serious*

Taxi drivers who 'do nights' in Montmartre don't need things spelled out to them and often get the point without a word being said.

When the shot was fired, one of the waiting drivers at the rank opposite Pickwick's Bar was about to open the passenger door for Maigret, not knowing who he was. But maybe he guessed from the way the inspector held himself that he was about to give a ride to a cop.

Customers at a small bar on the opposite side of the street came running. Soon there would be a whole crowd gathered round the wounded man. In the blink of an eye the driver lent a hand to the doorman who was propping up Maigret, without a clue what else to do. In less than half a minute the taxi was on its way with the inspector in the back.

The car drove on for ten minutes or so and came to a halt in an empty street. The driver got out the front, opened the passenger door, and saw his customer sitting in an almost normal posture, with one hand under his jacket.

'I can see it's no big deal, like I thought. Where can I take you?'

Still, Maigret looked quite upset, mainly because it was a flesh wound. His chest had been torn; the bullet had grazed a rib and exited near his shoulder blade.

'Quai des Orfèvres . . .'

The driver muttered something that couldn't be made out. En route, the inspector changed his mind.

'Take me to Hôtel Majestic . . . Drop me off at the service entrance on Rue de Ponthieu . . .'

He screwed up his handkerchief into a ball and stuffed it over his wound. He noted that the bleeding had stopped.

As he progressed towards the heart of Paris he appeared to be in less pain, but increasingly worried.

The taxi driver tried to help him out. Maigret brushed him off and crossed the pavement with a steady gait. In a narrow entranceway he found the watchman drowsing behind his counter.

'Anything happen?'

'What do you mean?'

It was cold. Maigret went back out to pay the driver, who grunted once again because all he was getting for his great exploit was a measly 100 franc tip.

In the state he was in, Maigret was an impressive sight. He was still pressing his handkerchief to his chest wound, under his jacket. He held one shoulder higher than the other, but all the same he was being careful to save his strength. He was slightly light-headed. Now and again he felt as if he was floating on air, and he had to make an effort to get a grip on himself so as to see clearly and move normally.

He climbed an iron stairway that led to the upper floors, opened a door, found he was in a corridor, got lost in the labyrinth and came upon another stairway identical to the first, except that it had a different number on it.

He was going round in circles in the hotel's back passages. Luckily he came across a chef in a white toque, who stared at him in fright.

'Take me to the first floor . . . Room next to the Mortimers' suite.'

In the first place, however, the chef wasn't privy to the names of the hotel guests. In the second place, he was awed by the five blood streaks that Maigret had put on his face when he'd wiped it with his hand. He was struck dumb by this giant of a man lost in a narrow servants' corridor with his coat worn over his shoulders and his hand permanently stuck to his chest, distorting the shape of his waistcoat and jacket.

'Police!'

Maigret was running out of patience.

He felt the threat of a dizzy spell coming on. His wound was burning hot and prickling, as if long needles were going through it.

At long last the chef set off without looking over his shoulder. Soon Maigret felt carpet beneath his feet, and he realized he'd left the service area and was in the hotel proper. He kept an eye on the room numbers. He was on the odd-numbered side.

Eventually he came across a terrified valet.

'The Mortimers' suite?'

'Downstairs . . . But . . . You . . .'

He went down a stairway, and meanwhile, the news spread among the staff that there was a strange wounded man wandering about the hotel like a ghost.

Maigret stopped to rest against a wall for a moment and left a bloodstain on it; three very dark red drops also fell on the carpet.

At last he caught sight of the Mortimers' suite and, beside it, the door of the room where Torrence was to be found. He got to the door, walking slightly crabwise, pushed it open . . .

'Torrence! . . .'

The lights were on. The table was still laden with food and drink. Maigret's thick eyebrows puckered. He could not see his partner. On the other hand he could smell something in the air that reminded him of a hospital.

He took a few more wobbly steps. And suddenly came to a stop by a settee.

A black-leather-shod foot was sticking out from under it.

He had to try three times over. As soon as he took his hand off his wound, blood spurted out of it at an alarming rate. Finally he took the towel that was lying on the table and wedged it under his waistcoat, which he fastened as tight as he could. The smell in the room made him nauseous.

He lifted one end of the settee with weak arms and swung it round on two of its legs. It was what he expected: Torrence, all crumpled up, with his shoulder twisted round as if he'd had his bones broken to make him fit into a small space.

There was a bandage over the lower part of his face, but it wasn't knotted. Maigret got down on his knees.

Every gesture was measured and even slow – no doubt because of the state he was in. His hand hovered over Torrence's chest before daring to feel for his heart. When it reached its target, Maigret froze. He didn't stir but stayed kneeling on the carpet and stared at his partner.

Torrence was dead! Involuntarily Maigret twisted his lips and clenched his fist. His eyes clouded over and he uttered a terrible oath in the shut and silent room.

It could have sounded merely grotesque. But it did not! It was fearsome! Tragic! Terrifying!

Maigret's face had hardened. He didn't cry. That must be something he was unable to do. But his expression was full of such anger and pain as well as astonishment that it came close to looking stunned.

Torrence was thirty years old. For the last five years he had worked pretty much exclusively for Inspector Maigret.

His mouth was wide open, as if he'd made a desperate attempt at getting his last gasp of air.

One floor up, a traveller was taking off his shoes, directly over the dead man's body.

Maigret looked around to seek out the enemy. He was breathing heavily.

Several minutes passed in this manner. Maigret got up only when he sensed some hidden process beginning to work inside him.

He went to the window, opened it and looked out on the empty roadway of the Champs-Élysées. He let the breeze cool his brow then went to pick up the gag he'd ripped off Torrence's mouth.

It was a damask table napkin embroidered with the monogram of the Majestic. It still gave off a faint whiff of chloroform. Maigret stayed upright. His mind was a blank, with just a few shapeless thoughts knocking about inside it and raising painful associations.

Once again, as he had done in the hotel passageway, he leaned his shoulder on the wall, and quite suddenly his features seemed to sink. He had aged; his spirits were low. Was he at that moment in time on the verge of bursting into tears? No, he was too big and substantial. He was made of a tougher cloth.

The settee was squint and touching the table that hadn't been cleared. On one plate chicken bones were mixed up with cigarette butts.

The inspector stretched out an arm towards the telephone. But he didn't pick up the receiver. Instead, he snapped his fingers in anger, turned back towards the corpse and stared at it.

He scowled bitterly and ironically when he thought of all the regulations, formal procedures and precautions he had to observe to please the examining magistrate.

Did any of that matter? It was Torrence, for heaven's sake! Almost the same as if it had been himself, dammit!

Torrence, who was part of the team, who . . .

Despite his apparent calm he unbuttoned his colleague's waistcoat with such feverish energy that he snapped off two of its buttons. That's when he saw something that made his face go quite grey.

On Torrence's shirt, *exactly over the centre of his heart*, there was a small brown mark.

Smaller than a chickpea! There was just one single drop of blood, and it had coagulated into a clot no larger than a pinhead. Maigret's eyes clouded over, and he twisted his face into a grimace of outrage he could not express in words.

It was disgusting, but in terms of crime it was the very apex of skill! He need look no further. He knew what the trick was, because he'd learned about it a few months earlier, in an article in a German crime studies journal.

First the chloroform towel, which overpowers the victim in twenty to thirty seconds. Then the long needle. The murderer can take his time and find just the right place between the ribs to get it straight into the heart, taking a life without any noise or mess.

Exactly the same method had been used in Hamburg six months earlier.

A bullet can miss its targets or just wound a man – Maigret was living proof of that. But a needle plunged into the heart of a man already made inert kills him scientifically, with no margin of error.

Inspector Maigret recalled one detail. That same evening, when the manager had reported that the Mortimers were leaving, he'd been sitting on the radiator, gnawing a chicken leg, and he'd been so overcome with his own comfort that he'd been on the verge of giving himself the hotel stake-out and sending Torrence to tail the millionaire at the theatre. That memory disturbed him. He felt awkward looking at his partner and felt nauseous, though he couldn't tell whether it was because of his wound, his emotions or the chloroform that was still hanging in the air.

It didn't even occur to him to start a proper methodical investigation.

It was Torrence lying there! Torrence, who'd been with him on all his cases these last few years! Torrence, a man who needed just one word, a single sign, to understand whatever he meant to say!

It was Torrence lying there with his mouth wide open as if he were still trying to suck in a bit of oxygen and keep on living! Maigret, who was unable to shed tears, felt sick and upset, with a weight on his shoulders, and nausea in his heart.

He went back to the telephone and spoke so quietly that he had to be asked to repeat his request.

'Police Judiciaire? . . . Yes . . . Hello! . . . Headquarters? . . . Who is that speaking? . . . What? . . . Tarraud? . . . Listen, my lad . . . You're going to run round to the chief's address . . . Yes, his home address . . . Tell him . . . Tell him to join me at the Majestic . . . Straight away . . . Room . . . I don't know the room number, but he'll be shown up . . . What? . . . No, nothing else . . . .

'Hello? . . . What's that? . . . No, nothing wrong with me . . .'

He hung up. His colleague had started asking questions, puzzled by the odd sound of Maigret's voice, and also because what he'd asked for was odder still.

He stood there for a while longer, with his arms swinging by his side. He tried not to look at the corner of the room where Torrence lay. He caught sight of himself in a mirror and realized that blood had soaked through the towel. So, with great difficulty, he took off his jacket.

One hour later the Superintendent of Criminal Investigation knocked at the door. Maigret opened it a slit and grunted at the valet who'd brought up the chief to say he was no longer needed. He only opened the door further when the flunkey had vanished. Only then did the super realize that Maigret was bare-chested. The door to the bathroom was wide open, and the floor was a puddle of reddish water.

'Shut the door, sharpish,' Maigret said, with no regard for hierarchy.

On the right side of his chest was an elongated and now swollen flesh wound. His braces were hanging down his legs.

He nodded towards the corner of the room where Torrence was lying and put a finger to his lips.

'Shush! . . .'

The superintendent shuddered. In sudden agitation, he inquired:

'Is he dead?'

Maigret's chin fell to his chest.

'Could you give me a hand, chief?' he mumbled gloomily.

'But . . . you're . . . It's a serious . . .'

'Shush! The bullet came out, that's the main thing. Help me wrap it up tight . . .'

He'd put the basin on the floor and cut the sheet in two.

'The Baltic gang . . .' he explained. 'They missed me . . . but they didn't miss my poor Torrence . . .'

'Have you disinfected the wound?'

'Yes, I washed it with soap then put some tincture of iodine on it . . .'

'Do you think . . .'

'That's enough for now! . . . With a needle, chief! . . . They anaesthetized him, then killed him with a needle . . .'

Maigret wasn't himself. It was as if he was on the other side of a net curtain that made him look and sound all fuzzy.

'Hand me my shirt . . .'

His voice was blank. His gestures were measured and imprecise. His face was without expression.

'You had to come here . . . Seeing as it's one of our own . . . Not to mention that I didn't want to make waves . . . You can have him taken away later . . . Keep all mention of it out of the papers . . . Chief, you do trust me, don't you?'

All the same there was a catch in Maigret's voice. It touched the super, who took him by the hand.

'Now tell me, Maigret . . . What's wrong?'

'Nothing . . . I'm quite calm, I swear . . . I don't think I've ever been so calm . . . But now, it's between them and me . . . Do you understand? . . .'

The superintendent helped him get his waistcoat and his jacket on. The dressing changed Maigret's appearance, broadening his waist and making his figure less neat, as if he had rolls of fat.

He looked at himself in the mirror and screwed up his face ironically. He was well aware that he now looked all soft. He'd lost that rock-solid, hard-cased look of a human mountain that he liked his enemies to see.

His face was pale, puffy and streaked with red. He was beginning to get bags under his eyes.

'Thank you, chief. Do you think you can do the necessary, as far as Torrence is concerned?'

'Yes, we can keep it out of the news . . . I'll alert the magistrates . . . I'll go to see the prosecutor in person.'

'Good! I'll get on with the job . . .'

He was tidying his mussed hair as he spoke. Then he walked over to the corpse, stopped in his tracks and asked his colleague:

'I'm allowed to close his eyes, aren't I? . . . I think he would have liked me to do it . . .'

His fingers were shaking. He kept them on the dead man's eyelids for a while, as if he was stroking them. The superintendent became agitated and begged him:

'Maigret! Please . . .'

The inspector got up and cast a last glance around the room.

'Farewell, chief . . . Don't let them tell my wife I've been hurt . . .'

His vast bulk filled the whole doorway for a moment. The Superintendent of Criminal Investigation almost called him back in, because he was a worrying sight.

During the war comrades in arms had said farewell to him just like that, calmly, with the same unreal gentleness, before going over the top.

Those men had never come back!

9. *The Hit-man*

International gangsters who engage in top-flight scams rarely commit murder. You can take it as a general rule that they never kill – at least, not the people they've chosen to unburden of a million or two. They use more scientific methods of thievery. Most of those gentlemen don't carry guns.

But they do sometimes use elimination to settle scores. Every year, one or two crimes that will never be properly solved take place somewhere. Most often, the victim is unidentifiable, and is buried under a patently false name.

The dead are either snitches, or men who drank too much and blabbed under the influence, or underlings aiming to rise, thus threatening the sitting hierarchy.

In America, the home of specialization, these kinds of execution are never carried out by a gang member. Specialists called hit-men are used. Like official executioners, they have their own teams and rates of remuneration.

The same has sometimes occurred in Europe, notably in the famous case of the Polish Connection (whose leaders all ended up on the scaffold). That set-up carried out several murders on behalf of more highly placed crooks who were keen not to have blood on their own hands.

Maigret knew all that as he went down the stairs towards the front desk of the Majestic.

'When a customer calls down for room service, where does his call get directed?' he asked.

'He gets connected to the room service manager.'

'At night, as well?'

'Sorry! After nine in the evening, night staff deal with it.'

'And where can I find the night staff?'

'In the basement.'

'Take me there.'

Maigret ventured once more into the innards of this hive of luxury designed to cater for a thousand guests. He found an employee sitting at a telephone exchange in a cubby-hole next to the kitchen. He had a register at his desk. It was the quiet time.

'Did Inspector Torrence call down between 9 p.m. and 2 a.m.?'

'Torrence?'

'The officer in the blue room, next door to suite 3 . . .' the receptionist explained in the language of the house.

The reasoning was elementary. Torrence had been attacked in the room by someone who had necessarily entered it. The murderer must have got behind his victim in order to put the chloroform gag over his face. And Torrence hadn't suspected a thing.

Only a hotel valet could have got away with it. He had either been called up by the policeman or else he'd come in unprompted, to clear the table.

Keeping quite calm, Maigret put the question another way round:

'Which member of staff knocked off early last night?'

The operator was taken aback by the question.

'How did you know? Sheer coincidence . . . Pepito got a call telling him his brother was sick . . .'

'What time?'

'Around ten . . .'

'Where was he, at that point?'

'Upstairs.'

'On which telephone did he take the call?'

They called the main exchange. The operator confirmed that he'd not put any call through to Pepito.

Things were moving fast! But Maigret remained placid and glum.

'His card? . . . You must have an employee card . . .'

'Not a proper one . . . We don't keep files on what we call room staff; there's too much turnover.'

They had to go to the hotel office, which was unmanned at that hour. Nonetheless Maigret had them open up the employee records, where he found what he was looking for:

Pepito Moretto, Hôtel Beauséjour, 3, Rue des Batignolles. Appointed on . . .

'Get me Hôtel Beauséjour on the telephone . . .'

Meanwhile Maigret interrogated another employee and learned that Pepito Moretto had been recommended by an Italian maître d'hôtel and had joined the staff of the Majestic three days before the Mortimer-Levingstons' arrival. No complaints about his work. He'd begun in the dining room, but then transferred to room service at his own request.

Hôtel Beauséjour came on the line.

'Hello! . . . Can you get Pepito Moretto to come to the phone? . . . Hello! . . . What was that? . . . His luggage too? . . . Three a.m.? . . . Thank you! . . . Hello? . . . One more thing . . . Did he get any mail at the hotel? . . . No letters at all? . . . Thank you! . . . That's all.'

Maigret hung up, remaining as unnaturally calm as he ever was.

'What's the time?' he asked.

'Five ten . . .'

'Call me a cab.'

He gave the driver the address of Pickwick's Bar.

'You know it closes at 4 a.m.?'

'Doesn't matter.'

The car came to a stop outside the nightclub. It was shuttered, but a streak of light could be seen coming from under the door. Maigret was aware that in most late-night venues the staff – often forty strong – usually has a meal before going home.

They eat in the same room that the customers have just vacated even while the streamers are being tidied away and the cleaners get to work.

Despite that, he didn't ring the bell at Pickwick's. He turned his back on the club, and his eye alighted on a café-tobacconist's at the corner of Rue Fontaine, the sort of place where nightclub staff often gather during intervals or after work.

The bar was still open. When Maigret walked in there were three men with their elbows on the counter, sipping coffee with something stronger in it, talking business.

'Is Pepito not in tonight?'

'He left quite a while ago,' the barman replied.

Maigret noticed that one of the customers who had perhaps recognized him was gesturing at the barman to keep his mouth shut.

'We had an appointment at two . . .' he said.

'He was here . . .'

'I know! . . . I told the dancer from over the road to bring a message to him.'

'You mean José . . . ?'

'Correct. He was supposed to tell Pepito I couldn't make it.'

'José did come over, actually . . . I think they had a chat . . .'

The customer who'd gestured to the barman was now drumming his fingers on the counter. He was pale with fury, because the few sentences that had just been said in the café were all that was needed to explain what had happened.

Around ten or a little before, Pepito had murdered Torrence at the Majestic. He must have had detailed instructions, because he knocked off work straight away, on the excuse that he'd had a phone call from his brother, and came straight to the bar at the corner of Rue Fontaine. Then he waited.

At some point the dancer who'd just been named as José came over the road and passed Pepito a message that a child could guess: shoot Maigret as soon as he steps outside Pickwick's Bar.

In other words, with two crimes in a few hours, the only two people who posed a threat to the Baltic gang would be got rid of!

Pepito fired his gun and fled. His role was over. He hadn't been seen. So he could go and get his bags from Hôtel Beauséjour . . .

Maigret paid for his drink, went out, looked back over his shoulder and saw the three customers vigorously upbraiding the barman.

He knocked at the door of Pickwick's Bar, and a cleaner opened it for him.

As he'd thought, the employees were having a late supper at tables that had been put end-to-end to make a refectory. Chicken leftovers, pieces of partridge, hors d'œuvres – everything that the customers hadn't eaten. Thirty pairs of eyes turned towards the inspector.

'Has José been gone long?'

'Sure! . . . Straight after . . .'

But the head waiter, recognizing Maigret, whom he'd served, stuck his elbow in the ribs of the man who was talking.

Maigret wasn't fooled.

'Give me his address! And it had better be the right one, OK? Or else you'll be sorry . . .'

'I don't have it . . . Only the boss has . . .'

'Where is he?'

'On his estate, at La Varenne.'

'Give me the books.'

'But . . .'

'Shut up!'

They pretended to look in the drawers of a small office desk behind the podium. Maigret shoved his way into the group that was fiddling about and found the staff register straight away.

José Latourie, 71, Rue Lepic

He exited in the same ponderous manner as he'd come in, while the still-worried waiters went back to their meal.

It was no distance to Rue Lepic. But no. 71 is a long way up the hillside street, and Maigret had to stop twice to get his puff back.

At last he got to the door of a lodging house of the same general kind as Hôtel Beauséjour, though more sordid still. He rang, and the front door opened automatically. He knocked at a glass window, and the night porter eventually got out of bed for him.

'José Latourie?'

'Still out. His key's here . . .'

'Hand it over! Police! . . .'

'But . . .'

'At the double! . . .'

The fact is, nobody could stand in Maigret's way that night. Yet he wasn't his usual stern and rigid self. Maybe people could sense something even worse?

'Which floor?'

'Fourth!'

The long and narrow room had a stuffy smell. The bed hadn't been made. Like most other people in the same line of trade, José must have slept until four in the afternoon, and hotels don't make up beds later than that.

An old pair of pyjamas that had worn through at the collar and elbows was flung across the sheets. On the floor lay a pair of moccasins with worn soles and broken uppers that must have been used as bedroom slippers. There was a travelling bag in imitation leather, but all it had in it were old newspapers and a patched-up pair of black trousers.

Over the sink was a bar of soap, a pot of skin cream, aspirin tablets and a tube of barbitone. Maigret picked up a ball of scrap paper from the floor and smoothed it out with care. He only needed one sniff to know that it had contained heroin.

Fifteen minutes later Inspector Maigret had gone through the room from top to bottom, but then he noticed a slit in the upholstery of the only armchair in the room. He slipped his finger inside the stuffing and pulled out, one by one, eleven one-gram packs of the same drug.

He put them in his wallet and went back down the stairs. He hailed a city policeman at Place Blanche and gave him instructions. The copper went to stand sentry next to no. 71.

Maigret thought back on the black-haired young man: an uneasy gigolo with unsteady eyes who'd bumped into his table out of agitation when he'd come back from his appointment with Moretto.

Once he'd done the job he hadn't dared go back home, as he would rather lose the few rags that he had and those eleven sachets, which must have had a street price of at least 1,000 francs. He'd be nabbed sooner or later, because he didn't have the nerve. He must have been scared stiff.

Pepito was a cooler kind of customer. Maybe he was in a railway station waiting for the first train out. Maybe he'd gone to ground in the suburbs. Or maybe he'd just moved to a different doss-house in another part of Paris.

Maigret hailed a cab and was on the point of asking for the Majestic when he reckoned they wouldn't have finished the job yet. That's to say, Torrence would still be there.

'Quai des Orfèvres . . .'

As he walked past Jean, Maigret realized that the doorman already knew, and he averted his eyes like a guilty man.

He didn't tend to his stove. He didn't take off his jacket or collar.

He sat at his desk, leaning on his elbows, stock still, for two hours. It was already light when he took notice of a screed that must have been put on his pad at some point during the night.

For the eyes of Detective Chief Inspector Maigret. Urgent.

Around 23.30 man in tails entered Hôtel du Roi de Sicile. Stayed ten minutes. Left in a limousine. The Russian did not exit.

Maigret took it in his stride. And then more news started flooding in. First there was a call from the Courcelles police station, in the seventeenth arrondissement:

'A man by the name of José Latourie, a professional dancer, has been found dead by the railings of Parc Monceau. Three knife wounds. His wallet was not taken. The time and circumstances of the crime have not been established.'

But Maigret knew what they were! He could see Pepito Moretto tailing the young man when he came out of Pickwick's and then, reckoning he was too upset and therefore likely to give the game away, Moretto took his life without even bothering to remove the man's wallet or ID – as a taunt, perhaps. As if to say, 'You think you can use this guy as a lead to get back to us? Be my guest! You can have him!'

Eight thirty. The manager of the Majestic was on the line:

'Hello? . . . Inspector Maigret? . . . It's unbelievable, incredible . . . A few minutes ago no. 17 rang! . . . No. 17! . . . Do you remember? . . . The man who . . .'

'Yes, he's called Oswald Oppenheim . . . Well?'

'I sent up a valet . . . Oppenheim was in bed, cool as a cucumber. He wanted his breakfast.'

10. *The Return of Oswald Oppenheim*

Maigret hadn't moved a muscle for two hours. When he wanted to get up he could barely lift his arm and he had to ring Jean to come and help him put on his overcoat.

'Get me a cab . . .'

A few minutes later he was in the surgery of Dr Lecourbe in Rue Monsieur-le-Prince. There were six people in the waiting room, but he was taken through the living quarters and, as soon as the doctor was free, he was shown into the consulting room.

It took an hour. His body was stiffer. The bags under his eyes were so deep that Maigret looked different, as if he'd got make-up on.

'Rue du Roi-de-Sicile! I'll tell you where to stop . . .'

From far off he caught sight of his two officers walking up and down opposite the lodging house. He got out of the car and went over to them.

'Still inside?'

'Yes . . . There's been one of us on duty at all times . . .'

'Who left the building?'

'A little old man all bent double, then two youngsters, then a woman of about thirty . . .'

'Did the old man have a beard?'

'Yes . . .'

He went off without saying another word, climbed the narrow staircase and went past the concierge's office. A moment later he was shaking the door of room 32. A woman's voice responded in a language he couldn't identify. The door gave way, and he set eyes on a half-naked Anna Gorskin getting out of bed.

'Where's your boyfriend?' he asked.

He spoke in staccato, like a man in a hurry, and didn't bother to look over the premises.

Anna Gorskin shouted:

'Get out of here! . . . You've no right . . .'

But he stayed unmoved, and picked up off the floor a trenchcoat he knew well. He seemed to be looking for something else. He noticed Fyodor Yurevich's dirty grey trousers at the foot of the bed.

On the other hand there were no men's socks to be found in the room.

The Jewish woman glowered ferociously at the inspector as she put on her dressing gown.

'You think that just because we're foreign . . .'

Maigret didn't give her time to throw a tantrum. He went out quietly and closed the door, which she opened again before he had gone down one flight. She stood on the landing just breathing heavily, not saying a word. She leaned over the railing, staring at him, and then, unable to contain her imperious need to do *something*, she spat on him.

Her spittle fell with a dull thud a metre away.

Inspector Dufour asked:

'Well? . . .'

'Keep a watch on the woman . . . At any rate, she can't disguise herself as an old man.'

'You mean that . . .'

No! He didn't mean anything! He wasn't up to having an argument. He got back in the taxi.

'To the Majestic . . .'

The junior detective was downcast as he watched Maigret leave.

'Do your best!' Maigret called out to him. He didn't want to take it out on the young man. It wasn't his fault if he'd been taken for a ride. After all, hadn't Maigret himself let Torrence get killed?

*

The manager was waiting for him at the door, which was a new departure for him.

'At last! . . . You see . . . I don't know what to do any more . . . They came to fetch your . . . your friend . . . They reassured me it would not be in the papers . . . But the *other one* is here! He's here! . . .'

'Nobody saw him come in?'

'Nobody! . . . That's what . . . Listen! . . . Like I told you on the telephone, he rang . . . When the valet went in, he ordered a coffee . . . He was in bed . . .'

'What about Mortimer? . . .'

'Do you think they're connected? . . . That's impossible! He's a well-known figure . . . He's had ministers and bankers call on him right here . . .'

'What's Oppenheim up to now? . . .'

'He's just had a bath . . . I think he's getting dressed . . .'

'And Mortimer?'

'The Mortimers haven't rung yet . . . They're still asleep . . .'

'Give me a description of Pepito Moretto . . .'

'Certainly . . . What I've heard . . . Actually, I never set eyes on him myself . . . I mean, noticed him . . . We have so many employees! . . . But I did some research . . . Short, dark skin, black hair, broad shoulders, could go for days without saying a word . . .'

Maigret copied it all down on a scrap of paper that he put in an envelope that he then addressed to the super. That ought to be enough, combined with the fingerprints that must have been found in the room where Torrence died.

'Have this taken to Quai des Orfèvres . . .'

'Certainly, sir . . .'

The manager was more pliant now because he sensed that events could easily get out of hand, to disastrous effect.

'What are you going to do, inspector?'

But Maigret had already moved off and was standing all clumsy and awkward in the middle of the lobby. He looked like a tourist in a historic church trying to work out without the help of a guide what there was to inspect.

There was a ray of sunshine shedding golden light on the entire lobby of the Majestic. At nine in the morning it was almost deserted. Just a few travellers at separate tables having breakfast while reading the papers.

In the end Maigret slumped into a wicker chair next to the fountain, which for one reason or another wasn't working that morning. The goldfish in the ceramic pond had decided to stop swimming about, and the only thing moving were fish-jaws going up and down, chewing water.

They reminded the inspector of Torrence's open mouth. That must have made a strong impression on him, because he wriggled about for a long time before finding a comfortable position.

A sprinkling of flunkeys passed by from time to time. Maigret did not take his eyes off them, because he knew that a bullet could fly at any moment.

The game he was in had got near to show-down.

The fact that Maigret had unmasked the identity of Oppenheim, alias Pietr the Latvian, was no big deal. In itself it didn't put the detective at risk.

The Latvian was hardly in hiding. On the contrary, he was flaunting himself in front of his trackers, as he was confident they had nothing on him.

The proof of that was the flurry of telegrams that had tracked him step by step from Krakow to Bremen, from Bremen to Amsterdam, and from Amsterdam to Brussels and Paris.

But then came the corpse on the Étoile du Nord! Most of all, there was Maigret's discovery of the unexpected relations between the East European and Mortimer-Levingston.

And that was a major discovery!

Pietr was a self-avowed crook who was happy to taunt international police forces: 'Just try to catch me red-handed!'

Mortimer was, in the eyes of the whole world, an honest and upright man!

There were just two people who might have guessed the connection between them.

That very evening, Torrence was murdered! And Maigret came under fire from a revolver in Rue Fontaine!

A third, bewildered person, who probably knew next to nothing but might serve as a lead to further investigation, had also been eliminated: José Latourie, a professional dancer.

So Mortimer and the Latvian, presumably reassured by the three disposals, had gone back to their allotted places. There they were upstairs, in their luxury suites, giving orders on the telephone to a whole team of domestics of a five-star hotel, taking baths, eating meals, getting dressed.

Maigret was waiting for them on his own. He wasn't comfortable in his wicker chair: one side of his chest was stiff and throbbing, and he could barely use his right arm, because it was wracked by persistent pain.

He could have arrested them there and then. But he knew that wouldn't be any use. At most he might get someone to testify against Pietr the Latvian, alias Fyodor Yurevich, alias Oswald Oppenheim, and who must have had many other identities as well, including that of Olaf Swaan.

But what had he got against the American millionaire Mortimer-Levingston? Within an hour of arrest, the US Embassy would lodge a protest! The French banks and companies and financial institutions on whose boards he sat would wheel in political support.

What evidence did he have? What clues? The fact that he'd vanished for a few hours when Pietr was also absent?

That he'd had supper at Pickwick's Bar and that his wife had danced with José Latourie?

That a police sergeant had seen him go into a scruffy lodging house at the sign of the Roi de Sicile?

It would all be torn to shreds! Apologies would have to be made and, to satisfy the Americans, there would have to be a scapegoat. Maigret would be sacked, at least for show.

But Torrence was dead!

He must have been carried across the hall at the crack of dawn on a stretcher. Or else the manager had warded off the possibility of an early riser seeing such an unpleasant spectacle by having the corpse taken out by the service entrance!

That was very likely! Narrow corridors, spiral staircases . . . the stretcher would have bumped into the railings . . .

Behind the mahogany counter the telephones rang. Comings and goings. Hurried commands. The manager came up to him:

'Mrs Mortimer-Levingston is leaving . . . They've just rung from upstairs to have her trunk brought down . . . The car is waiting . . .'

Maigret smiled faintly.

'Which train?'

'She's flying to Berlin from Le Bourget airfield . . .'

He'd barely finished his sentence when she appeared, dressed in a light-grey travelling cape, carrying a crocodile-skin handbag. She was moving quickly but when she got to the revolving door she couldn't resist turning round.

Maigret made a great effort to stand up so as to be certain she would see him. He was sure she had bitten her lip. Then she left even more hurriedly, waving her hands about and giving orders to her chauffeur.

The manager was wanted elsewhere. The inspector was all on his own beside the fountain, which suddenly began to spout. It must have been on a time-clock.

It was 10 a.m.

Maigret smiled inwardly, sat down weightily but with great care, because the slightest movement pulled on his wound, which was hurting him more and more.

'You get rid of the weakest links . . .'

That's what it was! First José Latourie, reckoned to be unreliable, had been got rid of with three stabs; and now Mrs Mortimer, who was also quite emotional. They were packing her off to Berlin! And doing her a favour.

The tough guys were staying behind: Pietr, who was taking ages to get dressed; Mortimer-Levingston, who had probably not lost an ounce of his aristocratic grandeur; and Pepito Moretto, the team's hit-man.

Connected by invisible threads, all three were gearing themselves up.

The enemy was in their midst, in a wicker armchair, sitting quite still with his legs stretched out in the middle of the lobby as the hotel began to get busier. Haze from the tinkling fountain misted his face.

The lift came down and stopped.

The first to emerge was Pietr, wearing a beautifully tailored cinnamon-coloured suit and smoking a Henry Clay cigar.

He was master of the house. That was what he paid for. Casually, confidently, he sauntered round the hall, stopped here and there, looked into the showcases that prestige shops set up in the lobbies of grand hotels, glanced at the board displaying the latest foreign currency rates and finally took up position less than three metres away from Maigret to stare at the artificial-looking goldfish in the pond. He flicked cigar ash into the water and then sailed off to the library.

11. *Arrivals and Departures*

Pietr glanced through a few newspapers, paying particular attention to the *Revaler Bote*, from Tallinn. There was only one out-of-date issue at the Majestic. It had probably been left behind by another guest.

He lit another cigar at a few minutes to eleven, went across the lobby and sent a bellhop to fetch his hat.

Thanks to the sun falling on one side of the Champs-Élysées, it was quite mild.

Pietr went out without his coat, with just a grey homburg on his head, and walked slowly up to the Arc de Triomphe like a man out for a breath of fresh air.

Maigret kept fairly close behind, making no effort to remain unseen. As the dressing on his wound made moving about uncomfortable, he did not appreciate the walk.

At the corner of Rue de Berry he heard a whistle that wasn't very loud and took no notice of it. Then another whistle. So he turned round and saw Inspector Dufour performing a mystifying dumb show so as to let him know he had something to tell him.

Dufour was in Rue de Berry, pretending to be fascinated by a pharmacist's window display, so his gesticulations appeared to be addressed to a waxwork female head, one of whose cheeks was covered with a meticulous simulation of eczema.

'Come over here . . . Come on! Quickly . . .'

Dufour was offended and indignant. He'd been prowling around the Majestic for an hour, using every trick of the trade – and now his chief was ordering him to break cover all at once!

'What's happened?'

'The Jewish woman . . .'

'She went out?'

'She's here . . . And since you made me cross over, she can see us, right now . . .'

Maigret looked around.

'Where from?'

'From Le Select . . . She's sitting inside . . . Look! The curtain's moving . . .'

'Carry on watching her . . .'

'Openly?'

'Have a drink at the table next to hers, if you like.'

At this point in the game there was no point playing hide-and-seek. Maigret walked on and caught up with Pietr in a couple of hundred metres. He hadn't tried to take advantage of Maigret's conversation with Dufour to slip away.

And why should he slip away? The match was being played on a new pitch. The two sides could see each other. Pretty much all the cards were on the table now.

Pietr walked up and down the Champs-Élysées twice over, from Étoile to the Rond-Point and back again, and by then Maigret had grasped his character, entirely.

He had a slender, tense figure that was fundamentally more thoroughbred than Mortimer's, but his breeding was of a kind particular to Northern peoples.

Maigret was already familiar with the type. He'd met others of the same ilk in the Latin Quarter during his days as a medical student (though he never completed the course), and they had baffled the Southerner that he was.

He had a particular recollection of one such, a skinny, blond Pole whose hair was already thinning at the age of twenty-two. He was the son of a cleaning lady, and for seven years he came to lectures at the Sorbonne without any socks, living on one egg with a slice of bread a day. He couldn't afford to buy the print versions of the lectures so he had to study in public libraries. He got to know nothing of Paris, of women, or of French ways. But scarcely had he got his degree than he was appointed a senior professor in Warsaw. Five years later Maigret saw him on a return visit to Paris, as a member of a delegation of foreign scientists. He was as skinny and icy as ever, but he went to a dinner at the presidential palace.

Maigret had met others, too. Not all of them were quite so special. But they were all amazingly keen to learn a huge range of different things. And learn they did!

To learn for the sake of learning! Like that Belgian professor who knew all the languages of the Far East – more than forty of them – without ever having set foot in Asia or being at all interested in the peoples whose languages he dissected, to amuse himself.

Ferocious will-power of the same kind could be seen in the grey-green eyes of Pietr the Latvian. But as soon as you thought you could pigeon-hole him in the category of intellectuals, you noticed other features that didn't fit at all.

In a sense you could feel the shadow of Fyodor Yurevich, the Russian vagrant in the trenchcoat, hovering over the neat figure of the guest at the Majestic.

It was a moral certainty that they were one and the same man; their identity was about to become a patent fact as well.

The evening he got to Paris, Pietr went missing. Next morning Maigret caught up with him in Fécamp in the shape of Fyodor Yurevich.

Fyodor returned to Rue du Roi-de-Sicile. A few hours later, Mortimer dropped in on him at his lodging. Several people then came out of the building, including a bearded old man.

Next morning Pietr was back in his place at Hôtel Majestic.

What was astounding was that, apart from a fairly striking physical resemblance, these two incarnations had absolutely nothing in common.

Fyodor Yurevich was a genuine Slavic vagrant, a sentimental and manic *déclassé*. Everything fitted perfectly. He didn't make the slightest error even when he leaned on the counter in the drinking hole in Fécamp.

On the other hand there wasn't a thread out of place in the character of the East European intellectual, breathing refinement from head to toe. The way he asked the bellhop for a light, the way he wore his top-quality English homburg, his casual stroll in the sun along the Champs-Élysées and the way he looked at window-displays – it was all quite perfect.

It was so perfect it had to go deeper than play-acting. Maigret had acted parts himself. Although the police use disguise and deep cover less often than people imagine, they still have to do it from time to time. But Maigret in make-up was still Maigret in some aspect of his being – in a glance, or a tic. When he'd dressed up as a cattle-dealer, for example (he had done that once, and got away with it), he was *acting the role* of a cattle-dealer. But he hadn't *become* a cattle-dealer. The persona he'd put on remained external to him.

Pietr-Fyodor was both Pietr and Fyodor *from inside*.

The inspector's view could be summed up this way: he was both one thing and the other not only in dress but in essence.

He'd been living two quite different lives in alternation for many years, that was clear, and maybe all his life long.

These were just the random thoughts that struck Maigret as he walked slowly through the sweet-smelling light air.

All of a sudden, though, the character of *Pietr the Latvian* cracked wide open.

What brought this about was significant in itself. He had paused opposite Fouquet's and was about to cross the street, manifestly intending to have an aperitif at the bar of that high-class establishment.

But then he changed his mind. He carried on along the same

side of the avenue, then suddenly began to hurry before darting down Rue Washington.

There was café nearby of the sort you find nestled in all the really plush areas of the city, to cater for taxi-drivers and domestic staff.

Pietr went in, and Maigret followed him, opening the door just as the Latvian was ordering an ersatz absinthe.

He was standing at the horseshoe counter. From time to time a waiter in a blue apron gave it a desultory wipe with a dirty dishcloth. There was a knot of dust-covered building workers to the Latvian's left, and, on his right, a gas company cashier.

The leader of the Baltic gang clashed with the surroundings in every detail of his impeccably tasteful and stylish attire.

His blond toothbrush moustache and his thin, almost transparent eyebrows caught the light. He stared at Maigret, not straight on, but in the mirror at the back of the bar.

That's when the inspector noticed a quiver in Pietr's lips and an almost imperceptible contraction of his nostrils.

Pietr must have been watching himself in the mirror too. He started drinking slowly, but soon he gulped down what was left in his glass in one go and waved a finger to say:

'Same again!'

Maigret had ordered a vermouth. He looked even taller and wider than ever in the confined space of the bar. He didn't take his eyes off the Latvian.

He was having something like double vision. Just as had happened to him in the hotel lobby, he could see one image superimposed on another: behind the current scene, he had a vision of the squalid bar in Fécamp. Pietr was going double. Maigret could see him in his cinnamon suit and in his worn-out raincoat at the same time.

'I'm telling you I'd rather do that than get beaten up!' one of the builders exclaimed, banging his glass down on the counter.

Pietr was now on his third glass of green liquid. Maigret could smell the aniseed in it. Because the gas company cashier had moved away, he was now shoulder to shoulder with his target, at touching distance.

Maigret was two heads taller than Pietr. They were both facing the mirror, and gazed at each other in that pewter-tinted screen.

The Latvian's face began to decompose, starting with his eyes. He snapped his white dry-skinned fingers, then wiped his forehead with his hand. A struggle then slowly began on his face. In the mirror Maigret saw now the guest of the Majestic, now the face of Anna Gorskin's tormented lover.

But the second visage didn't emerge in full. It kept getting pushed back by immense muscular effort. Only the eyes of Pietr's Russian self stayed stable.

He was hanging on to the edge of the counter with his left hand. His body was swaying.

Maigret tried out an experiment. In his pocket he still had the photograph of Madame Swaan that he'd extracted from the archive album of the photographer in Fécamp.

'How much do I owe you?' he asked the barman.

'Two francs twenty . . .'

He pretended to look for the money in his wallet and managed to drop the snapshot into a puddle of spilt drink between the counter's raised edges. He paid no attention to it, and held out a five franc note. But he looked hard at the mirror.

The waiter picked the photograph up and started wiping it clean, apologetically.

Pietr was squeezing the glass in his hand. His face was rigid and his eyes were hard.

Then suddenly there was an unexpected noise, a soft but sharp crack that made the barman at the cash register turn round with a start.

Pietr opened his fist. Shards of broken glass tinkled on to the counter.

He'd gradually crushed it. He was bleeding from a small cut on his index finger. He threw down a 100 franc note and left the bar without looking at Maigret.

Now he was striding straight towards the Majestic, showing no sign of drunkenness. His gait was just as neat and his posture just the same as when he had left it. Maigret stuck obstinately to his heels. As he got within sight of the hotel he recognized a car pulling away. It belonged to the forensics lab and must have been taking away the cameras and other equipment used for fingerprint detection.

This encounter stopped him in his tracks. His confidence sagged: he felt unmoored, without a post to lean on.

He passed by Le Select. Through the window Inspector Dufour waved his arm in what was supposed to be a confidential gesture but could be understood by anyone with eyes as an invitation to look at the table where the Jewish woman was sitting.

Maigret went up to the front desk at the Majestic:

'Mortimer?'

'He's just been driven to the American Embassy, where he's having lunch . . .'

Pietr was on his way to his seat in the empty dining room.

'Will you be lunching with us, sir?' the manager asked Maigret.

'Lay me a setting opposite that man, thank you.'

The hotelier found that hard to swallow.

'Opposite? . . .' he sputtered. 'I can't do that! The room is empty and . . .'

'I said, opposite.'

The manager would not give up and ran after the detective.

'Listen! It will surely cause a to-do . . . I can put you at a table where you'll be able to see him just as well.'

'I said, at his table.'

It was then, pacing about the lobby, that he realized he was weary. Weary with an insidious lassitude that affected him all over, and his whole self besides, body and soul.

He slumped into the wicker chair he had sat in that morning.

A couple consisting of a lady ripe in years and an overdressed young man stood up straight away. From behind her lorgnette the woman said in a voice that was meant to be overheard:

'These five-stars aren't what they used to be . . . Did you see that . . .'

'That' was Maigret. And he didn't even smile back.

12. *A Woman With a Gun*

'Hello! . . . Err . . . Um . . . Is that you?'

'Maigret speaking,' the inspector sighed. He'd recognized Dufour's voice.

'Shush! . . . I'll keep it short, chief . . . Went toilet . . . Handbag on table . . . Looked . . . Gun inside!'

'Is she still at Le Select?'

'She's eating . . .'

Dufour must have looked like a cartoon conspirator in the telephone booth, waving his arms about in mysterious and terrified ways. Maigret hung up without a word as he didn't have the heart to respond. Little foibles which usually made him smile now made him feel almost physically sick.

The manager had resigned himself to laying a place for Maigret opposite the Latvian, who'd asked the waiter:

'In whose honour . . . ?'

'I can't say, sir. I do as I'm told . . .'

So he let it drop. An English family group of five burst into the dining room and warmed up the atmosphere a bit.

Maigret deposited his overcoat and hat in the cloakroom, walked across the dining room and halted for a moment before sitting down. He even made as if to say hello.

But Pietr didn't seem to notice him. The four or five glasses of spirits he'd drunk seemed to have been forgotten. He conducted himself with icily impeccable manners.

He gave not the slightest hint of nerves. With his gaze on a far horizon, he looked more like an engineer trying to solve some technical problem in his head.

He drank modestly, though he'd selected one of the best burgundies of the last two decades.

He ate a light meal: omelette *aux fines herbes*, veal cutlet in crème fraîche.

In the intervals between the dishes he sat patiently with his two hands flat on the table, paying no attention to what was going on around him.

The dining room was beginning to fill up.

'Your moustache is coming unstuck', Maigret said suddenly.

Pietr didn't react. After a while he just stroked his lips with two fingers. Maigret was right, though it was hardly noticeable.

Maigret's imperturbability was legendary among his colleagues, but even so he was having trouble holding himself back.

He was going to have an even tougher time of it that afternoon.

Obviously he did not expect Pietr to do anything to put himself in jeopardy, given the close surveillance. All the same, he'd surely taken one step towards disaster in the morning. Wasn't it reasonable to hope he would be pushed all the way down by the unremitting presence of a man acting like a blank wall, shutting him off from the light?

Pietr had coffee in the lobby and then asked for his lightweight overcoat to be brought down. He strolled down the Champs-Élysées and a little after two went into a local cinema.

He didn't come out until six. He'd not spoken to anyone, not written anything, nor made a move that was in any way suspicious.

Sitting comfortably in his seat he'd concentrated on following the twists and turns of an infantile plot.

If he'd looked over his shoulder as he then sauntered towards Place de l'Opéra to have his aperitif he'd have realized that the figure behind him was made of tough, persistent stuff. But he might also have sensed that the inspector was beginning to doubt his own judgement.

That was indeed the case. In the darkness of the cinema, doing his best not to watch the images flickering on the screen, Maigret kept on thinking about what would happen if he were to make an arrest on the spot.

But he knew very well what would happen! No convincing material evidence on his side. On the other side, a heavy web of influence weighing on the examining magistrate, the prosecutor, going right up to the foreign minister and the minister of justice!

He was slightly hunched as he walked. His wound was hurting, and his right arm was getting even stiffer. The doctor had said firmly:

'If the pain starts to get worse, come back here straight away! It'll mean you've got an infection in the wound . . .'

So what? Did he have time to bother about that?

'Did you see that?' a guest at the Majestic had said that morning.

Heavens above, yes! 'That' was a cop trying to stop leading criminals from doing any more harm, a cop set on avenging a colleague who'd been murdered in that very same five-star hotel!

'That' didn't have a tailor in London, he didn't have time to get manicured every morning, and his wife had been cooking meals for him for three days in a row without knowing what was going on.

'That' was a senior detective earning 2,200 francs a month who, when he'd solved a case and put criminals behind bars, had to sit down with paper and pencil and itemize his expenses, clip his receipts and documentation to the claim, and then go and argue it out with accounts!

Maigret had no car of his own, no millions, not even a big team. If he commandeered a city policeman or two, he still had to justify the use he made of them.

Pietr, who was sitting a metre away from him, paid for a drink with a 50 franc note and didn't bother to pick up the change. It was either a habit or a trick. Then, presumably to irritate the inspector, he went into a shirt-maker's and spent half an hour picking twelve ties and three dressing gowns. He left his calling card on the counter while a smartly dressed salesman scurried after him.

The lesion was definitely becoming inflamed. Sometimes he had intense shooting pains in the whole of his shoulder and he felt like vomiting, as if he had a stomach infection as well.

Rue de la Paix, Place Vendôme, Faubourg Saint-Honoré! Pietr was gadding about . . .

Back to the Majestic at last . . . The bellhops rushed to help him with the revolving door.

'Chief . . .'

'You again?'

Officer Dufour emerged tentatively from the shadows with a worried look in his eyes.

'Listen . . . She's vanished . . .'

'What are you talking about?'

'I did my best, I promise! She left Le Select. A minute later she went into a couturier's at no. 52. I waited an hour and then interrogated the doorman. She hadn't been seen in the first-floor showroom. She'd simply walked straight through, because the building has a second exit on Rue de Berry.'

'That's enough!'

'What should I do?'

'Take a break!'

Dufour looked Maigret in the eye, then turned his gaze sharply aside.

'I swear to you that . . .'

To his amazement, Maigret patted him on the shoulder.

'You're a good lad, Dufour! Don't let it get you down . . .'

Then he went inside the Majestic, saw the manager making a face and smiled back.

'Oppenheim?'

'He's just gone up to his room.'

Maigret saw a lift that was free.

'Second floor . . .'

He filled his pipe and suddenly realized with another smile that was somewhat more ironical than the first that for the last several hours he'd forgotten to have a smoke.

He went to the door of no. 17 and didn't waver. He knocked. A voice told him to come in. He did so, closing the door behind him.

Despite the radiators a log fire had been lit in the lounge, for decoration. The Latvian was leaning on the mantelpiece and pushing a piece of paper towards the flames with his toe, to get it to light.

At a glance Maigret saw that he was not as cool as before, but he had enough self-control not to show how much that pleased him.

He picked up a dainty gilded chair with his huge hand, carried it to within a metre of the fire, set it down on its slender legs and sat astride it.

Maybe it was because he had his pipe back between his teeth. Or maybe because his whole being was rebounding from the hours of depression, or rather, of uncertainty, that he'd just been through.

In any case, the fact is he was now tougher and weightier than ever. He was Maigret twice over, so to speak. Carved from a single piece of old oak, or, better still, from very dense stone.

He propped his elbows on the back of the chair. You could feel that if he was driven to an extremity he could grab his target by the scruff of his neck with his two broad hands and bang his head against the wall.

'Mortimer is back,' he said.

The Latvian watched the paper burn, then slowly looked up.

'I'm not aware . . .'

It did not escape Maigret's eye that Pietr's fists were clenched. It also did not escape him that there was a suitcase next to the bedroom door that had not been in the suite before. It was a common suitcase that cost 100 francs at most, and it clashed with the surroundings.

'What's inside that?'

No answer. Just a nervous twitch. Then a question:

'Are you going to arrest me?'

He was anxious, to be sure, but there was also a sense of relief in his voice.

'Not yet . . .'

Maigret got up and pushed the suitcase across the floor with his foot, and then bent down to open it.

It contained a brand-new grey off-the-peg suit, with its tags still on it.

The inspector picked up the telephone.

'Hello! . . . Is Mortimer back? . . . No? . . . No callers for no. 17? Hello! . . . Yes . . . A parcel from a shirt-makers on the Grands Boulevards? . . . No need to bring it up . . .'

He put the phone down and carried on interrogating aggressively:

'Where is Anna Gorskin?'

At last he felt he was making progress!

'Look around . . .'

'You mean she's not in this suite . . . But she was here . . . She brought this suitcase, and a letter . . .'

The Latvian gave a quick stab at the charred paper to make it collapse. Now it was just a pile of ash.

Maigret was fully aware that this was no time for careless words. He was on the right track, but the slightest slip would give his advantage away.

Out of sheer habit he got up and went to the fire so abruptly that Pietr flinched and made as if to put up his arms in self-defence, then blushed with embarrassment. Maigret was only going to stand with his back to the fire! He took short, strong puffs at his pipe.

Silence ensued for such a long time and with so much unspoken that it strained nerves to breaking point.

The Latvian was on a tightrope and still putting on a show of balance. In response to Maigret's pipe he lit a cigar.

*

Maigret started to pace up and down and nearly broke the telephone table when he leaned on it. The Latvian didn't see that he'd pressed the call button without picking up the receiver. The result was instantaneous. The bell rang. It was reception.

'Hello! . . . You called?'

'Hello! . . . Yes . . . What was that?'

'Hello! . . . This is reception . . .'

Cool as a cucumber, Maigret went on:

'Hello! . . . Yes . . . Mortimer! . . . Thank you! . . . I'll drop in on him soon . . .'

'Hello! Hello! . . .'

He'd scarcely put the earpiece back on its hook when the telephone rang again. The manager was cross:

'What's going on? . . . I don't get it . . .'

'Dammit! . . .' Maigret thundered.

He stared heavily at the Latvian, who had gone even paler and who, for at least a second, wanted to make a dash for the door.

'No big deal,' Maigret told him. 'Mortimer-Levingston's just come in. I'd asked them to let me know . . .'

He could see sweat beading on Pietr's brow.

'We were discussing the suitcase and the letter that came with it . . . Anna Gorskin . . .'

'Anna's not involved . . .'

'Excuse me . . . I thought . . . Isn't the letter from her?'

'Listen . . .'

Pietr was shaking. Quite visibly shaking. And he was in a strangely nervous state. He had twitches all over his face and spasms in his body.

'Listen to me . . .'

'I'm listening,' Maigret finally conceded, still standing with his back to the fire.

He'd slipped his good hand into his gun pocket. It would take him no more than a second to aim. He was smiling, but behind the smile you could sense concentration taken to an utmost extreme.

'Well then? I said I was listening . . .'

But Pietr grabbed a bottle of whisky, muttering through clenched teeth:

'What the hell . . .'

Then he poured himself a tumbler and drank it straight off, looking at Maigret with the eyes of Fyodor Yurevich and a dribble of drink glinting on his chin.

13. *The Two Pietrs*

Maigret had never seen a man get drunk at such lightning speed. It's true he had also never seen anyone fill a tumbler to the brim with whisky, knock it back, refill it, knock the second glass back, then do the same a third time before shaking the bottle over his mouth to get the last few drops of 104 degrees proof spirit down his throat.

The effect was impressive. Pietr went crimson and the next minute he was as white as a sheet, with blotches of red on his cheeks. His lips lost their colour. He steadied himself on the low table, staggered about, then said with the detachment of a true drunk:

'This is what you wanted, isn't it? . . .'

He laughed uncertainly, expressing a whole range of things: fear, irony, bitterness and maybe despair. He tried to hold on to a chair but knocked it over, then wiped his damp brow.

'You do realize that you'd never have managed by yourself . . . Sheer luck . . .'

Maigret didn't move. He was so disturbed by the scene that he nearly put an end to it by having the man drink or inhale an antidote.

What he was watching was the same transformation he'd seen that morning, but on a scale ten times, a hundred times greater.

A few minutes earlier he'd been dealing with a man in control of himself, with a sharp mind backed up by uncommon will-power . . . A society man, a man of learning, of the utmost elegance.

Now there was just this bag of nerves tugged this way and that as if by a crazy puppeteer, with eyes like tempests set in a wan and twisted face.

And he was laughing! But despite his laughter and his pointless excitement, he had his ear open and was bending over as if he expected to hear something coming up from underneath.

Underneath was the Mortimers' suite.

'We had a first-rate set-up!' His voice was now hoarse. 'You'd never have got to the bottom of it. It was sheer chance, I'm telling you, or rather, several coincidences in a row!'

He bumped into the wall and leaned on it at an oblique angle, screwing up his face because his artificial intoxication – alcohol poisoning, to be more precise – must have given him a dreadful headache.

'Come on, then . . . While there's still time, try and work out which Pietr I am! Quite an actor, aren't I?'

He was sad and disgusting, comical and repulsive at the same time. His level of intoxication was increasing by the second.

'It's odd they're not here yet! But they will be! . . . And then . . . Come on, guess! . . . which Pietr will I be? . . .'

His mood changed abruptly and he put his head in his hands. You could see on his face that he was in pain.

'You'll never understand . . . The story of the two Pietrs . . . It's like the story of Cain and Abel . . . I suppose you're a Catholic . . . In our country we're Protestant and know the Bible by heart . . . But it's no good . . . I'm sure Cain was a good-natured boy, a trusting guy . . . Whereas that Abel . . .'

There was someone in the corridor. The door opened.

It even took Maigret aback, and he had to clench his pipe harder between his teeth.

For the person who had just come in was Mortimer, in a fur coat, looking as hale and ruddy as a man who has just come from a gourmet dinner.

He gave off a faint smell of liqueur and cigar.

His expression altered as soon as he got into the lounge. Colour drained from his face. Maigret noticed he was asymmetrical in a way that was difficult to place but which gave him a murky look.

You could sense he'd just come in from outside. There was still some cooler air in the folds of his clothes.

There were two sides to the scene. Maigret couldn't watch both simultaneously.

He paid more attention to the Latvian as he tried to clear his mind once his initial fright had passed. But it was already too late. The man had taken too large a dose. He knew it himself, even as he desperately applied all his willpower to the task.

His face was twisted. He could probably see people and things only through a distorting haze. When he let go of the table he tripped, came within a whisker of falling over but miraculously recovered his balance.

'My dear Mor . . .' he began.

His eyes crossed Maigret's and he spoke in a different voice:

'Too bad, eh! Too . . .'

The door slammed. Rapid footsteps going away. Mortimer had beaten a retreat. At that point Pietr fell into an armchair.

Maigret was at the door in a trice. Before setting off, he stopped to listen.

But the many different noises in the hotel made it impossible to identify the sound of Mortimer's footsteps.

'I'm telling you, this is what you wanted . . .' Pietr stuttered, and then with slurred tongue carried on speaking in a language Maigret didn't know.

The inspector locked the door behind him and went along the corridor until he got to a staircase. He ran down.

He got to the first-floor landing just in time to bump into a woman who was running away. He smelt gunpowder.

He grabbed the woman by her clothes with his left hand. With his right hand he hit her wrist hard, and a revolver fell to the floor. The gun went off, and the bullet shattered the glass pane in the lift.

The woman struggled. She was exceptionally strong. Maigret had no means to restrain her other than twisting her wrist, and she fell to her knees, hissing:

'Let go! . . .'

The hotel began to stir. An unaccustomed sound of excitement arose along all the corridors and filtered out all the exits.

The first person to appear was a chambermaid dressed in black and white. She raised her arms and fled in fright.

'Don't move!' Maigret ordered – not to the maid, but to his prisoner.

But both women froze. The chambermaid screamed:

'Mercy! . . . I haven't done anything . . .'

Then things turned quite chaotic. People started pouring in from every direction. The manager was waving his arms about in the middle of the crowd. Further down there were women in evening dress making a terrible din.

Maigret decided to bend over and put handcuffs on his prisoner, who was none other than Anna Gorskin. She fought back, and in the struggle her dress got torn, making her bosom visible, as it often was. A fine figure of a woman she was too, with her sparkling eyes and her twisted mouth.

'Mortimer's suite . . .' Maigret shouted to the manager.

But the poor man didn't know if he was coming or going. Maigret was on his own in the middle of a panicky crowd of people who kept bumping into each other, with womenfolk screaming, weeping and falling over.

The American's suite was only a few metres away. The inspector didn't need to open the door, it was swinging on its hinges. He saw a body on the floor, bleeding but still moving. Then he ran back up to the next floor, banged on the door he'd locked himself, got no response, and then forced it open.

Pietr's suite was empty!

The suitcase was still on the floor where he had left it, with the off-the-peg suit laid over it.

An icy blast came from the open window. It gave on to a courtyard no wider than a chimney. Down below you could make out the dark rectangular shapes of three doors.

Maigret went back down with heavy tread. The crowd had calmed down somewhat. One of the guests was a doctor. But the women – like the men, moreover! – weren't too bothered about Mortimer, to whom the doctor was attending. All eyes were on the Jewish woman slumped in the corridor with handcuffs on her wrists, snarling insults and threats at her audience. Her hat had slipped off and bunches of glossy hair fell over her face.

A desk interpreter came out of the lift with the broken glass, accompanied by a city policeman.

'Get them all out of here,' Maigret ordered. People protested behind his back. He looked big enough to fill the whole width of the corridor. Grumpily, obstinately, he went over to Mortimer's body.

'Well? . . .'

The doctor was a German with not much French, and he launched into a long explanation in a medley of two languages.

The millionaire's lower jaw had literally vanished. There was just a wide, red-black mess in its place. Despite this, his mouth was still moving, though it wasn't quite a mouth any more, and from it came a babbling sound, with a lot of blood.

Nobody could understand what it meant, neither Maigret nor the doctor who was, it turned out later, a professor at the University of Bonn; nor could the two or three other persons standing nearest.

Cigar ash was sprinkled over the fur coat. One of Mortimer's hands was wide open.

'Is he dead?' Maigret asked.

The doctor shook his head, and both men fell silent.

The noise in the corridor was abating. The policeman was moving the insistent rubberneckers down the corridor one pace at a time.

Mortimer's lips closed and then opened again. The doctor kept still for a few seconds. Then he rose and, as if relieved of a great weight, declared:

'Dead, *ja* . . . It was hard . . .'

Someone had stepped on the fur coat, which bore a clear imprint of the sole of a shoe.

The policeman, with his silver epaulettes, appeared in the open doorway and didn't say anything at first.

'What should I . . .'

'Get them all out of here, every single one . . .' Maigret commanded.

'The woman is screaming . . .'

'Let her scream . . .'

He went to stand in front of the fireplace. But there was no fire in this hearth.

14. *The Ugala Club*

Every race has its own smell, and other races hate it. Despite opening the window and puffing relentlessly at his pipe, Inspector Maigret could not get rid of the background odour that made him uncomfortable.

Maybe the whole of Hôtel du Roi de Sicile was impregnated with the smell. Perhaps it was the entire street. The first whiff hits you when the hotel-keeper with the skullcap opens his window, and the further you go up the stairs, the stronger it gets.

In Anna Gorskin's room, it was overpowering. That's partly because there was food all over the place. The *saucisson* was full of garlic but it had gone soft and turned an unprepossessing shade of pink. There were also some fried fish lying on a plate in a vinegary sauce.

Stubs from Russian cigarettes. Half a dozen cups with tea-dregs in them. Sheets and underwear that felt still damp. The tang of a bedroom that has never been aired.

He'd come across a small grey canvas bag inside the mattress that he'd taken apart. A few photos as well as a university diploma dropped out of it.

One of the photographs displayed a steep cobbled street of gabled houses of the kind you see in Holland, but painted a bright white to show off the neat black outlines of windows, doors and cornices.

On the house in the foreground was an inscription in ornate lettering reminiscent of Gothic and Cyrillic script at the same time

6
Rütsep
Max Johannson
Tailor

It was a huge building. There was a beam sticking out from the roof with a pulley on the end used to winch up wheat for storage in the loft. From street level, six steps with an iron railing led up to the main door.

On those steps a family group was gathered round a dull, grey little man of about forty – that must be the tailor – trying to look solemn and superior.

His wife, in a satin dress so tight it might burst, was sitting on a carved chair. She was smiling cheerfully at the photographer, though she'd pursed her lips to make herself look a little more distinguished.

The parents were placed behind two children holding hands. They were both boys, aged around six or eight, in short trousers, black long socks, in white embroidered sailor collar shirts with decorations on the cuffs.

Same age! Same height! A striking likeness between them, and with the tailor.

But you couldn't fail to notice the difference in their characters. One had a decisive expression on his face and was looking at the camera aggressively, with some kind of a challenge. The other was stealing a glance at his brother. It was a look of trust and admiration.

The photographer's name was embossed on the image: *K. Akel, Pskov*.

The second black-and-white photograph was bigger and more significant. Three refectory tables could be seen lengthwise, laden with bottles and plates, and, at their head, a display-piece made of six flags, a shield with a design that couldn't be made out, two crossed swords and a hunting horn. The diners were students between seventeen and twenty years of age, wearing caps with narrow silver-edged visors and velvet tops which must have been that acid shade of green which is the Germans' favourite colour, and their northern neighbours' too.

They all had short hair and most of their faces were fine-featured.

Some of them were smiling unaffectedly at the camera lens. Others were toasting it with an odd kind of beerstein made of turned wood. Some had shut their eyes against the magnesium flare.

Clearly visible in the middle of the table was a slate with the legend:

Ugala Club
Tartu

Students have clubs of that kind in universities all over the world. One young man, however, was separate from the others. He was standing in front of the display without his cap. His shaved head made his face stand out. Unlike most of the others, in lounge suits, this young man was wearing a dinner jacket – a little awkwardly, as it was still too big for his shoulders. Over his white waistcoat he wore a wide sash, as if he'd been made Knight Commander of something. It was the sash of office of the captain of the club.

Curiously, although most of those present looked at the photographer, the really shy ones had turned instinctively towards their leader. Looking at him with the greatest intensity from his side was his double, who had to twist his neck almost out of joint in order to keep his eyes on his brother.

The student with the sash and the one who was gazing at him were unquestionably the same as the lads in front of the house in Pskov, that's to say the sons of tailor Johannson.

The diploma was written in antique-looking script on parchment, in Latin. The text was larded with archaic formulas that appointed one Hans Johannson, a student of philosophy, as a Fellow of the Ugala Club. It was signed at the bottom by the *Grand Master of the Club, Pietr Johannson*.

In the same canvas bag there was another package tied up with string, also containing photographs as well as letters written in Russian.

The photographs were by a professional in Vilna. One of them portrayed a plump and stern-looking middle-aged Jewish lady bedecked with as many jewels as a Catholic reliquary.

A family resemblance with Anna Gorskin was obvious at first glance. There was a photo of her too, aged around sixteen, in an ermine toque.

The correspondence was on paper printed with the tri-lingual letterhead of

Ephraim Gorskin
Wholesale Furrier
Royal Siberian Furs a Specialty
Branches in Vilna and Warsaw

Maigret was unable to translate the handwritten part. But he did at least notice that one heavily underlined phrase recurred several times over.

He slipped these papers into his pocket and conscientiously went over the room one last time. It had been occupied by the same person for such a long time that it had ceased to be just a hotel room. Every object and every detail down to the stains on the wallpaper and the linen told the full story of Anna Gorskin.

There was hair everywhere: thick, oily strands, like Asian hair.

Hundreds of cigarette butts. Tins of dry biscuits; broken biscuits on the floor. A pot of dried ginger. A big preserving jar containing the remains of a goose confit, with a Polish label. Caviar.

Vodka, whisky, and a small vessel, which Maigret sniffed, holding some left-over opium in compressed sheets.

Half an hour later he was at Quai des Orfèvres, listening to a translation of the letters, and he hung on to sentences such as:

'. . . *Your mother's legs are swelling more and more* . . .'

'. . . *Your mother is asking if you still get swollen ankles when you walk a lot, because she thinks you have the same ailment as she does* . . .'

'. . . *We seem to be safe now, though the Vilna question hasn't been settled. We're caught between the Lithuanians and the Poles . . . But both sides hate the Jews . . .'*

'*. . . Could you check up on M. Levasseur, 65, Rue d'Hauteville, who has ordered some skins but has not provided any credit guarantee? . . .*'

'*. . . When you've got your degree, you must get married, and then the both of you must take over the business. Your mother isn't any use . . .*'

'*. . . Your mother won't get out of her chair all day long . . . She's becoming impossible to manage . . . You ought to come home . . .*'

'*. . . The Goldstein boy, who got back two weeks ago, says you're not enrolled at the University of Paris. I told him he was wrong and . . .*'

'*. . . Your mother's had her legs tapped and she . . .*'

'*. . . You've been seen in Paris in unsuitable company, I want to know what is going on . . .*'

'*. . . I've had more unpleasant information about you. As soon as business permits, I shall come and see for myself . . .*'

'*. . . If it wasn't for your mother, who does not want to be left alone and who according to the doctor will not recover, I would be coming to get you right now. I order you to come home . . .*'

'*. . . I'm sending you five hundred zloty for the fare . . .*'

'*. . . If you are not home within a month I will curse you . . .*'

Then more on the mother's legs. Then what a Jewish student on a home visit to Vilna told them about her bachelor life in Paris.

'*. . . Unless you come home straight away I want nothing more to do with you . . .*'

Then the final letter:

'*. . . How have you managed for a whole year since I stopped sending you any money? Your mother is very upset. She says it is all my fault . . .*'

Detective Chief Inspector Maigret did not smile once. He put the papers in his drawer and locked it, drafted a few telegrams and then went down to the police cells.

Anna Gorskin had spent the night in the common room. But Maigret had at last ordered them to put her in a private cell, and he went and peered at her through the grating in the door. Anna was sitting on the stool. She didn't jump but slowly turned her face towards the hatch, looked straight at Maigret and sneered at him.

He went into the cell and stood there looking at Anna for quite a while. He realized that there was no point trying to be clever or asking those oblique questions that sometimes prompt an inadvertent admission of guilt.

He just grunted:

'Anything to confess?'

'I admit nothing!'

'Do you still deny killing Mortimer?'

'I admit nothing!'

'Do you deny having bought grey clothes for your accomplice?'

'I admit nothing!'

'Do you deny having them taken up to his room at the Majestic together with a letter in which you declared you were going to kill Mortimer and also made an appointment to meet outside the hotel?'

'I admit nothing!'

'What were you doing at the Majestic?'

'I was looking for Madame Goldstein.'

'There's nobody of that name at the hotel.'

'I was unaware of that . . .'

'So why were you running away with a gun in your hand when I came across you?'

'In the first floor corridor I saw a man fire at someone and then drop his gun on the floor. I picked it up off the floor in case he decided to fire it at me. I was running to raise the alarm . . .'

'Had you ever set eyes on Mortimer?'

'No . . .'

'But he went to your lodgings in Rue du Roi-de-Sicile.'

'There are sixty tenants in the building.'

'Do you know Pietr the Latvian, or Oswald Oppenheim?'

'No . . .'

'That does not hold water . . .'

'I don't give a damn!'

'We'll find the salesman who brought up the grey suit.'

'Go ahead!'

'I've told your father, in Vilna . . .'

For the first time she tensed up. But she put on a grin straight away:

'If you want him to make the effort then you'd better send him the fare . . .'

Maigret didn't rise to the bait, but just carried on watching her – with interest, but also with some sympathy. You couldn't deny she had guts!

On first reading, her statement seemed insubstantial. The facts seemed to speak for themselves. But that's exactly the kind of situation where the police often lack sufficient solid evidence with which to confound the suspect's denials.

And in this case, they had no evidence at all! The revolver hadn't been supplied by any of the gunsmiths in Paris, so there was no way of proving it belonged to Anna Gorskin. Second: she'd been at the Majestic at the time of the murder, but it's not forbidden to walk in and around large hotels of that kind as if they were public spaces. Third: she claimed she'd been looking for someone, and that couldn't be ruled out.

Nobody had seen her pull the trigger. Nothing remained of the letter that Pietr had burned.

Circumstantial evidence? There was a ton of it. But juries don't reach a verdict on circumstantial evidence alone. They're wary of even the clearest proof for fear of making a judicial error, the ghost that defence lawyers are forever parading in front of them.

Maigret played his last card.

'Pietr's been seen in Fécamp . . .'

That got the response he wanted. Anna Gorskin shuddered. But she told herself he was lying, so she got a grip on herself and didn't rise to the bait.

'So what?'

'We have an anonymous letter – we're checking it out right now – that says he's hiding in a villa with someone called Swaan . . .'

Anna glanced up at him with her dark eyes. She looked grave, almost tragic.

Maigret was looking without thinking at Anna Gorskin's ankles and noticed that, as her mother feared, the young woman already had dropsy. Her scalp was visible through her thinning hair, which was in a mess. Her black dress was dirty. And there was a distinct shadow on her upper lip.

All the same she was a good-looking woman, in a common, feral way. Sitting sideways on the stool, or rather huddling up in self-defence, she fired daggers from her eyes as she scowled at the inspector.

'If you know all that already, why bother to ask me? . . .'

Her eyes flashed, and she added with an offensive laugh:

'Unless you're afraid of bringing *her* down too! . . . I'm right, aren't I? . . . Ha! Ha! . . . I don't matter . . . I'm just a foreigner . . . A ghetto girl living from hand to mouth . . . But she's different! . . . Oh well . . .'

She was going to talk. Jealousy had done it. Maigret sensed that he might scare her off if he seemed too interested, so he put on a nonchalant air and looked away. But she screamed out:

'Well . . . You get nothing! Did you hear me? Buzz off and leave me alone. I told you already, you get nothing! . . . Not a thing!'

She threw herself to the floor in a way that could not have been forestalled even by men well acquainted with this kind of woman. She was having a fit of hysterics! Her face was all distorted, her arms and legs were writhing on the floor, and her body juddered with muscular spasms.

What had been a beautiful woman was now a hideous hag tearing whole tufts of hair off her head with no thought for the pain.

Maigret wasn't alarmed, he'd seen a hundred fits of this kind already. He picked the water jug off the floor. It was empty. He called a guard:

'Fill this up, quickly.'

Within minutes he'd poured cold water over the woman's face. She gasped, greedily opened her mouth, looked at Maigret without knowing who he was, then fell into a deep slumber. Now and again small spasms ran across the surface of her body.

Maigret let down the bed, which had been raised against the wall as required by regulations, smoothed out the wafer-thin mattress and with great effort picked up Anna Gorskin and laid her on the bed.

He did all that without the slightest resentment, with a gentleness you'd never think he was capable of. He pulled the unhappy woman's dress down over her knees, took her pulse and watched over her for a long while.

In this light she had the look of a worn-out woman of thirty-five. Her forehead was full of tiny wrinkles you couldn't usually see. Conversely her chubby hands, with cheap varnish clumsily painted on her nails, had a delicate shape.

Maigret filled his pipe slowly with his index finger, like a man not sure what to do next. For a while he paced up and down the cell, with its door still ajar.

Suddenly he turned around, for he could hardly believe his eyes.

Anna Gorskin had just pulled the blanket up over her face. She was just a shapeless lump underneath the ugly grey cotton cover. A lump that was heaving up and down in staccato. If you strained your ear you could hear her muffled sobs.

Maigret went out noiselessly, shut the door behind him, went past the guard then, when he had gone ten metres further on, came back on his tracks.

'Have her meals sent over from Brasserie Dauphine!' he blurted out, grumpily.

15. Two Telegrams

Maigret read them aloud to Monsieur Coméliau, the examining magistrate, who had a bored expression on his face.

The first was a wire from Mrs Mortimer-Levingston in response to the message informing her of her husband's murder.

Berlin. Hotel Modern. Am sick with a high temperature, cannot travel. Stones will deal with it.

Maigret smiled sourly.

'Do you see? Here's the message from Wilhelmstrasse, for contrast. It's in IPC, I'll translate it for you:

> Mrs Mortimer arrived air, staying Hotel Modern, Berlin. Found message Paris on return from theatre. Took to bed and called American medic Pelgrad. Doctor claims confidentiality privilege. Query bring in second opinion? Hotel staff not aware any symptoms.

'As you can see, your honour, the lady is not keen to be questioned by French police. Mind you, I'm not claiming she's an accomplice. Quite the opposite, in fact. I'm sure Mortimer hid ninety-nine per cent of his activities from her. He wasn't the kind of man to trust a woman, especially not his wife. But the bottom line is that she passed on a message one evening at Pickwick's Bar to a professional dancer who's now on ice in the morgue . . . That might be the only time that Mortimer used her, out of sheer necessity . . .'

'What about Stones?' the magistrate inquired.

'Mortimer's principal secretary. He was in charge of communications between the boss and his various businesses. At the time of the murder he'd been in London for a week, staying at the Victoria Hotel. I was careful to keep him out of the picture. But I called

Scotland Yard and asked them to check the man out. Please note that when the English police turned up at the Victoria, news of Mortimer's death hadn't been released in the country, though it may have reached the news desks. Nonetheless the bird had flown. Stones did a bunk a few minutes before the police got there . . .'

The magistrate surveyed the pile of letters and telegrams cluttering his desk with a gloomy look on his face.

'Do you think we should foster the rumour that it was a love murder?' Coméliau asked, without conviction.

'I think that would be wise. Otherwise you'll set off a stock market panic and ruin a number of honourable businesses – first and foremost, those French companies that Mortimer had just bailed out.'

'Obviously, but . . .'

'Hang on a moment! The US Embassy will want proof . . . And you haven't got any! . . . And nor do I . . .'

The magistrate wiped his glasses.

'And the consequence is . . . ?'

'None . . . I'm waiting for news from Dufour, who's been in Fécamp since yesterday . . . Give Mortimer a fine funeral . . . Doesn't matter. With speeches and official delegations.'

The magistrate had been looking at Maigret with curiosity for the last few minutes.

'You look funny . . .' he said suddenly.

The inspector smiled and put on a confidential air:

'It's morphine!' he said.

'Eh? . . .'

'Don't worry! I'm not hooked on it yet! Just a little injection in my chest . . . The medics want to remove two of my ribs, they say it's absolutely necessary . . . But it's a huge job! . . . I'll have to go into a clinic and stay there for God knows how many weeks . . . I asked for sixty hours' stay of execution . . . The worst outcome would be losing a third rib . . . Two more than Adam! . . . That's all! Now you're treating this like a tragedy as well . . . It's obvious you haven't gone over the pros and cons with Professor Cochet, who's fiddled about with the innards of almost all the world's kings and masters . . . He'd have told you as he told me that there are thousands of people missing all sorts of bits and pieces in their bodies . . . Take the Czech premier . . . Cochet removed one of his kidneys . . . I saw it . . . He showed me all sorts of things, lungs, stomachs . . . And the people who had them before are still around, all over the world, getting on with their lives . . .'

He checked the time on his wristwatch, muttering:

'Come on, Dufour! . . .'

He was now looking serious again. The air in the magistrate's office was blue with the smoke from Maigret's pipe. The inspector perched on the edge of the desk; he had made himself quite at home. After a pause:

'I think I'd better pop down to Fécamp myself!' he sighed. 'There's a train in an hour . . .'

'Nasty business!' Coméliau said, as if to bring the case to an end, pushing the file away.

Maigret was lost in contemplation of the pall of smoke all around him. The only noise that broke the silence, or rather gave it a rhythm, was the gurgling of his pipe.

'Look at this photograph,' he said all of a sudden.

He held out the Pskov photograph showing the tailor's white-gabled house, the hoist, the six steps and the seated mother, with the father posing and the two lads in their embroidered sailor collar shirts.

'That's in Russia! I had to look it up in an atlas. Not far from the Baltic Sea. There are several small countries in those parts: Estonia, Lithuania, Latvia . . . With Poland and Russia surrounding them. The national borders don't match ethnic boundaries. From one village to the next you change language. And on top of that you've got Jews spread all over, constituting a separate race. And besides that, there are the communists! There are border wars going on all the time! And the armies of the ultra-nationalists . . . People live on pine-cones in the woods. The poor over there are poorer than anywhere else. Some of them die of cold and hunger. There are intellectuals defending German culture, others defending Slavic culture, and still others defending local customs and ancient dialects . . . Some of the peasants have the look of Lapps or Kalmyks, others are tall and blond, and then you've got mixed-race Jews who eat garlic and slaughter livestock their own special way . . .'

Maigret took the photograph back from the magistrate, who hadn't seemed very interested in it.

'What odd little boys!' was his only comment.

Maigret handed it back to the magistrate and asked:

'Can you tell me which of the two I'm looking for?'

Three-quarters of an hour remained before the train left. Magistrate Coméliau studied in turn the boy who seemed to be challenging the photographer and his brother, who could be turning towards the other one to ask for his advice.

'Photographs like that speak volumes!' Maigret continued. 'It makes you wonder why their parents and their teachers who saw them like that didn't guess right off what lay in store for these characters. Look closely at the father . . . He was killed in a riot one evening when the nationalists were fighting communists in the streets . . . He wasn't on either side . . . He'd just gone out to get a loaf of bread . . . I got the story by sheer chance from the landlord of the Roi de Sicile, who comes from Pskov . . . The mother's still alive and lives in the same house. On Sundays she puts on national dress, with a tall hat that comes down on the sides . . . And the boys . . .'

Maigret stopped. His voice changed entirely.

'Mortimer was born on a farm in Ohio and started out selling shoelaces in San Francisco. Anna Gorskin, who was born in Odessa, spent her early years in Vilna. Mrs Mortimer, lastly, is a Scot who emigrated to Florida when still a child. And the whole lot have ended up a stone's throw from Notre-Dame-de-Paris. Whereas I'm the son of a gamekeeper on a Loire Valley estate that goes back centuries.'

He looked at his watch again and pointed to the boy in the photograph who was staring admiringly at his brother.

'What I've got to do now is lay my hands on that boy there!'

He emptied his pipe into the coal bucket and almost began filling up the stove, out of habit.

A few minutes later Magistrate Coméliau was wiping his gold-rimmed spectacles and saying to his clerk:

'Don't you find Maigret changed? I though he was . . . how should I put it . . . rather excited . . . rather . . .'

He couldn't find the right word, and then cut to the main point:

'What the hell are all these foreigners doing here?'

Then he abruptly pulled over the Mortimer file and began to dictate:

'Take this down: *In the year nineteen . . .*'

Inspector Dufour was in the very same nook in the wall where Maigret had kept watch on the man in the trenchcoat one stormy day, because it was the only niche to be found in the steep alleyway that led first to the handful of villas on the cliff and then turned into a track that petered out in a grazed meadow.

Dufour was wearing black spats, a short, belted cloak and a sailor's cap, like everyone else in these parts. He must have acquired it on arrival at Fécamp.

'So? . . .' Maigret asked as he came upon him in the dark.

'All going fine, chief.'

He found that rather worrying.

'What's going fine?'

'The man hasn't come in or gone out . . . If he got to Fécamp before me and went to the villa, then that's where he is . . .'

'Give me the whole story, in detail.'

'Yesterday morning, nothing to report. The maid went to market. In the evening I had Detective Bornier relieve me. Nobody in or out all night long. Lights out at ten . . .'

'Next?'

'I returned to my post this morning, and Bornier went to bed . . . He'll come back and relieve me . . . Around nine, same as yesterday, the maid went off to the market . . . About half an hour ago a young lady came out . . . She'll be back shortly . . . I guess she's gone to call on someone . . .'

Maigret kept quiet. He realized how far the surveillance fell short of the mark. But how many men would he need to make a job like this completely watertight?

To keep the villa under permanent observation he would need at least three men. Then he'd need a detective to tail the maid, and another one for the 'young lady', as Dufour called her!

'She's been gone thirty minutes?'

'Yes . . . Look! Here comes Bornier . . . My turn for a meal break . . . I've only had a sandwich all day and my feet are freezing . . .'

'Off you go . . .'

Detective Bornier was a young man just starting out with the Flying Squad.

'I met Madame Swaan . . .' he said.

'Where? When?'

'At the dockside . . . Just now . . . She was going towards the outer pier . . .'

'On her own?'

'Yes, alone. I thought of tailing her . . . But then I remembered Dufour was expecting me . . . The pier's a dead end, so she can't get very far . . .'

'What was she wearing?'

'A dark coat . . . I didn't pay attention . . .'

'Can I go now?' Dufour asked.

'I told you already . . .'

'If anything comes up, you will let me know, won't you? . . . All you have to do is ring on the hotel bell three times in a row . . .'

What an idiot! Maigret was barely listening. He told Bornier: 'You stay here . . .' and then took off quite abruptly for the Swaans' villa, where he tugged at the bell-pull at the gate so hard that it nearly came off. He could see light on the ground floor, in the room he now knew to be the dining room.

Nobody came for five minutes, so he climbed over the low wall, got to the front door, and banged on it with his fist.

From inside a terrified voice wailed:

'Who's there?'

He could hear children crying as well.

'Police! Open up!'

There was a pause and the sound of scuffling feet.

'Open up! Get a move on!'

The hallway was unlit, but as he went in Maigret made out a white rectangle that could only be the maid's apron.

'Madame Swaan?'

At that point a door swung open and he saw the little girl he'd noticed on his first visit. The maid stood stock still with her back to the wall. You could tell she was rigid with fright.

'Who did you see this morning?'

'Officer, I swear I . . .'

She collapsed in tears.

'I swear . . . I swear . . .'

'Was it Captain Swaan?'

'No! . . . I . . . It was . . . madame's . . . brother-in-law . . . He gave me a letter to give to madame . . .'

'Where was he?'

'Opposite the butcher's . . . He was waiting for me there . . .'

'Was that the first time he's asked you to do jobs of that kind?'

'Yes, the first time . . . I never saw him before except in this house.'

' . . . Do you know where he planned to join up with Madame Swaan?'

'I don't know anything! . . . Madame has been in a nervous state all day . . . She asked me questions as well. She wanted to know how he looked . . . I told her the truth, I said he looked like he was on the edge . . . He scared me when he came up close.'

Maigret rushed out without closing the door behind him.

16. *On the Rocks*

Detective Bornier, a newcomer to the Squad, was quite horrified to see the chief run straight past, brushing him as he went without a word of apology and leaving the front door of the villa wide open. Twice he called out:

'Inspector Maigret! Inspector, sir!'

But Maigret did not turn back. He only slowed down a few minutes later, when he got to Rue d'Étretat, where there were some passers-by, then he turned to the right, sploshed through the mud at the dockside and started running again towards the outer pier.

He'd only gone 100 metres when he made out the figure of a woman. He switched to the other side so as to get nearer to her. There was a trawler with an acetylene lamp up in the rigging – that meant it was unloading its catch.

He stopped so as to allow the woman to reach the pool of light and he saw it was the face of Madame Swaan, in great distress. She was rolling her eyes and walking with a hurried and clumsy tread, as if she were hopping over deep ruts and by some miracle not falling into them.

The inspector was ready to tackle her and had already started to walk over. But the long black line of the deserted pier stretching out into the dark, with waves breaking over both sides, caught his eye. He rushed towards it. Beyond the trawler there wasn't a soul to be seen. The green and red flare of the harbour passage light cut through the night. The light was set on the rocks and every fifteen seconds it flashed over a wide stretch of water then lit up the outer cliff, which blinked on and off like a ghost.

Maigret stumbled over capstans as he found his way onto the pontoon, in the noise of crashing waves.

He strained his eyes to see in the dark. A ship's siren wailed a request to be let out of the lock.

In front of him was the blank and noisy sea. Behind him, the town with its shops and slippery pavements.

He strode on quickly, stopping at intervals to peer into the darkness, with increasing anxiety.

He didn't know the terrain and took what he thought was a short cut. The walkway on stilts led him to the foot of a lighthouse where there were three black cannonballs, which he counted without thinking why. Further on, he leaned over the railing and looked down on great pools of white foam settling between outcrops of rock.

The wind blew his hat off his head. He chased after it but couldn't stop it from falling into the sea. Seagulls screeched overhead, and every now and again he could make out a white wing flapping against the black sky.

Maybe Madame Swaan had found nobody waiting for her at the appointed place. Maybe her assignation had had time to get away? Maybe he was dead.

Maigret was hopping up and down, he was sure that every second counted.

He reached the green light and went round the steel platform on which it stood.

Nobody there! Waves raised their crests high, tottered, crashed down and retreated from the foamy hollow before renewing their attack on the breakwater. The sound of grinding shingle reached his ears in bursts. He could make out the vague outline of the deserted Casino.

Maigret was looking for a man!

He turned back and wandered along the shore among stones that in the dark all looked like huge potatoes. He was down at the waterline. Sea spray hit his face.

That was when he realized it was low tide, and that the pier stood on black rocks with swirling seawater in the hollows between them.

It was a complete miracle that he caught sight of the man. At first glance he looked like an inanimate object, just a blur among other blurry shapes in the dark.

He strained his eyes to see. It was something on the outermost rock, where breakers rose to their proudest height before collapsing into thousands of droplets.

But it was alive.

To get there Maigret had to slither through the struts holding up the walkway he'd run along a few minutes previously.

The rocks underfoot were covered in seaweed and Maigret's soles kept slipping and sliding. Hissing sounds came from all around – crabs fleeing in their hundreds, or air bubbles bursting, algae popping, mussels quivering on the wooden beams they'd colonized halfway to the top.

At one point Maigret lost his footing, plunging knee-deep into a rock pool.

He'd lost sight of the man but he knew he was going in the right direction. Whoever it was must have got to his spot when the tide had been even lower, because Inspector Maigret found himself held back by a pool that was now over two metres wide. He tested the depth with his right foot and nearly tipped right over. In the end he got across by hanging on to the ironwork supporting the stilts.

These are times when it's better not to be watched. You try out movements you've not been trained to do. You get them wrong every time, like a clumsy acrobat. But even so you make headway, pushed forwards by your own mass, so to speak. You fall and you get up again. There's no skill and no grace to it, but you splash on nonetheless.

Maigret got a cut in his cheek but he could never work out whether it was from a fall on the rocks or a graze from a nail in one of the beams.

He caught sight of the man again but wondered if he was seeing things: the man was so perfectly still that he could have been one of those rocks that from afar take on the shape of a human being.

He got to the point where he had water slapping about between his legs. Maigret was not the sea-going type.

He couldn't help himself but hurry on forwards.

At last he reached the outcrop where the man was sitting. He was one metre higher than his target, and three or four metres away.

He didn't think of getting his gun out, but insofar as the terrain allowed it he tiptoed forwards, knocking stones down into the water, whose roar covered the noise.

Then, suddenly, without transition, he pounced on the stationary figure, put his neck in an arm-lock and pulled him down backwards.

The pair of them almost slipped and disappeared into one of the big rollers that break over those rocks. They were spared by sheer chance.

Any attempt to repeat the exploit would surely have ended in disaster.

The man hadn't seen who was attacking him, and he slithered like a snake. He could not free his head, but he wriggled with what must surely be counted in those circumstances as superhuman agility.

Maigret didn't want to strangle him. He was only trying to overpower him. He'd hooked one of his feet behind a stilt, and that foot was all that was keeping the pair of them from falling off.

His opponent didn't struggle for long. He'd only fought out of spontaneous reaction, like an animal.

As soon as he'd had time to think, at any rate once he'd seen it was Maigret, whose face was right next to his, he stopped moving.

He blinked his eyes to indicate surrender and when his neck

was freed, he nodded towards the shifting and mountainous sea and blurted out in a still unsteady voice:

'Watch out . . .'

'Would you like to talk, Hans Johannson?'

Maigret was hanging on to a piece of slippery seaweed by his fingernails. When it was all over he confessed that at this precise moment his opponent could have easily kicked him into the water. It was only a second, but Johannson, squatting beside the last stilt of the pier, didn't take advantage of it. Later still, Maigret confessed with great honesty that he had had to hang on to his prisoner's foot to haul himself back up the slope.

Then the two of them began the return journey, without a word between them. The tide had risen further. A few metres from shore they were cut off by the same rock pool that had blocked the inspector on his way out, but it was deeper now.

Pietr went down first, stumbled when he was three metres in, slipped over, coughed up seawater, then stood up. It was only waist-deep. Maigret plunged in. At one point he closed his eyes as he felt he couldn't keep the huge weight of his body above the surface any more. But the two of them eventually found themselves dripping on the pebbles of the shore.

'Did she talk?' Pietr asked in a voice so blank that it seemed to be devoid of anything that might still harbour a will to live.

Maigret was entitled to lie but instead he declared:

'She told me nothing . . . But I know . . .'

They could not stay where they were. The wind was turning their wet clothes into an ice-jacket. Pietr's teeth started chattering. Even in the faint moonlight Maigret could see that the man's lips had turned blue.

He'd lost his moustache. He had the worried face of Fyodor Yurevich, the look of the little boy in Pskov gazing at his brother. But though his eyes were the same cloudy grey as before, they now stared with a harsh and unyielding gaze.

A three-quarters turn to the right would allow them to see the cliff and the two or three lights that twinkled on it. One of them came from Madame Swaan's villa.

Each time the beam of the harbour light went round, you caught a glimpse of the roof that shielded Madame Swaan, the two children and the frightened maid.

'Come on . . .' Maigret said.

'To the police station?'

Maigret sounded resigned, or rather, indifferent.

'No . . .'

He was familiar with one of the harbour-side hotels, Chez Léon, where he'd noticed an entrance that was used only in the summer, for the handful of holidaymakers who spend the season by the sea at Fécamp. The entrance gave onto a room that was turned into a fairly grand dining room in high season. In winter, though, sailors were happy to drink and eat oysters and herring in the main bar.

That was the door Maigret used. He crossed the unlit room with his prisoner and found himself in the kitchen. A maid screamed in stupefaction.

'Call the *patron* . . .'

She stood still and yelled:

'Monsieur Léon! . . . Monsieur Léon! . . .'

'Give me a room . . .' the inspector said when Léon came in.

'Monsieur Maigret! . . . But you're soaking! . . . Did you? . . .'

'A room, quickly! . . .'

'There's no fire made up in any of the rooms! . . . And a hot-water bottle will never . . .'

'Don't you have a pair of bathrobes?'

'Of course . . . My own . . . but . . .'

He was shorter than the inspector by three heads!

'Bring them down.'

They climbed a steep staircase with quaint bends in it. The room was decent. Monsieur Léon closed the shutters himself before suggesting:

'Hot toddy, right? . . . Full strength! . . .'

'Good idea . . . But get those bathrobes first . . .'

Maigret realized he was falling ill again, from the cold. The injured side of his chest felt like a block of ice.

For a few minutes he and his prisoner got on like room-mates. They got undressed. Monsieur Léon handed them his two bathrobes by stretching his arm around the door when it was ajar.

'I'll have the larger one,' the inspector said.

Pietr compared them for size. As he handed over the larger one to Maigret he noticed the wet bandage, and a nervous twitch broke out on his face.

'Is it serious?'

'Two or three ribs that'll have to be removed sooner or later . . .'

A silence ensued. It was broken by Monsieur Léon, who shouted from the other side of the door:

'Everything all right? . . .'

'Come in!'

Maigret's bathrobe barely covered his knees, leaving his thick, hairy calves for all to see.

Pietr, on the contrary, who was slim and pale with fair hair and feminine ankles, looked like a stylish clown.

'The toddy's on its way! I'll get your clothes dried, yes?'

Monsieur Léon gathered up the two soggy and dripping heaps on the floor and then shouted down from the top of the stairs:

'Come on then, Henriette . . . Where's that toddy?'

Then he tracked back to the bedroom and gave this advice:

'Don't talk too loud in here . . . There's a travelling salesman from Le Havre in the room next door . . . He's catching the 5 a.m. train . . .'

17. *And a Bottle of Rum*

It would be an exaggeration to say that in most criminal inquiries cordial relations arise between the police and the person they are trying to corner into a confession. All the same, they almost always become close to some degree (unless the suspect is just a glowering brute). That must be because for weeks and sometimes months on end the police and the suspect do nothing but think about each other.

The investigator strives to know all he can about the suspect's past, seeks to reconstitute his thinking and to foresee his reactions.

Both sides have high stakes in the game. When they sit down to a match, they do so in circumstances that are dramatic enough to strip away the veneer of polite indifference that passes for human relations in everyday life.

There have been cases of detectives who'd taken a lot of trouble to put a criminal behind bars growing fond of the culprit, to the extent of visiting him in prison and offering emotional support up to the moment of execution.

That partly explains the attitude that the two men adopted once they were alone in the hotel bedroom. The hotelier had brought up a portable charcoal stove, and a kettle was whistling on the hob. Beside it stood two glasses, a dish of sugar cubes and a tall bottle of rum.

Both men were cold. They huddled in their borrowed dressing gowns and leaned as close as they could to the little stove, which wasn't nearly strong enough to warm them up.

They were as casual with each other as if they were stuck in a dorm-room or a barracks, with the informality that arises between men only when social proprieties have become temporarily irrelevant.

In fact, it might have been simply because they were cold. Or more likely because of the weariness that overcame them at the same moment.

It was over! No words were needed to say that.

So each slumped into a chair and gazed at the blue enamel cooking stove that linked them together.

The Latvian was the one who took the bottle of rum and expertly mixed the toddy.

After taking a few sips, Maigret asked:

'Did you mean to kill her?'

The reply came straight away and it was just as straightforward:

'I couldn't do it.'

His face was all screwed up with nervous tics that gave the man no rest. His eyelids would bat up and down, his lips would go into spasms, his nostrils would twitch. The determined and intelligent face of Pietr started to dissolve into the face of Fyodor, the intensely agitated Russian vagrant. Maigret didn't bother to watch.

That's why he didn't realize that his opponent kept on taking the bottle of rum, filling his glass, and drinking it down. His eyes were beginning to shine.

'Was she married to Pietr? . . . He was the same as Olaf Swaan, wasn't he?'

The man from Pskov couldn't sit still, so he got up, looked for a packet of cigarettes but couldn't find any and seemed put out by that. As he came back past the table with the stove he poured himself some more rum.

'That's not the right starting point!' he said.

Then he looked Maigret straight in the eye:

'In a nutshell: you know the almost whole story already, don't you?'

'The two brothers of Pskov . . . Twins, I suppose? You're Hans, the one who was looking lovingly and tamely at the other one . . .'

'Even when we were kids he found it amusing to treat me as his servant . . . Not just between ourselves, but in front of classmates . . . He didn't call me his servant – he said: slave . . . He'd noticed I liked that . . . Because I did like it, I still don't know why . . . He was everything to me . . . I'd have got myself killed for his sake . . . When, later on . . .'

'Later on, when?'

He froze up. His eyelids flapped up and down. A swig of rum. Then he shrugged as if to say, what the hell. Then, controlling himself:

'When later on I came to love a woman, I don't think I was capable of any greater devotion . . . Probably less! I loved Pietr like . . . I can't find the word! . . . I got into fights with classmates who wouldn't grant that he was better than any of them, and as I was the least muscular boy in my class I got beaten up, and I got a kick out of it.'

'That kind of domination isn't uncommon between twins,' Maigret commented as he made himself a second glass of toddy. 'May I just take a moment?' He went to the door and called down to Léon to bring up the pipe he'd left in his clothes, together with some tobacco. Hans added:

'Can I have some cigarettes, do you mind?'

'And some cigarettes, Léon . . . Gauloises!'

He sat down again. They said nothing until the maid had brought up the supplies and withdrawn.

'You were both students at the University of Tartu . . .' Maigret resumed.

The other man couldn't sit still or stop moving around. He nibbled the end of his cigarette as he smoked and spat out scraps of tobacco, jiggled from side to side, picked up a vase from the mantelpiece and put it down somewhere else, and got more and more excited as he talked.

'Yes, that's where it all began! My brother was top of the class. All the professors paid attention to him. Students came under his spell. So although he was one of the youngest, he was made Captain of Ugala.

'We drank lots of beer in the taverns. I did, especially! I don't know why I started drinking so young. I had no special reason. In a word, I've been a drinker all my life.

'I think it was mainly because after a few glasses I could imagine a world to my own liking in which I would play a splendid part . . .

'Pietr was very hard on me. He called me a "dirty Russian". You can't know what that means. Our maternal grandmother was Russian. But in our part of the world, especially in the post-war years, Russians were treated as drunken dreamers and layabouts.

'At that time the communists were stoking up riots. My brother led the Ugala Fraternity. They went to get weapons from a barracks and faced the communists head-on in the centre of town.

'I was scared . . . It wasn't my fault . . . I was frightened . . . I couldn't use my legs . . . I stayed in the tavern with the shutters closed and drank my way through the whole thing.

'I thought I was destined to become a great playwright, like Chekhov. I knew all his plays by heart. Pietr just laughed at me.

'"You . . . You'll never make it!" he said.

'The disturbances and riots lasted a whole year, turning life upside down. The army wasn't up to maintaining order, so citizens got together in vigilante groups to defend the town.

'My brother, Captain of the Ugala Fraternity, became an important person, and he was taken seriously by people of substance. He didn't yet have any hair on his lip, but he was already being talked about as a potential leader of Free Estonia.

'But calm returned, and then a scandal erupted that had to be hushed up. When the accounts of the Ugala Club were done, it turned out that Pietr had used the group mainly to enrich himself.

'He was on several of the subcommittees and he'd fiddled all the books.

'He had to leave the country. He went to Berlin and wrote to ask me to join him there.

'That's where the two of us began.'

Maigret watched the man's face. It was too agitated by half.

'Which of you was the forger?'

'Pietr taught me how to mimic anybody's handwriting, and made me take a course in chemistry . . . I lived in a little room, and he gave me 200 marks a week to live on . . . But he soon bought himself a car, to take girls out for rides . . .

'Mainly, we doctored cheques . . . I could turn a cheque for ten marks into a cheque for ten thousand, and Pietr would cash it in Switzerland or Holland or even, one time, in Spain . . .

'I was drinking heavily. He despised me and treated me spitefully. One day I nearly got him caught accidentally, because one of my forgeries wasn't quite up to the mark.

'He beat me with his walking stick . . .

'And I said nothing! I still looked up to him . . . I don't know why . . . He impressed everyone, actually . . . At one point, if he'd wanted to, he could have married the daughter of a Reichsminister . . .

'Because of the dud forgery we had to get to France. To begin with I lived in Rue de l'École-de-Médecine . . .

'Pietr wasn't on his own. He'd linked up with several international gangs . . . He travelled abroad a lot and he used me less and less. Only occasionally, for forgeries, because I'd got very good at that . . .

'He gave me small amounts of money. He always said: "You'll never do more than drink, you filthy Russian!" . . .

'One day he told me he was going to America for a huge deal which would make him super-rich. He ordered me to go live in the country because I'd already been picked up several times in Paris by the immigration authorities. "All I'm asking is for you to lie low! . . . Not too much to ask, is it?" But he also asked me to supply him with a set of false passports, which I did.'

'And that's how you met the woman who became Madame Swaan . . .'

'Her name was Berthe . . .'

A pause. The man's Adam's apple was bouncing up and down. Then he blurted it all out:

'You can't imagine how much I wanted to *be something*! She was the cashier at the hotel where I was staying . . . She saw me coming back drunk every night . . . She would scold me . . .

'She was very young, but a serious person. She made me think of having a house and children . . .

'One evening she was lecturing me when I wasn't too drunk. I wept in her arms and I think I promised I would start over and become a new man.

'I think I would have kept my word. I was sick of everything! I'd had enough of the low life! . . .

'It lasted almost a month . . . Look! It was stupid . . . On Sundays we went to the bandstand together . . . It was autumn . . . We would walk back by way of the harbour and look at the boats . . .

'We didn't talk about love . . . She said she was my chum . . . But I knew that one day . . .

'That's right! One day my brother did come back. He needed me right away . . . He had a whole suitcase of cheques that needed doctoring . . . It was hard to imagine how he'd got hold of so many! . . . They were drawn on all the major banks in the world . . .

'He'd become a merchant seaman for the time being under the alias of Olaf Swaan . . . He stayed at my hotel . . . While I sweated over the cheques for weeks on end – doctoring cheques is tricky work! – he toured the Channel ports looking for boats to buy . . .

'His new business was booming. He told me he'd done a deal with a leading American financier, who would obviously be kept at arm's length from the scam.

'The aim was to get all the main international gangs to pull together.

'The bootleggers had already agreed to cooperate. Now they needed small boats to smuggle the alcohol . . .

'Do I need to tell you the rest? Pietr had cut off supplies of drink, to make me work harder . . . I lived alone in my little room with weaver's glasses, acids, pens and inks of every kind. I even had a portable printing press . . .

'One day I went into my brother's room without knocking. He had Berthe in his arms . . .'

He grabbed the almost empty bottle and poured the last dregs down his throat.

'I walked out,' he concluded in a peculiar tone. 'I had no option. I walked out . . . I got on a train . . . I tottered round every bar in Paris for days on end . . . and washed up in Rue du Roi-de-Sicile, dead drunk and sick as a dog!'

18. Hans at Home

'I suppose I can only make women feel sorry for me. When I woke up there was a Jewish girl taking care of me . . . She got the idea she should stop me drinking, just like the last one! . . . And she treated me like I was a child, as well! . . .'

He laughed. His eyes were misty. His restless fidgeting and twitching was exhausting to watch.

'Only this girl stuck it out. As for Pietr . . . I guess our being twins isn't insignificant, and we do have things in common . . .

'I told you he could have married a German society figure . . . Well, he didn't! He married Berthe, some while later, when she'd changed job and was working in Fécamp . . . He never told her the truth . . . I can see why not! . . . He needed a quiet, neat little place of his own . . . He had children with her! . . .'

That seemed to be more than he could bear. His voice broke. Real tears came to his eyes but they dried up straight away: maybe his eyelids were so hot they just evaporated.

'Right up to this morning she really believed she'd married the master of an ocean-going vessel . . . He would turn up now and again and spend a weekend or a month with her and the kids . . . Meanwhile, I was stuck with the other woman . . . with Anna . . . It's a mystery why she loved me . . . But she did love me, no doubt about that . . . So I treated her the way my brother had always treated me . . . I threw insults at her . . . I was constantly humiliating her . . .

'When I got drunk, she would weep . . . So I drank *on purpose* . . . I even took opium and other kinds of crap . . . *On purpose* . . . Then I would get ill, and she would look after me for weeks on end . . . I was turning into a wreck . . .'

He waved at his own body with an expression of disgust. Then he wheedled:

'Could you get me something to drink?'

Maigret hesitated only briefly, then went to the landing:

'*Patron*, send up some rum!' he shouted.

The man from Pskov didn't say thank you.

'I used to run away now and again, to Fécamp, where I prowled around the villa where Berthe lived . . . I remember her walking her first baby in the pram . . . Pietr had had to tell her I was his brother, because we looked so similar . . . Then I got an idea. When we were kids I'd learned to imitate Pietr, out of admiration . . . Anyway, one day, with all those dark thoughts in my mind, I went down to Fécamp dressed in clothes like his . . .

'The maid fell for it . . . As I went into the house the kid came up to me and cried "Papa!" . . . What a fool I was! I ran away! But all the same it stuck in my mind . . .

'From time to time Pietr made appointments to see me . . . He needed me to forge things for him . . . And I said yes! Why? I hated him, but I was under his thumb . . . He was swimming in money, swanning around in five-star hotels and high society . . .

'He was caught twice, but he got off both times . . .

'I was never involved in what he was up to, but you must have seen through it as I did. When he'd been working on his own or with just a handful of accomplices, he only did things on a modest scale . . . But then Mortimer, whom I met only recently, got him in his sights . . . My brother had skills, cheek and maybe a touch of genius. Mortimer had scope and a rock-solid reputation the world over . . . Pietr's job was to get the top crooks to work in cahoots on Mortimer's behalf and to set up the scams. Mortimer was the banker . . .

'I didn't give a damn . . . As my brother had told me when I was a student at Tartu, I was a nobody . . . As I was a nobody, I drank, and alternated between moods of depression and periods of high spirits . . . Meanwhile there was one lifebuoy on these stormy seas – I still don't know why, maybe because it was the only time I'd ever glimpsed a prospect of happiness – and that was Berthe . . .

'I was stupid enough to come down to Fécamp last month . . . Berthe gave me some advice . . . Then she added: "Why aren't you more like your brother?"

'Something suddenly occurred to me. I didn't understand why I hadn't thought of it before . . . I could *be* Pietr, whenever I liked!

'A few days later I got a message from him saying he was coming to France and would have need of me.

'I went to Brussels to wait for him. I crossed the tracks and boarded his train from the wrong side. I hid behind the luggage until I saw him get up from his seat to go to the toilet. I got there before he did.

'I killed him! I'd just drunk a litre of Belgian gin. The hardest part was to get his clothes off and then dress him up in mine.'

He was drinking greedily, with an appetite Maigret had never imagined possible.

'At your first meeting in the Majestic, did Mortimer suspect anything?'

'I think he did. But only vaguely. I had only one thing in my mind at that time: to see Berthe again . . . I wanted to tell her the truth . . . I had no real feelings of remorse, yet I felt unable to take advantage of the crime I'd committed . . . There were all sorts of clothes in Pietr's trunk . . . I dressed up as a tramp, the way I'm used to dressing . . . I went out by the back door . . . I sensed that Mortimer was on my tail, and it took me two hours to throw him off the scent . . .

'Then I got a car to drive me to Fécamp . . .

'Berthe was bewildered when I got there . . . And once I was standing in front of her, with her asking me to explain, I didn't have the heart to tell her what I'd done!

'Then you turned up . . . I saw you through the window . . . I told Berthe I was wanted for theft and I asked her to save me. When you'd gone, she said: "Be off with you now! You are bringing dishonour on your brother's house . . . "

'That's right! That's exactly what she said! And I did go off! That's when you and I went back to Paris together . . .

'I went back to Anna . . . We had a row, obviously . . . Screaming and crying . . . Mortimer turned up at midnight, since he'd now seen through the whole thing, and he threatened to kill me unless I took over Pietr's place completely . . .

'It was a huge issue for him . . . Pietr had been his only channel of communication with the gangs . . . Without him, Mortimer would lose his hold over them.

'Back to the Majestic . . . with you right behind me! Someone said something about a dead policeman . . . I could see you'd got a bandage under your jacket . . .

'You'll never know how much life itself disgusted me . . . And the idea that I was condemned to acting the part of my brother for ever more . . .

'Do you remember when you dropped a photograph on the counter of a bar?

'When Mortimer came to the Roi de Sicile, Anna was up in arms . . . She saw it would put paid to her plan . . . She realized my new role would take me away from her . . . Next evening, when I got back to my room at the Majestic, I found a package and a letter . . .'

'A grey off-the-peg suit, and a note from Anna saying she was going to kill Mortimer,' Maigret said. 'And also making an appointment to see you somewhere . . .'

The air was now thick with smoke, which made the room feel warmer. Things looked less clear-cut in the haze. But Maigret spelled it out:

'You came here to kill Berthe . . .'

Hans was having another drink. He finished his glass, gripped the mantelpiece, and said:

'So as to be rid of everybody! Myself included! . . . I'd had enough! . . . All I had in my mind was what my brother would call a Russian idea – to die with Berthe, in each other's arms . . .'

He switched to a different tone of voice.

'That's stupid! You only get that kind of idea from the bottom of a bottle of spirits . . . There was a cop outside the gate . . . I'd sobered up . . . I scouted around . . . That morning I gave a note to the maid, asking my sister-in-law to meet me on the outer pier, saying that if she didn't come in person with some money, I'd be done for . . . That was base of me, wasn't it? But she came . . .'

All of a sudden he put his elbows on the marble mantelpiece and burst into tears, not like a man, but like a child. But, despite his sobs, he went on with his story.

'I wasn't up to it! We were in a dark spot . . . The roar of the sea . . . She was looking worried . . . I told her everything. All of it! Including the murder . . . Yes, changing clothes in the cramped train toilet . . . Then, because she looked like she was going mad with grief, I swore to her that it wasn't true! . . . Wait a moment! I didn't deny the murder! . . . What I retracted was that Pietr was a piece of scum . . . I yelled that I'd made that up to get my own back on him . . . I suppose she believed me . . . *People always believe things like that* . . . She dropped the bag she'd brought with the money in it. Then she said . . . No! She had nothing else to say . . .'

He raised his head and looked at Maigret. His face was contorted, he tried to take a step but couldn't keep his balance and had to steady himself on the mantelpiece.

'Hand me the bottle, pal! . . .'

'Pal' was said with a kind of grumpy affection.

'Hang on! . . . Let me see that photo again . . . The one . . .'

Maigret got out the snapshot of Berthe. That was the only mistake he had made in the whole case: believing that at that moment Hans's mind was on the woman.

'No, not that one. The other one . . .'

The picture of the two boys in their embroidered sailor collar shirts!

The Latvian gazed on it like a man possessed. Inspector Maigret could only see it upside down, but even so the fairer boy's hero-worship of his brother stood out.

'They took my gun away with my clothes!' Hans blurted out in a blank and steady voice as he looked around the room.

Maigret had gone crimson. He nodded awkwardly towards the bed, where his own service revolver lay.

The native of Pskov let go of the mantelpiece. He wasn't swaying now. He must have summoned up his last scrap of energy.

He went right past the inspector, less than a metre from him. They were both in dressing gowns. They'd drunk rum together.

Their two chairs were still facing each other, on opposite sides of the charcoal heater.

Their eyes met. Maigret couldn't bring himself to look away. He was expecting Hans to stop.

But Hans went on past him as stiff as a pike and sat on the bed, making its springs creak.

There was still a drop left in the second bottle. Maigret took it, clinking its neck against the glass.

He sipped it slowly. Or was he just pretending to drink? He was holding his breath.

Then the bang. He gulped his drink down.

Administratively speaking, the events were as follows:

> On . . . 19 November . . . at 10 p.m. verified, an individual by the name of Hans Johannson, born Pskov, Russian Empire, of Estonian nationality, unemployed, residing at Rue du Roi-de-Sicile, Paris, after confessing to the murder of his brother, Pietr Johannson, on . . . November of the same year in the train Étoile du Nord, took his own life by shooting himself in the mouth shortly after his arrest in Fécamp by Detective Chief Inspector Maigret of the Flying Squad.

The 6 mm bullet traversed the palate and lodged in the brain. Death was instantaneous.

As a precaution the body has been taken to the morgue. Receipt of corpse has been acknowledged.

19. *The Injured Man*

The male nurses left, but not before Madame Maigret had treated them to a glass of plum liqueur, which she made herself every year on her summer holiday back home in the country in Alsace.

When she'd closed the door behind them and heard them going down the stairs, she went back into the bedroom with the rose-pattern wallpaper.

Maigret was lying in the double bed under an impressive red silk eiderdown. He looked rather tired; there were little bags under his eyes.

'Did they hurt you?' his wife inquired as she went around, tidying things up in the room.

'Not a lot . . .'

'Can you eat?'

'A bit . . .'

'It's amazing you had the same surgeon as crowned heads and people like Clemenceau and Courteline . . .'

She opened a window to shake out a rug on which a nurse had left the mark of his shoe. Then she went to the kitchen, moved a pot from one ring to another and put the lid at a slant.

'I say, Maigret . . .' she said as she came back into the bedroom.

'What?' he asked.

'Do you really believe that it was a crime of passion?'

'What are you talking about?'

'About the Jewish woman, Anna Gorskin, who's on trial today. A woman from Rue du Roi-de-Sicile who claims she was in love with Mortimer and killed him in a fit of jealousy . . .'

'Ah, that starts today, does it?'

'The story doesn't hold water.'

'Mmm . . . You know, life is a complicated thing . . . You'd better raise my pillow.'

'Might she get an acquittal?'

'Lots of other people have been acquitted.'

'That's what I mean . . . Wasn't she connected to your case?'

'Vaguely . . .' he sighed.

Madame Maigret shrugged.

'A fat lot of use it is being married to an inspector!' she grumbled. With a smile, all the same. 'When there's something going on, I get my news from the door-lady . . . One of her nephews is a journalist, so there!'

Maigret smiled too.

Before having his operation he'd been to see Anna twice, at the Saint-Lazare prison.

The first time she had clawed his face.

The second time she had given him information that led to the immediate arrest at his lodgings in Bagnolet of Pepito Moretto, the murderer of Torrence and José Latourie.

Day after day, and no news! A telephone call now and again, from God knows where, then one fine morning Maigret turns up like a man at the end of his rope, slumps into an armchair and mumbles:

'Get me a doctor . . .'

Now she was happy to be bustling around the flat, pretending to be grumpy just for show, stirring the crackling Swiss fries in the pan, hauling buckets of water around, opening and closing windows and asking now and again:

'Time for a pipe?'

Last time she asked she got no answer.

Maigret was asleep. Half of him was buried under the red eiderdown, and his head was sunk deep in a feather pillow, while all these sounds fluttered over his resting face.

In the central criminal court Anna Gorskin was fighting for her life.

In the prison, in a top-security cell, Pepito Moretto knew what fate awaited him. He walked in circles around his cell under the glum gaze of the guard, whose face could only be seen through the grid pattern on the wire screen over the hatch.

In Pskov, an old lady in a folk hat that came down over both cheeks must have been on her way to church in a sled behind a drunken coachman whipping a pony trotting across the snow like a mechanical toy.

The Hanged Man of Saint-Pholien

Translated by LINDA COVERDALE

LECRAM

LE PENDU

DE

SAINT PHOLIEN

ROMAN

PAR

GEORGES SIMENON

A. FAYARD & CIE - PARIS

PRIX : 6 FR.

1. *The Crime of Inspector Maigret*

No one noticed what was happening. No one suspected that something serious was taking place in the small station's waiting room, where only six passengers sat dejectedly among odours of coffee, beer and lemonade.

It was five in the afternoon, and night was falling. The lamps had been lighted, but through the windows one could still see both German and Dutch railway and customs officials pacing along the platform, stamping their feet for warmth in the grey dusk.

For Gare de Neuschanz is at the northern tip of Holland, on the German border.

A railway station of no importance. Neuschanz is barely a village. It isn't on any main railway line. A few trains come through mostly in the morning and evening, carrying German workers attracted by the high wages paid in Dutch factories.

And the same ceremony is performed every time: the German train stops at one end of the platform; the Dutch train waits at the other end. The train staff in orange caps and the ones wearing the dull green or Prussian blue uniforms get together to pass the time during the hour allotted for customs formalities.

As there are only twenty or so passengers per train, mostly regular commuters on a first-name basis with the customs men, such formalities do not take long.

The passengers go and sit in the station restaurant, which resembles all those found at international borders. The prices are marked in *cents* and *Pfennige*. A display case contains Dutch chocolate and German cigarettes. Gin and schnapps are served.

That evening, the place felt stuffy. A woman dozed at the cash register. Steam was shooting from the coffee percolator. Through the open kitchen door came the whistling of a wireless as a boy fiddled with its knobs.

A cosy scene, and yet a few small things were enough to insinuate an uneasy sense of mystery and adventure into the atmosphere: the two different national uniforms, for example, and the posters, some advertising German winter sports, others a trade fair in Utrecht.

Off in a corner was a man of about thirty, his face wan and stubbled, in threadbare clothing and a soft felt hat of some vague grey, someone who might well have drifted all around Europe.

He had arrived on the Holland train. When he had produced a ticket for Bremen, the conductor had explained in German that he had chosen a roundabout route without any express trains.

The man had indicated that he did not understand. He had ordered coffee, in French, and everyone had considered him with curiosity.

His eyes were feverish, too deeply sunk in their orbits. He smoked with his cigarette stuck to his lower lip, a small detail that spoke volumes about his weariness or indifference.

At his feet was a small suitcase of the kind sold in any cheap store, made of cardboard treated to look like leather. It was new.

When his coffee arrived, he pulled a handful of loose change from his pocket: French and Belgian tokens, some tiny silver Dutch coins.

The waitress had to select the correct amount herself.

People paid less attention to a traveller sitting at the neighbouring table, a tall, heavy fellow, broad in the shoulders. He wore a thick black overcoat with a velvet collar and a celluloid protector cradled the knot of his necktie.

The first man kept anxiously watching the railway employees through the glass door, as if he feared missing a train.

The second man studied him, calmly, almost implacably, puffing on his pipe.

The nervous traveller left his seat for two minutes to go to the toilet. Without even leaning down, simply by moving a foot, the other man then drew the small suitcase towards him and replaced it with one exactly like it.

Thirty minutes later, the train left. The two men took seats in the same third-class compartment, but without speaking to each other.

At Leer, the other passengers left the train, which still continued along its way for the two remaining travellers.

At ten o'clock it pulled in beneath the monumental glass roof of Bremen Station, where the arc-lamps made everyone's face look deathly pale.

The first traveller must not have known a word of German, because he headed several times in the wrong direction, went into the first-class restaurant and managed only after much coming and going to find the third-class buffet, where he did not sit down. Pointing at some sausages in bread rolls, he gestured to explain that he wished to take them with him and once again paid by holding out a handful of coins.

Carrying his small suitcase, he wandered for more than half an hour through the wide streets near the station, as if he were looking for something.

And when the man with the velvet collar, who was following him patiently, saw him finally turn left and walk quickly into a poorer neighbourhood, he understood that the fellow had simply been seeking an inexpensive hotel.

The younger man's pace was slowing down, and he examined several such establishments suspiciously before choosing a seedy-looking one with a large white globe of frosted glass over the front door.

He was still carrying his suitcase in one hand and his little sausages in bread rolls wrapped in tissue paper in the other.

The street was bustling. Fog began to drift in, dimming the light from the shop windows.

The man with the heavy overcoat finally managed to obtain the room next to that of the first traveller.

A poor room, like all the other poor rooms in the world, except, perhaps, that poverty is nowhere more dispiriting than in northern Germany.

But there was a communicating door between the two rooms, a door with a keyhole.

The second man was thus able to witness the opening of the suitcase, which turned out to contain only old newspapers.

He saw the other fellow turn so white that it was painful to witness, saw him turn the suitcase over and over in his trembling hands, scattering the newspapers around the room.

The rolls and sausages sat on the table, still in their wrapping, but the young man, who had not eaten since four that afternoon, never even gave them a glance.

He rushed back to the station, losing his way, asking for directions ten times, blurting out over and over in such a strong accent that he could barely be understood: '*Bahnhof?*'

He was so upset that, to make himself better understood, he imitated the sound of a train!

He reached the station. He wandered in the vast hall, spotted a pile of luggage somewhere and stole up to it like a thief to make sure that his suitcase wasn't there.

And he gave a start whenever someone went by with the same kind of suitcase.

The second man followed him everywhere, keeping a sombre eye on him.

Not until midnight, one following the other, did they return to the hotel.

The keyhole framed the scene: the young man collapsed in a chair, his head in his hands. When he stood up, he snapped his fingers as if both enraged and overcome by his fate.

And that was the end. He pulled a revolver from his pocket, opened his mouth as wide as he could and pressed the trigger.

A moment later there were ten people in the room, although Detective Chief Inspector Maigret, still in his overcoat with its velvet collar, was attempting to keep them out. *Polizei*, they kept saying, and *Mörder*.

The young man was even more pitiful dead than alive. The soles of his shoes had holes in them, and one leg of his trousers had been pushed up by his fall, revealing an incongruously red sock on a pale, hairy shin.

A policeman arrived and with a few imperious words sent the crowd out on to the landing, except for Maigret, who produced his detective chief inspector's badge of the Police Judiciaire in Paris.

The officer did not speak French. Maigret could venture only a few words of German.

Within ten minutes, a car pulled up outside the hotel, and some officials in civilian clothes rushed in.

Out on the landing, the onlookers now discussed the *Franzose* instead of the *Polizei* and watched the inspector with interest. As if snapping off a light, however, a few orders put an end to their excited speculation, and they returned to their rooms. Down in the street, a silent group of bystanders kept a respectful distance.

Inspector Maigret still clenched his pipe between his teeth, but it had gone out. And his fleshy face, which seemed punched out of dense clay by strong thumbs, bore an expression bordering on fear or disaster.

'I would like permission to conduct my own inquiry while you are conducting yours,' he announced. 'One thing is certain: this man committed suicide. He is a Frenchman.'

'You were following him?'

'It would take too long to explain. I would like your technicians to photograph him from all angles and with as much clarity of detail as possible.'

Commotion had given way to silence in the hotel room; only Maigret and two policemen were left.

One of the Germans, a fresh-faced young man with a shaved head, wore a morning coat and striped trousers. His official title was something like 'doctor of forensic science', and every now and then he wiped the lenses of his gold-rimmed spectacles.

The other man, equally rosy but less formal in his attire, was rummaging around everywhere and making an effort to speak French.

They found nothing except a passport in the name of Louis Jeunet, mechanic, born in Aubervilliers. As for the revolver, it carried the mark of a firearms manufacturer in Herstal, Belgium.

That night, back at the headquarters of the Police Judiciaire on Quai des Orfèvres, no one would have pictured Maigret, silent and seemingly crushed by the turn of events, watching his German colleagues work, keeping out of the way of the photographers and forensic pathologists, waiting with stubborn concern, his pipe still out, for the pathetic harvest handed over to him at around three in the morning: the dead man's clothes, his passport and a dozen photos taken by magnesium flashlights to hallucinatory effect.

Maigret was not far from – indeed quite close to – thinking that he had just killed a man.

A man he didn't know! He knew nothing about him! There was no proof whatsoever that he was wanted by the law!

It had all begun the previous day in Brussels, in the most unexpected way. Maigret happened to have been sent there to confer with the Belgian police about some Italian refugees who had been expelled from France and whose activities were now cause for concern.

An assignment that had seemed like a pleasure trip! The meetings had taken less time than anticipated, leaving the inspector a few hours to himself.

And simple curiosity had led him to step inside a small café in Rue Montagne aux Herbes Potagères.

It was ten in the morning; the café was practically deserted. While the jovial proprietor was talking his ear off in a friendly way, however, Maigret had noticed a customer at the far end of the room, where the light was dim, who was absorbed in a strange task.

The man was shabby and looked for all the world like one of the chronically unemployed found in every big city, always on the lookout for an opportunity.

Except that he was pulling thousand-franc notes from his pocket and counting them, after which he wrapped them in grey paper, tied the package with string and addressed it. At least thirty notes, 30,000 Belgian francs! Maigret had frowned at that, and when the unknown man left after paying for his coffee, the inspector had followed him to the nearest post office.

There he had managed to read the address over the man's shoulder, an address written in a handwriting much more sophisticated than a simple schoolboy scrawl:

> Monsieur Louis Jeunet
> 18, Rue de la Roquette, Paris

But what struck Maigret the most was the description: *Printed matter.*

Thirty thousand francs travelling as simple newsprint, as ordinary brochures – because the parcel hadn't even been sent via registered mail!

A postal clerk weighed it: 'Seventy centimes . . .'

The sender paid and left. Maigret had noted down the name and address. He then followed his man and had been amused – for a moment – at the thought of making a present of him to the Belgian police. Later on he would go to find the chief commissioner of the Brussels police and casually remark, 'Oh, by the way, while I was having a glass of your delicious gueuze beer, I spotted a crook . . . All you'll have to do is pick him up at such-and-such a place . . .'

Maigret was feeling positively cheerful. A gentle play of autumn sunshine sent warm air wafting through the city.

At eleven o'clock, the unknown man spent thirty-two francs on a suitcase of imitation leather – perhaps even imitation canvas – in a shop in Rue Neuve. And Maigret, playing along, bought the same one, with no thought of what might come next.

At half past eleven, the man turned into a little alley and entered a hotel, the name of which Maigret couldn't manage to see. The man shortly reappeared and at Gare du Nord took the train to Amsterdam.

This time, the inspector hesitated. Was his decision influenced, perhaps, by the feeling that he had already seen that face somewhere?

'It probably isn't anything important. But – what if it is?'

No urgent business awaited him in Paris. At the Dutch border, he had been intrigued by the way the man, with what was clearly practised skill, heaved his suitcase up on to the roof of the train before it stopped at the customs station.

'We'll see what happens when he gets off somewhere . . .'

Except that he did not stay in Amsterdam, where he simply purchased a third-class ticket for Bremen. Then the train set off across the Dutch plain, with its canals dotted with sailboats that seemed to be gliding along right out in the fields.

Neuschanz . . . Bremen . . .

Just on the off chance, Maigret had managed to switch the suitcases. For hours on end, he had tried without success to classify this fellow with one of the familiar police labels.

'Too nervous for a real international criminal. Or else he's the kind of underling who gets his bosses nabbed . . . A conspirator? Anarchist? He speaks only French, and we've hardly any conspirators in France these days, or even any militant anarchists! Some petty crook off on his own?'

Would a crook have lived so cheaply after mailing off 30,000-franc notes in plain grey paper?

In the stations where there was a long wait, the man drank no alcohol, consuming simply coffee and the occasional roll or brioche.

He was not familiar with the line, because at every station he would ask nervously – even anxiously – if he was going in the right direction.

Although he was not a strong, burly man, his hands bore the signs of manual labour. His nails were black, and too long as well, which suggested that he had not worked for a while.

His complexion indicated anaemia, perhaps destitution.

And Maigret gradually forgot the clever joke he'd thought of playing on the Belgian police by jauntily presenting them with a trussed-up crook.

This conundrum fascinated him. He kept finding excuses for his behaviour.

'Amsterdam isn't that far from Paris . . .'

And then . . .

'So what! I can take an express from Bremen and be back in thirteen hours.'

The man was dead. There was no compromising paper on him, nothing to reveal what he had been doing except an ordinary revolver of the most popular make in Europe.

He seemed to have killed himself only because someone had stolen his suitcase! Otherwise, why would he have bought rolls from the station buffet but never eaten them? And why spend a day travelling, when he might have stayed in Brussels and blown his brains out just as easily as in a German hotel?

Still, there was the suitcase, which might hold the solution to this puzzle. And that's why – after the naked body had been photographed and examined from head to toe, carried out wrapped in a sheet, hoisted into a police van and driven away – the inspector shut himself up in his hotel room.

He looked haggard. Although he filled his pipe as always, tapping gently with his thumb, he was only trying to persuade himself that he felt calm.

The dead man's thin, drawn face was haunting him. He kept seeing him snapping his fingers, then immediately opening his mouth wide for the gunshot.

Maigret felt so troubled – indeed, almost remorseful – that only after painful hesitation did he reach for the suitcase.

And yet that suitcase would supposedly prove him right! Wasn't he going to find there evidence that the man he was weak enough to pity was a crook, a dangerous criminal, perhaps a murderer?

The keys still hung from a string tied to the handle, as they had in the shop in Rue Neuve. Maigret opened the suitcase and first took out a dark-grey suit, less threadbare than the one the dead man had been wearing. Beneath the suit were two dirty shirts frayed at the collar and cuffs, rolled into a ball, and a detachable collar with thin pink stripes that had been worn for at least two weeks, because it was quite soiled wherever it had touched the wearer's neck . . . Soiled and shoddy . . .

That was all. Except for the bottom of the suitcase: green paper lining, two brand-new straps with buckles and swiveling tabs that hadn't been used.

Maigret shook out the clothing, checked the pockets. Empty! Seized with a choking sense of anguish, he kept looking, driven by his desire – his need – to find something.

Hadn't a man killed himself because someone had stolen this suitcase? And there was nothing in it but an old suit and some dirty laundry!

Not even a piece of paper. Nothing in the way of documents. No sign of any clue to the dead man's past.

The hotel room was decorated with new, inexpensive and aggressively floral wallpaper in garish colours. The furniture, however, was old and rickety, broken-down, and the printed calico draped over the table was too filthy to touch.

The street was deserted, the shutters of the shops were closed, but a hundred metres away there was the reassuring thrum of steady traffic at a crossroads.

Maigret looked at the communicating door, at the keyhole he no longer dared to peek through. He remembered that the technicians had chalked the outline of the body on the floor of the neighbouring room for future study.

Carrying the dead man's suit, still wrinkled from the suitcase, he went next door on tiptoe so as not to awaken other guests, and perhaps because he felt burdened by this mystery.

The outline on the floor was contorted, but accurately drawn.

When Maigret tried to fit the jacket, waistcoat and trousers into the outline, his eyes lit up, and he bit down hard on his pipe-stem. The clothing was at least three sizes too large: it did not belong to the dead man.

What the tramp had been keeping so protectively in his suitcase, a thing so precious to him that he'd killed himself when it was lost, was someone else's suit!

2. *Monsieur Van Damme*

The Bremen newspapers simply announced in a few lines that a Frenchman named Louis Jeunet, a mechanic, had committed suicide in a hotel in the city and that poverty seemed to have been the motive for his act.

But by the time those lines appeared the following morning, that information was no longer correct. In fact, while leafing through Jeunet's passport, Maigret had noticed an interesting detail: on the sixth page, in the column listing *age*, *height*, *hair*, *forehead*, *eyebrows* and so on for the bearer's description, the word *forehead* appeared before *hair* instead of after it.

It so happened that six months earlier, the Paris Sûreté had discovered in Saint-Ouen a veritable factory for fake passports, military records, foreign residence permits and other official documents, a certain number of which they had seized. The counterfeiters themselves had admitted, however, that hundreds of their forgeries had been in circulation for several years and that, because they had kept no records, they could not provide a list of their customers.

The passport proved that Louis Jeunet had been one of them, which meant that his name was not Louis Jeunet.

And so, the single more or less solid fact in this inquiry had melted away. The man who had killed himself that night was now a complete unknown.

Having been granted all the authorization he needed, at nine o'clock the next morning Maigret arrived at the morgue, which the general public was free to visit after it opened its doors for the day.

He searched in vain for a dark corner from which to keep watch, although he really didn't expect much in the way of results. The morgue was a modern building, like most of the city and all its public buildings, and it was even more sinister than the ancient morgue in Quai de l'Horloge, in Paris. More sinister precisely because of its sharp, clean lines and perspectives, the uniform white of the walls, which reflected a harsh light, and the refrigeration units as shiny as machines in a power station. The place looked like a model factory: one where the raw material was human bodies.

The man who had called himself Louis Jeunet was there, less disfigured than might have been expected, because specialists had partially reconstructed his face. There were also a young woman and a drowned fellow who'd been fished from the harbour.

Brimming with health and tightly buttoned into his spotless uniform, the guard looked like a museum attendant.

In the space of an hour, surprisingly enough, some thirty people passed through the viewing hall. When one woman asked to see a body that was not on display, electric bells rang and numbers were barked into a telephone.

In an area on the first floor, one of the drawers in a vast cabinet filling an entire wall glided out into a freight lift, and a few moments later a steel box emerged on the ground floor just as books in some libraries are delivered to reading rooms.

It was the body that had been requested. The woman bent over it – and was led away, sobbing, to an office at the far end of the hall, where a young clerk took down her statement.

Few people took any interest in Louis Jeunet. Shortly after ten o'clock, however, a smartly attired man arrived in a private car, entered the hall, looked around for the suicide and examined him carefully.

Maigret was not far away. He drew closer and, after studying the visitor, decided that he didn't look German.

As soon as this visitor noticed Maigret approaching, moreover, he started uneasily, and must have come to the same conclusion as Maigret had about him.

'Are you French?' he asked bluntly.

'Yes. You, too?'

'Actually, I'm Belgian, but I've been living in Bremen for a few years now.'

'And you knew a man named Jeunet?'

'No! I . . . I read in this morning's paper that a Frenchman had committed suicide in Bremen . . . I lived in Paris for a long time . . . and I felt curious enough to come and take a look.'

Maigret was completely calm, as he always was in such moments, when his face would settle into an expression of such stubborn density that he seemed even a touch bovine.

'Are you with the police?'

'Yes! The Police Judiciaire.'

'So you've come up here because of this case? Oh, wait: that's impossible, the suicide only happened last night . . . Tell me, do you have any French acquaintances in Bremen? No? In that case, if I can assist you in any way . . . May I offer you an aperitif?'

Shortly afterwards, Maigret followed the other man outside and joined him in his car, which the Belgian drove himself.

And as he drove he chattered away, a perfect example of the enthusiastic, energetic businessman. He seemed to know everyone, greeted passers-by, pointed out buildings, provided a running commentary.

'Here you have Norddeutscher Lloyd . . . Have you heard about the new liner they've launched? They're clients of mine . . .'

He waved towards a building in which almost every window displayed the name of a different firm.

'On the fifth floor, to the left, you can see my office.'

Porcelain sign letters on the window spelled out: *Joseph Van Damme, Import-Export Commission Agent*.

'Would you believe that sometimes I go a month without having a chance to speak French? My employees and even my secretary are German. That's business for you!'

It would have been hard to divine a single one of Maigret's thoughts from his expression; he seemed a man devoid of subtlety. He agreed; he approved. He admired what he was asked to admire, including the car and its patented suspension system, proudly praised by Van Damme.

The inspector followed his host into a large brasserie teeming with businessmen talking loudly over the tireless efforts of a Viennese orchestra and the clinking of beer mugs.

'You'd never guess how much this clientele is worth in millions!' crowed the Belgian. 'Listen! You don't understand German? Well, our neighbour here is busy selling a cargo of wool currently on its way to Europe from Australia; he has thirty or forty ships in his fleet, and I could show you others like him. So, what'll you have? Personally, I recommend the Pilsner. By the way . . .'

Maigret's face showed no trace of a smile at the transition.

'By the way, what do you think about this suicide? A poor man down on his luck, as the papers here are saying?'

'It's possible.'

'Are you looking into it?'

'No: that's a matter for the German police. And as it's a clear case of suicide . . .'

'Oh, obviously! Of course, the thing that struck me was only that he was French, because we get so few of them up in the North!'

He rose to go and shake the hand of a man who was on his way out, then hurried back.

'Please excuse me – he runs a big insurance company, he's worth a hundred million . . . But listen, inspector: it's almost noon, you must come and have lunch with me! I'm not married, so I can only invite you to a restaurant, and you won't eat as you would in Paris, but I'll do my best to see that you don't do too badly. So, that's settled, right?'

He summoned the waiter, paid the bill. And when he pulled his wallet from his pocket, he did something that Maigret had often seen when businessmen like him had their aperitifs in bars around the Paris stock exchange, for they had that inimitable way of leaning backwards, throwing out their chests while tucking in their chins and opening with careless satisfaction that sacred object: the leather *portefeuille* plump with money.

'Let's go!'

Van Damme hung on to the inspector until almost five o'clock, after sweeping him along to his office – three clerks and a typist – but by then he'd made him promise that if he did not leave Bremen that evening, they would spend it together at a well-known cabaret.

Maigret found himself back in the crowd, alone with his thoughts, although they were in considerable disarray. Strictly speaking, were they even really thoughts?

His mind was comparing two figures, two men, and trying to establish a relationship between them.

Because there was one! Van Damme hadn't gone to the trouble of driving to the morgue simply to look at the dead body of a stranger. And the pleasure of speaking French was not the only reason he had invited Maigret to lunch. Besides, he had gradually revealed his true personality only after becoming increasingly persuaded that his companion had no interest in the case. And perhaps not much in the way of brains, either!

That morning, Van Damme had been worried. His smile had seemed forced. By the end of the afternoon, on the other hand, he had resurfaced as a sharp little operator, always on the go, busy, chatty, enthusiastic, mixing with financial big shots, driving his car, on the phone, rattling off instructions to his typist and hosting expensive dinners, proud and happy to be what he was.

And the second man was an anaemic tramp with grubby

clothes and worn-out shoes, who had bought some sausages in rolls without the faintest idea that he would never get to eat them!

Van Damme must have already found himself another companion for the evening aperitif, in the same atmosphere of Viennese music and beer.

At six o'clock, a cover would close quietly on a metal bin, shutting away the naked body of the false Louis Jeunet, and the lift would deliver it to the freezer to spend the night in a numbered compartment.

Maigret went along to the Polizeipräsidium. Some officers were exercising, stripped to the waist in spite of the chill, in a courtyard with vivid red walls.

In the laboratory, a young man with a faraway look in his eye was waiting for him near a table on which all the dead man's possessions had been laid out and neatly labelled.

The man spoke perfect textbook French and took pride in coming up with *le mot juste*.

Beginning with the nondescript grey suit Jeunet had been wearing when he died, he explained that all the linings had been unpicked, every seam examined, and that nothing had been found.

'The suit comes from La Belle Jardinière in Paris. The material is fifty per cent cotton, so it is a cheap garment. We noticed some grease spots, including stains of mineral jelly, which suggest that the man worked in or was often inside a factory, workshop or garage. There are no labels or laundry marks in his linen. The shoes were purchased in Rheims. Same as the clothing: mass-produced, of mediocre quality. The socks are of cotton, the kind peddled in the street at four or five francs a pair. They have holes in them but have never been mended.

'All these clothes have been placed in a strong paper bag and shaken, and the dust obtained was analysed.

'We were thus able to confirm the provenance of those grease stains. The clothes are in fact impregnated with a fine metallic powder found only on the belongings of fitters, metal-workers, and, in general, those who labour in machine shops.

'These elements are absent from the items I will call clothing B, items which have not been worn for at least six years.

'One more difference: in the pockets of suit A we found traces of French government-issue tobacco, what you call shag tobacco. In the pockets of clothing B, however, there were particles of yellowish imitation Egyptian tobacco.

'But now I come to the most important point. The spots found on clothing B are not grease spots. They are old human bloodstains, probably from arterial blood.

'The material has not been washed for years. The man who wore this suit must have been literally drenched in blood. And finally, certain tears suggest that there may have been a struggle, because in various places, for example on the lapels, the weave of the cloth has been torn as if it had been clawed by fingernails.

'The items of clothing B have labels from the tailor Roger Morcel, Rue Haute-Sauvenière, in Liège.

'As for the revolver, it's a model that was discontinued two years ago.

'If you wish to leave me your address, I will send you a copy of the report I'll be drawing up for my superiors.'

By eight that evening, Maigret had finished with the formalities. The German police had handed the dead man's clothes over to him along with the ones in the suitcase, which the technician had referred to as clothing B. And it had been decided that, until further notice, the body would be kept at the disposition of the French authorities in the mortuary refrigerator unit.

Maigret had a copy of Joseph Van Damme's public record: born in Liège of Flemish parents; travelling salesman, then director of a commission agency bearing his name.

He was thirty-two. A bachelor. He had lived in Bremen for only three years and, after some initial difficulties, now seemed to be doing nicely.

The inspector returned to his hotel room, where he sat for a long time on the edge of his bed with the two cheap suitcases in front of him. He had opened the communicating door to the neighbouring room, where nothing had been touched since the previous day, and he was struck by how little disorder the tragedy had left behind. In one place on the wallpaper, beneath a pink flower, was a very small brown spot, the only bloodstain. On the table lay the two sausage bread rolls, still wrapped in paper. A fly was sitting on them.

That morning, Maigret had sent two photos of the dead man to Paris and asked that the Police Judiciaire publish them in as many newspapers as possible.

Should the search begin there? In Paris, where the police at least had an address, the one where Jeunet had sent himself the thirty thousand-franc notes from Brussels?

Or in Liège, where clothing B had been bought a few years before? In Rheims, where the dead man's shoes had come from? In Brussels, where Jeunet had wrapped up his package of 30,000 francs? Bremen, where he had died and where a certain Joseph Van Damme had come to take a look at his corpse, denying all the while that he had ever known him?

The hotel manager appeared, made a long speech in German and, as far as the inspector could tell, asked him if the room where the tragedy had taken place could be cleaned and rented out.

Maigret grunted his assent, washed his hands, paid and went off with his two suitcases, their obviously poor quality in stark contrast with his comfortably bourgeois appearance.

There was no clear reason to tackle his investigation from one angle or another. And if he chose Paris, it was above all because of the strikingly foreign atmosphere all around him that constantly disturbed his habits, his way of thinking and, in the end, depressed him.

The local tobacco – rather yellow and too mild – had even killed his desire to smoke!

He slept in the express, waking at the Belgian border as day was breaking, and passed through Liège thirty minutes later. He stood at the door of the carriage to stare half-heartedly out at the station, where the train halted for only thirty minutes, not enough time for a visit to Rue Haute-Sauvenière.

At two that afternoon he arrived at Gare du Nord and plunged into the Parisian crowds, where his first concern was to visit a tobacconist.

He was groping around in his pockets for some French coins when someone jostled him. The two suitcases were sitting at his feet. When he bent to retrieve them, he could find only one, and looking around in vain for the other, he realized that there was no point in alerting the police.

One detail, in any case, reassured him. The remaining suitcase had its two keys tied to the handle with a small string. That was the suitcase containing the clothing.

The thief had carried off the one full of old newspapers.

Had he been simply a thief, the kind that prowl through stations? In which case, wasn't it odd that he'd stolen such a crummy-looking piece of luggage?

Maigret settled into a taxi, savouring both his pipe and the familiar hubbub of the streets. Passing a kiosk, he caught a glimpse of a front-page photograph and even at a distance recognized one of the pictures of Louis Jeunet he had sent from Bremen.

He considered stopping by his home on Boulevard Richard-Lenoir to kiss his wife and change his clothes, but the incident at the station was bothering him.

'If the thief really was after the second suit of clothes, then how was he informed in Paris that I was carrying them and would arrive precisely when I did?'

It was as if fresh mysteries now hovered around the pale face and thin form of the tramp of Neuschanz and Bremen: shadowy forms were shifting, as on a photographic plate plunged into a developing bath.

And they would have to become clearer, revealing faces, names, thoughts and feelings, entire lives.

For the moment, in the centre of that plate lay only a naked body, and a harsh light shone on the face German doctors had done their fumbling best to make look human again.

The shadows? First, a man in Paris who was making off with the suitcase at that very moment. Plus another man who – from Bremen or elsewhere – had sent him instructions. The convivial Joseph Van Damme, perhaps? Or perhaps not! And then there was the person who, years ago, had worn clothing B . . . and the one who, during the struggle, had bled all over him. And the person who had supplied the 30,000 francs to 'Louis Jeunet' – or the person from whom they had been stolen!

It was sunny; the café terraces, heated by braziers, were thronged with people. Drivers were hailing one another. Swarms of people were pushing their way on to buses and trams.

From among all this seething humanity, here and in Bremen, Brussels, Rheims and still other places, the hunt would have to track down two, three, four, five individuals . . .

Fewer, perhaps? Or maybe more . . .

Maigret looked up fondly at the austere façade of police headquarters as he crossed the front courtyard carrying the small suitcase. He greeted the office boy by his first name.

'Did you get my telegram? Did you light a stove?'

'There's a lady here, about the picture! She's in the waiting room, been there for two hours now.'

Maigret did not stop to take off his hat and coat. He didn't even set down the suitcase.

The waiting room, at the end of the corridor lined with the chief inspectors' offices, is almost completely glassed-in and furnished with a few chairs upholstered in green velvet; its sole brick wall displays the list of policemen killed while on special duty.

On one of the chairs sat a woman who was still young, dressed with the humble care that bespeaks long hours of sewing by lamp-light, making do with the best one has.

Her black cloth coat had a very thin fur collar. Her hands, in their grey cotton gloves, clutched a handbag made, like Maigret's suitcase, of imitation leather.

Did the inspector notice a vague resemblance between his visitor and the dead man?

Not a facial resemblance, no, but a similarity of expression, of social *class*, so to speak.

She, too, had the washed-out, weary eyes of those whose courage has abandoned them. Her nostrils were pinched and her complexion unhealthily dull.

She had been waiting for two hours and naturally hadn't dared change seats or even move at all. She looked at Maigret through the glass with no hope that he might at last be the person she needed to see.

He opened the door.

'If you would care to follow me to my office, madame.'

When he ushered her in ahead of him she appeared astonished at his courtesy and hesitated, as if confused, in the middle of the room. Along with her handbag she carried a rumpled newspaper showing part of Jeunet's photograph.

'I'm told you know the man who—'

But before he could finish she bit her lips and buried her face in her hands. Almost overcome by a sob she could not control, she moaned, 'He's my husband, monsieur.'

Hiding his feeling, Maigret turned away, then rolled a heavy armchair over for her.

3. The Herbalist's Shop in Rue Picpus

'Did he suffer much?' she asked, as soon as she could speak again.

'No, madame. I can assure you that death was instantaneous.'

She looked at the newspaper in her hand. The words were hard to say.

'In the mouth?'

When the inspector simply nodded, she stared down at the floor, suddenly calm, and as if speaking about a mischievous child she said solemnly, 'He always had to be different from everyone else . . .'

She spoke not as a lover, or even a wife. Although she was not yet thirty, she had a maternal tenderness about her, and the gentle resignation of a nun.

The poor are used to stifling any expression of their despair, because they must get on with life, with work, with the demands made of them day after day, hour after hour. She wiped her eyes with her handkerchief, and her slightly reddened nose erased any prettiness she possessed.

The corners of her mouth kept drooping sadly though she tried to smile as she looked at Maigret.

'Would you mind if I asked you a few questions?' he said, sitting down at his desk. 'Was your husband's name indeed Louis Jeunet? And . . . when did he leave you for the last time?'

Tears sprang to her eyes; she almost began weeping again. Her fingers had balled the handkerchief into a hard little wad.

'Two years ago . . . But I saw him again, once, peering in at the shop window. If my mother hadn't been there . . .'

Maigret realized that he need simply let her talk. Because she would, as much for herself as for him.

'You want to know all about our life, isn't that right? It's the only way to understand why Louis did that . . . My father was a male nurse in Beaujon. He had set up a small herbalist's shop in Rue Picpus, which my mother managed.

'My father died six years ago, and Mama and I have kept up the business.

'I met Louis . . .'

'That was six years ago, did you say?' Maigret asked her. 'Was he already calling himself Jeunet?'

'Yes!' she replied, in some astonishment. 'He was a milling machine operator in a workshop in Belleville . . . He earned a good living . . . I don't know why things happened so quickly, you can't imagine – he was in a hurry about everything, as if some fever were eating at him.

'I'd been seeing him for barely a month when we got married, and he came to live with us. The living quarters behind the shop are too small for three people; we rented a room for Mama over in Rue du Chemin-Vert. She let me have the shop, but as she hadn't saved enough to live on, we gave her 200 francs every month.

'We were happy, I swear to you! Louis would go off to work in the morning; my mother would come to keep me company. He stayed home in the evenings.

'I don't know how to explain this to you, but – I always felt that something was wrong!

'I mean, for example . . . it was as if Louis didn't belong to our world, as if the way we lived was sometimes too much for him.

'He was very sweet to me . . .'

Her expression became wistful; she was almost beautiful when she confessed, 'I don't think many men are like this: he would take me suddenly in his arms, looking so deeply into my eyes that it hurt. Then sometimes, out of the blue, he would push me away – I've never seen such a thing from anyone else – and he'd sigh to himself, "Yet I really am fond of you, my little Jeanne . . . "

'Then it was over. He'd keep busy with this or that without giving me another glance, spend hours repairing a piece of furniture, making me something handy for housework, or fixing a clock.

'My mother didn't much care for him, precisely because she understood that he wasn't like other people.'

'Among his belongings, weren't there some items he guarded with particular care?'

'How did you know?'

She started, a touch frightened, and blurted out, 'An old suit! Once he came home when I'd taken it from a cardboard box on top of the wardrobe and was brushing it. The suit would have been still good enough to wear around the house. I was even going to mend the tears. Louis grabbed it from me, he was furious, shouting cruel things, and that evening – you'd have sworn he hated me!

'We'd been married for a month. After that . . .'

She sighed and looked at Maigret as if in apology for having nothing more for him than this poor story.

'He became more and more strange?'

'It isn't his fault, I'm sure of that! I think he was ill, he worried so . . . We were often in the kitchen, and whenever we'd been happy for a little while, I used to see him change suddenly: he'd stop speaking, look at things – and me – with a nasty smile, and go and throw himself down on his bed without saying goodnight to me.'

'He had no friends?'

'No! No one ever came to see him.'

'He never travelled, received any letters?'

'No. And he didn't like having people in our home. Once in a while, a neighbour who had no sewing machine would come over to use mine, and that was guaranteed to enrage Louis. But he didn't become angry like everyone else, it was something shut up inside . . . and he was the one who seemed to suffer!

'When I told him we were going to have a child, he stared at me like a madman . . .

'That was when he started to drink, fits of it, binges, especially after the baby was born. And yet I know that he loved that child! Sometimes he used to gaze at him in adoration, the way he did with me at first . . .

'The next day, he'd come home drunk, lie down, lock the bedroom door and spend hours in there, whole days.

'The first few times, he'd cry and beg me to forgive him. Maybe if Mama hadn't interfered I might have managed to keep him, but my mother tried to lecture him, and there were awful arguments. Especially when Louis went two or three days without going to work!

'Towards the end, we were desperately unhappy. You know what it's like, don't you? His temper got worse and worse. My mother threw him out twice, to remind him that he wasn't the lord and master there.

'But I just know that it wasn't his fault! Something was pushing him, driving him! He would still look at me, or our son, in that old way I told you about . . .

'Only now not so often, and it didn't last long. The final quarrel was dreadful. Mama was there. Louis had helped himself to some money from the shop, and she called him a thief. He went so pale, his eyes all red, as on his bad days, and a crazed look in those eyes . . .

'I can still see him coming closer as if to strangle me! I was terrified and screamed, "Louis!"

'He left, slamming the door so hard the glass shattered.

'That was two years ago. Some neighbourhood women saw him around now and again . . . I went to that factory in Belleville, but they told me he didn't work there any more.

'Someone saw him, though, in a small workshop in Rue de la Roquette where they make beer pumps.

'Me, I saw him once more, maybe six months ago now, through the shop window. Mama is living with me and the child again, and she was in the shop . . . she kept me from running to the door.

'You swear to me that he didn't suffer? That he died instantly? He was an unhappy, unfortunate man, don't you see? You must have understood that by now . . .'

She had relived her story with such intensity, and her husband had had such a strong hold on her, that, without realizing it, she had been reflecting all the feelings she was describing on her own face.

As in his first impression, Maigret was struck by an unnerving resemblance between this woman and the man in Bremen who had snapped his fingers before shooting a bullet into his mouth.

What's more, that raging fever she had just evoked seemed to have infected her. She fell silent, but all her nerves remained on edge, and she almost gasped for breath. She was waiting for something, she didn't know what.

'He never spoke to you about his past, his childhood?'

'No. He didn't talk much. I only know that he was born in Aubervilliers. And I've always thought he was educated beyond his station in life; he had lovely handwriting, and he knew the Latin names of all the plants. When the woman from the haberdashery next door had a difficult letter to write, he was the one she came to.'

'And you never saw his family?'

'Before we were married, he told me he was an orphan. Chief inspector, there's one more thing I'd like to ask you. Will he be brought back to France?'

When Maigret hesitated to reply, she turned her face away to hide her embarrassment.

'Now the shop belongs to my mother. And the money, too. I know she won't want to pay anything to bring the body home – or give me enough to go and see him! Would it be possible, in this case . . .'

The words died in her throat, and she quickly bent down to retrieve her handkerchief, which had fallen to the floor.

'I will see to it that your husband is brought home, madame.'

She gave him a touching smile, then wiped a tear from her cheek.

'You've understood, I can tell! You feel the same way I do, chief inspector! It wasn't his fault . . . He was an unhappy man . . .'

'Did he ever have any large sums of money?'

'Only his wages. In the beginning, he gave everything to me. Later on, when he began drinking . . .'

Another faint smile, very sad, and yet full of pity.

She left somewhat calmer, gathering the skimpy fur collar tightly round her neck with her right hand, still clutching the handbag and the tightly folded newspaper in the other.

Maigret found a seedy-looking hotel at 18, Rue de la Roquette, right where it joins Rue de Lappe, with its accordion-band dance halls and squalid housing. That stretch of Roquette is a good fifty metres from Place de la Bastille. Every ground floor hosts a bistro, every house a hotel frequented by drifters, immigrants, tarts and the chronically unemployed.

Tucked away within these vaguely sinister haunts of the underclass, however, are a few workshops, their doors wide open to the street, where men wield hammers and blowtorches amid a constant traffic of heavy trucks.

The contrast is striking: these steady workers, busy employees with waybills in hand, and the sordid or insolent creatures who hang around everywhere.

'Jeunet!' rumbled the inspector, pushing open the door of the hotel office on the ground floor.

'Not here!'

'He's still got his room?'

He'd been spotted for a policeman, and got a reluctant reply.

'Yes, room 19!'

'By the week? The month?'

'The month!'

'You have any mail for him?'

The manager turned evasive, but in the end handed over to Maigret the package Jeunet had sent himself from Brussels.

'Did he receive many like this?'

'A few times . . .'

'Never any letters?'

'No! Maybe he got three packages, in all. A quiet man. I don't see why the police should want to come bothering him.'

'He worked?'

'At number 65, down the street.'

'Regularly?'

'Depended. Some weeks yes, others, no.'

Maigret demanded the key to the room. He found nothing there, however, except a ruined pair of shoes with flapping soles, an empty tube of aspirin and some mechanic's overalls tossed into a corner.

Back downstairs, he questioned the manager again, learning that Louis Jeunet saw no one, did not go out with women and basically led a humdrum life, aside from a few trips lasting three or four days.

But no one stays in one of these hotels, in this neighbourhood, unless there's something wrong somewhere, and the manager knew that as well as Maigret.

'It's not what you think,' he admitted grudgingly. 'With him, it's the bottle! And how – in binges. Novenas, my wife and I call them. Buckle down for three weeks, go off to work every day, then . . . for a while he'd drink until he passed out on his bed.'

'You never saw anything suspicious about his behaviour?'

But the man shrugged, as if to say that in his hotel everyone who walked through the door looked suspicious.

At number 65, in a huge workshop open to the street, they made machines to draw off beer. Maigret was met by a foreman, who had already seen Jeunet's picture in the paper.

'I was just going to write to the police!' he exclaimed. 'He was still working here last week. A fellow who earned eight francs fifty an hour!'

'When he was working.'

'Ah, you already know? When he was working, true! There are lots of them like that, but in general those others regularly take one drink too many, or they splurge on a champion hangover every Saturday. Him, it was sudden-like, no warning: he'd drink for a solid week. Once, when we had a rush job, I went to his hotel room. Well! There he was, all alone, drinking right out of a bottle set on the floor by his bed. A sorry sight, I swear.'

In Aubervilliers, nothing. The registry office held a single record of one Louis Jeunet, son of Gaston Jeunet, day labourer, and Berthe Marie Dufoin, domestic servant. Gaston Jeunet had died ten years earlier; his wife had moved away.

As for Louis Jeunet, no one knew anything about him, except that six years before he had written from Paris to request a copy of his birth certificate.

But the passport was still a forgery, which meant that the man who had killed himself in Bremen – after marrying the herbalist woman in Rue Picpus and having a son – was not the real Jeunet.

The criminal records in the Préfecture were another dead end: nothing indexed under the name of Jeunet, no fingerprints matching the ones of the dead man, taken in Germany. Evidently this desperate soul had never run afoul of the law in France or abroad, because headquarters kept tabs on the police records of most European nations.

The records went back only six years. At which point, there was a Louis Jeunet, a drilling machine operator, who had a job and lived the life of a decent working man.

He married. He already owned clothing B, which had provoked the first scene with his wife and years later would prove the cause of his death.

He had no friends, received no mail. He appeared to know Latin and therefore to have received an above-average education.

Back in his office, Maigret drew up a request for the German police to release the body, disposed of a few current matters and, with a sullen, sour face, once again opened the yellow suitcase, the contents of which had been so carefully labelled by the technician in Bremen.

To this he added the package of thirty Belgian thousand-franc notes – but abruptly decided to snap the string and copy down the serial numbers on the bills, a list he sent off to the police in Brussels, asking that they be traced.

He did all this with studied concentration, as if he were trying to convince himself that he was doing something useful.

From time to time, however, he would glance with a kind of bitterness at the crime-scene photos spread out on his desk, and his pen would hover in mid-air as he chewed on the stem of his pipe.

Regretfully, he was about to set the investigation aside and leave for home when he learned that he had a telephone call from Rheims.

It was about the picture published in the papers. The proprietor of the Café de Paris, in Rue Carnot, claimed to have seen the man in question in his establishment six days earlier – and had remembered this because the man got so drunk that he had finally stopped serving him.

Maigret hesitated. The dead man's shoes had come from Rheims – which had now cropped up again.

Moreover, these worn-out shoes had been bought months earlier, so Louis Jeunet had not just happened to be in Rheims by accident.

One hour later, the inspector took his seat on the Rheims express, arriving there at ten o'clock. A fashionable establishment favoured by the bourgeoisie, the Café de Paris was crowded that evening; three games of billiards were in full swing, and people at a few tables were playing cards.

It was a traditional café of the French provinces, where customers shake hands with the cashier and waiters know all the regulars by name: local notables, commercial travellers and so forth. It even had the traditional round nickel-plated receptacles for the café dishcloths.

'I am the inspector whom you telephoned earlier this evening.'

Standing by the counter, the proprietor was keeping an eye on his staff while he dispensed advice to the billiard players.

'Ah, yes! Well, I've already told you all I know.'

Somewhat embarrassed, he spoke in a low voice.

'Let me think . . . He was sitting over in that corner, near the third billiard table, and he ordered a brandy, then another, and a third . . . It was at about this same time of night. People were giving him funny looks because – how shall I put this? – he wasn't exactly our usual class of customer.'

'Did he have any luggage?'

'An old suitcase with a broken lock. I remember that when he left, the suitcase fell open and some old clothes spilled out. He even asked me for some string to tie it closed.'

'Did he speak to anyone?'

The proprietor glanced over at one of the billiard players, a tall, thin young man, a snappy dresser, the very picture of a sharp player whose every bank shot would be studied with respect.

'Not exactly . . . Won't you have something, inspector? We could sit over here, look!'

He chose a table with trays stacked on it, off to one side.

'By about midnight, he was as white as this marble tabletop. He'd had maybe eight or nine brandies. And I didn't like that stare he had – it takes some people that way, the alcohol. They don't get agitated or start rambling on, but at some point they simply pass out cold. Everyone had noticed him. I went over to tell him that I couldn't serve him any more, and he didn't protest in any way.'

'Was anyone still playing billiards?'

'The fellows you see over at that third table. Regulars, here every evening: they have a club, organize competitions. Well, the man left – and that's when there was that business with the suitcase falling open. The state he was in, I don't know how he managed to tie the string. I closed up a half-hour later. These gentlemen here shook my hand leaving, and I remember one of them said, 'We'll find him off somewhere in the gutter!'

The proprietor glanced again at the smartly dressed player with the white, well-manicured hands, the impeccable tie, the polished shoes that creaked each time he moved around the billiard table.

'I might as well tell you everything, especially since it's probably some fluke or a misunderstanding . . . The next day, a travelling salesman who drops by every month and who was here that night, well, he told me that at about one in the morning he'd seen the drunk and Monsieur Belloir walking along together. He even saw them both go into Monsieur Belloir's house!'

'That's the tall blond fellow?'

'Yes. He lives five minutes from here, in a handsome house in Rue de Vesle. He's the deputy director of the Banque de Crédit.'

'Is the salesman here tonight?'

'No, he's off on his regular tour through his eastern territories, won't be back until mid-November or so. I told him he must have been mistaken, but he stuck to his story. I almost mentioned it to Monsieur Belloir, as a little joke, but thought, better not. He might have been offended, right? In fact, I'd appreciate it if you wouldn't make a big deal out of what I just told you – or at least don't make it look as if it came from me. In my profession . . .'

Having just scored a break of forty-eight points, the player in question was looking around to gauge everyone's reaction while he rubbed the tip of his cue with green chalk. He frowned almost imperceptibly when he noticed Maigret sitting with the proprietor.

For, like most people trying to appear relaxed, the café owner looked worried, as if he were up to something.

Belloir called out to him from across the room.

'It's your turn, Monsieur Émile!'

4. The Unexpected Visitor

The house was new, and there was something in the studied refinement of its design and building materials that created a feeling of comfort, of crisp, confident modernism and a well-established fortune.

Red bricks, freshly repointed; natural stone; a front door of varnished oak, with brass fittings.

It was only 8.30 in the morning when Maigret turned up at that door, half hoping to catch a candid glimpse of the Belloir family's private life.

The façade, in any case, seemed suitable for a bank deputy director, an impression increased by the immaculately turned-out maid who opened the door. The entrance hall was quite large, with a door of bevelled glass panes at the end. The walls were of faux marble, and geometric patterns in two colours embellished the granite floor.

To the left, two sets of double doors of pale oak, leading to the drawing room and dining room.

Among the clothes hanging from a portmanteau was a coat for a child of four or five. A big-bellied umbrella stand held a Malacca cane with a gold pommel.

Maigret had only a moment to absorb this atmosphere of flawless domesticity, for he had barely mentioned Monsieur Belloir when the maid replied, 'If you'd be so good as to follow me, *the gentlemen* are expecting you.'

She walked towards the glass-paned door. Passing another, half-open door, the inspector caught a glimpse of the dining room, cosy and neat, where a young woman in a peignoir and a little boy of four were having their breakfast at a nicely laid table.

Beyond the last door was a staircase of pale wooden panelling with a red floral carpet runner fixed to each step by a brass rod.

A large green plant sat on the landing. The maid was already turning the knob of another door, to a study, where three men turned as one towards their visitor.

There was a reaction of shock, deep unease, even real distress that froze the looks in their eyes, which only the maid never noticed as she asked in a perfectly natural voice, 'Would you like me to take your coat?'

One of the three gentlemen was Belloir, perfectly dressed, with not a blond hair out of place. The man next to him was a little more casually attired, and a stranger to Maigret. The third man, however, was none other than Joseph Van Damme, the business-man from Bremen.

Two of the men spoke simultaneously.

With a dry hauteur in keeping with the décor and frowning as he stepped forwards, Belloir inquired, 'Monsieur?' – while at the same time Van Damme, in an effort to summon up his usual bonhomie, held out his hand to Maigret and exclaimed, 'What a surprise! Imagine seeing you here!'

The third man silently took in the scene in what looked like complete bafflement.

'Please excuse me for disturbing you,' began the inspector. 'I did not expect to be interrupting a meeting this early in the morning . . .'

'Not at all! Not at all!' replied Van Damme. 'Do sit down! Cigar?'

There was a box on the mahogany desk. He hurried to open it and select a Havana, talking all the while.

'Hold on, I'm looking for my lighter . . . You're not going to write me a ticket because these are missing their tobacco tax stamp, are you? But why didn't you tell me in Bremen that you knew Belloir! When I think that we might have made the trip together! I left a few hours after you did: a telegram, some business requiring my presence in Paris. And I've taken advantage of it to come and say hello to Belloir . . .'

The latter, having lost none of his starchy manner, kept looking from one to the other of the two men as if waiting for an explanation, and it was towards him that Maigret turned and spoke.

'I'll make my visit as short as possible, given that you're expecting someone . . .'

'I am? How do you know?'

'Simple! Your maid told me that I was expected. And as I cannot be the person in question, then clearly . . .'

His eyes were laughing in spite of himself, but his face stayed perfectly blank.

'Inspector Maigret, of the Police Judiciaire. Perhaps you noticed me yesterday evening at the Café de Paris, where I was seeking information relevant to an ongoing investigation.'

'It can't be that incident in Bremen, surely?' remarked Van Damme, with feigned indifference.

'The very one! Would you be so kind, Monsieur Belloir, as to look at this photograph and tell me if this is indeed the man you invited into your home one night last week?'

He held out a picture of the dead man. The deputy bank director looked at it, but vacantly, without seeing it.

'I don't know this person!' he stated, returning the photo to Maigret.

'You're certain this isn't the man who spoke to you when you were returning home from the Café de Paris?'

'What are you talking about?'

'Forgive me if I seem to labour the point, but I need some information that is, after all, of only minor importance, and I took the liberty of disturbing you at home because I assumed you would not mind helping us in our inquiries. On that evening, a drunk was sitting near the third billiard table, where you were playing. All the customers noticed him. He left shortly before you did, and later on, after you'd left your friends, he approached you.'

'I have a vague recollection . . . He asked me for a light.'

'And you came back here with him, isn't that right?'

Belloir smiled rather nastily.

'I've no idea who told you such nonsense. I'm hardly the sort of person to bring home tramps.'

'You might have recognized him – as an old friend, or . . .'

'I have better taste in friends!'

'You're saying that you went home alone?'

'Absolutely.'

'Was that man the same one in the photo I just showed you?'

'I have no idea. I never even looked at him.'

Listening with obvious impatience, Van Damme had been on the verge of interrupting several times. As for the third man, who had a short brown beard and was dressed all in black in a bygone but 'artistic' fashion, he was looking out of the window, occasionally wiping away the fog his breath left on the pane.

'In which case, I must now simply thank you and apologize once again, Monsieur Belloir.'

'Just a minute, inspector!' exclaimed Joseph Van Damme. 'You're not going to leave just like that? Please, do stay here with us for a moment, and Belloir will offer us some of that fine brandy he always keeps on hand . . . Do you realize that I'm rather put out with you for not coming to dinner with me, in Bremen? I waited for you all evening!'

'Did you travel here by train?'

'By plane! I almost always fly, like most businessmen, in fact! Then, in Paris, I felt like dropping in on my old friend Belloir. We were at university together.'

'In Liège?'

'Yes. And it's almost ten years now since we last saw each other. I didn't even know that he'd got married! It's odd to find him again – with a fine young son! But . . . are you really still working on that suicide of yours?'

Belloir had rung for the maid, whom he told to bring brandy

and some glasses. His every move was made slowly and carefully, but with each move he betrayed the gnawing uncertainty he felt.

'The investigation has only just begun,' said Maigret quietly. 'It's impossible to tell if it will be a long one or if the case will be all wrapped up in a day or two.'

When the front doorbell rang, the other three men exchanged furtive glances. Voices were heard; then someone with a strong Belgian accent asked, 'Are they all upstairs? Don't bother, I know the way.'

From the doorway he called out, 'Hello, fellows!'

And met with dead silence. When he saw Maigret, he looked questioningly at the others.

'Weren't you . . . expecting me?'

Belloir's expression tightened. Walking over to the inspector, he said, as if through clenched teeth, 'Jef Lombard, a friend.'

Then, pronouncing every syllable distinctly: 'Inspector Maigret, of the Police Judiciaire.'

The new arrival gave a little start, and stammered in a flat voice that squeaked in the most peculiar way, 'Aha! . . . I see . . . Well, fine . . .'

After which, in his bewilderment, he gave his overcoat to the maid, only to chase after her to retrieve the cigarettes he had left in a pocket.

'Another Belgian, inspector,' observed Van Damme. 'Yes, you're witnessing a real Belgian reunion! You must think this all looks like a conspiracy . . . What about that brandy, Belloir? Inspector, a cigar? Jef Lombard is the only one who still lives in Liège. It just so happens that business affairs have brought us all to the same place at the same moment, so we've decided to celebrate, and have a grand old time! And I wonder if . . .'

He hesitated for a moment, looking around at the others.

'You skipped that dinner I wanted to treat you to in Bremen. Why not have lunch with us later today?'

'Unfortunately, I have other engagements,' replied Maigret. 'Besides, I've already taken enough of your time.'

Jef Lombard had gone over to a table. He was pale, with irregular features, so tall and thin that his limbs seemed too long for his body.

'Ah! Here's the picture I was looking for,' muttered Maigret, as if to himself. 'I won't ask you, Monsieur Lombard, if you know this man, because that would be one chance in a million . . .'

But he contrived to show him the photo anyway – and saw the man's Adam's apple seem to swell, bobbing weirdly up and down.

'Don't know him,' Lombard managed to croak.

Belloir's manicured fingers were drumming on his desk, while Van Damme cast about for something to say.

'So, inspector, I won't have the pleasure of seeing you again? You're going straight back to Paris?'

'I'm not sure yet. My apologies, gentlemen.'

Van Damme shook hands with him, so the others had to as well. Belloir's hand was hard and dry. The bearded man's handshake was more hesitant, and Jef Lombard was off in a corner of the study lighting a cigarette, so he simply nodded towards Maigret and grunted.

Maigret brushed past the green plant in its enormous porcelain pot and went back down the stairs with their brass carpet rods. In the front hall, over the shrill scraping of a violin lesson, he heard a woman's voice saying, 'Slow down . . . Keep your elbow level with your chin . . . Gently!'

It was Madame Belloir and her son. He caught sight of them from the street, through the drawing-room curtains.

It was 2 p.m., and Maigret had just finished lunch at the Café de Paris when he noticed Van Damme come in and look around as if searching for someone. Spotting Maigret, he smiled and came over with his hand outstretched.

'So this is what you call having other engagements! Eating alone in a restaurant! I understand: you wanted to leave us in peace.'

He was clearly one of those people who latch on to you without any invitation, ignoring any suggestion that their attentions might be unwelcome.

Maigret took selfish pleasure in his chilly response, but Van Damme sat down at his table anyway.

'You've finished? In that case, allow me to offer you a *digestif* . . . Waiter! Well, what will you have, inspector? An old Armagnac?'

He called for the drinks list, and after consultation with the proprietor, chose an 1867 Armagnac, to be served in snifters.

'I was wondering: when are you returning to Paris? I'm going there this afternoon, and since I cannot bear trains, I'll be hiring a car . . . If you like, I'll take you along. Well, what do you think of my friends?'

He inhaled the aroma of his brandy with a critical air, then pulled a cigar case from his pocket.

'Please, have one, they're quite good. There's only one place in Bremen where you can get them, and they're straight from Havana!'

Maigret had emptied his eyes of all thought and made his face a blank.

'It's funny, meeting again years later,' remarked Van Damme, who seemed unable to cope with silence. 'At the age of twenty, starting out, we're all on the same footing, so to speak. Time passes, and when we get together again, it's astonishing how far away from one another we seem . . . I'm not saying anything against them, mind you, it's just that, back at Belloir's house, I felt . . . uncomfortable. That stifling provincial atmosphere! And Belloir himself, quite the clothes horse! Although he hasn't done badly for himself, seeing as he married the daughter of Morvandeau, the one who's in sprung mattresses. All Belloir's brothers-in-law are in industry. And him? He's sitting pretty in the bank, where he'll wind up director one of these days.'

'And the short man with the beard?' asked Maigret.

'That one . . . He may yet find his way and make good. Meanwhile, I think he's feeling the pinch, poor devil. He's a sculptor, in Paris. And talented, it seems – but what do you expect? You saw him, in that get-up from another century . . . Nothing modern about him! And no business sense.'

'Jef Lombard?'

'They don't make them any better! In his younger days, he was a real joker, could keep you laughing yourself silly for hours on end. He was going to be a painter . . . He earned a living as a newspaper artist, then worked as a photoengraver in Liège. He's married. I believe they're expecting their third child.

'What I'm saying is, when I was with them I felt as if I couldn't breathe! Those petty lives, with their petty preoccupations and worries . . . It isn't their fault, but I can't wait to get back to the business world.'

He drained his glass and considered the almost deserted room, where a waiter at a table in the back was reading a newspaper.

'It's settled, then? You're returning to Paris with me?'

'But aren't you travelling with the short bearded fellow who came with you?'

'Janin? No, by this time he has already taken the train back.'

'Married?'

'Not exactly. But he always has some girlfriend or other who lives with him for a week, a year – and then he gets a new one! Whom he always introduces as "Madame Janin". Oh, waiter! The same again, here!'

Maigret had to be careful, at times, not to let his eyes give away how keenly he was listening. He had left the address of the Café de Paris back at headquarters, and the proprietor now came over to tell him personally that he was wanted on the phone.

News had been wired from Brussels to the Police Judiciaire: *The 30,000-franc notes were handed over by the Banque Générale de Belgique to one Louis Jeunet in payment of a cheque signed by Maurice Belloir.*

Opening the door to leave the telephone booth, Maigret saw that Van Damme, unaware that he was being observed, had allowed himself to drop his mask – and now seemed deflated and, above all, less glowing with health and optimism.

He must have felt those watchful eyes on him, however, for he shuddered, automatically becoming the jovial businessman once again.

'We're set, then?' he called out. 'You're coming with me? *Patron!* Would you arrange for us to be picked up here by car and driven to Paris? A comfortable car! See to it, will you? And in the mean-time, let's have another.'

He chewed on the end of his cigar and just for an instant, as he stared down at the marble table, his eyes lost their lustre, while the corners of his mouth drooped as if the tobacco had left a bitter taste in his mouth.

'It's when you live abroad that you really appreciate the wines and liqueurs of France!'

His words rang hollow, echoing in the abyss lying between them and the man's troubled mind.

Jef Lombard went by in the street, his silhouette slightly blurred by the tulle curtains. He was alone. He walked with long strides, slowly and sadly, seeing nothing of the city all around him.

He was carrying an overnight bag, and Maigret found himself thinking about those two yellow suitcases . . . Lombard's was of better quality, though, with two straps and a sleeve for a calling card. The man's shoe heels were starting to wear down on one side, and his clothes did not look as if anyone brushed them regu-larly. Jef Lombard was walking all the way to the station.

Van Damme, sporting a large platinum signet ring on one finger, was wreathing himself in a fragrant cloud of cigar smoke height-ened by the alcohol's sharp bouquet. Off in the background, the proprietor could be heard on the phone, arranging for the car.

Belloir was probably setting out from his new house for the marble portal of the bank, while his wife took their son for a walk along the avenues. Everyone would wish Belloir a good afternoon. His father-in-law was the biggest businessman around. His brothers-in-law were 'in industry'. A bright future lay ahead of him.

As for Janin, with his black goatee and his artistic *lavallière* bow tie, he was on his way to Paris – in third class, Maigret would have bet on it.

And down at the bottom of the heap was the pale traveller of Neuschanz and Bremen, the husband of the herbalist in Rue Picpus, the milling machine operator from Rue de la Roquette, the solitary drinker who went to gaze at his wife through the shop window, sent himself banknotes as if they were a package of old newspapers, bought sausages in rolls at a station buffet and shot himself in the mouth because he'd been robbed of an old suit that wasn't even his.

'Ready, inspector?'

Maigret flinched and stared in confusion at Van Damme, his gaze so vacant that the other man tried uneasily to laugh and botched it, stammering, 'Were you daydreaming? Wherever you were, it was far away . . . I suspect it's that suicide of yours you're still worried about.'

Not entirely. When startled from his reverie, Maigret – and even he did not know why – had been concentrating on an unusual list, counting up the children involved in this case: one in Rue Picpus, a small figure between his mother and grandmother in a shop smelling of mint and rubber; one in Rheims, who was learning to hold his elbow up by his chin while drawing his bow across the strings of a violin; two in Liège, in the home of Jef Lombard, where a third was on the way . . .

'One last Armagnac, what do you say?'

'Thank you: I've had enough.'

'Come on! We'll have a stirrup cup, or in our case one for the road!'

Only Joseph Van Damme laughed, as he constantly felt he must, like a little boy so afraid to go down into the cellar that he tries to whistle up some courage.

5. Breakdown at Luzancy

As they drove at a fast clip through the gathering dusk, there was hardly a moment's silence. Joseph Van Damme was never at a loss for words and, fuelled by the Armagnac, he managed to keep up a stream of convivial patter. The vehicle was an old sedan, a saloon car with worn cushions, flower holders and marquetry side pockets. The driver was wearing a trench coat, with a knitted scarf around his neck.

They had been driving for about two hours when the driver pulled over to the side of the road and stopped at least a kilometre from a village, a few lights of which gleamed in the misty evening.

After inspecting the rear wheels, the driver informed his passengers that he had found a flat tyre, which it would take him fifteen minutes or so to repair.

The two men got out. The driver was already settling a jack under the rear axle and assured them that he did not need any help.

Was it Maigret or Van Damme who suggested a short walk? Neither of them, actually; it seemed only natural for them to walk a little way along the road, where they noticed a path leading down to the rushing waters of a river.

'Look! The Marne!' said Van Damme. 'It's in spate . . .'

As they strolled slowly along the little path, smoking their cigars, they heard a noise that puzzled them until they reached the riverbank.

A hundred metres away, across the water, they saw the lock at Luzancy: its gates were closed, and there was no one around. Right at their feet was a dam, with its milky overspill, churning waters and powerful current. The Marne was running high.

In the darkness they could just make out branches, perhaps

entire trees, smashing repeatedly into the barrier until swept at last over its edge.

The only light came from the lock, on the far side of the river.

Joseph Van Damme kept talking away.

'Every year the Germans make tremendous efforts to harness the energy of rivers, and the Russians are right behind them: in the Ukraine they're constructing a dam that'll cost 120 million dollars but will provide electricity to three provinces.'

It was almost unnoticeable, the way his voice faltered – briefly – at the word *electricity.* And then, coughing, Van Damme had to take out his handkerchief to blow his nose.

They were on the very brink of the river. Shoved suddenly from behind, Maigret lost his balance, turning as he fell forwards, and grabbed the edge of the grassy riverbank with both hands, his feet now in the water, while his hat was already plunging over the dam.

The rest happened quickly, for he had been expecting that push. Clods of earth were giving way under his right hand, but he had spotted a branch sturdy enough for him to cling to with his other hand.

Only seconds later, he was on his knees on the towpath and then on his feet, shouting at a figure fading away.

'Stop!'

It was strange: Van Damme didn't dare run. He was heading towards the car in only a modest hurry and kept looking back, his legs wobbly with shock.

And he allowed himself to be overtaken. With his head down and pulled like a turtle's into the collar of his overcoat, he simply swung his fist once through the air, in rage, as if he were pounding on an imaginary table and growled through clenched teeth, 'Idiot!'

Just to be safe, Maigret had brought out his revolver. Gun in hand, without taking his eyes off the other man, he shook the legs of his trousers, soaked to the knees, while water spurted from his shoes.

Back at the road, the driver was tapping on the horn to let them know that the car was roadworthy again.

'Let's go!' said the inspector.

And they took their same seats in the car, in silence. Van Damme still had his cigar between his teeth but he would not meet Maigret's eyes.

Ten kilometres. Twenty kilometres. They slowed down to go through a town, where people were going about their business in the lighted streets. Then it was back to the highway.

'You still can't arrest me, though,' said Van Damme abruptly, and Maigret started with surprise. And yet these words – so unexpected, spoken so slowly, even stubbornly – had echoed his own misgivings . . .

They reached Meaux. Countryside gave way to the outer suburbs. A light rain began to fall, and whenever the car passed a streetlamp, each drop became a star. Then the inspector leaned forwards to speak into the voice-pipe.

'You're to take us to the Police Judiciaire, Quai des Orfèvres.'

He filled a pipe he could not smoke because his matches were now wet. Van Damme's face was almost completely turned away from him and further obscured in the dim light, but he could sense the man's fury.

There was now a hard edge to the atmosphere, something rancorous and intense.

Maigret himself had his chin thrust out belligerently.

This tension led to a ridiculous incident after the car pulled up in front of the Préfecture and the men got out, the inspector first.

'Come along!'

The driver was waiting to be paid, but Van Damme was ignoring him. There was a moment of hesitation, indecision.

'Well?' said Maigret, not unaware of the absurdity of the situation. 'You're the one who hired the car.'

'Pardon me: if I travelled as your prisoner, it's up to you to pay.'

A small matter, but didn't it show how much had happened since Rheims and, most importantly, how much the Belgian businessman had changed?

Maigret paid and silently showed Van Damme to his office. After closing the door behind him, the first thing he did was to stir up the fire in the stove.

Next he took some clothing from a cupboard and, without a glance at the other man, changed his trousers, shoes and socks and placed his damp things near the stove to dry.

Van Damme had sat down without waiting to be asked. In the bright light, the change in him was even more striking: he'd left his bogus bonhomie, his open manner and somewhat strained smile back at Luzancy and now, with a grim and cunning look, he was waiting.

Pretending to pay him no attention, Maigret kept busy for a little while around his office, organizing dossiers, telephoning his boss for some information that had nothing to do with the current case.

Finally, he went over to confront Van Damme.

'When, where and how did you first meet the man who committed suicide in Bremen and who was travelling with a passport in the name of Louis Jeunet?'

The other man flinched almost imperceptibly but faced his challenger with bold composure.

'Why am I here?'

'You refuse to answer my question?'

Van Damme laughed, but now his laughter was cold and sarcastic.

'I know the law as well as you do, inspector. Either you charge me and must show me the arrest warrant, or you don't charge me and I don't have to answer you. And in the first case, the law allows me to wait for the assistance of a lawyer before speaking to you.'

Maigret did not seem angry or even annoyed by the man's attitude. On the contrary! He studied him with curiosity and perhaps a certain satisfaction.

Thanks to the incident at Luzancy, Joseph Van Damme had been forced to abandon his play-acting and the pretence he had kept up not only with Maigret, but with everyone else and even, in the end, with himself.

There was almost nothing left of the jolly, shallow businessman from Bremen, constantly on the go between his modern office and the finest taverns and restaurants. Gone was the happy-go-lucky operator raking in money with zestful energy and a taste for the good life. All that remained was a haggard face drained of colour, and it was uncanny how quickly dark, puffy circles seemed to have appeared under his eyes.

Only an hour earlier, hadn't Van Damme still been a free man who, although he did have something on his conscience, yet enjoyed the self-assurance guaranteed by his broker's licence, his reputation, his money and his shrewdness?

And he himself had emphasized this change.

In Rheims, he was used to standing round after round of drinks. He offered his guests the finest cigars. He had only to give an order, and a café proprietor would hasten to curry favour, phoning a garage to hire their most comfortable car.

He was somebody!

In Paris? He had refused to pay for the trip. He invoked the law. He appeared ready to argue, to defend himself at every turn, fiercely, like a man fighting for his life.

And he was furious with himself! His angry exclamation after what had happened on the bank of the Marne was proof of that. There had been no premeditation. He hadn't known the driver. Even when they had stopped for the flat tyre, he hadn't immediately realized how that might work to his advantage.

Only when they had reached the water . . . The swirling current, the trees swept by as if they were simply dead leaves . . . Like a fool, without thinking twice, he'd given that push with his shoulder.

Now he was beside himself. He was sure that the inspector had been waiting for that move! He probably even realized that he was done for – and was all the more determined to strike back with everything he had.

When he went to light a new cigar, Maigret snatched it from

his mouth, tossed it into the coal scuttle – and for good measure removed the hat Van Damme hadn't bothered to take off.

'For your information,' said the Belgian, 'I have business to attend to. If you do not mean to officially arrest me in accordance with the regulations, I must ask you to be good enough to release me. If you don't, I'll be forced to file a complaint for false imprisonment.

'With regard to your little dip in the river, I might as well tell you that I'll deny everything: the towpath was soggy and you slipped in the mud. The driver will confirm that I never tried to run away, as I would have if I'd really tried to drown you.

'As for the rest, I still don't know what you might have against me. I came to Paris on business and I can prove that. Then I went to Rheims to see an old friend, an upstanding citizen like myself.

'After meeting you in Bremen, where we don't often see Frenchmen, I was trusting enough to consider you a friend, taking you out for dinner and drinks and then offering you a ride back to Paris.

'You showed me and my friends the photograph of a man we do not know. A man who killed himself! That's been materially proved. No one has lodged a complaint, so you have no grounds for taking action.

'And that's all I have to say to you.'

Maigret stuck a twist of paper into the stove, lit his pipe and remarked, almost as an afterthought, 'You're perfectly free to go.'

He could not help smiling to see Van Damme so dumbfounded by his suspiciously easy victory.

'What do you mean?'

'That you're free, that's all! May I add that I'm quite ready to return your hospitality and invite you to dinner.'

Rarely had he felt so light-hearted. The other man gaped at him in amazement, almost in fear, as if the inspector's words had been heavy with hidden threats. Warily, Van Damme rose to his feet.

'I'm free to return to Bremen?'

'Why not? You just said yourself that you've committed no crime.'

For an instant, it seemed that Van Damme might recover his confidence and bluster, might even accept that dinner invitation and explain away the incident at Luzancy as clumsiness or a momentary aberration . . .

But the smile on Maigret's face snuffed out that flicker of optimism. Van Damme grabbed his hat and clapped it on to his head.

'How much do I owe you for the car?'

'Nothing at all. Only too happy to have been of service.'

Van Damme was at such a loss for words that his lips were trembling, and he had no idea how to leave gracefully. In the end he shrugged and walked out, muttering, 'Idiot!'

But it was impossible to tell what or whom he meant by that.

Out on the staircase, as Maigret leaned over the handrail to watch him go, he was still saying it over and over . . .

Sergeant Lucas happened along with some files, on his way to his boss's office.

'Quick! Get your hat and coat: follow that man to the ends of the earth if you have to . . .'

And Maigret plucked the files from his subordinate's hands.

The inspector had just finished filling out various requests for information, each headed by a different name. Sent out to the appropriate divisions, these forms would return to him with detailed reports on these persons of interest: Maurice Belloir, a native of Liège, deputy director of a bank, Rue de Vesle, Rheims; Jef Lombard, photo-engraver in Liège; Gaston Janin, sculptor, Rue Lepic, Paris; and Joseph Van Damme, import-export commission agent in Bremen.

He was filling out the last form when the office boy announced that a man wanted to see him regarding the suicide of Louis Jeunet.

It was late. Headquarters was practically deserted, although an inspector was typing a report in the neighbouring office.

'Come!'

Ushered in, his visitor stopped at the door, looking awkward and ill at ease, as if he might already be sorry to have come.

'Sit down, why don't you!'

Maigret had taken his measure: tall, thin, with whitish-blond hair, poorly shaved, wearing shabby clothes rather like Louis Jeunet's. His overcoat was missing a button, the collar was soiled, and the lapels in need of a brushing.

From a few other tiny signs – a certain attitude, a way of sitting down and looking around – the inspector recognized an ex-con, someone whose papers may all be in order but who still cannot help being nervous around the police.

'You're here because of the photo? Why didn't you come in right away? That picture appeared in the papers two days ago.'

'I don't read them,' the man explained. 'But my wife happened to bring some shopping home wrapped in a bit of newspaper.'

Maigret realized that he'd seen this somewhere before, this constantly shifting expression, this nervous twitching and most of all, the morbid anxiety in the man's eyes.

'Did you know Louis Jeunet?'

'I'm not sure. It isn't a good photo. But I think . . . I believe he's my brother.'

Maigret couldn't help it: he sighed with relief. He felt that this time the whole mystery would be cleared up at last. And he went to stand with his back to the stove, as he often did when in a good mood.

'In which case, your name would be Jeunet?'

'No, but that's it, that's why I hesitated to come here, and yet – he really is my brother! I'm sure of that, now that I see a better photo on the desk . . . That scar, for example! But I don't understand why he killed himself – or why in the world he would change his name.'

'And yours is . . .'

'Armand Lecocq d'Arneville. I brought my papers.'

And there again, that way he reached into his pocket for a grimy passport betrayed his status on the margins of society, someone used to attracting suspicion and proving his identity.

'D'Arneville with a small *d* and an apostrophe?'

'Yes.'

'You were born in Liège,' continued the inspector, consulting the passport. 'You're thirty-five years old. Your profession?'

'At present, I'm an office messenger in a factory at Issy-les-Moulineaux. We live in Grenelle, my wife and I.'

'It says here you're a mechanic.'

'I was one. I've done this and that . . .'

'Even some prison time!' exclaimed Maigret, leafing through the passport. 'You're a deserter.'

'There was an amnesty! Just let me explain . . . My father had money, he ran a tyre business, but I was only six when he abandoned my mother, who'd just given birth to my brother Jean. That's where it all started!

'We moved to a little place in Rue de la Province, in Liège, and in the beginning my father sent us money to live on fairly regularly. He liked to live it up, had mistresses; once, when he came by to drop off our monthly envelope, there was a woman in the car waiting for him down in the street. There were scenes, arguments, and my father stopped paying, or maybe he began paying less and less. My mother worked as a cleaning woman and she gradually went half-mad, not crazy enough to be shut away, but she'd go up to people and pour out her troubles, and she used to roam the streets in tears . . .

'I hardly ever saw my brother. I was off running with the local kids. They must have hauled us in to the police station ten times. Then I was sent to work in a hardware store. My mother was always crying, so I stayed away from home as much as I could. She liked all the old neighbour women to come over so she could wail her heart out with them.

'I joined the army when I was sixteen and asked to be sent to the Congo, but I only lasted a month. For about a week I hid in Matadi, then I stowed away on a passenger steamer bound for Europe. I got caught, served some time, escaped and made it to France, where I worked at all sorts of jobs. I've gone starving hungry, slept in the market here at Les Halles.

'I haven't always been on the up and up, but I swear to you, I've buckled down and been clean for four years. I'm even married now! To a factory worker. She's had to keep her job because I don't earn much and sometimes there's nothing for me . . .

'I've never tried to go back to Belgium. Someone told me that my mother died in a lunatic asylum but that my father's still alive. He never wanted to bother with us, though. He has a second family.'

And the man gave a crooked smile, as if to apologize.

'What about your brother?'

'It was different with him: Jean was serious. He won a scholarship as a boy and went on to secondary school. When I left Belgium for the Congo he was only thirteen, and I haven't seen him since. I heard news now and again, whenever I ran into anyone from Liège. Some people took an interest in him, and he went on to study at the university there. That was ten years ago . . . After that, any Belgians I saw told me they didn't know anything about him, that he must have gone abroad, because he'd dropped out of sight.

'It was a real shock to see the photograph, and especially to think that he'd died in Bremen, under a false name. You can't have any idea . . . Me, I got off to a bad start, I messed up, did stupid things, but when I remember Jean, at thirteen . . . He was like me, but steadier, more serious, already reading poetry. He used to study all by himself at night, reading by the light of candle ends he got from a sacristan. I was sure he'd make it. Listen, even when he was little, he would never have been a street kid, not at any price – and the neighbourhood bad boys even made fun of him!

'But me, I was always short of money, and I wasn't ashamed to hound my mother for it. She used to go without to give me some . . . She adored us. At sixteen, you don't understand! But now I can remember a time when I was mean to her simply because I'd promised some girl I'd take her to the movies . . . Well, my mother had no money. I cried, I threatened her! A charity had just got some medicines for her – and she went and sold them.

'Can you understand? And now it's Jean who's dead, like that, up there, with someone else's name! I don't know what he did. I cannot believe he went down the same wrong road I did. You wouldn't believe it either if you'd known him as a child . . .

'Please, can you tell me anything?'

But Maigret handed the man's passport back to him and asked, 'In Liège, do you know any Belloirs, Van Dammes, Janins, Lombards?'

'A Belloir, yes: the father was a doctor, in our neighbourhood. The son was a student. But they were well-to-do, respectable people, out of my league.'

'And the others?'

'I've heard the name Van Damme before. I think there was a big grocery store in Rue de la Cathédrale by that name. Oh, it's so long ago now . . .' He seemed to hesitate.

And then Armand Lecocq d'Arneville asked, 'Could I see Jean's body? Has it been brought here?'

'It will arrive in Paris tomorrow.'

'Are you sure that he really did kill himself?'

Maigret looked away, disturbed by the thought that he was more than sure of it: he had witnessed the tragedy and been the unwitting cause of it.

The other man was twisting his cap in his hands, shifting from one foot to the other, awaiting his dismissal. Lost within pale lids, his deep-set eyes with their pupils flecked grey like confetti reminded Maigret so poignantly of the humble, anxious eyes of the traveller from Neuschanz that within his breast the inspector felt a sharp pang that was very like remorse.

6. *The Hanged Men*

It was nine o'clock in the evening. Maigret was at home in Boulevard Richard-Lenoir in his shirt-sleeves, his collar off, and his wife was sewing when Lucas came in soaked from the downpour outside, shrugging the rain from his shoulders.

'The man left town,' he said. 'Seeing as I wasn't sure if I was supposed to follow him abroad . . .'

'Liège?'

'That's it! You already knew? His luggage was at the Hôtel du Louvre. He had dinner there, changed and took the 6.19 Liège express. Single ticket, first class. He bought a whole slew of magazines at the station newsstand.'

'You'd think he was trying to get underfoot on purpose!' groused the inspector. 'In Bremen, when I've no idea he even exists, he's the one who shows up at the morgue, invites me to lunch and plain latches on to me. I get back to Paris: he's here a few hours before or after I arrive . . . Probably before, because he took a plane. I go to Rheims; he's already there. An hour ago, I decided to return to Liège tomorrow – and he'll be there by this evening! And the last straw? He's well aware that I'm coming and that his presence there almost amounts to an accusation against him.'

Lucas, who knew nothing about the case, ventured a suggestion.

'Maybe he wants to draw suspicion on himself to protect somebody else?'

'Are you talking about a crime?' asked Mme Maigret peaceably, without looking up from her sewing.

But her husband rose with a sigh and looked back at the armchair in which he'd been so comfortable just a moment before.

'How late do the trains run to Belgium?'

'Only the night train is left, at 9.30. It arrives in Liège at around 6 a.m.'

'Would you pack my bag?' Maigret asked his wife. 'Lucas, a little something? Help yourself, you know where everything is in the cabinet. My sister-in-law has just sent us some plum brandy, and she makes it herself, in Alsace. It's the bottle with the long neck . . .'

He dressed, removed clothing B from the yellow suitcase and placed it, well wrapped, in his travel bag. Half an hour later, he left with Lucas, and they waited outside for a taxi.

'What case is this?' Lucas asked. 'I haven't heard anything about it around the shop.'

'I hardly know myself!' the inspector exclaimed. 'A very strange fellow died, in a way that makes no sense, right in front of me – and *that* incident is all tied up in the most ungodly tangle of events, which I'm attempting to figure out. I'm charging blindly at it like a wild boar and wouldn't be surprised if I wound up getting my knuckles rapped . . . Here's a taxi. Shall I drop you off somewhere?'

It was eight in the morning when Maigret left the Hôtel du Chemin de Fer, across from Gare des Guillemins, in Liège. He'd taken a bath, shaved and was carrying a package containing not all of clothing B, just the suit jacket.

He found Rue Haute-Sauvenière, a steep and busy street, where he asked for directions to Morcel's. In the dim light of the tailor's shop, a man in shirt-sleeves examined the jacket, turning it over and over carefully while questioning the inspector.

'It's old,' he finally announced, 'and it's torn. That's about all I can tell you.'

'Nothing else comes to mind?'

'Not a thing. The collar's poorly cut. It's imitation English woollen cloth, made in Verviers.'

And then the man became more chatty.

'You're French? Does this jacket belong to someone you know?'

With a sigh, Maigret retrieved the suit jacket as the man nattered on and at last wound up where he ought to have started.

'You see, I've only been here for the past six months. If I'd made the suit in question, it wouldn't have had time to wear out like that.'

'And Monsieur Morcel?'

'In Robermont!'

'Is that far from here?'

The tailor laughed, tickled by the misunderstanding.

'Robermont, that's our cemetery. Monsieur Morcel died at the beginning of this year, and I took over his business.'

Back out in the street with his package under his arm, Maigret headed for Rue Hors-Château, one of the oldest streets in the city, where, at the far end of a courtyard, he found a zinc plaque announcing: *Photogravure Centrale – Jef Lombard – Rapid results for work of all kinds.*

The windows had small panes, in the style of historic Liège, and in the centre of the courtyard of small, uneven paving stones was a fountain bearing the sculpted coat of arms of some great lord of long ago.

The inspector rang. He heard footsteps coming down from the first floor, and an old woman peeked out from the ancient-looking door.

'Just push it open,' she said, pointing to a glazed door. 'The workshop's all the way at the end of the passage.'

A long room, lit by a glass roof; two men in blue overalls working among zinc plates and tubs full of acids; a floor strewn with photographic proofs and paper smeared with thick, greasy ink.

The walls were crowded with posters, advertisements, magazine covers.

'Monsieur Lombard?'

'He's in the office, with a gentleman. Please come this way – and don't get any ink on you! Take a left turn, then it's the first door.'

The building must have been constructed piecemeal; stairs went up and down, and doors opened on to abandoned rooms.

The feeling was both antiquated and weirdly cheerful, like the old woman who'd greeted him downstairs and the atmosphere in the workroom.

Coming to a shadowy corridor, the inspector heard voices and thought he recognized that of Joseph Van Damme. He tried in vain to make out the words, and when he took a few steps closer, the voices stopped. A man stuck his head out of the half-open door: it was Jef Lombard.

'Is it for me?' he called, not recognizing his visitor in the half-light.

The office was smaller than the other rooms and furnished with two chairs, shelves full of photographic negatives and a table cluttered with bills, prospectuses and business letters from various companies.

And perched on a corner of the table was Van Damme, who nodded vaguely in Maigret's direction and then sat perfectly still, scowling and staring straight ahead.

Jef Lombard was in his work clothes; his hands were dirty, and there were tiny blackish flecks on his face.

'May I help you?'

He cleared papers off a chair, which he pushed over to his visitor, and then he looked around for the cigarette butt he'd left balanced on the edge of a wooden shelf now beginning to char.

'Just some information,' replied the inspector, without sitting down. 'I'm sorry to bother you, but I'd like to know if, a few years ago, you ever knew a certain Jean Lecocq d'Arneville . . .'

There was a quick, distinct change. Van Damme shuddered, but resisted turning towards Maigret, while Lombard bent abruptly down to pick up a crumpled paper lying on the floor.

'I . . . may have heard that name before,' murmured the photoengraver. 'He . . . From Liège, isn't he?'

The colour had drained from his face. He moved a pile of plates from one spot to another.

'I don't know what became of him. I . . . It was so long ago . . .'

'Jef! Jef, hurry!'

It was a woman's voice, coming from the labyrinth of stairs and corridors, and she arrived at the open door breathless from running, so excited that her legs were shaky and she had to wipe her face with a corner of her apron. Maigret recognized the old lady he'd seen downstairs.

'Jef!'

And he, now even whiter from emotion, his eyes gleaming, gasped, 'Well?'

'A girl! Hurry!'

The man looked around, stammered something impossible to decipher and dashed out of the door.

Alone with Maigret, Van Damme pulled a cigar from his pocket, lit it slowly, crushed out the match with his shoe. He wore the same wooden expression as in Maigret's office: his mouth was set in the same hard line, and he ground his jaws in the same way.

But the inspector pretended not to notice him and, hands in his pockets, pipe between his teeth, he began to walk around the office, examining the walls.

Very little of the original wallpaper was still visible, however, because any space not taken up by shelves was covered with drawings, etchings, and paintings that were simply canvases on stretchers without frames, rather plodding landscapes in which the tree foliage and grass were of the same even, pasty green.

There were a few caricatures signed *Jef*, some of them touched up with watercolours, some cut from a local paper.

What struck Maigret, though, was how many of the drawings were all variations on one particular theme. The drawing paper had yellowed with age, and a few dates indicated that these sketches had been done about ten years earlier.

They were executed in a different style as well, with a more darkly Romantic sensibility, and seemed like the efforts of a young art student imitating the work of Gustave Doré.

A first ink drawing showed a hanged man swinging from a gallows on which perched an enormous crow. And there were at least twenty other etchings and pen or pencil sketches that had the same leitmotif of hanging.

On the edge of a forest: a man hanging from every branch.

A church steeple: beneath the weathercock, a human body dangling from each arm of the cross.

There were hanged men of all kinds. Some were dressed in the fashions of the sixteenth century and formed a kind of Court of Miracles, where everybody was swinging a few feet above the ground.

There was one crazy hanged man in a top hat and tails, cane in hand, whose gallows was a lamp post.

Below another sketch were written four lines from François Villon's *Ballad of the Hanged Men*.

There were dates, always from around the same time, and all these macabre pictures from ten years earlier were now displayed along with captioned sketches for comic papers, drawings for calendars and almanacs, landscapes of the surrounding Ardennes and advertising posters.

Another recurrent theme was the steeple – in fact, so was the whole church, depicted from the front, from the sides, from below. The church portal, on its own. The gargoyles. The parvis, with its six steps looming large in perspective . . .

Always the same church! And as Maigret moved from one wall to another, he could sense Van Damme's growing agitation, an uneasiness fuelled, perhaps, by the same temptation that had overwhelmed him by the dam at Luzancy.

A quarter of an hour passed like this, and then Jef Lombard returned, his eyes moist with emotion, wiping his hand across his forehead and brushing away a stray lock of hair.

'Please forgive me,' he said. 'My wife has just given birth. A girl!'

There was a hint of pride in his voice, but, as he spoke, he was looking anxiously back and forth between Maigret and Van Damme.

'Our third child. But I'm still as excited as I was the first time! You saw my mother-in-law, well – she had eleven and she's sobbing with joy, she's gone to give the workmen the good news and wants them to see our baby girl.'

His eyes followed Maigret's gaze, now fixed upon the two men hanging from the church-steeple cross, and he became even more nervous.

'The sins of my youth,' he murmured, clearly uncomfortable. 'Terrible stuff. But at the time I thought I was going to be a great artist . . .'

'It's a church in Liège?'

Jef didn't answer right away. And when he finally did, it was almost with regret.

'It's been gone for seven years. They tore it down to build a new church. The old one wasn't beautiful, it didn't even have any style to speak of, but it was very old, with a touch of mystery in all its lines and in the little streets and alleys around it . . . They've all been levelled now.'

'What was its name?'

'The Church of Saint-Pholien. The new one is in the same place and bears the same name.'

Still seated on the corner of Lombard's table, Joseph Van Damme was fidgeting as if his nerves were burning him inside, an inner turmoil betrayed only by the faintest of movements, uneven breathing, a trembling in his fingers, and the way one foot was jiggling against a table leg.

'Were you married at that time?' continued Maigret.

Lombard laughed.

'I was nineteen! I was studying at the Académie des Beaux-Arts. Look over there . . .'

And he pointed, with a look of fond nostalgia, to a clumsy portrait in gloomy colours that was nevertheless recognizable as him, thanks to the telling irregularity of his features. His hair was almost shoulder length; he wore a black tunic buttoned up to his neck and an ample *lavallière* bow tie.

The painting was flagrantly Romantic, even to the traditional death's-head in the background.

'If you'd told me back then that I'd wind up a photoengraver!' he marvelled, with helpless irony.

Jef Lombard seemed equally unsettled by Van Damme and Maigret, but he clearly had no idea how to get them to leave.

A workman came for advice about a plate that wasn't ready.

'Have them come back this afternoon.'

'But they say that will be too late!'

'So what! Tell them I've just had a daughter . . .'

Lombard's eyes, his movements, the pallor of his complexion pocked with tiny acid marks – everything about him reflected a disturbing confusion of joy, anxiety, perhaps even anguish.

'If I may, I'd like to offer you something . . . We'll go down to the house.'

The three men walked back along the maze of corridors and through the door where the old woman had spoken to Maigret. There were blue tiles in the hall and a clean smell faintly scented, however, with a kind of staleness, perhaps from the stuffiness of the lying-in room.

'The two boys are at my brother-in-law's. Come through here . . .'

He opened the door to the dining room, where the small panes of the windows admitted a dim, bleak light that glinted off the many copper pieces on display everywhere. The furniture was dark.

On the wall was a large portrait of a woman, signed *Jef*, full of awkward passages but imbued with a clear desire to present the model – presumably the artist's wife – in a flattering way.

When Maigret looked around the room he was not surprised to find more hanged men. The best ones, considered good enough to frame!

'You'll have a glass of genever?'

The inspector could feel Van Damme glaring coldly at him, obviously infuriated by the whole situation.

'You were saying a moment ago that you knew Jean Lecocq d'Arneville . . .'

Steps sounded on the floor above, probably from the lying-in room.

'But only casually,' the distracted father replied, listening intently to the faint whimpering of the new-born infant.

And raising his glass, he exclaimed, 'To the health of my little girl! And my wife!'

Turning abruptly away, he drained his glass in one go, then went to the sideboard and pretended to look for something while he recovered from his emotions, but Maigret still caught the soft hiccup of a stifled sob.

'I'm sorry, I have to go up there! On a day like today . . .'

Maigret and Van Damme had not exchanged one word. As they crossed the courtyard, passing by the fountain, the inspector glanced with a faint smile at the other man, wondering what he would do next.

Once out in the street, however, Van Damme simply touched the brim of his hat and strode off to the right.

There aren't many taxis in Liège. Unfamiliar with the tram lines, Maigret walked back to the Hôtel du Chemin de Fer, where he had lunch and made inquiries about the local newspapers.

At two o'clock, he entered the *La Meuse* newspaper building at the very moment when Joseph Van Damme was leaving it: the two men passed silently within arm's reach of each other.

'He's still one step ahead of me!' Maigret grumbled under his breath.

When he asked the usher with his silver chain of office about consulting the newspaper's archives, he was told to fill out an authorization form and wait for its approval.

Maigret thought over certain striking details in his case: Armand Lecocq d'Arneville had told him that his brother had left Liège at around the same time that Jef Lombard was drawing hanged men with such morbid fascination.

And clothing B, which the tramp of Neuschanz and Bremen had carried around in the yellow suitcase, was at least six years old, according to the German technician, *and perhaps even ten . . .*

And now Joseph Van Damme had turned up at *La Meuse*! Didn't that tell the inspector something?

The usher showed Maigret into a room with heavy formal furniture, where the parquet gleamed like a skating rink.

'Which year's collection do you wish to consult?'

Maigret had already noticed the enormous cardboard cases arrayed around the entire room, each containing the issues of a particular year.

'I'll find it myself, thank you.'

The room smelled of polish, musty paper and formal luxury. On the moleskin tabletop were reading stands to hold the cumbersome volumes. Everything was so neat, so clean, so austere that the inspector hardly dared take his pipe from his pocket.

In a few moments he was leafing page by page through the newspapers of the 'year of the hanged men'.

Thousands of headlines streamed past his gaze, some recalling events of worldwide importance, others dealing with local incidents: a big department store fire (a full page for three days running), an alderman's resignation, an increase in tram fares.

Suddenly: torn newsprint, all along the binding. The daily paper for 15 February had been ripped out.

Hurrying into the reception room, Maigret fetched the usher.

'Someone came here before I did, isn't that right? And it was this same collection he asked for?'

'Yes. He was here only five minutes or so.'

'Are you from Liège? Do you remember what happened back then?'

'Ten years ago? Hmm . . . That's the year my sister-in-law died . . . I know! The big floods! We even had to wait a week for the burial because the only way you could get around in the streets down by the Meuse was by boat. Here, look at these articles: *The King and Queen visit the disaster victims* . . . There are photos, and – wait, we're missing an issue. How extraordinary! I'll have to inform the director about this . . .'

Maigret picked up a scrap of newsprint that had fallen to the floor while Joseph Van Damme – and there was no doubt about it – had been tearing out the pages for 15 February.

7. The Three Men

There are four daily papers in Liège. Maigret spent two hours checking their archives one after the other and, as he expected, they were all missing the 15 February issue.

With its luxury department stores, popular brasseries, cinemas and dance halls, the place to see and be seen in Liège is the busy quadrangle of streets known as the Carré. At least three times, the inspector caught sight of Joseph Van Damme strolling around there, walking stick in hand.

When Maigret returned to the Hôtel du Chemin de Fer, he found two messages waiting for him. The first was a telegram from Lucas, to whom he had given certain instructions just before leaving Paris.

> Stove ashes found room Louis Jeunet Rue Roquette analysed by technician stop Identified remains Belgian and French banknotes stop Quantity suggests large sum

The other was a letter delivered to the hotel by messenger, typed on ordinary typing paper without any heading.

> Detective Chief Inspector,
>
> I beg to inform you that I am prepared to furnish the answers you seek in your inquiry.
>
> I have my reasons for being cautious, and I would be obliged, if my proposal interests you, if you would meet me this evening at around eleven o'clock, at the Café de la Bourse, which is behind the Théâtre Royal.
>
> Until then, I remain, sir, your most humble, loyal and obedient servant, etc., etc.

No signature. On the other hand, a rather surprising number of business turns of phrase for a note of this kind: *I beg to inform you . . . I would be obliged . . . if my proposal interests you . . . your most humble, loyal and obedient servant, etc., etc. . . .*

Dining alone at his table, Maigret realized that, although he hadn't much noticed it before, the focus of his attention had shifted somewhat away from Jean Lecocq d'Arneville, who had killed himself in a hotel room in Bremen under the name of Louis Jeunet.

Now the inspector found himself haunted by the images Jef Lombard had hung up everywhere, those hanged men dangling from a church-steeple cross, from the trees in a wood, from a nail in an attic room, grotesque or sinister hanged men in the garb of many centuries, their faces livid or flushed crimson.

At half past ten he set out for the Théâtre Royal; it was five to eleven when he pushed open the door of the Café de la Bourse, a quiet little place frequented by locals and by card players in particular.

And there he found a surprise waiting for him. Three men were sitting at a table off in a corner, over by the counter: Maurice Belloir, Jef Lombard and Joseph Van Damme.

Things seemed to hang fire for a moment while the waiter helped Maigret out of his overcoat. Belloir automatically rose halfway in greeting. Van Damme didn't move a muscle. Lombard, grimacing with extraordinary nervous tension, could not keep still as he waited for his companions to make a move.

Was Maigret going to come over, shake hands, sit down with them? He knew them all: he had accepted Van Damme's invitation to lunch in Bremen, he'd had a glass of brandy at Belloir's house in Rheims, and only that morning he had visited Lombard's home.

'Good evening, gentlemen.'

He shook their hands with his customary firmness, which could at times seem vaguely threatening.

'Imagine, meeting you all again like this!'

There was space next to Van Damme on the banquette, so Maigret parked himself there.

'A glass of pale ale!' he called to the waiter.

Then silence fell. A strained, oppressive silence. Van Damme stared straight ahead, his teeth clenched. Lombard was still fidgeting, as if his clothes were too tight at his armpits. Belloir, cold and distant, was studying his fingertips and ran a wooden match end under the nail of one index finger to remove a speck.

'Madame Lombard is doing well?'

Jef Lombard darted a glance all around, as if seeking something to cling to, then stared at the stove and stammered, 'Very well . . . Thank you.'

By the wall clock behind the counter, Maigret counted five whole minutes without anyone saying a word.

Van Damme, who had let his cigar go out, was the only man who allowed his face to burn with undisguised hatred.

Lombard was the most interesting one to observe. Everything that had happened that day had surely rubbed his nerves raw, and even the tiniest muscle in his face was twitching.

The four men were sitting in an absolute oasis of silence in a café where everyone else was loudly chattering away.

'And *belote* again!' crowed a card player on the right.

'High *tierce*,' said a fellow cautiously on the left. 'We're all agreed on that?'

'Three beers! Three!' shouted the waiter.

The whole café was a beehive of noise and activity except for that one table of four, around which an invisible wall seemed to be growing.

Lombard was the one who broke the spell. He'd been chewing on his lower lip when suddenly he leaped to his feet and gasped, 'The hell with it!'

After glancing briefly but piercingly at his companions, he grabbed his hat and coat and, flinging the door violently open, left the café.

'I bet he bursts into tears as soon as he gets off on his own,' said Maigret thoughtfully.

He'd sensed it, that sob of rage and despair swelling inside the man's throat until his Adam's apple quivered.

Turning to Van Damme, who was staring at the marble tabletop, Maigret tossed down half his beer and wiped his lips with the back of his hand.

The atmosphere was the same – but ten times more concentrated – as in the house in Rheims, where the inspector had first imposed himself on these three people. And the man's imposing bulk itself helped make his stubborn presence all the more menacing.

Maigret was tall and wide, particularly broad-shouldered, solidly built, and his run-of-the-mill clothes emphasized his peasant stockiness. His features were coarse, and his eyes could seem as still and dull as a cow's. In this he resembled certain figures out of children's nightmares, those monstrously big blank-faced creatures that bear down upon sleepers as if to crush them. There was something implacable and inhuman about him that suggested a pachyderm plodding inexorably towards its goal.

He drank his beer, smoked his pipe, watched with satisfaction as the minute hand of the café clock snapped onwards with a metallic click. On a livid clock face!

He seemed to be ignoring everyone and yet he kept an eye on the slightest signs of life to either side.

This was one of the most extraordinary hours of his career. For this stand-off lasted almost one hour: exactly fifty-two minutes! A war of nerves.

Although Jef Lombard had been *hors de combat* practically from the outset, the other two men were hanging on.

Maigret sat between them like a judge, but one who made no accusations and whose thoughts could not be divined. What did he know? Why had he come? What was he waiting for? A word, a gesture that would corroborate his suspicions? Had he already found out the whole truth – or was his confident manner simply a bluff?

And what could anyone say? More musings on coincidence and chance encounters?

Silence reigned. They waited even without any idea of what they were waiting for. They were waiting for something, and nothing was happening!

With each passing minute, the hand on the clock quivered as the mechanism within creaked faintly. At first no one had paid any attention. Now, the sound was incredibly loud – and the event had even separated into three stages: an initial click; the minute hand beginning to move; then another click, as if to slide the hand into its new slot. And as an obtuse angle slowly became an acute angle, the clock face changed: the two hands would eventually meet.

The waiter kept looking over at this gloomy table in astonishment. Every once in a while, Maurice Belloir would swallow – and Maigret would know this without even looking. He could hear him live, breathe, wince, carefully shift his feet a little now and again, as if he were in church.

Not too many customers were left. The red cloths and playing cards were vanishing from the pale marble tabletops. The waiter stepped outside to close the shutters, while the *patronne* sorted the chips into little piles, according to their value.

'You're staying?' Belloir finally asked, in an almost unrecognizable voice.

'And you?'

'I'm . . . not sure.'

Then Van Damme tapped the table sharply with a coin and called to the waiter, 'How much?'

'For the round? Nine francs seventy-five.'

The three of them were standing now, avoiding one another's eyes, and the waiter helped each of them in turn into his overcoat.

'Goodnight, gentlemen.'

It was so foggy outside that the streetlamps were almost lost in the mist. All the shutters were closed. Somewhere in the distance, footsteps echoed along the pavement.

There was a moment's hesitation, for none of the men wanted to take responsibility for deciding in which direction they would go. Behind them, someone was locking the doors of the café and setting the security bars in place.

Off to the left lay an alley of crookedly aligned old houses.

'Well, gentlemen,' announced Maigret at last, 'the time has come to wish you goodnight.'

He shook Belloir's hand first; it was cold, trembling. The hand Van Damme grudgingly extended was clammy and soft.

The inspector turned up the collar of his overcoat, cleared his throat and began walking alone down the deserted street. And all his senses were attuned to a single purpose: to perceive the faintest noise, the slightest ruffle in the air that might warn him of any danger.

His right hand gripped the butt of the revolver in his pocket. He had the impression that in the network of alleys laid out on his left, enclosed within the centre of Liège like a small island of lepers, people were trying to hurry along without making a sound.

He could just make out a low murmur of conversation but couldn't tell whether it was very near or far away, because the fog was muffling his senses.

Abruptly, he pitched to one side and flattened himself against a door just as a sharp report rang out – and someone, off in the night, took to his heels.

Advancing a few steps, Maigret peered down the alley from which the shot had come but saw only some dark blotches that probably led into blind side alleys and, at the far end 200 metres away, the frosted-glass globe announcing a shop selling *pommes frites*.

A few moments later, as he was walking past that shop, a girl emerged from it with a paper cone of golden *frites*. After propositioning him for form's sake, she headed off to a brighter street.

*

Grinding the pen-nib down on to the paper with his enormous index finger, Maigret was peacefully writing, pausing from time to time to tamp down the hot ashes in his pipe.

He was ensconced in his room in the Hôtel du Chemin de Fer and according to the illuminated station clock, which he could see from his window, it was two in the morning.

Dear old Lucas,

As one never knows what may happen, I'm sending you the following information so that, if necessary, you will be able to carry on the inquiry I have begun.

1. Last week, in Brussels, a shabbily dressed man who looks like a tramp wraps up thirty thousand-franc notes and sends the package to his own address, Rue de la Roquette, in Paris. The evidence will show that he often sent himself similar sums but that *he did not make any use of the money himself.* The proof is that charred remains of large amounts of banknotes burned on purpose have been found in his room.

He goes by the name of Louis Jeunet and is more or less regularly employed by a workshop on his street.

He is married (contact Mme Jeunet, herbalist, Rue Picpus) and has a child. After some acute episodes of alcoholism, however, he leaves his wife and child under mysterious and troubling circumstances.

In Brussels, after posting the money, he buys a suitcase in which to transport some things he's been keeping in a hotel room. While he is on his way to Bremen, I replace his suitcase with another.

Then Jeunet, *who does not appear to have been contemplating suicide and who has already bought something for his supper*, kills himself upon realizing that the contents of his suitcase have been stolen.

The stolen property is an old suit that does not belong to him and which, years earlier, had been torn as if in a struggle and drenched with blood. This suit *was made in Liège.*

In Bremen, a man comes to view the corpse: Joseph Van Damme, an import-export commission agent, *born in Liège.*

In Paris, I learn that Louis Jeunet is in reality Jean Lecocq d'Arneville, *born in Liège*, where he studied to graduate level. He disappeared from Liège about ten years ago and no one there has had any news of him, but he has no black marks against his name.

2. In Rheims, before he leaves for Brussels, Jean Lecocq d'Arneville is observed one night entering the home of Maurice Belloir, deputy director of a local bank and *born in Liège*, who denies this allegation.

But the thirty thousand francs sent from Brussels were supplied by this same Belloir.

At Belloir's house I encounter: Van Damme, who has flown in from Bremen; Jef Lombard, a photoengraver *in Liège*; and Gaston Janin, who was also born *in that city.*

As I am travelling back to Paris with Van Damme, he tries to push me into the Marne.

And I find him again *in Liège*, in the home of Jef Lombard, who was an active painter around ten years ago and has covered the walls of his home with works from that period depicting hanged men.

When I consult the local newspaper archives, I find that all the papers of 15 February in the year of the hanged men have been stolen by Van Damme.

That evening, an unsigned letter promises to tell me everything and gives me an appointment in a local café. There I find not one man, but three: Belloir (in from Rheims), Van Damme and Jef Lombard.

They are not pleased to see me. I have the feeling that it's one of these men who has decided to talk; the others seem to be there simply to prevent this.

Lombard cracks under the strain and leaves abruptly. I stay with the other two men. Shortly past midnight, I take leave of them outside, in the fog, and a few moments later a shot is fired at me.

I conclude both that one of the three tried to talk to me and that one of the same three tried to eliminate me.

And clearly, given that this last action amounts to a confession, *the person in question has no recourse but to try again and not miss me.*

But who is it? Belloir, Van Damme, Lombard?

I'll find out when he tries again. Since accidents do happen, I'm sending you these notes on the off chance, so that you will be familiar with the inquiry from the very beginning.

To see the human side of this case, look in particular at Mme Jeunet and Armand Lecocq d'Arneville, the dead man's brother.

And now I'm going to bed. Give my best to everybody back there.

Maigret

The fog had faded away, leaving beads of pearly hoarfrost on the trees and every blade of grass in Square d'Avroy. A chilly sun gleamed in the pale-blue sky as Maigret crossed the square, and with each passing minute the melting frost fell in limpid drops to the gravel.

It was eight in the morning when the inspector strode through the still-deserted Carré, where the folded sandwich boards of film posters stood propped against closed shutters.

When Maigret stopped at a mailbox to post his letter to Sergeant Lucas, he took a moment to look around him and felt a pang at the thought that somewhere in the city, in those streets bathed in sunlight, a man was at that very moment thinking about him, a man whose salvation depended upon killing him. And the man had the home-ground advantage over the inspector, as he had proved the night before by vanishing into the maze of alleys.

He knew Maigret, too, and was perhaps even watching him where he stood, whereas the inspector did not know who he was.

Could he be Jef Lombard? Did the danger lie in the ramshackle house in Rue Hors-Château, where a woman and her newborn lay sleeping upstairs, watched over by her loving old mother, while her husband's employees worked nonchalantly among the acid baths, hustled along by bicycle messengers from the newspapers?

Joseph Van Damme, a bold, moody and aggressive man, always scheming: was he not lying in wait for the inspector in a place *where he knew Maigret would eventually appear*?

Because that fellow had foreseen everything ever since Bremen! Three lines in a German newspaper – and he showed up at the morgue! He had lunch with Maigret and then beat him to Rheims! And beat him again to Rue Hors-Château! Beat the investigator to the newspaper archives!

He was even at the Café de la Bourse!

True, there was nothing to prove that he was the one who had decided to talk to Maigret. But there was nothing to prove that he wasn't!

Perhaps it was Maurice Belloir, so cold and formal, the haughty provincial *grand bourgeois*, who had taken a shot at him in the fog. Maybe he was the one whose only hope was to polish off Maigret.

Or Gaston Janin, the little sculptor with the goatee: he hadn't been at the Café de la Bourse, but he could have been lying in ambush in the street . . .

And what connected all that to a hanged man swinging from a church-steeple cross? Or to clusters of hanged men? Or to forests of trees that bore no fruit but hanged men? Or to an old blood-stained suit with lapels clawed by desperate fingernails?

Typists were going off to work. A municipal street sweeper rolled slowly past, its double-nozzle sprayer and brush roller pushing rubbish into the gutter. At street corners, the local police in their white enamel helmets directed traffic with their shiny white gauntlets.

'Police headquarters?' Maigret inquired.

He followed the directions and arrived while the cleaning ladies were still busy, but a cheerful clerk welcomed his French colleague and, upon the inspector's request to examine some ten-year-old police records, but only for the month of February, the man exclaimed in surprise: 'You're the second person in twenty-four hours! You want to know if a certain Joséphine Bollant was in fact arrested for domestic larceny back then, right?'

'Someone came here?'

'Yesterday, towards five in the afternoon. A citizen of Liège who's made it big abroad even though he's still quite a young man! His father was a doctor, and him, he's got a fine business going, in Germany.'

'Joseph Van Damme?'

'The very man! But no matter how hard he looked, he couldn't find what he wanted.'

'Would you show me?'

It was a green index-book of daily reports bound in numerical order. Five entries were listed for 15 February: two for drunkenness and breach of the peace at night, one for shoplifting, one for assault and battery and the last one for breach of close and stealing rabbits.

Maigret didn't bother to look at them. He simply checked the numbers at the top of each form.

'Did Monsieur Van Damme consult the book himself?'

'Yes. He took it into the office next door.'

'Thank you!'

The five reports were numbered 237, 238, 239, 241 and 242.

In other words, number 240 was missing and had been torn out just as the archived newspapers had been ripped from their bindings.

A few minutes later, Maigret was standing in the square behind the town hall, where cars were pulling up to deliver a wedding party. In spite of himself, he was straining to catch the faintest sound, unable to shake a slight feeling of anxiety that he didn't like at all.

8. *Little Klein*

He had made it just in time: it was nine o'clock. The employees of the town hall were arriving for work, crossing the main courtyard there and pausing a moment to greet one another on the handsome stone steps, at the top of which a doorkeeper with a braided cap and nicely groomed beard was smoking his pipe.

It was a meerschaum. Maigret noticed this detail, without knowing why; perhaps because it was glinting in the morning sun, because it looked well seasoned and because for a moment the inspector envied this man who was smoking in voluptuous little puffs, standing there as a symbol of peace and joie de vivre.

For that morning the air was like a tonic that grew more bracing as the sun rose higher into the sky. A delightful cacophony reigned, of people shouting in a Walloon dialect, the shrill clanging of the red and yellow streetcars, and the splashing of the four jets in the monumental Perron Fountain doing its best to be heard over the hubbub of the surrounding Place du Marché.

And when Maigret happened to see Joseph Van Damme head up one side of the double staircase leading to the main lobby, he hurried after him. Inside the building, the two staircases continued up on opposite sides, reuniting on each floor. On one landing, the two men found themselves face to face, panting from their exertion, struggling to appear perfectly at ease before the usher with his silver chain of office.

What happened next was short and swift. A question of precision, of split-second timing.

While dashing up the stairs, Maigret had realized that Van Damme had come only to make something disappear, as he had at police headquarters and the newspaper archives.

One of the police reports for 15 February had already been torn out. But in most cities, didn't the police send a copy of all daily reports to the mayor the next morning?

'I would like to see the town clerk,' announced Maigret, with Van Damme only two steps behind him. 'It's urgent . . .'

Their eyes met. They hesitated. The moment for shaking hands passed. When the usher turned expectantly to the businessman from Bremen, he simply murmured, 'It's nothing, I'll come back later.'

He left. The sound of his footsteps died away as he crossed the lobby downstairs.

Shortly afterwards, Maigret was shown into an opulent office, where the town clerk – ramrod straight in his morning coat and a *very* high collar – quickly began the search for the ten-year-old daily police reports.

The room was warm, the carpets soft and springy. A sunbeam lit up a bishop's crozier in a historical painting that took up one whole section of wall.

After half an hour's hunting and a few polite exchanges, Maigret found the reports about the stolen rabbits, the public drunkenness, the shoplifting and then, between two minor incidents, the following lines:

> Officer Lagasse, of Division No. 6, was proceeding this morning at six o'clock to the Pont des Arches to take up his post there when, on passing the main door of the Church of Saint-Pholien, he observed a body hanging from the door knocker.
>
> A doctor was immediately summoned but could only confirm the death of the young man, one Émile Klein, born in Angleur, twenty years old, a house painter living in Rue du Pot-au-Noir.
>
> Klein had hanged himself, apparently around the middle of the night, with the aid of a window-blind cord. His pockets held only a few items of no value and some small change.
>
> The inquiry established that the deceased had not been regularly

employed for three months, and he seems to have been driven to his action by destitution.

His mother, Madame Klein, a widow who lives in Angleur on a modest pension, has been notified.

There followed hours of feverish activity. Maigret vigorously pursued this new line of inquiry and yet, without being really aware of it, he was less interested in finding out about Klein than he was in finding Van Damme.

For only then, when he had the businessman again in his sights, would he be closing in on the truth. Hadn't it all started in Bremen? And from then on, whenever Maigret scored a point, hadn't he come up against Van Damme?

Van Damme, who had seen him at the town hall, now knew that he'd read the report, that he was tracking down Klein.

At Angleur, nothing! The inspector had taken a taxi deep into an industrial area where small working-class houses, all cast from the same mould in the same sooty grey, lined up on dismal streets at the feet of factory chimneys.

A woman was washing the doorstep of one such house, where Madame Klein had lived.

'It's at least five years since she passed away.'

Van Damme would not be skulking around that neighbourhood.

'Didn't her son live with her?'

'No! And he made a bad end of it: he did away with himself, at the door of a church.'

That was all. Maigret learned only that Klein's father had been a foreman in a coalfield and that after his death his wife lived off a small pension, occupying only a garret in the house, which she sublet.

'To Police Division No. 6,' he told the taxi driver.

As for Officer Lagasse, he was still alive, but he hardly remembered anything.

'It had rained the whole night, he was soaked, and his red hair was sticking to his face.'

'He was tall? Short?'

'Short, I'd say.'

Maigret went next to the gendarmerie, spending almost an hour in offices that smelled of leather and horse sweat.

'If he was twenty years old at the time, he must have been seen by an army medical board . . . Did you say Klein, with a K?'

They found Form 13, in the 'registrant not acceptable' file, and Maigret copied down the information: *height* 1.55 metres, *chest* .80 metres, and a note mentioning 'weak lungs'.

But Van Damme had still not shown up. Maigret had to look elsewhere. The only result of that morning's inquiries was the certainty that clothing B had never belonged to the hanged man of Saint-Pholien, who had been just a shrimp.

Klein had killed himself. There had been no struggle, not a drop of blood shed.

So what tied him to the Bremen tramp's suitcase and the suicide of Lecocq d'Arneville, alias Louis Jeunet?

'Drop me off here . . . And tell me how to find Rue Pot-au-Noir.'

'Behind the church, the street that runs down to Quai Sainte-Barbe.'

After paying off his taxi in front of Saint-Pholien, Maigret took a good look at the new church standing alone in a vast stretch of waste land.

To the right and left of it were boulevards lined by apartment houses built at about the same time as the present church, but behind it there still remained part of the old neighbourhood the city had cut into to make room for Saint-Pholien.

In a stationery shop window, Maigret found some postcards showing the old church, which had been lower, squatter and completely black. One wing had been shored up with timbers. On three sides, dumpy, mean little houses backed up against its walls and gave the whole place a medieval look.

Nothing was left of this Court of Miracles except a sprawl of old houses threaded with alleys and dead ends, all giving off a nauseating odour of poverty.

A stream of soapy water was running down the middle of Rue du Pot-au-Noir, which wasn't even two paces wide. Kids were playing on the doorsteps of houses teeming with life. And although the sun was shining brightly, its rays could not reach down into the alley. A cooper busy hooping barrels had a brazier burning right out in the street.

The house numbers had worn away, so the inspector had to ask for directions to number 7, which turned out to be all the way down a blind alley echoing with the whine of saws and planes, a workshop with a few carpenter's benches at which three men were labouring away. All the shop doors were open, and some glue was heating on a stove.

Looking up, one of the men put down his dead cigarette butt and waited for the visitor to speak.

'Is this the place where a man named Klein used to live?'

The man glanced knowingly at his companions, pointed to the open door of a dark staircase and grumbled, 'Upstairs! Someone's already there.'

'A new tenant?'

The man gave an odd little smile, which Maigret would understand only later.

'Go see for yourself . . . On the first floor, you can't miss it: there's only the one door . . .'

One of the other workmen shook with silent laughter as he worked his long, heavy plane. Maigret started up the stairs, but after a few steps there was no more banister, and the stairwell was completely shrouded in darkness. He struck a match and saw up ahead a door with no lock or doorknob, and only a string to secure it to a rusty nail.

With his hand in his revolver pocket, Maigret nudged the door open with his knee – and was promptly dazzled by light pouring in from a bay window missing a good third of its panes, a sight so surprising that, when he looked around, it took him a few moments to actually focus on anything.

Finally he noticed, off in a corner, a man leaning against the wall and glowering at him with savage fury: it was Joseph Van Damme.

'We were bound to wind up here, don't you think?' said the inspector, in a voice that resonated strangely in the raw, vacant air of the room.

Saying nothing, staring at him venomously, Van Damme never moved.

To understand the layout of the place, one would have had to know what kind of building – convent, barracks, private house – had once contained these walls, not one of which was smooth or square. And although half the room had wooden flooring, the rest was paved with uneven flagstones, as if it were an old chapel.

The walls were whitewashed, except for a rectangular patch of brown bricks apparently blocking up what had once been a window. The view from the bay window was of a gable, a gutter, and beyond them, some crooked roofs off in the direction of the Meuse.

But by far the most bizarre thing of all was that the place was furnished so incoherently that it might have been a lunatic asylum – or some elaborate practical joke.

Strewn in disorder on the floor were new but unfinished chairs, a door lying flat with one panel repaired, pots of glue, broken saws and crates from which straggled straw or shavings.

Yet off in one corner there was a kind of divan or, rather, a box spring, partly draped with a length of printed calico. And directly overhead hung a slightly battered lantern with coloured glass, the kind sometimes found in second-hand shops.

Separate sections of an incomplete skeleton like the ones medical students use had been tossed on to the divan, but the ribs and the pelvis were still hooked together and sat slumped forward like an old rag doll.

And then there were the walls! White walls, covered with drawings and even painted frescoes that presented perhaps the most arrestingly absurd aspect of the whole room: grinning, grimacing figures and inscriptions along the lines of *Long live Satan, grandfather of the world!*

On the floor lay a bible with a broken back. Elsewhere were crumpled-up sketches and papers yellow with age, all thick with dust.

Over the door, another inscription: *Welcome, damned souls!*

And amid this chaos of junk sat the unfinished chairs, the glue pots, the rough pine planks, smelling like a carpenter's shop. A stove lay on its side, red with rust.

Finally, there was Joseph Van Damme, meticulously groomed in his well-tailored overcoat and impeccable shoes, Van Damme who in spite of everything was still the man-about-town with a modern office at a prestigious address, at home in the great brasseries of Bremen, a lover of fine food and aged Armagnac . . .

. . . Van Damme who called and waved to the leading citizens of Liège from the wheel of his car, remarking that that man in the fur-lined coat was worth millions, that that one over there owned a fleet of thirty merchant ships, Van Damme who would later, serenaded by light music amid the clinking of glasses and saucers, shake the hands of all these magnates with whom he felt a growing fraternity . . .

. . . Van Damme who suddenly looked like a hunted animal, still frozen with his back against the wall, with white plaster marks on his shoulder and one hand in his overcoat pocket, glaring steadily at Maigret.

'How much?'

Had he really spoken? Could the inspector, in that unreal atmosphere, have been imagining things?

Startled, Maigret knocked over a chair with a caved-in seat, which landed with a loud clatter.

Van Damme had flushed crimson, but not with the glow of health: his hypertensive face betrayed panic – or despair – as well as rage and the desire to live, to triumph at any cost, and he concentrated all his remaining will to resist in his defiant gaze.

'What do you mean?' asked Maigret, going over to the pile of crumpled sketches swept into a corner by the bay window, where he began spreading them out for a look. They were studies of a nude figure, a girl with coarse features, unruly hair, a strong, healthy body with heavy breasts and broad hips.

'There's still time,' Van Damme continued. 'Fifty thousand? . . . A hundred?'

When the inspector gave him a quizzical look, Van Damme, in a fever of ill-concealed anxiety, barked, 'Two hundred thousand!'

Fear shivered in the air within the crooked walls of that miserable room. A bitter, sick, morbid fear.

And perhaps there was something else, too: a repressed desire, the intoxicating temptation of murder . . .

Yet Maigret went on examining the old figure drawings, recognizing in various poses the same voluptuous girl, always staring sullenly into the distance. Once, the artist had tried draping her in the length of calico covering the divan. Another time, he had sketched her in black stockings. Behind her was a skull, which now sat at the foot of the box spring. And Maigret remembered having seen that macabre death's-head in Jef Lombard's self-portrait.

A connection was arising, still only vaguely, among all these people, these events, across time and space. With a faint tremor of excitement, the inspector smoothed out a charcoal sketch depicting a young man with long hair, his shirt collar wide open across his chest and the beginnings of a beard on his chin. He had chosen a Romantic pose: a three-quarter view of the head, and he seemed to be facing the future the way an eagle stares into the sun.

It was Jean Lecocq d'Arneville, the suicide of the sordid hotel in Bremen, the tramp who had never got to eat his last dinner.

'Two hundred thousand francs!'

And the voice added, even now betraying the businessman who thinks of every detail, of the fluctuations in the exchange rate, 'French francs! . . . Listen, inspector . . .'

Maigret sensed that pleading would give way to threats, that the fear quivering in his voice would soon become a growl of rage.

'There's still time, no official action has been taken, and we're in Belgium . . .'

There was a candle end in the lantern; beneath the pile of papers on the floor, the inspector found an old kerosene stove.

'You're not here in an official capacity . . . and even if . . . I'm asking you for a month.'

'Which means it happened in December . . .'

Van Damme seemed to draw back even closer to the wall and stammered, 'What do you mean?'

'It's November now. In February, it will have been ten years since Klein hanged himself, and you're asking me for only one month.'

'I don't understand . . .'

'Oh yes you do!'

And it was maddening, frightening, to see Maigret go on leafing through the old papers with his left hand – and the papers were crackling, rustling – while his right hand remained thrust into his overcoat pocket.

'You understand perfectly, Van Damme! If the problem were Klein's death, and if – for example – he'd been murdered, the statute of limitations would apply only in February, meaning ten years afterwards. Whereas you are asking me for only one month. So *whatever happened* . . . happened in December.'

'You'll never find out anything . . .'

His voice quavered like a wobbly phonograph record.

'Then why are you afraid?'

The inspector lifted up the box spring, underneath which he saw only dust and a greenish, mouldy crust of something barely recognizable as bread.

'Two hundred thousand francs! We could arrange it so that, later on . . .'

'Do you want me to slap your face?'

Maigret's threat had been so blunt and unexpected that Van Damme panicked for a moment, raised his arm to protect himself and, in so doing, unintentionally pulled out the revolver he'd been clutching in his coat pocket. Realizing what he'd done, he was again overcome for a few seconds by that intoxicating temptation . . . but must have hesitated to shoot.

'Drop it!'

He let go. The revolver fell to the floor, near a pile of wood shavings.

And, turning his back to the enemy, Maigret kept on rummaging through the bewildering collection of incongruous things. He picked up a yellowish sock, also marbled with mildew.

'So tell me, Van Damme . . .'

Sensing a change in the silence, Maigret turned round and saw the man pass a hand over his face, where his fingers left wet streaks on his cheeks.

'You're crying?'

'Me?'

He'd said this aggressively, sardonically, despairingly.

'What branch of the army were you in?'

Van Damme was baffled by the inspector's question, but ready to snatch at any scrap of hope.

'I was in the École des Sous-Lieutenants de Réserve, at Beverloo.'

'Infantry?'

'Cavalry.'

'So you must have been between one metre sixty-five and one metre seventy. And you weren't over seventy kilos. It was later that you put on some weight.'

Maigret pushed away a chair he'd bumped into, then picked up another scrap of paper – it looked like part of a letter – with only a single line on it: *Dear old thing* . . .

But he kept an eye on Van Damme, who was still trying to figure out what Maigret had meant and who – in sudden understanding, his face haggard – cried out in horror, 'It wasn't me! I swear I've never worn that suit!'

Maigret's foot sent Van Damme's revolver spinning to the other side of the room.

Why, at that precise moment, did he count up the children again? A little boy in Belloir's house. Three kids in Rue Hors-Château, and the newest hadn't even opened her eyes yet! Plus the son of the false Louis Jeunet . . .

On the floor, the beautiful naked girl was arching her back, throwing out her chest on an unsigned sketch in red chalk.

There were hesitant footsteps, out on the stairs; a hand fumbled at the door, feeling for the string that served as a latch.

9. The Companions of the Apocalypse

In what happened next, everything mattered: the words, the silences, the looks they gave one another, even the involuntary twitch of a muscle. Everything had great meaning, and there was a sense that behind the actors in these scenes loomed an invisible pall of fear.

The door opened. Maurice Belloir appeared, and his first glance was for Van Damme, over in the corner with his back to the wall. The second glance took in the revolver lying on the floor.

It was enough; he understood. Especially when he saw Maigret, with his pipe, still calmly going through the pile of old sketches.

'Lombard's coming!' announced Belloir, without seeming to address anyone in particular. 'I grabbed a taxi.'

Hearing this was enough to tell Maigret that the bank deputy director had just given up. The evidence was slight: a gentle easing of tension in his face; a hint of shame in his tired voice.

The three of them looked at one another. Joseph Van Damme spoke first.

'What is he . . . ?'

'He's gone crazy. I tried to calm him down, but he got away from me. He went off talking to himself, waving his arms around . . .'

'He has a gun?' asked Maigret.

'He has a gun.'

Maurice Belloir tried to listen carefully, with the strained look of a stunned man struggling in vain to recover control of himself.

'Both of you were down in Rue Hors-Château? Waiting for the result of my conversation with . . .'

He pointed to Van Damme, and Belloir nodded.

'And all three of you agreed to offer me . . . ?'

He didn't need to say everything; they understood right away. They all understood even the silences and felt as if they could hear one another think.

Suddenly footsteps were racing up the stairs. Someone tripped, must have fallen, then moaned with rage. The next moment the door was kicked open and framed the figure of Jef Lombard, stock still for an instant as he gazed at the three men with terrifying intensity.

He was shaking, gripped by fever, perhaps by some kind of insanity.

What he saw must have been a mad vision of Belloir backing away from him, Van Damme's congested face, and then Maigret, broad-shouldered and absolutely immobile, holding his breath.

And there was all that bewildering junk to boot, with the lantern and the broken-down divan and the spread-out drawings covering all but the breasts and chin of the naked girl in that sketch . . .

The scene lasted for mere fractions of a second. Jef Lombard's long arm was holding out a revolver. Maigret watched him quietly. Still, he did heave a sigh when Lombard threw the gun to the floor, grabbed his head with both hands and burst into great raw sobs.

'I can't, I can't!' he groaned. 'You hear me? God damn it, I can't!'

And he turned away to lean both arms against the wall, his shoulders heaving. They could hear him snuffling softly.

The inspector went over and closed the door, to shut off the noise of sawing and planing downstairs and the distant cries of children out in the street.

Jef Lombard wiped his face with his handkerchief, tossed back his hair and looked around with the empty eyes of someone whose nerves have just given way. He was not completely calm; his fingers were flexing like claws, he was breathing heavily, and when he tried to speak he had to bite his lip to suppress the sob welling in his throat.

'To end up like this!' he finally said, his voice dark and biting.

He tried to laugh, but sounded desperate.

'Nine years! Almost ten! I was left all alone, with no money, no job . . .'

He was talking to himself, probably unaware that he was staring hard at the figure drawing of the nude with that bare flesh . . .

'Ten years of slogging away, every day, with difficulties and disappointments of all kinds, but I got married anyway, I wanted kids . . . I drove myself like an animal to give them a decent life. A house! And the workshop! Everything – you saw that! But what you didn't see is what it cost me to build it all, and the *heartbreaks* . . . The bills that kept me awake at night when I was just getting started . . .'

Passing his hand over his forehead, he swallowed hard, and his Adam's apple rose and fell.

'And now look: I've just had a baby girl and I can't remember if I've even seen her! My wife is lying in bed unable to understand what's going on, she sneaks frightened looks at me, she doesn't recognize me any more . . . My men ask me questions, and I don't know what to tell them.

'All gone! Suddenly, in a few days: wrecked, ruined, done for, smashed to pieces! *Everything!* Ten years of work! And all because . . .'

Clenching his fists, he looked down at the gun on the floor, then up at Maigret. He was at the end of his rope.

'Let's get it over with,' he sighed, wearily waving a hand. 'Who's going to do the talking? It's so stupid!'

And he might have been speaking to the skull, the heap of old sketches, the wild, outlandish drawings on the walls.

'Just so stupid . . .'

He seemed on the verge of tears again, but no, he was all done in. The fit had passed. He went over to sit on the edge of the divan, planted his elbows on his bony knees, his chin in his hands, and sat there, waiting.

He moved only to scrape a bit of mud off the bottom of a trouser leg with a fingernail.

'Am I disturbing you?' asked a cheery voice.

The carpenter entered, covered in sawdust, and, after looking around at the drawings decorating the walls, he laughed.

'So, you came back to look at all this?'

No one moved. Only Belloir tried to look as if nothing were wrong.

'Do you remember about those twenty francs you still owe me for that last month? Oh, not that I've come to ask you for them. It just makes me laugh, because when you left without taking all this old junk, I recall you saying, "Maybe one day a single one of these sketches might well be worth as much as this whole dump." I didn't believe you. Still, I did put off whitewashing the walls. One day I brought up a framer who sells pictures and he went off with two or three drawings. Gave me a hundred sous for them. Do you still paint?'

It finally dawned on him that something was wrong. Van Damme was staring stubbornly at the floor. Belloir was impatiently snapping his fingers.

'Aren't you the one who set himself up in Rue Hors-Château?' asked the carpenter, turning to Jef Lombard. 'I've a nephew worked with you. A tall blond fellow . . .'

'Maybe,' sighed Lombard, turning away.

'You I don't recognize. . . Were you with this lot?'

Now the landlord was speaking to Maigret.

'No.'

'What a weird bunch! My wife didn't want me to rent to them, and then she advised me to throw them out, especially since they didn't pay up very often. But they amused me. Always looking to be the one wearing the biggest hat, or smoking the longest clay pipe. And they used to sing together and drink all night long! And some pretty girls would show up sometimes . . . Speaking of which, Monsieur Lombard, that one there, on the floor, do you know what happened to her? . . .

'She married a shop walker at Le Grand Bazar and she lives about two hundred metres down the street from here. She has a son who goes to school with mine . . .'

Lombard stood up, went over to the bay window, and retraced his steps in such agitation that the carpenter decided to beat a retreat.

'Maybe I am disturbing you after all, so I'll leave you to it. And you know, if you're interested in anything here . . . Of course, I never held on to this stuff on account of the twenty francs! All I took was one landscape, for my dining room.'

Out on the landing, he seemed about to start chatting again, but was summoned from downstairs.

'Someone to see you, *patron*!'

'Later, then, gentlemen. Glad to have met—'

The closing door cut off his voice. Although inopportune, the carpenter's visit had eased some of the tension, and while he'd been talking, Maigret had lit his pipe.

Now he pointed to the most puzzling drawing on the wall, an image encircled by an inscription that read: *The Companions of the Apocalypse*.

'Was this the name of your group?'

Sounding almost like himself again, it was Belloir who replied.

'Yes. I'll explain . . . It's too late for us, isn't it – and tough luck for our wives and children . . .'

But Lombard broke in: 'Let me tell him, I want to . . .'

And he began pacing up and down the room, now and then looking over at some object or other, as if to illustrate his story.

'Just over ten years ago, I was studying painting at the Académie, where I used to go around in a wide-brimmed hat and a *lavallière* . . . Two others there with me were Gaston Janin, who was studying sculpture, and little Émile Klein. We would parade proudly around the Carré – because we were *artists*, you understand? Each of us thought he'd be at least another Rembrandt!

'It all started so foolishly . . . We read a lot, and favoured the

Romantic period. We'd get carried away and idolize some writer for a week, then drop that one and adopt another . . .

'Little Klein, whose mother lived in Angleur, rented this studio we're in, and we started meeting here. We were really impressed by the medieval atmosphere of the neighbourhood, especially on winter evenings. We'd sing old songs and recite Villon's poetry . . .

'I don't remember any more who discovered the Book of Revelation – the Apocalypse of John – and insisted on reading us whole chapters from it.

'One evening we met a few university students: Belloir, Lecocq d'Arneville, Van Damme, and a Jewish fellow named Mortier, whose father has a shop selling tripe and sausage casings not far from here.

'We got to drinking and wound up bringing them back to the studio. The oldest of them wasn't even twenty-two. That was you, Van Damme, wasn't it?'

It was doing Lombard good to talk. His movements were less abrupt, his voice less hoarse, but his face was still blotched with red and his lips swollen from weeping.

'I think it was my idea to found a group, a society! I'd read about the secret societies in German universities during the eighteenth century. A club that would unite Science and Art!'

Looking around the studio walls, he couldn't help sneering.

'Because we were just full of that kind of talk! Hot air that puffed up our pride. On the one side were Klein, Janin and me, the paint-pushers: we were Art! On the other side, our new university friends. We drank to that. Because we drank a lot . . . We drank to feel even more gloriously superior! And we'd dim the lights to create an atmosphere of mystery.

'We'd lounge around right here, look: some of us on the divan, the others on the floor. We'd smoke pipe after pipe, until the air became a thick haze. Then we'd all start singing. There was almost always someone feeling sick who'd have to go and throw up in the courtyard. We'd still be going strong at two, three in the morning, working ourselves up into a frenzy. Helped along by the wine, some cheap rotgut that upset our stomachs, we used to soar off into the realm of metaphysics . . .

'I can still see little Klein . . . He was the most excitable one, the nervous type. He wasn't well. His mother was poor and he lived on nothing, went without food so he could drink. Because when we'd been drinking, we all felt like real geniuses!

'The university contingent was a little more level-headed, because they weren't as poor, except for Lecocq d'Arneville. Belloir would swipe a bottle of nice old Burgundy or liqueur from his parents, and Van Damme used to bring some charcuterie . . .

'We were convinced that people used to look at us out in the street with fear and admiration, and we chose an arcane, sonorous, lofty name: *The Companions of the Apocalypse*. Actually, I don't think any of us had read the Book of Revelation all the way through . . . Klein was the only one who could recite a few passages by heart, when he was drunk.

'We'd all decided to split the rent for the room, but Klein was allowed to live here.

'A few girls agreed to come pose for us for free . . . Pose and all the rest, naturally! And we tried to think of them as *grisettes* from *La Bohème*! And all that half-baked folderol . . .

'There's one of the girls, on the floor. Dumb as they come. But we painted her as a Madonna anyway.

'Drinking – that was the main thing. We had to ginger up the atmosphere at all costs. Klein once tried to achieve the same effect by pouring sulphuric ether on the divan. And I remember all of us, working ourselves up, waiting for intoxication, expecting visions . . . Oh God Almighty!'

Lombard went over to cool his forehead against a misty windowpane, but when he came back there was a new quaver in his voice.

'Chasing after this frenzied exaltation, we wound up nervous wrecks – especially those of us who weren't eating enough, you understand? Little Klein, among others: a poor kid going without food to over-stimulate himself with drink . . .

'And it was as if we were rediscovering the world all on our own, naturally! We were full of opinions on every great problem, and full of scorn for society, established truths and everything bourgeois. When we'd had a few drinks and smoked up a storm, we'd spout the most cock-eyed nonsense, a hodgepodge of Nietzsche, Karl Marx, Moses, Confucius, Jesus Christ . . .

'Here's an example: I don't remember which one of us discovered that *pain doesn't exist*, the brain's simply imagining it. One night I became so enthralled with the idea that, surrounded by my excited audience, I stabbed myself in the upper arm with a pocket knife *and forced myself to smile about it*!

'And we had other wild inspirations like that . . . We were an elite, a coterie of geniuses who'd come together by chance and were way above the conventional world with its laws and preconceived opinions. A gathering of the gods, hey? Gods who were sometimes dying of hunger but who strode through the streets with their heads high, crushing passers-by with their contempt.

'And we had the future completely in hand: Lecocq d'Arneville would become a new Tolstoy, while Van Damme, who was taking boring courses at our university business school, would fundamentally redefine economics and upend all the accepted ideas about the social workings of humanity. And each one of us had a role to play, as poets, painters and future heads of state.

'All fuelled by booze! Or just fumes! Because by the end we were so used to flying high here that simply by walking through that door, into the alchemical light of the lantern, with a skeleton in the shadows and the skull we used as a communal drinking bowl, we'd catch the little fever we craved, all on our own.

'Even the most modest among us could already envision the marble plaque that would one day adorn this house: *Here met the famous Companions of the Apocalypse* . . . We all tried to come up with the newest great book or amazing idea. It's a miracle we didn't all wind up anarchists! Because we actually discussed that question, quite seriously. There'd been an incident in Seville;

someone read the newspaper article about it aloud, and I don't remember any more who shouted, "True genius is destructive!"

'Well, our kiddy club debated this subject for hours. We came up with ways to make bombs. We cast about for interesting things to blow up.

'Then little Klein, who was on his sixth or seventh glass, became ill, but not like the other times. This was some kind of nervous fit: he was writhing on the floor, and all we could think of any more was what would happen to us if something happened to him! And that girl was there! Henriette, her name was. She was crying . . .

'Oh, those were some nights, all right . . . It was a point of honour with us not to leave until the lamplighter had turned off the gas streetlamps, and then we'd head out shivering into the dreary dawn. Those of us who were better off would sneak home through a window, sleep, eat and more or less recover from our nightly excesses, but the others – Klein, Lecocq d'Arneville and I – would drag ourselves through the streets, nibbling on a roll and looking longingly into shop windows . . .

'That year I didn't have an overcoat because I wanted to buy a wide-brimmed hat that cost a hundred and twenty francs, and I pretended that, like everything else, cold was an illusion. And primed by all our discussions, I announced to my father, a good, honest man, a gunsmith's assistant – he's dead, now – that parental love is the worst form of selfishness and that a child's first duty is to reject his family.

'He was a widower. He used to go off to work in the morning at six o'clock, just when I was getting home. Well, he took to setting out earlier so he wouldn't run into me, because my big speeches frightened him. And he would leave me little notes on the table: *There's some cold meat in the cupboard. Father . . .*'

Lombard's voice broke for a moment. He looked over at Belloir, who was sitting on the edge of a staved-in chair, staring at the floor, and then at Van Damme, who was shredding a cigar to bits.

'There were seven of us,' said Lombard dully. 'Seven supermen! Seven geniuses! Seven kids!

'Janin's still sculpting, off in Paris – or rather, he makes shop-window mannequins for a big factory. Now and then he works off his frustration by doing something from a real model, his mistress of the moment . . . Belloir's in banking, Van Damme's in business, I'm a photoengraver . . .'

The fear in that silent room was now palpable. Lombard swallowed hard but went on, and his eyes seemed to sink even deeper into their dark sockets.

'Klein hanged himself at the church door . . . Lecocq d'Arneville shot himself in the mouth in Bremen . . .'

Another silence. This time, unable to sit still, Belloir stood up, hesitated, then went to stand by the bay window. A strange noise seemed to be rumbling in his chest.

'And the last one?' inquired Maigret. 'Mortier, I believe? The tripe dealer's son.'

Lombard now stared at him so frantically that the inspector thought he might have another fit. Van Damme somehow knocked over a chair.

'It was in December, wasn't it?'

As he was speaking, Maigret kept a close eye on the three men.

'In a month it will have been ten years. The statute of limitations will come into effect.'

He went first to pick up Van Damme's automatic, then collected the revolver Lombard had thrown away after he arrived.

Maigret had seen it coming: Lombard was breaking down, holding his head in his hands and wailing, 'My children! My three little ones!'

And with renewed hysteria, unashamed to show the tears streaming down his face, he yelled, 'It's because of you, you, only because of you, that I haven't even seen my newborn child, my little girl! I couldn't even say what she looks like . . . *Do you understand?*'

10. *Christmas Eve in Rue du Pot-au-Noir*

There must have been a passing shower, some swift low-lying clouds, because all the sunshine glinting off objects in the room vanished in an instant. As if a switch had been flicked, the light turned uniformly grey, while the clutter took on a glum look.

Maigret understood why those who'd gathered there had felt the need to doctor the light with a lantern of many colours, set their stage with mysterious shadows and muddle the atmosphere with drink and tobacco smoke.

And he could imagine how Klein would awaken in the morning after those sad orgies to find himself surrounded by empty bottles, broken glasses and rancid odours, all bathed in the murk from the bay window, which had no curtains.

Jef Lombard was too upset to go on, and it was Maurice Belloir who took up the story.

Everything shifted, as if they'd moved to a different register. Lombard had been shaken to his very core, his emotion expressed through wrenching sobs, shrill, wheezing catches in his voice, nervous pacing and periods of alternating agitation and calm that could have been plotted on a medical chart, while Belloir's entire person – his voice, his gaze, his every move – was under such taut control that it was painful to see, for it clearly demanded a gruelling effort of will and concentration.

This man could never have cried, or even tried to smile: he held himself completely still.

'May I take over, inspector? It will be dark soon and we'll have no light here.'

It was not Belloir's fault that he'd brought up a practical detail, and it wasn't from lack of feeling, for it was actually his own way of showing how he felt.

'I believe that we were all sincere in our arguments and endless discussions, and when we were dreaming out loud. But there were different degrees of sincerity involved.

'Jef has mentioned this. On the one hand, there were the wealthy ones, who went home afterwards to recover their balance in a stable environment: Van Damme, Willy Mortier and I. And even Janin, who had everything he needed.

'Willy Mortier was in a class by himself, however. A case in point: he was the only one who chose his mistresses from among professional nightclub singers and the dancers in second-rate theatres. He paid them.

'He was a practical, unsentimental person, like his father, who arrived in Liège with empty pockets, matter-of-factly chose the sausage-casing business – and made a fortune.

'Willy received a monthly allowance of 500 francs, which seemed a fabulous sum to the rest of us. He never set foot inside the university, paid poorer students to take notes for him in lectures and "arranged" to pass his exams through favours and bribes.

'He came here simply out of curiosity, because he never shared our tastes or ideas. Look at his father: he'd buy paintings from artists even though he despised them, and he "bought" city councilmen and even aldermen as well, to get what he wanted. He despised them, too.

'Well, Willy despised us in the same way. He was a rich boy who came here to see just how different he was from the rest of us.

'He didn't drink. And those who got drunk here disgusted him. During our epic discussions, he'd say only a few words, but they were like ice water, the kind of words that hurt because they're too blunt, because they ruined the fake poetic atmosphere we'd managed to create.

'He hated us! And we hated him! On top of everything else, he was stingy – and cynical about it. Klein didn't always get something to eat every day, so one or the other of us would help him out now and then. Mortier? He'd announce, "I don't want any difficulties about money to come between us. I don't want to be welcomed simply because I'm well off."

'And he'd cough up *exactly* his share when we were all turning our pockets inside out to buy something to drink.

'It was Lecocq d'Arneville who used to take lecture notes for him, and I once overheard Willy refuse to give him an advance on his payment.

'He was the alien, hostile element that crops up almost every time when men get together. We put up with him. Klein, though, when he was drunk, used to attack him savagely, really let everything that bothered him come pouring out. Mortier would go a bit pale but he'd just listen, with a faint sneer . . .

'I mentioned various kinds of sincerity. Klein and Lecocq d'Arneville were definitely the most forthright, unpretentious members of our group. They were close, like brothers. They'd both had difficult childhoods, with their mothers watching every sou . . . Both these fellows were desperate to better themselves and agonized over anything that stood in their way.

'Klein had to work during the day as a house painter to pay for his evening classes at the Académie, and he did tell us that it made him dizzy when he had to climb a ladder. Lecocq took lecture notes for others, gave French lessons to foreign students; he often came here to eat. The stove must still be around here somewhere . . .'

It was lying on the floor near the divan, where Lombard gave it a gloomy kick.

Not one hair was out of place on Maurice Belloir's sleek head, and his voice was flat, stripped down.

'Since those days, I've heard people in the middle-class drawing rooms of Rheims ask jokingly, "In such-and-such a situation, would you be able to kill someone?" Sometimes it's the mandarin question, you know the one: *If all you had to do was push a button to kill a wealthy mandarin way off in China to inherit his riches, would you do it?*

'We took up the weirdest ideas here and talked for nights on end, so we inevitably came around to the enigma of life and death . . .

'It was almost Christmas; it had been snowing. A short item in a newspaper started us off. We always had to challenge the status quo, right? So we went all out on this idea: mankind is just a patch of mould on the earth's crust. So human life and death don't matter, pity is only a sickness, big animals eat the little ones, and we eat the big ones.

'Lombard told you about the pocket knife: stabbing himself to prove that pain didn't exist!

'Well, that night, shortly before Christmas, with three or four empty bottles lying around on the floor, we seriously debated the idea of killing someone. After all, weren't we off in the realm of pure theory, where anything goes? All bright-eyed, we kept quizzing one another with shivers of guilty excitement.

'"Would *you* be brave enough?"

'"Why not? If life is nothing, just some accident, a blemish on the face of the earth . . . "

'"A stranger, passing in the street?"

'And Klein – so pale, with those dark rings under his eyes – he'd drunk the most. And he yelled, "Yes!"

'We were afraid to take another step: it felt like being at the edge of a cliff. We were dicing with danger, joking around with this murder we'd conjured up, and now that murder seemed to be stalking *us* . . .

'Someone who'd been an altar boy – I think it was Van Damme – started singing the *Libera nos*, which the priest chants over a coffin, and we all took up the chorus, playing this ghoulish game with real relish.

'But we didn't kill anyone that night! At four a.m. I went over the garden wall to sneak home. By eight I was having coffee with my family. The whole thing was only a memory, you understand? Like remembering being scared watching a play in a theatre.

'But Klein stayed here, at Rue du Pot-au-Noir, where all those ideas kept seething in his sickly, swollen head. They were eating him alive. We could tell what was worrying him from the questions he kept popping at us over the next few days.

'"Do you really think it's hard to kill someone?"

'We weren't drunk any more but we didn't want to back down, so we blustered, we said, "Of course it isn't!"

'Maybe we were even getting a thrill out of his childish excitement, but get this straight: we had no intention of causing a tragedy! We were still seeing how far we could go . . .

'When there's a fire, onlookers can't help wanting it to last, to be a *spectacular* fire, and when the river is rising, newspaper readers hope for *major* flooding they can talk about for the next twenty years. *They want something interesting, and it doesn't matter what!*

'Christmas Eve arrived. Everybody brought some bottles. We drank, we sang, and Klein, already half-soused, kept pulling one after another of us aside.

'"Do you think I'd be able to kill someone?"

'We weren't worried about it. By midnight no one was sober. We talked about going out for more bottles.

'That's when Willy Mortier showed up, in a dinner jacket, with a broad white shirt front that seemed to soak up all the light. His face was rosy, he was wearing scent, and he announced that he'd just come from a fancy society reception.

'"Go and get some booze!" Klein yelled at him.

'"You're drunk, chum! I just came along to pay my respects."

'"No, to look down your nose at us!"

'There still wasn't any reason to suspect that something might happen, although Klein's face was more frightening than it had ever been during his other drunken spells. He was so small, so thin next to the other man . . . His hair was a mess, his forehead was all sweaty, and he'd yanked his tie off.

'"Klein," said Willy, "you're stinking drunk!"

'"So what! This stinking drunk's telling you to go and get some booze!"

'I think that scared Willy. He'd begun to sense that this was no laughing matter, but he still tried to bluff his way out . . . His black hair had been curled and perfumed . . .

'"You fellows don't seem to be having much fun here," he told us. "It was livelier back with the stuffed shirts I just left!"

'"Go and get some booze . . ."

'Now Klein was circling him, staring at him, all wound up. A few of us were off in a corner, talking about some Kantian theory or other. Someone else was weeping and swearing that he wasn't fit to live.

'Not one of us had all his wits about him, and no one saw the whole thing: Klein darting forward abruptly, a furious little bundle of nerves, and striking Mortier . . .

'It looked as if he'd butted him in the chest with his head, but we saw blood spurting out! Willy opened his mouth so wide . . .'

'No!' Lombard begged suddenly, now standing and staring at Belloir as if in a daze.

Van Damme had retreated back to the wall, his shoulders slumping. But nothing could have stopped Belloir, not even if he had wanted to himself. It was growing dark. Everyone's face looked grey.

'We were all frantic!' the voice went on. 'And Klein huddled there with a knife in his hand, stunned, gaping at Willy, who just stood swaying, tottering . . . These things don't happen the way people imagine – I can't explain . . .

'Mortier was still on his feet in spite of the blood streaming from the hole in his shirt front. He said – and I'm sure of this – "Bastards!" And he kept standing in the same place, his legs slightly apart, as if to keep his balance. If he hadn't been bleeding, you'd have thought *he* was the drunk.

'He had big eyes, and now they seemed even bigger . . . His left hand was clutching the button of his dinner jacket, while his right was fumbling around the back of his trousers.

'Someone – I think it was Jef – shouted in terror, and we saw Mortier's right hand pull a revolver slowly from a pocket, a small black thing, made of steel, that looked so *hard* . . .

'Klein was rolling on the floor in a fit. A bottle fell, smashing into pieces.

'And Willy was still alive! Just barely swaying, he looked at us, one after the other! Although he couldn't have been seeing clearly . . . He raised the revolver . . .

'Then someone stepped forwards to grab the gun from him, slipped in the blood, and the two of them fell to the floor.

'Mortier must have gone into convulsions – because he still wasn't dead, you hear me? His eyes, those big eyes, were wide open! He kept trying to shoot, and he said it again: "Bastards!"

'The other man's hand was able to grip his throat . . . He hadn't much longer to live, anyway . . .

'I got completely soaked . . . while the dinner jacket just lay there on the floor.'

Van Damme and Lombard were now looking at their companion in horror. And Belloir finished what he had to say.

'That hand around his neck, it was mine! I was the man who slipped in that pool of blood . . .'

He was standing in the same place as he had then. Now, though, he was dapper and soigné, his shoes polished, his suit impeccable. He wore a large gold signet ring on his white, well-cared-for hand with its manicured nails.

'We were in a state of shock. We made Klein go to bed, even though he wanted to go and give himself up. No one spoke. Again, I can't explain . . . And yet I was quite lucid! I'll say it again: people don't understand what such tragedies are really like. I dragged Van Damme out on to the landing, where we talked quietly, while Klein kept howling and struggling.

'The church bells rang the hour while three of us were going down the alley carrying the body, but I don't remember what time it was. The Meuse was in spate – Quai Sainte-Barbe was under half a metre of water – and the current was running fast. Both upstream and down, the barrage gates were open. We just caught a glimpse of a dark mass being swept past the nearest lamp post by the rushing water.

'My suit was stained and torn; I left it at the studio after Van Damme went home to get me some of his clothes. The next day, I concocted a story for my parents . . .'

'Did you all get together again?' Maigret asked slowly.

'No. Most of us bolted from Rue du Pot-au-Noir. Lecocq d'Arneville stayed on with Klein. And ever since then, we've all avoided one another, as if by mutual agreement. Whenever any of us met up by accident in town, we looked the other way.

'It turned out that Willy's body was never found, thanks to the flood. Since he hadn't been proud of knowing us, he'd always been careful never to mention us at home. People thought he'd simply run off for a few days. Later, they did look for him in the seedy parts of town, where they thought he might have finished up that evening.

'I was the first to leave Liège, three weeks later. I suddenly broke off my studies and announced to my family that I wanted to pursue my career in France. I found work in a bank in Paris.

'I learned from the newspapers that Klein had hanged himself that February at the door of Saint-Pholien.

'One day I ran into Janin, in Paris. We didn't talk about the tragedy, but he told me that he, too, had moved to France.'

'I stayed on in Liège, alone,' muttered Lombard resentfully, his head hanging.

'You drew hanged men and church steeples,' Maigret said. 'Then you did sketches for the newspapers. Then . . .'

And he recalled the house in Rue Hors-Château, the windows with the small, green-tinged panes, the fountain in the courtyard, the portrait of the young woman, the photoengraving workshop, where posters and magazine illustrations were gradually invading the walls of hanged men . . .

And the kids! The newest one born only yesterday . . .

Hadn't ten years gone by? And little by little, more or less clumsily, hadn't life returned to normal everywhere?

Van Damme had roamed around Paris, like the other two. By chance, he'd wound up in Germany. His parents had left him an inheritance. He had become an important businessman in Bremen.

Maurice Belloir had made a fine marriage. Moving up the ladder, he was now a bank deputy director! Then there was the lovely new house in Rue de Vesle, where a little boy was studying the violin.

In the evening he played billiards with other town luminaries in the comfortable ambience of the Café de Paris.

Janin got by with a series of mistresses, earned his living by making shop-window mannequins and relaxed by working on portrait busts of his lady friends.

And hadn't even Lecocq d'Arneville got married? Didn't his wife and child live in the back of the herbalist's shop in Rue Picpus?

Willy Mortier's father was still buying, cleaning and selling whole truckloads of pig's entrails, bribing city councilmen and growing ever richer.

His daughter had married a cavalry officer, who hadn't wanted to join the family business, whereupon Mortier had refused to hand over the agreed-upon dowry.

The couple lived off somewhere in a small garrison town.

11. *The Candle End*

It was nearly dark. Their faces were receding into the shadows, but their features seemed all the more sharply etched.

Lombard was the one who burst out, as if alarmed by the gathering dusk, 'We need some light!'

There was still a candle end, left in the lantern that had hung from the same nail for ten years, kept along with the broken-down divan, the length of calico, the battered skeleton, the sketches of the girl with naked breasts and everything else saved as security by the landlord still waiting for his rent.

When Maigret lit the stump, shadows danced on the walls, which shone red, yellow and blue in light glowing through the tinted glass panes, as if from a magic lantern.

'When did Lecocq d'Arneville come to see you for the first time?' the inspector asked, turning towards Belloir.

'It must be about three years ago. I hadn't been expecting it . . . The house you saw had just been finished. My boy was barely walking yet.

'I was struck by how much he'd grown to resemble Klein: not so much physically as in his nature. That same feverish intensity, the same morbid uneasiness. He came as an enemy. He was furious and embittered, or desperate – I can't find exactly the right word. He sniggered at me, spoke aggressively, he was on edge; he pretended to admire my home, my position, my life and character, and yet . . . I had the feeling he might burst into tears, like Klein when he was drunk!

'He thought that I'd forgotten. Not true! I simply wanted to live, you understand me? And that's why I worked like a dog: to live . . .

'But he hadn't been able to get on with his life. He had lived with Klein for two months after that Christmas Eve, it's true . . . We left, they stayed behind: the two of them, here in this room, in . . .

'I can't explain what I felt in his presence. So many years had passed, but I had the feeling Lecocq d'Arneville had remained exactly the same. It was as if life had moved on for some, and stopped short for others.

'He told me that he'd changed his name because he didn't want to keep anything that reminded him of that awful night. He'd even changed his life! He'd never opened another book. He'd got it into his head to build a new life by becoming a manual labourer.

'I had to glean all this information on my own, weeding it out from all his reproaches, caustic remarks and truly monstrous accusations.

'He'd failed! Been a disaster at everything! And part of him was still rooted right here. It was the same for the rest of us, I think, but in our case it was less intense, not as painful, as unhealthy. I believe Klein's face haunted him even more than Willy's did.

'Married, with a kid, he'd been through some tough times and had turned to drink. He was unable, not only to be happy, but even to be at any kind of peace. He screamed at me that he adored his wife and had left her because when he was near her, he felt like a thief! A thief stealing happiness! Happiness stolen from Klein . . . And the other man.

'You see, I've thought a lot about this since then. And I think I understand. We were fooling around with dangerous ideas, with mysticism and morbid thoughts. It was only a game, and we were just kids, playing, but at least two of us let themselves fall into the trap. The most excitable, fanatical ones.

'Klein and Lecocq d'Arneville. We'd all talked about killing someone? Klein went on to do it! And then he killed himself! And Lecocq, appalled, a broken man, was chained to this nightmare for the rest of his life.

'The others and I tried to escape, to find our way back to a normal life, whereas Lecocq d'Arneville threw himself recklessly into his remorse, in a rage of despair. He destroyed his own life! Along with those of his wife and son . . .

'So he turned on us. Because that's why he'd come looking for me. I hadn't understood that at first. He looked around at *my* house, *my* family, *my* bank. And I really did feel that he considered it his duty to destroy all that.

'To avenge Klein! To avenge himself.

'He threatened me. He had kept the suit, with the rips, the bloodstains, and it was the only physical proof of what happened that Christmas Eve. He asked me for money. Lots of it! And asked for more later on.

'Because wasn't that where we were vulnerable? Van Damme, Lombard, myself, even Janin: everything we had achieved depended on money.

'It was the beginning of a new nightmare! Lecocq had known what he was doing, and he went from one to another of us, lugging along that sinister ruined suit. With diabolical cunning, he calculated precisely how much to ask us for, to make us feel the pinch.

'You saw my house, inspector. It's mortgaged! My wife thinks her dowry is sitting untouched at the bank, but there's not a centime of it left. And I've done other things like that.

'He went twice to Bremen, to see Van Damme. He came to Liège. Still consumed with fury, bent on destroying every last scrap of happiness.

'There were six of us around Willy's corpse. Klein was dead; Lecocq was trapped in a living nightmare. So we all had to be equally miserable. And he didn't even spend the money! He lived as wretchedly as before, when he was sharing a bit of cheap sausage with Klein. He burned all the money! And every banknote he burned meant unbelievable hardship for us all.

'For three years we've been struggling, each off in his own corner: Van Damme in Bremen, Jef in Liège, Janin in Paris, myself in Rheims. For three years we've hardly dared write to one another, while Lecocq d'Arneville was forcing us back into the madness of the Companions of the Apocalypse.

'I have a wife. So does Lombard. We've got kids. So we're trying to hang on, for them.

'The other day Van Damme sent us telegrams saying Lecocq had killed himself, and he told us to meet.

'We were all together when you turned up. After you left, we learned that you were the one who now had the bloodstained suit, and that you were determined to track down the truth.'

'Who stole one of my suitcases at Gare du Nord?' Maigret asked, and it was Van Damme who answered.

'Janin. I'd arrived before you and was hiding on one of the station platforms.'

Everyone was exhausted. The candle end would probably last about another ten minutes, if that. The inspector accidentally knocked over the skull, which fell to the floor and seemed to be trying to bite it.

'Who wrote to me at the Hôtel du Chemin de Fer?'

'I did,' Lombard replied without looking up. 'Because of my little girl. My little daughter I haven't seen yet . . . But Van Damme suspected as much. Belloir, too. Both of them were waiting at the Café de la Bourse.'

'And it was you who fired the shot?'

'Yes . . . I couldn't take it any more. I wanted to live! Live! With my wife, my kids . . . So I was waiting for you outside. I've debts of 50,000 francs at the moment. Fifty thousand francs that Lecocq d'Arneville burned to ashes! But that's nothing – I'll pay the debts, I'll do whatever it takes, but to know that you were out there, hunting us . . .'

Maigret looked at Van Damme.

'And you were racing on ahead of me, trying to destroy the clues?'

No one spoke. The candle flame wavered . . . Lombard was

the only one still illuminated, by a fading red gleam from the lantern.

It was then, for the first time, that Belloir's voice faltered.

'Ten years ago, right after the . . . the thing . . . I would have accepted my fate. I'd bought a revolver, in case anyone came to arrest me. But after ten years of living, striving, struggling! And with a wife and child now, well – I think I could have shoved you into the Marne myself. Or taken a shot at you that night outside the Café de la Bourse.

'Because in a month – not even that, in twenty-six days – the statute will be in force . . .'

Silence fell, and it was then that the candle suddenly flamed up and went out. They were left in utter darkness.

Maigret did not move. He knew that Lombard was standing at his left, Van Damme was leaning against the wall in front of him, with Belloir barely a step behind him.

He waited, without even bothering to slip his hand into the pocket holding his revolver. He definitely sensed that Belloir was trembling all over, even panting.

Maigret struck a match and said, 'Let's go, shall we?'

In the glimmer of the match, everyone's eyes seemed to shine especially brightly. The four of them brushed against one another in the doorway, and again on the stairs. Van Damme fell, because he'd forgotten that there was no handrail after the eighth step.

The carpenter's shop was closed. Through the curtains of one window, they could see an old woman knitting by the light of a small paraffin lamp.

'Was it along there?' asked Maigret, pointing to the roughly paved street leading to the embankment a hundred metres away, where a gas lamp was fixed to the corner of a wall.

'The Meuse had reached the third house,' Belloir replied. 'I had to wade into the water up to my knees to . . . so that he would go off with the current.'

Turning round, they walked back, passing the new church looming in the middle of vacant ground that was still bare and uneven dirt.

Suddenly they found themselves amid the bustle of passers-by, red and yellow trams, cars, shop windows.

To get to the centre of town they had to cross the Pont des Arches and heard the rushing river crashing noisily into the piers.

Back in Rue Hors-Château, people would be waiting for Jef Lombard: his men downstairs, amid their acid baths, their photo-engraved plates waiting to be picked up by bicycle messengers; the new mother upstairs, with the sweet old mother-in-law and, nestled in the white bed sheets, the tiny girl who hadn't yet opened her eyes; the two older boys, trying not to make too much noise in the dining room decorated with hanged men.

And wasn't there another mother, in Rheims, giving her son a violin lesson, while the maid was polishing all the brass stair-rods and dusting the china pot holding the big green plant?

In Bremen, the commercial building was closing up for the day. The typist and two clerks were leaving their modern office, and when they turned off the electricity, the porcelain letters spelling *Joseph Van Damme, Import-Export Commission Agent* would vanish into the night.

Perhaps, in the brasseries alive with Viennese music, some businessman with a shaved head would remark, 'Huh! That Frenchman isn't here . . .'

In Rue Picpus, Madame Jeunet was selling a toothbrush, or a hundred grams of dried chamomile, its pale flowers crackling in their packet.

The little boy was doing his homework in the back of the shop.

The four men were walking along in step. A breeze had come up and was driving so many clouds through the sky that the bright moon shone through for only a few seconds at a time.

Did they have any idea where they were going?

When they passed in front of a busy café, a drunk staggered out.

'I'm due back in Paris!' Maigret announced, stopping abruptly.

And while the other three stood staring at him, not daring to speak and uncertain whether to rejoice or despair, he shoved his hands into his coat pockets.

'There are five kids at stake here . . .'

The men weren't even sure they'd heard him correctly, because Maigret had been muttering to himself through clenched teeth.

And the last they saw of him was his broad back in his black overcoat with the velvet collar, walking away.

'One in Rue Picpus, three in Rue Hors-Château, one in Rheims . . .'

In Rue Lepic, where he went after leaving the train station, the concierge told him, 'There's no point in going upstairs, Monsieur Janin isn't there. They thought he had bronchitis, but now that it's turned into pneumonia, they've taken him off to the hospital.'

So the inspector had himself driven to Quai des Orfèvres, where he found Sergeant Lucas phoning the owner of a bar that had racked up some violations.

'Did you get my letter, *vieux*?'

'It's all over? You figured it out?'

'Fat chance!'

It was one of Maigret's favourite expressions.

'They ran off? You know, that letter really had me worried . . . I almost dashed up to Liège. Well, what was it? Anarchists? Counterfeiters? An international gang?'

'Kids,' he sighed.

And he tossed into his cupboard the suitcase containing what a German technician had called, in a long and detailed report, clothing B.

'Come along and have a beer, Lucas.'

'You don't look too happy . . .'

'Says who? There's nothing funnier than life, *vieux*! Well, are you coming?'

A few moments later, they were pushing through the revolving door of Brasserie Dauphine.

Lucas had seldom felt so anxious and bewildered. Skipping the beer, his companion put away six ersatz absinthes just about non-stop, which didn't prevent him from announcing in a fairly steady voice, and with only a slightly blurry and most unfamiliar look in his eye, 'You know, *vieux*, ten more cases like that one and I'll hand in my resignation. Because it would prove that there's a good old Good Lord up there who's decided to take up police work.'

When he called over the waiter, though, he did add, 'But don't you worry! There won't be ten like that one . . . So, what's new around the shop?'

The Carter of La Providence

Translated by DAVID COWARD

LE CHARRETIER
DE
"LA PROVIDENCE"

ROMAN
PAR
GEORGES SIMENON

1. *Lock 14*

The facts of the case, though meticulously reconstructed, proved precisely nothing – except that the discovery made by the two carters from Dizy made, frankly, no sense at all.

On the Sunday – it was 4 April – it had begun to rain heavily at three in the afternoon.

At that moment, moored in the reach above Lock 14, which marks the junction of the river Marne and the canal, were two motor barges, both heading downstream, a canal boat which was being unloaded and another having its bilges washed out.

Shortly before seven, just as the light was beginning to fade, a tanker-barge, the *Éco-III*, had hooted to signal its arrival and had eased itself into the chamber of the lock.

The lock-keeper had not been best pleased, because he had relatives visiting at the time. He had then waved 'no' to a boat towed by two plodding draught horses which arrived in its wake only minutes later.

He had gone back into his house but had not been there long when the man driving the horse-drawn boat, who he knew, walked in.

'Can I go through? The skipper wants to be at Juvigny for tomorrow night.'

'If you like. But you'll have to manage the gates by yourself.'

The rain was coming down harder and harder. Through his window, the lock-keeper made out the man's stocky figure as he trudged wearily from one gate to the other, driving both horses on before making the mooring ropes fast to the bollards.

The boat rose slowly until it showed above the lock side. It wasn't the barge master standing at the helm but his wife, a large woman from Brussels, with brash blonde hair and a piercing voice.

By 7.20 p.m., the *Providence* was tied up by the Café de la Marine, behind the *Éco-III*. The tow-horses were taken on board. The carter and the skipper headed for the café where other boat men and two pilots from Dizy had already assembled.

At eight o'clock, when it was completely dark, a tug arrived under the lock with four boats in tow.

Its arrival swelled the crowd in the Café de la Marine. Six tables were now occupied. The men from one table called out to the others. The newcomers left puddles of water behind them as they stamped the mud off their boots.

In the room next door, a store lit by an oil-lamp, the women were buying whatever they needed.

The air was heavy. Talk turned to an accident that had happened at Lock 8 and how much of a hold-up this would mean for boats travelling upstream.

At nine o'clock, the wife of the skipper of the *Providence* came looking for her husband and their carter. All three of them then left after saying goodnight to all.

By ten o'clock, the lights had been turned out on most of the boats. The lock-keeper accompanied his relations as far as the main road to Épernay, which crosses the canal two kilometres further on from the lock.

He did not notice anything out of the ordinary. On his way back, he walked past the front of the café. He looked in and was greeted by a pilot.

'Come and have a drink! Man, you're soaked to the skin . . .'

He ordered rum, but did not sit down. Two carters got up, heavy with red wine, eyes shining, and made their way out to the stable adjoining the café, where they slept on straw, next to their horses.

They weren't exactly drunk. But they had had enough to ensure that they would sleep like logs.

There were five horses in the stable, which was lit by a single storm lantern, turned down low.

At four in the morning, one of the carters woke his mate, and both began seeing to their animals. They heard the horses on the *Providence* being led out and harnessed.

At the same time, the landlord of the café got up and lit the lamp in his bedroom on the first floor. He also heard the *Providence* as it got under way.

At 4.30, the diesel engine of the tanker-barge spluttered into life, but the boat did not leave for another quarter of an hour, after its skipper had swallowed a bracing hot toddy in the café which had just opened for business.

He had scarcely left and his boat had not yet got as far as the bridge when the two carters made their discovery.

One of them was leading his horses out to the towpath. The other was ferreting through the straw looking for his whip when one hand encountered something cold.

Startled, because what he had touched felt like a human face, he fetched his lantern and cast its light on the corpse which was about to bring chaos to Dizy and disrupt life on the canal.

Detective Chief Inspector Maigret of the Flying Squad was running through these facts again, putting them in context.

It was Monday evening. That morning, magistrates from the Épernay prosecutor's office had come out to make the routine inspection of the scene of the crime. The body, after being checked by the people from Criminal Records and examined by police surgeons, had been moved to the mortuary.

It was still raining, a fine, dense, cold rain which had gone on falling without stopping all night and all day.

Shadowy figures came and went around the lock gates, where a barge was rising imperceptibly.

The inspector had been there for an hour and had got no further than familiarizing himself with a world which he was suddenly discovering and about which, when he arrived, he had had only mistaken, confused ideas.

The lock-keeper had told him:

'There was hardly anything in the canal basin: just two motor barges going downstream, one motorized barge heading up, which had gone through the lock in the afternoon, one boat cleaning out its bilges and two panamas. Then the tin tub turned up with four vessels in tow . . .'

In this way did Maigret learn that a 'tin tub' is a tug and a 'panama' a boat without either an engine or its own horses on board, which employs a carter with his own animals for a specified distance, known in the trade as 'hitching a lift'.

When he arrived at Dizy all he'd seen was a narrow canal, three miles from Épernay, and a small village near a stone bridge.

He had had to slog through the mud of the towpath to reach the lock, which was two kilometres from Dizy.

There he had found the lock-keeper's house. It was made of grey stone, with a board that read: 'Office'.

He had walked into the Café de la Marine, which was the only other building in the area.

On his left was a run-down café-bar with brown oilcloth-covered tables and walls painted half brown and half a dirty yellow.

But it was full of the characteristic odour which marked it out as different from the usual run of country cafés. It smelled of stables, harness, tar, groceries, oil and diesel.

There was a small bell just by the door on the right. Transparent advertisements had been stuck over the glass panels.

Inside was full of stock: oilskins, clogs, canvas clothes, sacks of potatoes, kegs of cooking oil and packing cases containing sugar, dried peas and beans cheek-by-jowl with fresh vegetables and crockery.

There were no customers in sight. The stable was empty except for the horse which the landlord only saddled up when he went to market, a big grey as friendly as a pet dog. It was not tethered and at intervals would walk around the yard among the chickens.

Everywhere was sodden with rainwater. It was the most striking thing about the place. And the people who passed by were black, gleaming figures who leaned into the rain.

A hundred metres away, a narrow-gauge train shunted backwards and forwards in a siding. The carter had rigged up an umbrella on the back of the miniature engine and he crouched under it, shivering, with shoulders hunched.

A barge hauled by boat hooks slid along the canal bank heading for the lock chamber, from which another was just emerging.

How had the woman got here? And why? That was what had baffled the police at Épernay, the prosecutor's people, the medics and the specialists from Records. Maigret was now turning it over and over in his heavy head.

She had been strangled, that was the first sure fact. Death had occurred on the Sunday evening, probably around 10.30.

And the body had been found in the stable a little after four in the morning.

There was no road anywhere near the lock. There was nothing there to attract anyone not interested in barges and canals. The towpath was too narrow for a car. On the night in question anyone on foot would have had to wade knee deep through the puddles and mud.

It was obvious that the woman belonged to a class where people were more likely to ride in expensive motor-cars and travel by sleeper than walk.

She had been wearing only a beige silk dress and white buckskin shoes designed more for the beach than for city streets.

The dress was creased, but there was no trace of mud on it. Only the toe of the left shoe was wet when she was found.

'Between thirty-eight and forty,' the doctor had said after he'd examined the body.

Her earrings were real pearls worth about 15,000 francs. Her bracelet, a mixture of gold and platinum worked in the very latest style, was more artistic than costly even though it was inscribed with the name of a jeweller in the Place Vendôme.

Her hair was brown, waved and cut very short at the nape of the neck and temples.

The face, contorted by the effects of strangulation, must have been unusually pretty.

No doubt a bit of a tease.

Her manicured, varnished fingernails were dirty.

Her handbag had not been found near her. Police officers from Épernay, Rheims and Paris, armed with a photograph of the body, had been trying all day to establish her identity but without success.

Meanwhile the rain continued to fall with no let-up over the dreary landscape. To left and right, the horizon was bounded by chalk hills streaked with white and black, where at this time of year the vines looked like wooden crosses in a Great War cemetery.

The lock-keeper, recognizable only because he wore a silver braided cap, trudged wearily around the chamber of the lock, in which the water boiled every time he opened the sluices.

And every time a vessel was raised or lowered he told the tale to each new bargee.

Sometimes, after the official papers had been signed, the two of them would hurry off to the Café de la Marine and down a couple or three glasses of rum or a half litre of white wine.

And every time, the lock-keeper would point his chin in the direction of Maigret, who was prowling around with no particular purpose and thus probably made people think he did not know what he was doing.

Which was true. There was nothing normal about the case. There was not even a single witness who could be questioned.

For once the people from the prosecutor's office had interviewed the lock-keeper and spoken to the Waterways Board's civil engineer, they had decided that all the boats were free to go on their way.

The two carters had been the last to leave, around noon, each in charge of a 'panama'.

Since there is a lock every three or four kilometres, and given that they are all connected by telephone, the location of any boat at any given time could be established and any vessel stopped.

Besides which, a police inspector from Épernay had questioned everyone, and Maigret had been given transcripts of their written statements, which told him nothing except that the facts did not add up.

Everyone who had been in the Café de la Marine the previous day was known either to the owner of the bar or the lock-keeper and in most cases to both.

The carters spent at least one night each week in the same stable and invariably in the same, semi-drunken state.

'You know how it is! You take a drop at every lock . . . Nearly all the lock-keepers sell drink.'

The tanker-barge, which had arrived on Sunday afternoon and moved on again on Monday morning, was carrying petrol and was registered to a big company in Le Havre.

The *Providence*, which was owned by the skipper, passed this way twenty times a year with the same pair of horses and its old carter. And this was very much the case with all the others.

Maigret was in a tetchy mood. He entered the stable and from there went to the café or the shop any number of times.

He was seen walking as far as the stone bridge looking as though he was counting his steps or looking for something in the mud. Grimly, dripping with water, he watched as ten vessels were raised or lowered.

People wondered what he had in mind. The answer was: nothing. He didn't even try to find what might be called clues, but rather to absorb the atmosphere, to capture the essence of canal life, which was so different from the world he knew.

He had made sure that someone would lend him a bicycle if he should need to catch up with any of the boats.

The lock-keeper had let him have a copy of the *Official Handbook of Inland Waterways*, in which out-of-the-way places like Dizy take on an unsuspected importance for topographical reasons or for some particular feature: a junction, an intersection, or because there is a port or a crane or even an office.

He tried to follow in his mind's eye the progress of the barges and carters:

Ay – Port – Lock 13.

Mareuil-sur-Ay – Shipyard – Port – Turning dock – Lock 12 – Gradient 74, 36 . . .

Then Bisseuil, Tours-sur-Marne, Condé, Aigny . . .

Right at the far end of the canal, beyond the Langres plateau, which the boats reached by going up through a series of locks and then were lowered down the other side, lay the Sâone, Chalon, Mâcon, Lyons . . .

'What was the woman doing here?'

In a stable, wearing pearl earrings, her stylish bracelet and white buckskin shoes!

She must have been alive when she got there because the crime had been committed after ten in the evening.

But how? And why? And no one had heard a thing! She had not screamed. The two carters had not woken up.

If the whip had not been mislaid, it was likely the body might not have been discovered for a couple of weeks or a month, by chance when someone turned over the straw.

And other carters passing through would have snored the night away next to a woman's corpse!

Despite the cold rain, there was still a sense of something heavy, something forbidding in the atmosphere. And the rhythm of life here was slow.

Feet shod with boots or clogs shuffled over the stones of the lock or along the towpath. Tow-horses streaming with water waited while barges were held at the lock before setting off again, taking the strain, thrusting hard with their hind legs.

Soon evening would swoop down as it had the previous day. Already, barges travelling upstream had come to a stop and were tying up for the night, while their stiff-limbed crews made for the café in groups.

Maigret followed them in to take a look at the room which had been prepared for him. It was next door to the landlord's. He remained there for about ten minutes, changed his shoes and cleaned his pipe.

At the same time as he was going back downstairs, a yacht steered by a man in oilskins close to the bank slowed, went into reverse and slipped neatly into a slot between two bollards.

The man carried out all these manoeuvres himself. A little later, two men emerged from the cabin, looked wearily all round them and eventually made their way to the Café de la Marine.

They too had donned oilskins. But when they took them off, they were seen to be wearing open-necked flannel shirts and white trousers.

The watermen stared, but the newcomers gave no sign that they felt out of place. The very opposite. Their surroundings seemed to be all too familiar to them.

One was tall, fleshy, turning grey, with a brick-red face and prominent, greenish-blue eyes, which he ran over people and things as if he weren't seeing them at all.

He leaned back in his straw-bottomed chair, pulled another to him for his feet and summoned the landlord with a snap of his fingers.

His companion, who was probably twenty-five or so, spoke to him in English in a tone of snobbish indifference.

It was the younger man who asked, with no trace of an accent:

'You have still champagne? I mean without bubbles?'

'I have.'

'Bring us a bottle.'

They were both smoking imported cork-tipped Turkish cigarettes.

The watermen's talk, momentarily suspended, slowly started up again.

Not long after the landlord had brought the wine, the man who had handled the yacht arrived, also in white trousers and wearing a blue-striped sailor's jersey.

'Over here, Vladimir.'

The bigger man yawned, exuding pure, distilled boredom. He emptied his glass with a scowl, indicating that his thirst was only half satisfied.

'Another bottle!' he breathed at the young man.

The young man repeated the words more loudly, as if he was accustomed to passing on orders in this way.

'Another bottle! Of the same!'

Maigret emerged from his corner table, where he had been nursing a bottle of beer.

'Excuse me, gentlemen, would you mind if I asked you a question?'

The older man indicated his companion with a gesture which meant:

'Talk to him.'

He showed neither surprise nor interest. The sailor poured himself a drink and cut the end off a cigar.

'Did you get here along the Marne?'

'Yes, of course, along the Marne.'

'Did you tie up last night far from here?'

The big man turned his head and said in English:

'Tell him it's none of his business.'

Maigret pretended he had not understood and, without saying any more, produced a photograph of the corpse from his wallet and laid it on the brown oilcloth on the table.

The bargees, sitting at their tables or standing at the bar, followed the scene with their eyes.

The yacht's owner, hardly moving his head, looked at the photo. Then he stared at Maigret and murmured:

'Police?'

He spoke with a strong English accent in a voice that sounded hoarse.

'Police Judiciaire. There was a murder here last night. The victim has not yet been identified.'

'Where is she now?' the other man asked, getting up and pointing to the photo.

'In the morgue at Épernay. Do you know her?'

The Englishman's expression was impenetrable. But Maigret registered that his huge, apoplectic neck had turned reddish blue.

The man picked up his white yachting cap, jammed it on his balding head, then muttered something in English as he turned to his companion.

'More complications!'

Then, ignoring the gawping watermen, he took a strong pull on his cigarette and said:

'It's my wife!'

The words were less audible that the patter of the rain against the window panes or even the creaking of the windlass that opened the lock gates. The ensuing silence, which lasted a few seconds, was absolute, as if all life had been suspended.

'Pay the man, Willy.'

The Englishman threw his oilskin over his shoulders, without putting his arms in the sleeves, and growled in Maigret's direction.

'Come to the boat.'

The sailor he had called Vladimir polished off the bottle of champagne and then left, accompanied by Willy.

The first thing the inspector saw when he arrived on board was a woman in a dressing gown dozing on a dark-red velvet bunk. Her feet were bare and her hair uncombed.

The Englishman touched her on the shoulder and with the same poker face he had worn earlier he said in a voice entirely lacking in courtesy:

'Out!'

Then he waited, his eye straying to a folding table, where there was a bottle of whisky and half a dozen dirty glasses plus an ashtray overflowing with cigarette ends.

In the end, he poured himself a drink mechanically and pushed the bottle in Maigret's direction with a gesture which meant:

'If you want one . . .'

A barge passed on a level with the portholes, and fifty metres further on the carter brought his horses to a halt. There was the sound of bells on their harness jangling.

2. *The Passengers on Board the* Southern Cross

Maigret was almost as tall and broad as the Englishman. At police headquarters on Quai des Orfèvres, his imperturbability was legendary. But now he was exasperated by the calm of the man he wanted to question.

Calm seemed to be the order of the day on the boat. From Vladimir, who sailed it, to the woman they had roused from her sleep, everyone on board seemed either detached or dazed. They were like people dragged out of bed after a night of serious drinking.

One detail among many: as she got up and looked round for a packet of cigarettes, the woman noticed the photo which the Englishman had put down on the table. During the short walk from the Café de la Marine to the yacht, it had got wet.

'Mary?' She put the question scarcely batting an eye.

'Yes. Mary.'

And that was it! She went out through a door which opened into the cabin and presumably was the door to the bathroom.

Willy appeared on deck and poked his head in through the hatchway. The cabin was cramped. Its varnished mahogany walls were thin and anyone forward could hear every word, for its owner looked first in that direction, frowning, then at the young man saying impatiently:

'Come in . . . and sharp about it!'

Then, turning to Maigret, he added curtly:

'Sir Walter Lampson, Colonel, Indian Army, retired.'

He accompanied this introduction of himself with a stiff little bow and a motion of the hand towards the bench seat along the cabin wall.

'And you are . . .?' said the inspector, turning towards Willy.

'A friend . . . Willy Marco.'

'Spanish?'

The colonel gave a shrug. Maigret scanned the young man's visibly Jewish features.

'My father is Greek and my mother Hungarian.'

'Sir Walter, I'm afraid I have to ask you some questions.'

Willy had sat down casually on the back of a chair and was rocking backwards and forwards, smoking a cigarette.

'I'm listening.'

But just as Maigret was about to open his mouth, the yacht's owner barked:

'Who did it? Do you know?'

He meant the perpetrator of the crime.

'We haven't come up with anything so far. That's why you can be useful to our inquiries by filling me in on a number of points.'

'Was it a rope?' he continued, holding one hand against his throat.

'No. The murderer used his hands. When was the last time you saw Mrs Lampson?'

'Willy . . . ?'

Willy was obviously his general factotum, expected to order the drinks and answer questions put to the colonel.

'Meaux. Thursday evening,' he said.

'And you did not report her disappearance to the police?'

Sir Walter helped himself to another whisky.

'Why should I? She was free to do whatever she pleased.'

'Did she often go off like that?'

'Sometimes.'

The sound of rain pattered on the deck overhead. Dusk was turning into night. Willy Marco turned the electric light on.

'Batteries been charged up?' the colonel asked him in English. 'It's not going to be like the other day?'

Maigret was trying to maintain a coherent line of questioning. But he was constantly being distracted by new impressions.

Despite his best efforts, he kept looking at everything, thinking about everything simultaneously. As a result his head was filled with a jumble of half-formed ideas.

He was not so much annoyed as made to feel uneasy by this man who, in the Café de la Marine, had cast a quick glance at the photo and said without flinching:

'It's my wife.'

And he recalled the woman in the dressing gown saying:

'Mary?'

Willy went on rocking to and fro, a cigarette glued to his lips, while the colonel was worrying about the boat's batteries!

In the neutral setting of his office, the inspector would have doubtless conducted a properly structured interview. But here, he began by taking off his overcoat without being invited to and picked up the photo, which was disturbing in the way all photographs of corpses are disturbing.

'Do you live here, in France?'

'In France, England . . . Sometimes Italy . . . Always on my boat, the *Southern Cross*.'

'And you've just come from . . . ?'

'Paris!' replied Willy who had got the nod from the colonel to do the talking. 'We stayed there two weeks after spending a month in London.'

'Did you live on board?'

'No. The boat was moored at Auteuil. We stayed at the Hotel Raspail, in Montparnasse.'

'You mean the colonel, his wife, the lady I saw just now, plus yourself?'

'Yes. The lady is the widow of a member of the Chilean parliament, Madame Negretti.'

Sir Walter gave an impatient snort and lapsed into English again:

'Get on with it or else he'll still be here tomorrow morning.'

Maigret did not flinch. But from then on, he put his questions with more than a touch of bloody-mindedness.

'So Madame Negretti is no relation?' he asked Willy.

'Absolutely not.'

'So she is not connected in any way with you and the colonel . . . Would you tell me about accommodation arrangements on board?'

Sir Walter swallowed a mouthful of whisky, coughed and lit a cigarette.

'Forward are the crew's quarters. That's where Vladimir sleeps. He's a former cadet in the Russian navy . . . He served in Wrangel's White Russian fleet.'

'Any other crew? No servants?'

'Vladimir does everything.'

'Go on.'

'Between the crew's quarters and this cabin are, on the right, the galley, and on the left the bathroom.'

'And aft?'

'The engine.'

'So there were four of you in this cabin?'

'There are four bunks . . . First, the two that you see. They convert to day couches . . . Then . . .'

Willy crossed to a wall panel, pulled out a kind of deep drawer which was in fact a bed.

'There's one of these on each side . . . Do you see?'

Actually, Maigret was indeed beginning to see a little more clearly. He was beginning to feel that it wouldn't be long before he got to the bottom of these unusual living arrangements.

The colonel's eyes were a dull grey and watered like a drunk's. He seemed to have lost interest in the conversation.

'What happened at Meaux? But first, when exactly did you get there?'

'Wednesday evening . . . Meaux is a one-day stage from Paris. We'd brought along a couple of girls, just friends, with us from Montparnasse.'

'And?'

'The weather was marvellous. We played some records and danced outside, on deck. Around four in the morning I took the girls to their hotel, and they must have caught the train back the next morning.'

'Where was the *Southern Cross* moored?'

'Near the lock.'

'Anything happen on Thursday?'

'We got up very late, we were woken several times in the night by a crane loading stone into a barge nearby. The colonel and I went for a drink before lunch in town. Then, in the afternoon, let me see . . . the colonel had a nap . . . and I played chess with Gloria . . . Gloria is Madame Negretti.'

'On deck?'

'Yes. I think Mary went for a walk.'

'And she never came back?'

'Yes she did: she had dinner on board. The colonel suggested we all spend the evening at the palais de danse. Mary didn't want to come with us . . . When we got back, which was around three in the morning, she wasn't here.'

'Didn't you look for her?'

Sir Walter was drumming his fingers on the polished top of the table.

'As the colonel told you, his wife was free to come and go as she pleased. We waited for her until Saturday and then we moved on . . . She knew our route and could have caught up with us later.'

'Are you going down to the Mediterranean?'

'Yes, to the island of Porquerolles, off Hyères. It's where we spend most of the year. The colonel bought an old fort there. It's called the Petit Langoustier.'

'Did everybody stay on board all day Friday?'

Willy hesitated for a moment then almost blurted out his answer:

'I went to Paris.'

'Why?'

He laughed unpleasantly, which gave his mouth an odd twist.

'I mentioned our friends, the two girls . . . I wanted to see them again. Or at least one of them.'

'Can you give me their names?'

'First names . . . Suzy and Lia . . . You'll find them any night at La Coupole. They live at the hotel on the corner of Rue de la Grande-Chaumière.'

'Working girls?'

'They're both decent sorts . . .'

The door opened. It was Madame Negretti. She had put on a green silk dress.

'May I come in?'

The colonel answered with a shrug. He must now have been on to his third whisky and was drinking them more or less neat.

'Willy . . . Ask him . . . The formalities . . .'

Maigret had no need to have it translated to understand. But this roundabout, offhand way of being asked questions was beginning to irritate him.

'Obviously as a first step you will be expected to identify the body. After the post-mortem, you will no doubt be given a death certificate authorizing burial. You will choose the cemetery and . . .'

'Can we go now, straightaway? Is there a garage around here where I can hire a car?'

'There's one in Épernay.'

'Willy, phone for a car . . . right now.'

'There's a phone at the Café de la Marine,' said Maigret while the young man badtemperedly put on his oilskin jacket.

'Where's Vladimir?'

'I heard him come back a little while ago.'

'Tell him we'll have dinner at Épernay.'

Madame Negretti, who was running to fat and had glossy black hair and very light skin, had found a chair in a corner, under the barometer, and had observed what was happening with her chin cupped in one hand. She looked as if her mind was elsewhere or perhaps she was deep in thought.

'Are you coming with us?' asked Sir Walter.

'I'm not sure . . . Is it still raining?'

Maigret was already bristling, and the colonel's last question did nothing to calm him down.

'How many days do think you'll need us for? To wind everything up?'

To this came the blunt answer:

'Do you mean including the funeral?'

'Yes . . . Three days?'

'If the police doctors produce a burial certificate and if the examining magistrate has no objection, you could be all done in practical terms inside twenty-four hours.'

Did the colonel feel the bitter sarcasm of the words?

Maigret needed to take another look at the photo: a body that was broken, dirty, crumpled, a face which had once been pretty, carefully made up, with scented rouge applied to lips and cheeks, and a macabre grimace which you couldn't look at without feeling an icy chill run up and down your spine.

'Like a drink?'

'No thanks.'

'In that case . . .'

Sir Walter stood up to indicate that he considered that the interview was over. Then he called:

'Vladimir! . . . A suit!'

'I'll probably have to question you again,' the inspector said. 'I may even need to have your boat thoroughly searched.'

'Tomorrow . . . Épernay first, right? . . . How long will the car be?'

'Will I have to stay here by myself?' said Madame Negretti in alarm.

'With Vladimir . . . But you can come . . .'

'I'm not dressed.'

Willy suddenly burst in and shrugged off his streaming oilskins.

'The car will be here in ten minutes.'

'Perhaps, inspector, if you wouldn't mind . . . ?'

The colonel motioned to the door.

'We must dress.'

As he left, Maigret felt so frustrated that he would gladly have punched someone on the nose. He heard the hatch close behind him.

From the outside, all that could be seen was the glow of eight portholes and the light of the white lantern fixed to the mast. Not ten metres away was the outline of the squat stern of a barge and, on the left, a large heap of coal.

Perhaps it was an illusion but Maigret had the impression that the rain was coming down twice as hard and that the sky was the darkest and most threatening he'd ever seen.

He made his way to the Café de la Marine, where everyone stopped talking the moment he walked in. All the watermen were there, huddled round the cast-iron stove. The lock-keeper was leaning against the bar, near the landlord's daughter, a tall girl with red hair who wore clogs.

The tables were covered with waxy cloths and were littered with wine bottles, tumblers and standing pools of drink.

'So, was it his missus?' the landlord finally asked, taking his courage in both hands.

'Yes. Give me a beer. On second thoughts, no. Make it something hot. A grog.'

The watermen's talk started up again, very gradually. The girl brought Maigret the steaming glass and in doing so brushed against his shoulder with her apron.

The inspector imagined those three characters getting dressed in that cramped space. Vladimir too.

He imagined a number of other things, idly and without great relish.

He was familiar with the lock at Meaux, which is bigger than most locks because, like the one at Dizy, it is situated at the junction of the Marne and the canal, where there is a crescent-shaped port which is always full of barges packed closely together.

There, among the watermen, the *Southern Cross* would have been moored, all lit up, and on board the two women from Montparnasse, the curvaceous Gloria Negretti, Madame Lampson, Willy and the colonel dancing on the deck to the strains of the gramophone and drinking . . .

In a corner of the Café de la Marine, two men in blue overalls were eating sausage and bread, cutting slices off each with their knives and drinking red wine.

And someone was talking about an accident which had happened that morning in the 'culvert', that is a stretch of the canal which, as it crosses the high part of the Langres plateau, passes through a tunnel for eight kilometres.

A barge hand had got one foot caught in the horses' tow-line. He'd called out but hadn't been able to make the carter hear. So when the animals set off again after a rest stop, he'd been yanked into the water.

The tunnel was not lit. The barge carried only one lamp which reflected faintly in the water. The barge hand's brother – the boat was called *Les Deux Frères* – had jumped into the canal.

Only one of them had been fished out, and he was dead. They were still looking for the other.

'They only had two more instalments on the boat to pay. But it looks like, going by the contract, that the wives won't have to fork out another penny.'

A taxi-driver wearing a leather cap came in and looked round.

'Who was it ordered a car?'

'Me!' said Maigret.

'I had to leave it at the bridge. I didn't fancy finishing up in the canal.'

'Will you be eating here?' the landlord asked the inspector.

'I don't know yet.'

He went out with the taxi-driver. Through the rain, the white-painted *Southern Cross* was a milky stain. Two boys from a nearby barge, out despite the downpour, were staring at it admiringly.

'Joseph!' came a woman's voice. 'Bring your brother here! . . . You're going to get a walloping! . . .'

'*Southern Cross*,' the taxi-driver read on the bow. 'English, are they?'

Maigret walked across the gangplank and knocked. Willy opened the door. He was already dressed, looking elegant in a dark suit. Inside, Maigret saw the colonel, red-faced and jacketless, having his tie knotted by Gloria Negretti. The cabin smelled of eau de Cologne and brilliantine.

'Has the car come?' asked Willy. 'Is it here?'

'It's at the bridge, a short distance from here.'

Maigret stayed outside. He half heard the colonel and the young man arguing in English. Eventually Willy came out.

'He won't traipse through mud,' he said. 'Vladimir's going to launch the dinghy. We'll meet you there.'

'Thought so,' muttered the taxi-driver, who had heard.

Ten minutes later, Maigret and he were walking to and fro on the stone bridge just by the parked taxi, which had its sidelights on. Nearly half an hour went by before they heard the putt-putt of a small two-stroke engine.

Eventually Willy's voice shouted:

'Is this the place? . . . Inspector!'

'Yes, over here!'

The dinghy, powered by a removable motor, turned a half circle and pulled in to the bank. Vladimir helped the colonel out and made arrangements to pick them up when they got back.

In the car, Sir Walter did not speak. Despite his bulk, he was remarkably elegant. Ruddy-faced, well turned-out and impassive, he was every inch the English gentleman as portrayed in nineteenth-century prints.

Willy was chain-smoking.

'Some jalopy!' he muttered as they lurched over a drain.

Maigret noticed he was wearing a platinum ring set with a large yellow diamond.

When they got to the town, where the cobbled streets gleamed in the rain, the taxi-driver lifted the glass separating him and his fare and asked:

'Where do you want me to . . . ?'

'The mortuary!' replied the inspector.

It didn't take long. The colonel barely said a word. There was only one attendant in the building, where three bodies were laid out on stone slabs.

All the doors were locked. The locks creaked as they were opened. The light had to be switched on.

It was Maigret who lifted the sheet.

'Yes!'

Willy was the most upset, the most anxious to turn away from the sight.

'Do you recognize her too?'

'It's her all right . . . She looks so . . .'

He did not finish. The colour was visibly draining from his face. His lips were dry. If the inspector had not dragged him away, he would probably have passed out.

'You don't know who . . . ?' the colonel said distinctly.

Was a barely noticeable hint of distress just detectable in his tone of voice? Or wasn't it just the effect of all those glasses of whisky?

Even so, Maigret made a mental note of this small shift.

Then they were outside, on a pavement poorly lit by a single lamp-post near the car. The driver had not budged from his seat.

'You'll have dinner with us, won't you?' Sir Walter asked, again without turning to face Maigret.

'Thank you, no. Since I'm here, I'll make the most of it to sort out a few matters.'

The colonel bowed and did not insist.

'Come, Willy.'

Maigret remained for a moment in the doorway of the mortuary while the young man, after conferring with the Englishman, turned to the taxi-driver.

He was obviously asking which was the best restaurant in town. People walked past while brightly lit, rattling trams trundled by.

A few kilometres from there, the canal stretched away, and all along it, near the locks, there were barges now asleep which would set off at four in the morning, wrapped in the smell of hot coffee and stables.

3. Mary Lampson's Necklace

When Maigret got into bed, in his room, with its distinctive, slightly nauseating smell, he lay for some time aligning two distinct mental pictures.

First, Épernay: seen through the large, brightly lit windows of La Bécasse, the best restaurant in town, the colonel and Willy elegantly seated at a table surrounded by high-class waiters . . .

It was less than half an hour after their visit to the mortuary. Sir Walter Lampson was sitting ramrod straight, and the aloof expression on that ruddy face under its sparse thatch of silver hair was phenomenal.

Beside his elegance, or more accurately his pedigree, Willy's smartness, though he wore it casually enough, looked like a cheap imitation.

Maigret had eaten elsewhere. He had phoned the Préfecture and then the police at Meaux.

Then, alone and on foot, he had headed off into the rainy night along the long ribbon of road. He had seen the illuminated portholes of the *Southern Cross* opposite the Café de la Marine.

He had been curious and called in, using a forgotten pipe as an excuse.

It was there that he had acquired the second mental picture: in the mahogany cabin, Vladimir, still wearing his striped sailor's jersey, a cigarette hanging from his lips, was sitting opposite Madame Negretti, whose glossy hair again hung down over her cheeks.

They were playing cards – 'sixty-six', a game popular in central Europe.

There had been a brief moment of utter stupefaction. But

no shocked reaction! Both had just stopped breathing for a second.

Then Vladimir had stood up and begun hunting for the pipe. Gloria Negretti had asked, in a faint lisp:

'Aren't they back yet? Was it Mary?'

The inspector had thought for a moment of getting on his bicycle, riding along the canal and catching up with the barges which had passed through Dizy on Sunday night. The sight of the sodden towpath and the black sky had made him change his mind.

When there was a knock on the door of his room, he was aware, even before he opened his eyes, that the bluey-grey light of dawn was percolating through the window of his room.

He had spent a restless night full of the sound of horses' hooves, confused voices, footsteps on the stairs, clinking glass in the bar underneath him and finally the smell of coffee and hot rum which had wafted up to him.

'What is it?'

'Lucas! Can I come in?'

Inspector Lucas, who almost always worked with Maigret, pushed the door open and shook the clammy hand which his chief held out through a gap in the bedclothes.

'Got something already? Not too worn out, I hope?'

'I'll survive, sir. After I got your phone call, I went straight to the hotel you talked about, on the corner of Rue de la Grande-Chaumière. The girls weren't there, but at least I got their names. Suzanne Verdier, goes under the name of Suzy, born at Honfleur in 1906. Lia Lauwenstein, born in the Grand Duchy of Luxembourg in 1903. The first arrived in Paris four years ago, started as a housemaid, then worked for a while as a model. The Lauwenstein girl has been living mainly on the Côte d'Azur . . . Neither, I checked, appears in the Vice Squad's register of prostitutes. But they might as well be on it.'

'Lucas, would you pass me my pipe and order me coffee?'

The sound of rushing water came from the chamber of the lock and over it the chug of a diesel engine idling. Maigret got out of bed and stood at a poor excuse for a washstand where he poured cold water into the bowl.

'Don't stop.'

'I went to La Coupole, like you said. They weren't there, but the waiters all knew them. They sent me to the Dingo, then La Cigogne. I ended up at a small American bar, I forget what it's called, in Rue Vavin, and found them there, all alone, looking very sorry for themselves. Lia is quite a looker. She's got style. Suzy is blonde, girl-next-door type, not a nasty bone in her body. If she'd stayed back in the sticks where she came from, she'd have got married and made a good wife and mother. She had got freckles all over her face and . . .'

'See a towel anywhere?' interrupted Maigret. His face was dripping with water, and his eyes were shut. 'By the way, is it still raining?'

'It wasn't raining when I got here, but it looks like it could start up again at any moment. At six this morning there was a fog which almost froze your lungs . . . Anyway, I offered to buy the girls a drink. They immediately asked for sandwiches, which didn't surprise me at first. But after a while I noticed the pearl necklace the Lauwenstein girl was wearing. As a joke I managed to get a bite on it. They were absolutely real! Not the necklace of an American millionairess, but even so it must have been worth all of 100,000 francs. Now when girls of that sort prefer sandwiches and hot chocolate to cocktails . . .'

Maigret, who was smoking his first pipe of the day, answered the knock of the girl who had brought his coffee. Then he glanced out of the window and registered that there was as yet no sign of life outside. A barge was passing close to the *Southern Cross*. The man leaning his back against the tiller was staring at the yacht with reluctant admiration.

'Right. Go on.'

'I drove them to another place, a quiet café.

'There, without warning, I flashed my badge, pointed to the necklace and asked straight out: "Those are Mary Lampson's pearls, aren't they?"

'I don't suppose they knew she was dead. But if they did, they played their parts to perfection.

'It took them a few moments to admit everything. In the end it was Suzy who said to her friend: "Best tell him the truth, seeing as he knows so much about it already."

'And a pretty tale it was too . . . Need a hand, chief?'

Maigret was flailing his arms wildly in his efforts to catch his braces, which were dangling down his thighs.

'The main point first. They both swore that it was Mary Lampson herself who gave them the pearls last Friday, in Paris, where she'd come to meet them. You'll probably understand this better than I do, because all I know about the case is what you told me over the phone.

'I asked if Madame Lampson had come there with Willy Marco. They said no. They said they hadn't seen Willy since last Thursday, when they left him at Meaux.'

'Just a moment,' Maigret broke in as he knotted his tie in a milky mirror which distorted his reflection. 'The *Southern Cross* arrives at Meaux on Wednesday evening. Our two girls are on board. They spend a lively night with the colonel, Willy, Mary Lampson and Gloria.

'It's very late when Suzy and Lia are taken off to a hotel, and they leave by train on Thursday morning . . . Did anyone give them money?'

'They said 500 francs.'

'Had they got to know the colonel in Paris?'

'A few days earlier.'

'And what happened on the yacht?'

Lucas gave a knowing smile.

'Assorted antics, none very savoury. Apparently the Englishman lives only for whisky and women. Madame Negretti is his mistress.'

'Did his wife know?'

'Oh, she knew all right! She herself was Willy's mistress. None of which stopped them bringing Suzy and Lia to join the party, if you follow me. And then there was Vladimir, who danced with all the women. In the early hours there was a row because Lia Lauwenstein said that 500 francs was charity. The colonel did not answer, leaving that to Willy. They were all drunk. The Negretti woman fell asleep on the roof, and Vladimir had to carry her into the cabin.'

Standing at the window, Maigret let his eye wander along the black line of the canal. To his left, he could see the small-gauge railway, which was still used to transport earth and gravel.

The sky was grey and streaked low down with shreds of blackish cloud. But it had stopped raining.

'What happened then?'

'That's more or less it. On Friday, Mary Lampson supposedly travelled to Paris and met up with both girls at La Coupole, when she must have given them the necklace.'

'My, my! A teeny-weeny little present . . .'

'Not a present. She handed it over for them to sell on. They were to give her half of whatever cash they got for it. She told them her husband didn't let her have much in the way of ready money.'

The paper on the walls of the room was patterned with small yellow flowers. On it the basin was a splash of dirty white.

Maigret saw the lock-keeper hurrying his way along with a bargee and his carter, clearly intending to drink a tot of rum at the bar.

'That's all I could get out of them,' said Lucas in conclusion. 'I left them at two this morning. I sent Inspector Dufour to keep a discreet eye on their movements. Then I went back to the Préfecture to check the records as per your instructions. I found the file on Willy Marco, who was kicked out of Monaco four years ago after some murky business to do with gambling. The following year he was questioned after an American woman claimed he had relieved her of some items of jewellery. But the charge was dropped, I don't know why, and Marco stayed out of jail. Do you think that he's . . .'

'I don't think anything. And that's the honest truth, I swear. Don't forget the murder was committed on Sunday after ten at night, when the *Southern Cross* was moored at La Ferté-sous-Jouarre.'

'What do you make of the colonel?'

Maigret shrugged his shoulders and pointed to Vladimir, who had just popped out through the forward hatch and was making for the Café de la Marine. He was wearing white trousers, rope sandals and a sweater. An American sailor's cap was pulled down over one ear.

'Phone call for Monsieur Maigret,' the red-haired serving girl called through the door.

'Come down with me, Lucas.'

The phone was in the corridor, next to a coat stand.

'Hello? . . . Meaux? . . . What was that? . . . Yes, the *Providence* . . . At Meaux all day Thursday loading? . . . Left at three o'clock Friday morning . . . Did any others? . . . The *Éco-III* . . . That's a tanker-barge, right? . . . Friday night at Meaux . . . Left Saturday morning . . . Thanks, inspector! . . . Yes, carry on with the questioning, you never know . . . Yes, I'll still be at this address . . .'

Lucas had listened to this conversation without understanding a word of it. Before Maigret could open his mouth to tell him, a uniformed officer on a bicycle appeared at the door.

'Message from Records . . . It's urgent!'

The man was spattered with mud to the waist.

'Go and dry off for a moment and while you're at it drink my health with a hot grog.'

Maigret led Lucas out on to the towpath, opened the envelope and read out in a half-whisper:

Summary of preliminary analyses relating to inquiries into the murder at Dizy:

— victim's hair shows numerous traces of resin and also the presence of horsehairs, dark brown in colour;
— the stains on the dress are fuel oil;
— stomach contents at time of death: red wine and tinned meat similar in type to what is commercially available as corned beef.

'Eight out of ten horses have dark brown coats!' sighed Maigret.

In the café, Vladimir was asking what was the nearest place where he could buy the supplies he needed. There were three people who were telling him, including the cycling policeman from Épernay, who eventually set off with the Russian in the direction of the stone bridge.

Maigret, with Lucas in tow, headed for the stable, where, in addition to the landlord's grey, a broken-kneed mare possibly intended for slaughter had been kept since the night before.

'It wasn't here that she would have picked up traces of resin,' said the inspector.

He walked twice along the path that led round the buildings from the canal to the stable.

'Do you sell resin?' he asked when he saw the landlord pushing a wheelbarrow full of potatoes.

'It's not exactly proper resin . . . We call it Norwegian pitch. It's used for coating the sides of wooden barges above the waterline. Below it they use coal-tar, which is twenty times cheaper.'

'Have you got any?'

'There are still about twenty cans in the shop . . . But in this sort of weather there's no call for it. The bargees wait for the sun to come out before they start doing up their boats.'

'Is the *Éco-III* made of wood?'

'Iron, like most boats with motors.'

'How about the *Providence*?'

'Wood. Have you found out something?'

Maigret did not reply.

'You know what they're saying?' said the man, who had set down his wheelbarrow.

'Who are "they"?'

'Everybody on the canal, the bargees, pilots, lock-keepers. Goes without saying that a car would have a hard time driving along the towpath, but what about a motorbike? A motorbike could come from a long way off and leave no more trace than a push-bike.'

The door of the *Southern Cross*'s cabin opened. But no one came out.

For one brief moment, a patch of sky turned yellowish, as if the sun was at last about to break through. Maigret and Lucas walked up and down the canal bank without speaking.

No more than five minutes had gone by before the wind was bending the reeds flat, and one minute later rain was coming down in earnest.

Maigret held out one hand, an automatic reaction. With an equally mechanical gesture Lucas produced a packet of grey pipe tobacco from his pocket and handed it to his companion.

They paused a moment by the lock. The chamber was empty but it was being made ready, for an invisible tug still some distance off had hooted three times, which meant that it was towing three boats.

'Where do you reckon the *Providence* is now?' Maigret asked the lock-keeper.

'Half a mo' . . . Mareuil, Condé . . . and just before Aigny there's a string of about ten boats. That'll hold her up . . . Only two sluices of the lock at Vraux are working . . . So I'd say she's at Saint-Martin.'

'Is that far?'

'Exactly thirty-two kilometres.'

'And the *Éco-III*?'

'Should be at La Chaussée. But a barge coming downstream told us last night that she'd broken her propeller at Lock 12. Which means you'll find her at Tours-sur-Marne, which is fifteen kilometres upstream. It's their own fault . . . It's clear. Regulations state no loads should exceed 280 tons, but they all go on doing it.'

It was ten in the morning. As Maigret clambered on to the bicycle he had hired, he saw the colonel sitting in a rocking chair on the deck of the yacht. He was opening the Paris papers, which the postman had just delivered.

'No special orders,' he told Lucas. 'Stay around here. Don't let them out of your sight.'

The showers became less frequent. The towpath was dead straight. When he reached the third lock, the sun came out, still rather watery, but making the droplets of water on the reeds sparkle.

From time to time, Maigret had to get off his bike to get past horses towing a barge. Harnessed side by side, they took up the full width of the towpath and plodded forward, one step at a time, with an effort which made their muscles swell visibly.

Two of these animals were being driven by a little girl of eight or ten. She wore a red dress and carried a doll which dangled at the end of one arm.

The villages were, for the most part, some distance from the canal so that the long ribbon of flat water seemed to unfurl in an absolutely empty landscape.

Here and there was an occasional field with men bent over the dark earth. But most of it was woods. Reeds a metre and a half or two metres high further added to the mood of calm.

A barge taking on a cargo of chalk near a quarry sent up clouds of dust which whitened its hull and the toiling men.

There was a boat in the Saint-Martin lock, but it wasn't the *Providence*.

'They'll have stopped for their dinners in the reach above Châlons!' the lock-keeper's wife said as she went, with two young children clinging to her skirts, from one dock-gate to the other.

Maigret was not a man who gave up easily. Around eleven o'clock he was surprised to find himself in springlike surroundings, where the air pulsed with sun and warmth.

Ahead of him, the canal cut a straight line across a distance of six kilometres. It was bordered with woods of fir on both sides.

At the far end the eye could just make out the light-coloured stonework of a lock. Through its gates spurted thin jets of water.

Halfway along, a barge had halted, at a slight angle. Its two horses had been unharnessed and, their noses in a feedbag, were munching oats and snorting.

The first impression was cheerful or at least restful. Not a house in sight. The reflections in the calm water were wide and slow.

A few more turns of the pedals and the inspector saw a table set up under the awning over the tiller in the stern of the barge. On it was a blue and white checked waxed tablecloth. A woman with fair hair was setting a steaming dish in the middle of it.

He got off his bike after reading, on the rounded bows in gleaming polished letters: *Providence*.

One of the horses, taking its time, stared at him, then twitched its ears and let out a peculiar growl before starting to eat again.

Between the barge and the side of the canal was a thin, narrow plank, which sagged under Maigret's weight. Two men were eating, following him with their eyes, while the woman advanced towards him.

'Yes, what do you want?' she asked as she buttoned her blouse, which was part open over her ample bosom.

She spoke with a singsong intonation almost as strong as a southern accent. But she wasn't at all bothered. She waited. She seemed to be protecting the two men with the fullness of her brazen flesh.

'Information,' said the inspector. 'I expect you know there was a murder at Dizy?'

'The crew of the *Castor et Pollux* told us about it. They overtook us this morning. Is it true? It doesn't hardly seem possible, does it? How could anybody have done such a thing? And on the canal too, where it's always so peaceful.'

Her cheeks were blotchy. The two men went on eating, never taking their eyes off Maigret, who glanced involuntarily down at the dish which contained dark meat and gave off an aroma which startled his nostrils.

'A kid goat. I bought it this morning at the lock at Aigny . . . You were looking for information? About us, I suppose? We'd gone long before any dead body was discovered. Speaking of which, anybody know who the poor woman was?'

One of the men was short, dark-haired, with a drooping moustache and a soft, submissive air about him.

He was the husband. He'd merely nodded vaguely at the intruder, leaving his wife to do the talking.

The other man was around sixty years of age. His hair, thick and badly cut, was white. A beard three or four centimetres long covered his chin and most of his cheeks, and he had very thick eyebrows. He looked as hairy as an animal.

In contrast, his eyes were bright but without expression.

'It's your carter I'd like to talk to.'

The woman laughed.

'Talk to Jean? I warn you, he don't talk much to anyone. He's our tame bear! Look at the way he's eating! But he's also the best carter you could hope to find.'

The old man's fork stopped moving. He looked at Maigret with eyes that were disturbingly clear.

Village idiots sometimes have eyes like that. And also animals who are used to being treated with kindness and then without warning are beaten without pity.

There was something vacant about them. But something else too, something beyond words, almost withdrawn.

'What time did you get up to see to your horses?'

'Same time as always . . .'

Jean's shoulders were unusually broad and looked even broader because his legs were short.

'Jean gets up every day at half past two!' the woman broke in. 'Take a look at the horses. They are groomed every day like they're thoroughbreds. And of an evening, you won't get him to go near a drop of white wine until he's rubbed them down.'

'Do you sleep in the stable?'

Jean did not seem to understand. So it was again the woman who pointed to a structure, taller than the rest, in the middle of the boat.

'That's the stable,' she said. 'He always sleeps there. Our cabin is in the stern. Would you like to see it?'

The deck was spotlessly clean, the brasses more highly polished than those on the *Southern Cross*. And when the woman opened a double door made of pine with a skylight of coloured glass over it, Maigret saw a touching sight.

Inside was a small parlour. It contained exactly the same oak Henri III-style furniture as is found in the most traditional of lower-middle-class front rooms. The table was covered with a cloth embroidered with silks of various colours, and on it were vases, framed photographs and a stand overflowing with green-leaved plants.

There was more embroidery on a dresser. Over the armchairs were draped thin dust covers.

'If Jean had wanted, we could have rigged up a bed for him near us . . . But he always says he can only sleep in the stable, though we're afraid that he'll get kicked one of these days. No good saying the horses know him, is it? When they're sleeping . . .'

She had started eating, like the housewife who makes other people's dinners and gives herself the worst portion without a second thought . . .

Jean had stood up and kept staring at his horses and then at the inspector while the skipper rolled a cigarette.

'And you didn't see anything, or hear anything?' asked Maigret, looking the carter directly in the eye.

The man turned to the skipper's wife, who replied with her mouth full:

'If he'd seen something, he'd have said, 'course he would.'

'Here's the *Marie*!' said her husband anxiously.

The chugging of an engine had become audible in the last few moments. Now the form of a barge could be made out astern of the *Providence*.

Jean looked at the woman, who was looking uncertainly at Maigret.

'Listen,' she said finally, 'if you've got to talk to Jean, would you mind doing it as we go? The *Marie* has got an engine, but she's slower than us. If she gets in front of us before we get to the lock, she'll hold us up for two days.'

Jean had not waited to hear her last words. He had already taken the feedbags containing the horses' oats from over their heads and was now driving them a hundred metres ahead of the barge.

The bargee picked up a tin trumpet and blew a few quavering notes.

'Are you staying on board? Listen, we'll tell you what we know. Everybody on the canals knows who we are, from Liège to Lyons.'

'I'll meet up with you at the lock,' said Maigret, whose bicycle was still on the bank.

The gangplank was stowed on board. A distant figure had just appeared on the lock gates, and the sluices started to open. The horses set off with a jangle of tinkling bells, and the red pompons tied to the top of their heads bobbed and jounced.

Jean walked by the side of them, unconcerned.

Two hundred metres astern, the motor barge slowed as it realized it had come too late.

Maigret followed, holding the handlebars of his bicycle with one hand. He could see the skipper's wife rushing to finish eating and her husband, short, thin and frail, leaning, almost lying, on the long tiller, which was too heavy for him.

4. The Lover

'I've had lunch,' said Maigret as he strode into the Café de la Marine, where Lucas was sitting at a table in the window.

'At Aigny?' asked the landlord. 'My brother-in-law's the inn-keeper at Aigny . . .'

'Bring us two beers.'

It had been a narrow escape. The inspector, pedalling hard, was barely in sight of Dizy when the weather had turned overcast again. And now thick rain was being drawn like curtains over the last rays of the sun.

The *Southern Cross* was still in its berth. There was no one to be seen on deck. And no sound came from the lock so that, for the first time, Maigret was aware of being truly in the country. He could hear chickens clucking in the yard outside.

'Got anything for me?' he asked Lucas.

'The Russian came back with supplies. The woman put in a brief appearance in a blue dressing gown. The colonel and Willy came for a drink before lunch. They gave me some odd looks, I think.'

Maigret took the tobacco pouch which his companion was holding out for him, filled his pipe and waited until the landlord, who had served them, had vanished into his shop.

'I didn't get anything either,' he muttered. 'Of the two boats which could have brought Mary Lampson here, one has broken down about fifteen kilometres from here, and the other is ploughing along the canal at three kilometres an hour.'

'The first one is iron-built, so no chance of the body coming into contact with pitch there.

'The other one is made of wood . . . The master and his wife are called Canelle. A fat motherly sort, who tried her level best to get me to drink a glass of disgusting rum, with a pint-sized husband who runs round after her like a spaniel.

'Which leaves just their carter.

'Either he's pretending to be stupid, in which case he does a brilliant turn, or else he's a complete half-wit. He's been with them for eight years. If the husband is a spaniel, he's a bulldog.

'He gets up at half past two every morning, sees to his horses, downs a bowl of coffee and then starts walking alongside his animals.

'He does his daily thirty or forty kilometres like that, every day, at the same pace, with a swig of white wine at every lock.

'Every evening he rubs the horses down, eats without speaking a word and then collapses on to a straw truss, most times still in his clothes.

'I've checked his papers. An old army pay book with pages so stuck together with filth they can hardly be opened. The name in it is Jean Liberge, born in Lille in 1869.

'And that's it . . . no, just a moment. The *Providence* would have had to get Mary Lampson on board on Thursday evening at Meaux. So she was alive then. She was still alive when she got here on Sunday evening.

'It would be physically impossible to hide a grown woman for two days against her will in the stable on the boat.

'In which case all three of them would be guilty.'

The scowl on Maigret's face showed that he did not believe that was the case.

'But let's suppose the victim did get on the boat of her own free will. Do you know what you are going to do, Lucas? You're going to ask Sir Walter what his wife's maiden name was. Then get on the phone and find out what you can about her.'

There were two or three patches of sky where the sunlight still lingered, but the rain was coming down more and more heavily. Lucas had hardly left the Café de la Marine and was heading towards the yacht, when Willy Marco stepped off it, wearing a suit and tie, loose-limbed and casual, looking at nothing in particular.

It was definitely a trait shared by all the passengers on the *Southern Cross* that they always looked as though they hadn't had enough sleep or as if large amounts of alcohol did not agree with them.

The two men passed each other on the towpath. Willy appeared to hesitate when he saw Lucas go aboard. Then, lighting a fresh cigarette with the one he had just finished, he made straight for the café.

He was looking for Maigret and did not pretend otherwise.

He did not take off his soft felt hat but touched it absently with one finger as he murmured:

'Hello, inspector. Sleep well? I wanted a quick word . . .'

'I'm listening.'

'Not here, if it's all the same to you. Could we possibly go up to your room, do you think?'

He had lost nothing of his relaxed, confident manner. His small eyes sparkled with something not far from gleeful elation, or perhaps it was malevolence.

'Cigarette?'

'No thanks.'

'Of course! You're a pipe man.'

Maigret decided to take him up to his room, though it hadn't yet been cleaned. After a glance out at the yacht, Willy sat down at once on the edge of the bed and began:

'Naturally you've already made inquiries about me.'

He looked round for an ashtray, failed to locate one and flicked his ash on to the floor.

'Not much to write home about, eh? But I've never claimed to be a saint. Anyway the colonel tells me what a rotter I am three times a day.'

What was remarkable about this was the completely frank

expression on his face. Maigret was forced to admit that he was beginning to warm to Willy, who he hadn't been able to stomach at first.

A strange mixture. Sly and foxy. Yet at the same time a spark of decency which redeemed the rest, plus an engaging touch of humour.

'But you will have noted that I went to Eton, like the Prince of Wales. If we'd been the same age, we would have been the best of pals. But the truth is my father is a fig wholesaler in Smyrna. I can't bear the thought! I've been in some scrapes. The mother of one of my Eton friends, if you must know, got me out of one of them.

'You do understand if I don't give you her name, don't you? A delectable lady . . . But her husband became a government minister, and she was afraid of compromising his position.

'After that . . . They must have told you about Monaco, then that unpleasantness in Nice. Actually the truth isn't as bad as all that . . . Here's a tip: never believe anything you're told by a middle-aged American woman who lives it up on the Riviera and has a husband who arrives unexpectedly from Chicago. Stolen jewels have not always been stolen. But let's move on.

'Now, about the necklace. Either you know already or maybe you've not yet heard. I would have preferred to talk to you about it last night, but in the circumstances it might not have been the decent thing to do.

'The colonel is nothing if not a gentleman. He may be a touch over-fond of whisky, I grant. But he has some justification.

'He should have ended up a general. He was one of the men most in the public eye in Lima. But there was a scandal involving a woman, the wife of a highly placed local bigwig, and he was pensioned off.

'You've seen him. A magnificent specimen, with vigorous appetites. Out there, he had thirty native boys, orderlies, secretaries and God knows how many cars and horses for his own use.

'Then all of a sudden, all gone! Something like a hundred thousand francs a year, wiped out.

'Did I say that he'd already been married twice before he met Mary? His first wife died in India. Second time round, he got a divorce by taking all the fault on himself after finding his lady in bed with one of the boys.

'A real gentlemen!'

Willy, now leaning well back, was swinging one leg lethargically, while Maigret, his pipe between his teeth, stood with his back against the wall without moving.

'That's how it goes. Nowadays, he passes the time as well as he can. Down at Porquerolles, he lives in his old fort, which the locals call the Petit Langoustier. When he's saved up enough money, he goes to Paris or London.

'And just think that in India he used to give dinners for thirty or forty guests every week!'

'Was it about the colonel you wanted to talk to me?' murmured Maigret.

Willy did not bat an eyelid.

'Actually, I was trying to put you in the picture. I mean, you've never lived in India or London or had thirty native servants and God knows how many pretty girls at your beck and call . . . I'm not trying to get under your skin . . .

'Be that as it may, I met him two years ago.

'You didn't know Mary when she was alive . . . An adorable creature but a brain like a bird's . . . And a touch loud. If you weren't waiting hand and foot on her all the time, she'd have a fit or cause a scene.

'By the way, do you know how old the colonel is? Sixty-eight.

'She wore him out, if you follow me. She happily indulged his fantasies – he's not past it yet! – but she could be a bit of a nuisance.

'Then she got a thing about me. I quite liked her.'

'I take it that Madame Negretti is Sir Walter's mistress?'

'Yes,' the young man agreed with a scowl. 'It's hard to explain . . .

He can't live or drink on his own. He has to have people round him. We met her when we put in once at Bandol. The next morning, she didn't leave. As far as he's concerned, that was it. She'll stay as long as she likes.

'But me, I'm different. I'm one of those rare men who can hold his whisky as well as the colonel.

'Except perhaps for Vladimir, who you've seen. Nine times out of ten, he's the one who puts us both to bed in our bunks.

'I don't know if you have grasped my position. It's true that I have no material worries. Still, there are times when we get stuck in a port for a fortnight waiting for a cheque from London so that we can buy petrol!

'Yes, and that necklace, which I shall come back to in a moment, has seen the inside of a pawnshop a score of times.

'Never mind! The whisky rarely runs out.

'It's not exactly a lavish lifestyle. But we sleep for as long as we want. We come and we go.

'Speaking personally, I much prefer it to being knee-deep in my father's figs.

'At the beginning, the colonel bought several items of jewellery for his wife. From time to time she would ask him for money.

'To buy clothes and so that she had a little pocket-money, if you follow me.

'But whatever you might think, I swear I got a colossal shock yesterday when I realized it was her in that awful photo! So did the colonel, actually . . . But he'd go through fire and water rather than show his feelings. That's his style. And so very English!

'When we left Paris last week – it's Tuesday today, isn't it – the cash was running low. The colonel sent a cable to London asking for an advance on his pension. We waited for it at Épernay. The draft arrived at around this time of day, I think.

'Thing is, I'd left a few debts unpaid in Paris. I'd asked Mary once or twice why she didn't sell her necklace. She could easily have told her husband she'd lost it or said it had been stolen.

'Thursday evening was the party, as you know. But you really shouldn't get any wrong ideas about what went on. The moment Lampson catches sight of pretty women, he has to invite them on board.

'Then a couple of hours later, when he's had too much to drink, he tells me to get rid of them as cheaply as possible.

'On Thursday, Mary got up much earlier than usual, and by the time we'd all staggered out of our bunks, she'd already gone outside.

'After lunch, there was a brief moment when the two of us were alone. She was very affectionate. Affectionate in a special way, a sad way.

'At one point, she put her necklace in my hand and said: "Just sell it."

'I'm sorry if you don't believe me . . . I felt awkward, had a qualm or two. If you'd known her, you'd understand.

'Although she could be a real bitch at times, at others she could be quite touching.

'Don't forget that she was over forty. She was looking out for herself. But she must have had an inkling that her time had gone.

'Then someone came in. I slipped the necklace into my pocket. In the evening, the colonel dragged us all off to the palais de danse, and Mary stayed on board by herself.

'When we got back, she wasn't there. Lampson wasn't worried. It wasn't the first time she'd run off like that.

'And not for the reasons you might think. On one occasion, for instance, during the festival of Porquerolles, there was a rather jolly orgy at the Petit Langoustier which lasted the best part of a week. For the first couple of days, Mary was the life and soul of the party. But on day three, she disappeared.

'And do you know where we found her? Staying at an inn at Giens, where she was happily passing the time playing mummies with a couple of unwashed brats.

'I was not comfortable with the business of the necklace. On

Friday, I went up to Paris. I nearly sold it. But then I told myself that if there were problems I could land myself in serious trouble.

'Then I remembered the two girls from the night before. With girls like that, you can get away with anything. Besides, I'd already met Lia in Nice and knew I could count on her.

'I gave the necklace to her. Just in case, I told her that if anyone asked, she was to say that Mary herself had given it to her to sell.

'It's as simple as that, and very stupid! I would have been far better off keeping quiet. All the same, if I come up against policemen who aren't very bright, it's the sort of thing that could well land me in court.

'I realized this yesterday the minute I heard that Mary had been strangled.

'I won't ask you what you think. To be honest, I'm expecting to be arrested.

'That would be a mistake, a big mistake! Look, if you want me to help, I'm ready to lend you a hand.

'There are things that may strike you as odd but are quite straightforward really.'

He was now almost flat on the bed, still smoking, with his eyes fixed on the ceiling.

Maigret took up a position by the window to cover his perplexity.

'Does the colonel know that you're here telling me all this?' he asked, turning round suddenly.

'No more than he knows about the business with the necklace. Actually, though I'm obviously in no position to ask, I would prefer if he went on not knowing.'

'And Madame Negretti?'

'A dead weight. A beautiful woman who is incapable of existing except on a couch, smoking cigarettes and drinking sweet liqueurs. She started the day she first came on board and has been doing it ever since . . . Oh sorry: she also plays cards. I think it's the only thing that really interests her.'

The screech of rusted iron indicated that the lock gates were being opened. Two mules trudged past the front of the house then stopped a little further on, while an empty barge continued moving, swinging as it lost its way, looking as though it were trying to climb up the bank.

Vladimir, bent double, was baling out the rainwater which threatened to swamp the dinghy.

A car crossed the stone bridge, attempted to drive on to the towpath, stopped, then made several clumsy attempts to turn before coming to a complete stop.

A man dressed all in black got out. Willy, who had got off the bed, glanced out of the window and said:

'It's the undertaker.'

'When is the colonel thinking of leaving?'

'Immediately after the funeral.'

'Which will take place here?'

'Anywhere'll do! He already has one wife buried near Lima and another now married to a New Yorker who will finish up under six feet of American soil.'

Maigret glanced across at him instinctively, as if he was trying to work out if he was joking. But Willy Marco was perfectly serious, though that little ambiguous spark still flickered in his eye.

'If, that is, the money draft has come through! Otherwise, the funeral will have to wait.'

The man in black halted uncertainly by the yacht, put a question to Vladimir, who answered without stopping what he was doing, then finally climbed aboard and vanished into the cabin.

Maigret had not seen Lucas come out.

'You'd better go,' he said to Willy.

Willy hesitated. For a moment, a look of anxiety flitted across his face.

'Are you going to ask him about the necklace?'

'I don't know.'

The moment had passed. Willy, his usual cool self once more, knocked out the dent in his felt hat, waved a goodbye with one hand and went downstairs.

When, shortly after, Maigret followed him down, there were two bargees leaning on the bar nursing bottles of beer.

'Your mate's on the phone,' said the landlord. 'Asked for a Moulins number.'

A tug sounded its hooter several times in the distance. Maigret counted mechanically and muttered:

'Five.'

On the canal it was business as usual. Five barges approaching. The lock-keeper, wearing clogs, emerged from his house and made for the sluices.

Lucas came out of the phone booth. His face was red.

'Whew! That was hard work . . .'

'What is it?'

'The colonel told me his wife's maiden name was Marie Dupin. For the wedding, she produced a birth certificate with that name on it issued at Moulins. Now I've just phoned them there, pulling rank . . .'

'And?'

'There's only one Marie Dupin on their register. She is forty-two years old, has three children and is married to a man called Piedbœuf, who is a baker in the high street. The clerk in the town hall I talked to said she had seen her serving in the shop only yesterday. Apparently she weighs all of 180 pounds.'

Maigret said nothing. Looking like a well-to-do bystander with time on his hands, he wandered over to the lock without another thought for his companion and followed every stage of the operation closely. All the while, one thumb angrily tamped down the tobacco in his pipe.

A little later, Vladimir approached the lock-keeper. He touched his white forage cap with one hand and asked where he could fill up with fresh water.

5. The YCF Badge

Maigret had gone to bed early, while Inspector Lucas, who had his orders, went off to Meaux, Paris and Moulins.

When he left the bar, there had been three customers, two bargees and the wife of one of them who had joined her husband and was sitting in a corner, knitting.

The atmosphere was cheerless and heavy. Outside, a barge had tied up less than two metres from the *Southern Cross*, whose portholes were all lit up.

Now, suddenly, the inspector was dragged from a dream so confused that even as he opened his eyes he could remember nothing of it. Someone was knocking urgently on his door, and a voice was calling in a panic:

'Inspector! Inspector! Come quickly! My father . . .'

He ran to the door in his pyjamas and opened it. Outside he was surprised to see the landlord's daughter looking distraught. She leaped on him and literally buried herself in his arms.

'Ah! . . . You must go, hurry! . . . No, stay here! . . . Don't leave me by myself! . . . I couldn't bear it! . . . I'm scared! . . .'

He had never paid much attention to her. He'd thought she was a sturdy girl, well upholstered, but without a nerve in her body.

And here she was, face convulsed, heaving for breath, hanging on to him with an insistence that was embarrassing. Still trying to extricate himself, he moved towards the window and opened it.

It was probably about six in the morning. It was barely first light and cold as a winter dawn.

A hundred metres beyond the *Southern Cross*, in the direction of the stone bridge and the Épernay road, four or five men were using a heavy boat hook to fish out something floating in the water, while one of the barge men untied his dinghy and began rowing across.

Maigret's pyjamas had seen better days. He threw his overcoat over his shoulders, located his ankle boots and inserted his bare feet into them.

'You realize . . . It's *him*! . . . They've . . .'

With a sudden movement, he broke free of the clutches of this strange girl, hurried down the stairs and was going outside just as a woman carrying a baby in her arms was bearing down on the group.

He hadn't been there when Mary Lampson's body had been found. But this new discovery was if anything more grim because, as an effect of this recurrence of crime, a feeling of almost mystical anguish now hung over this stretch of the canal.

The men called to each other. The landlord of the Café de la Marine, who had been first to spot a body floating in the water, was directing operations.

Twice the boat hook had snagged the corpse and each time the metal end had slipped. Each time, the body had dipped a few centimetres before returning to the surface.

Maigret had already recognized Willy's dark suit. He could not see the face because the head, being heavier, remained submerged.

The man in the dinghy suddenly nudged it, grabbed the body by the chest and raised it with one hand. But he had to haul it over the side of the boat.

The man was not squeamish. He lifted the legs one after the other, threw his mooring rope on to the bank then wiped his streaming forehead with the back of his hand.

For one moment, Maigret had a glimpse of Vladimir's sleep-dulled head appearing through a hatch on the yacht. The Russian rubbed his eyes. Then he vanished.

'Don't touch anything!'

Behind him, one of the men protested, saying that back in

Alsace his brother-in-law had been revived after being in the water for nearly three hours.

The landlord of the café pointed to the corpse's throat. There was no doubt: two finger marks, black, just like the ones on the neck of Mary Lampson.

This death was the more shocking of the two. Willy's eyes were wide open, looking much, much larger than usual. His right hand was still clutching a handful of reeds.

Maigret suddenly sensed an unexpected presence behind him. He turned and saw the colonel, also in pyjamas with a silk dressing gown thrown over them and blue kid slippers on his feet.

His silver hair was dishevelled and his face slightly puffy. He was a strange sight dressed like that, surrounded by canal men wearing clogs and thick coarse clothes, in the mud and damp of the early morning.

He was the tallest and broadest there. He gave off a faint whiff of eau de Cologne.

'It's Willy!' he said in a hoarse whisper.

Then he said a few words in English, too fast for Maigret to understand, bent down and touched the face of the young man.

The girl who had woken the inspector was leaning on the café door for support, sobbing. The lock-keeper came running.

'Phone the police at Épernay . . . And a doctor . . .'

Even Madame Negretti came out, barely decent, with nothing on her feet. But she did not dare leave the bridge of the yacht and called to the colonel:

'Walter! Walter!'

In the background were people who had arrived unseen: the driver of the little train, a group of navvies and a man with a cow which went ambling along the towpath by itself.

'Take him inside the café . . . And don't touch him more than you have to.'

He was obviously dead. The elegant suit, now no more than a limp rag, trailed along the ground when the body was lifted.

The colonel followed slowly. His dressing gown, blue slippers and ruddy scalp, across which the wind stirred a few long wisps of hair, made him an absurd but also priestly figure.

The girl's sobs came faster when the body passed in front of her. Then she ran off and shut herself away in the kitchen. The landlord was yelling down the phone:

'No, operator! . . . Police! . . . Hurry up! . . . There's been a murder! . . . Don't hang up! . . . Hello? Hello?'

Maigret kept most of the onlookers out. But the barge men who had discovered the body and helped to fish it out had all crowded into the café where the tables were still littered with glasses and bottles from the night before. The stove roared. A broom was lying in the middle of the floor.

The inspector caught a glimpse of Vladimir peering in through one of the windows. He'd had time to put his American sailor's forage cap on his head. The barge men were talking to him, but he was not responding.

The colonel was still staring at the body, which had been laid out on the red stone flags of the café floor. Whether he was upset or bored or scared it was impossible to say. Maigret went up to him:

'When was the last time you saw him?' he asked.

Sir Walter sighed and seemed to look around him for the man he usually relied on to answer for him.

'It's all so very terrible . . .' he said eventually.

'Didn't he sleep on board last night?'

With a gesture of the hand, the Englishman pointed to the barge men who were listening to them. It was like a reminder of the conventions. It meant: 'Do you think it right and proper for these people . . .'

Maigret ordered them out.

'It was ten o'clock last night. We had no whisky left on board. Vladimir hadn't been able to get any at Dizy. I decided to go to Épernay.'

'Did Willy go with you?'

'Not very far. He went off on his own just after the bridge.'

'Why?'

'We had words . . .'

And as the colonel said this, his eyes still drawn to the pinched, pallid, twisted features of the dead man, his own face crumpled.

Was it because he had not slept enough and that his flesh was puffy that he looked more upset? Perhaps. But Maigret would have sworn that there were tears lurking under those heavy eyelids.

'Did you have a bust-up?'

The colonel gave a shrug, as if resigning himself to hearing such a vulgar, ugly expression.

'Were you angry with him about something?'

'No! I wanted to know . . . I kept saying: "Willy, you're a rotter . . . But you've got to tell me . . ."'

He stopped, overcome. He looked around him so that he would not be mesmerized by the dead man.

'Did you accuse him of murdering your wife?'

He shrugged and sighed:

'He went off by himself. It's happened before, now and again. Next morning we'd drink the first whisky of the day together and put it out of our minds . . .'

'Did you walk all the way to Épernay?'

'Yes.'

'Did you drink a lot?'

The lingering look which the colonel turned on the inspector was abject.

'I also tried my luck at the tables, at the club . . . They'd told me at La Bécasse that there was a gambling club . . . I came back in a cab.'

'At what time?'

With a motion of the hand he intimated that he had no idea.

'Willy wasn't in his bunk?'

'No. Vladimir told me as he was helping me undress for bed.'

A motorcycle and sidecar pulled up outside the door. A police sergeant dismounted, and the passenger, a doctor, climbed out. The café door opened and then closed.

'Police Judiciaire,' said Maigret, introducing himself to his colleague from Épernay. 'Could you get these people to keep back and then phone the prosecutor's office . . . ?'

The doctor needed only a brief look at the body before saying:

'He was dead before he hit the water. Take a look at these marks.'

Maigret had already seen them. He knew. He glanced mechanically at the colonel's right hand. It was muscular, with the nails cut square and prominent veins.

It would take at least an hour to get the public prosecutor and his people together and ferry them to the crime scene. Policemen on cycles arrived and formed a cordon around the Café de la Marine and the *Southern Cross*.

'May I get dressed?' the colonel asked.

Despite his dressing gown, slippers and bare ankles, he made a surprisingly dignified figure as he passed through the crowd of bystanders. He had no sooner gone into the cabin than he poked his head out again and shouted:

'Vladimir!'

Then all the hatches on the yacht were shut.

Maigret was interviewing the lock-keeper, who had been called out to man his gates by a motorboat.

'I imagine that there is no current in a canal? So a body will stay in the place where it was thrown in?'

'In long stretches of the canal, ten or fifteen kilometres, that would be true. But this particular stretch doesn't go even five. If a boat passes through Lock 13, which is the one above mine, I smell water that's released arrive here a few minutes later. And if I put a boat going downstream through my lock, I take a lot of water out of the canal, and that creates a short-lived current.'

'What time do you start work?'

'Officially at dawn but actually a lot earlier. The horse-drawn boats, which move pretty slowly, set off at about three in the morning. More often than not, they put themselves through the lock without me hearing a thing . . . Nobody says anything because we know them all . . .'

'So this morning . . . ?'

'The *Frédéric*, which spent the night here, must have left around half past three and went through the lock at Ay at five.'

Maigret turned and retraced his steps. Outside the Café de la Marine and along the towpath, a few groups of men had gathered. As the inspector passed them on his way to the stone bridge, an old pilot with a grog-blossom nose came up to him:

'Want me to show you the spot where that young feller was thrown into the water?'

And looking very proud of himself, he glanced round at his comrades, who hesitated a moment before falling into step behind him.

The man was right. Fifty metres from the stone bridge, the reeds had been trampled over an area of several metres. They hadn't simply been walked on. A heavy object had been dragged across the ground. The tracks were wide where the reeds had been flattened.

'See that? I live half a kilometre from here, in one of the first houses you come to in Dizy. When I was coming in this morning, to check if there were any boats going down the Marne that needed me, it struck me as unusual. And then I found this on the towpath just by it.'

The man was tiresome, for he kept pulling funny faces and looking back at his companions, who were following at a distance.

But the object he produced from his pocket was of the greatest interest. It was a finely worked enamel badge. On it was a kedge anchor and the initials 'YCF'.

'Yachting Club de France,' said the pilot. 'They all wear them in their lapels.'

Maigret turned to look at the yacht, which was clearly visible some two kilometres away. Under the words *Southern Cross* he could just make out the same initials: YCF.

Paying no further attention to the man who had given him the badge, he walked slowly to the bridge. On his right, the Épernay road stretched away in a straight line, still glistening with last night's rain. Traffic drove along it at high speeds.

To the left, the road formed a bend as it entered the village of Dizy. On the canal beyond, several barges were lying up, undergoing repairs, just by the yards owned by the Compagnie Générale de Navigation.

Maigret walked back the way he'd come, feeling the tension mounting. The public prosecutor's officials would be arriving soon, and for an hour or two there would be the usual chaos, questions, comings and goings and a spate of wild theories.

When he was level with the yacht, everything was still all closed up. A uniformed officer was pacing up and down a little distance away, telling bystanders to move along, but failing to prevent two journalists from Épernay taking pictures.

The weather was neither fine nor foul. A luminous grey morning sky, unbroken, like a frosted glass ceiling.

Maigret walked across the gangplank and knocked on the door.

'Who is it?' came the colonel's voice.

He went in. He was in no mood to argue. He saw the Negretti woman, wearing no more clothes than before, hair hanging down over her face and neck, wiping away her tears and snivelling.

Sir Walter was sitting on the bench seat, holding out his feet to Vladimir, who was helping him on with a pair of chestnut-brown shoes.

Water had to be boiling somewhere on a stove because there was the hiss of escaping steam.

The two bunks slept in by the colonel and Gloria were still unmade. Playing cards were scattered on the table beside a map of France's navigable waterways.

And still there was that elusive, spicy smell which evoked bar, boudoir and secret amours. A white canvas yachting cap hung from the hat stand next to a riding crop with an ivory handle.

'Was Willy a member of the Yacht Club de France?' asked Maigret in as neutral a tone as he could manage.

The way the colonel shrugged his shoulders told him his question was absurd. And so it was. The YCF is one of the most exclusive clubs.

'But I am,' Sir Walter said casually. 'And of the Royal Yacht Club in England.'

'Would you mind showing me the jacket you were wearing last night?'

'Vladimir . . .'

He now had his shoes on. He stood up, bent down and opened a small cupboard, which had been turned into a liquor cabinet. There was no whisky in sight. But there were other bottles of spirits, over which he hesitated.

Finally he brought out a bottle of liqueur brandy and murmured offhandedly:

'What will you have?'

'Not for me, thanks.'

He filled a silver goblet which he took from a rack above the table, looked for the siphon, and frowned darkly like a man all of whose habits have been turned upside down and who feels hard done by.

Vladimir emerged from the bathroom with a black tweed suit. A nod from his master instructed him to hand it to Maigret.

'The YCF badge was usually pinned to the lapel of this jacket?'

'Yes. How long are they going to be over there? Is Willy still on the floor of that café?'

He had emptied his glass while still standing, a sip at a time, and hesitated about whether he'd pour himself another.

He glanced out of the porthole, saw legs and grunted indistinctly.

'Will you listen to me for a moment, colonel?'

The colonel indicated that he was listening. Maigret took the enamel badge from his pocket.

'This was found this morning at the spot where Willy's body was dragged through a bank of reeds and dumped in the canal.'

Madame Negretti uttered a cry, threw herself on the plum-coloured plush of the bench seat and there, holding her head in her hands, she began to sob convulsively.

Vladimir, however, did not move. He waited for the jacket to be returned to him so that he could hang it back up in its place.

The colonel gave an odd sort of laugh and repeated four or five times:

'Yes! Yes!'

As he did so, he poured himself another drink.

'Where I come from, the police ask questions differently. They have to say that everything you say may be used as evidence against you. I'll say it once . . . Shouldn't you be writing this down? I won't say it again . . .

'I was with Willy. We had words. I asked . . . It doesn't matter what I asked.

'He wasn't a rotter like the rest of them. Some rotters are decent fellows.

'I spoke too harshly. He grabbed my jacket just here . . .'

He indicated the lapels and looked out irritably at the feet encased in clogs or heavy shoes which were still visible through the portholes.

'That's all. I don't know, maybe the badge fell off then . . . It happened on the other side of the bridge.'

'Yet the badge was found on this side.'

Vladimir hardly seemed to be listening. He gathered up things that were lying about, went forward and returned unhurriedly.

In a very strong Russian accent, he asked Gloria, who wasn't crying any more but was lying flat on her back without moving, clutching her head with both hands:

'You want anything?'

Steps were heard on the gangplank. There was a knock on the door, and the sergeant said:

'Are you in there, inspector? It's the prosecutor's office . . .'

'I'm coming!'

The sergeant did not move, an unseen presence behind the mahogany door with brass handles.

'One more thing, colonel. When is the funeral?'

'Three o'clock.'

'Today?'

'Yes! I have no reason to stay on here.'

When he had drunk his third glass of three-star cognac, his eyes looked more clouded. Maigret had seen those eyes before.

Then, just as the inspector was about to leave, he asked, cool, casual, every inch the master of all he surveyed:

'Am I under arrest?'

At once, Madame Negretti looked up. She was deathly pale.

6. The American Sailor's Cap

The conclusion of the interview between the magistrate and the colonel was almost a solemn moment. Maigret, who stood slightly apart, was not the only one to notice it.

He caught the eye of the deputy public prosecutor and saw that he too had picked up on it.

The public prosecutor's team had gathered in the bar room of the Café de la Marine. One door led to the kitchen, from which came the clatter of saucepans. The other door, glass-panelled, was covered with stuck-on transparent adverts for pasta and rock soap through which the sacks and boxes in the shop could be seen.

The peaked cap of a policeman in uniform marched to and fro outside the window. Onlookers, silent but determined, had grouped a little further away.

A half-litre glass, with a small amount of liquid in it, was still standing beside a pool of wine on one of the tables.

The clerk of the court, seated on a backless bench, was writing. There was a peevish look on his face.

Once the statements had all been taken, the body had been placed as far from the stove as possible and temporarily covered with one of the brown oilcloths taken from a tabletop, leaving its disjointed boards exposed.

The smell had not gone away: spices, stables, tar and wine lees.

The magistrate, who was reckoned to be one of the most unpleasant in Épernay – he was a Clairfontaine de Lagny and proud of the aristocratic 'de' in the name – stood with his back to the fire and wiped his pince-nez.

At the start of the proceedings, he had said in English:

'I imagine you'd prefer us to use your language?'

He himself spoke it quite well with, perhaps, a hint of affectation, a slight screw of the lips standard among those who try – and fail – to reproduce the correct accent.

Sir Walter had accepted the offer. He had responded to every question slowly, his face turned to the clerk, who was writing, pausing from time to time to allow him to catch up.

He had repeated, without adding anything new, what he had told Maigret during their two interviews.

For the occasion, he had chosen a dark-blue double-breasted suit of almost military cut. To one lapel was pinned a single medal: the Order of Merit.

In one hand he held a peaked cap. On it was a broad gilt crest bearing the insignia of the Yachting Club de France.

It was very simple. One man asked questions and the other man invariably gave a slight, deferential nod before answering.

Even so, Maigret looked on admiringly but could not help feeling mortified as he remembered his own intrusive probings on board the *Southern Cross.*

His English was not good enough for him to grasp all the finer points. But he at least understood the broad meaning of the concluding exchanges.

'Sir Walter,' said the magistrate, 'I must ask you to remain available until we have got to the bottom of both these appalling crimes. I am afraid, moreover, that I have no choice but to withhold permission for the burial of Lady Lampson.'

Another slight bow of the head.

'Do I have your authorization to leave Dizy in my boat?'

With one hand the colonel gestured towards the onlookers who had gathered outside, the scenery, even the sky.

'My home is on Porquerolles . . . it will take me a week just to reach the Saône.'

This time it was the turn of the magistrate to offer a respectful nod.

They did not shake hands, though they almost did. The colonel looked around him, appeared not to see either the doctor, who seemed bored, or Maigret, who avoided his eye, but he did acknowledge the deputy prosecutor.

The next moment he was walking the short distance between the Café de la Marine and the *Southern Cross*.

He made no attempt to go inside the cabin. Vladimir was on the bridge. He gave him his orders and took the wheel.

Then, to the amazement of the canal men and the bargees, they saw the Russian in the striped jersey disappear into the engine room, start the motor and then, from the deck, with a neat flick of the wrist, yank the mooring ropes free of the bollards.

Within moments, a small, gesticulating group began moving off towards the main road, where their cars were waiting. It was the public prosecutor's team.

Maigret was left standing on the canal bank. He had finally managed to fill his pipe and now thrust both hands into his pockets with a gesture that was distinctly proletarian, even more proletarian than usual, and muttered:

'Well, that's that!'

It was back to square one!

The investigation of the prosecutor's office had come up with only a few points. It was too early to tell if they were significant.

First: the body of Willy Marco, in addition to the marks of strangulation, also had bruises to the wrists and torso. The police surgeon ruled out an ambush but thought that a struggle with an exceptionally strong attacker was more likely.

Second: Sir Walter had stated that he had met his wife in Nice, where, although she had divorced her Italian husband, she was still using her married name of Ceccaldi.

The colonel's account had not been clear. His wilfully ambiguous statement let it be supposed that Marie Dupin, or Ceccaldi, was at that time virtually destitute and living on the generosity of a few friends, though without ever actually selling her body.

He had married her during a trip to London, and it was then

that she had obtained from France a copy of her birth certificate in the name of Marie Dupin.

'She was a most enchanting woman.'

In his mind's eye Maigret saw the colonel's fleshy, dignified, ruddy face as he said these words, without affectation and with a sober simplicity which had seemed to impress the magistrate favourably.

He stepped back to allow the stretcher carrying Willy's body to pass.

Suddenly he shrugged his shoulders and went into the café, sat down heavily on a bench and called:

'Bring me a beer!'

It was the girl who served him. Her eyes were still red, and her nose shone. He looked up at her with interest and, before he could question her, she looked this way and that to make sure no one was listening, then murmured:

'Did he suffer much?'

She had a lumpish, unintelligent face, thick ankles and red beefy arms. Yet she was the only one who had given a second thought to the suave Willy, who perhaps had squeezed her waist as a joke the evening before – if, indeed, he had.

Maigret was reminded of the conversation he had had with the young man when he had been half stretched out on the unmade bed in his room, chain-smoking.

The girl was wanted elsewhere. One of the watermen called to her:

'Seems like you're all upset, Emma!'

She tried to smile and gave Maigret a conspiratorial look.

The canal traffic had been held up all morning. There were now seven vessels, three with engines, tied up outside the Café de la Marine. The bargees' wives came to the shop, and each one made the door bell jangle.

'When you're ready for lunch . . .' the landlord said to Maigret.

'In a while.'

And from the doorway, he looked at the spot where the *Southern Cross* had been moored only that morning.

The previous evening, two men, two healthy men, had stepped off it. They had walked off towards the stone bridge. If the colonel was to be believed, they'd separated after an argument, and Sir Walter had gone on his way along the three kilometres of empty, dead-straight road which led to the first houses of Épernay.

No one had ever seen Willy alive again. When the colonel had returned in a cab, he had not noticed anything unusual.

No witnesses! No one had heard anything! The butcher at Dizy, who lived 600 metres from the bridge, said his dog had barked, but he hadn't investigated and could not say what time it had been.

The towpath, awash with puddles and pools, had been used by too many men and horses for there to be any hope of finding any useful tracks.

The previous Thursday, Mary Lampson, also fit and well to all appearances, had left the *Southern Cross*, where she had been alone.

Earlier – according to Willy – she had given him a pearl necklace, the only valuable item of jewellery she owned.

After this there was no trace of her. She had not been seen alive again. Two days had gone by when no one had reported seeing her.

On Sunday evening, she lay strangled under a pile of straw in a stable at Dizy, a hundred kilometres from her point of departure, with two carters snoring just feet from her corpse.

That was all! The Épernay magistrate had ordered both bodies to be transferred to cold storage in the Forensic Institute.

The *Southern Cross* had just left, heading south, for Porquerolles, for the Petit Langoustier, which was no stranger to orgies.

Maigret, head down, walked all round the building of the Café de la Marine. He beat off a bad-tempered goose which bore down on him, its beak open and shrieking with rage.

There was no lock on the stable door, only a simple wooden

latch. The hunting dog with an overfed paunch, which prowled round the yard, turned joyful circles and greeted him deliriously, as it did all visitors.

When he opened the door, the inspector was confronted by the landlord's grey horse, which was no more tethered now than on the other days, and made the most of the opportunity to go for a walk outside.

The broken-winded mare was still lying in its box, looking miserable.

Maigret moved the straw with his foot, as though hoping to find something he had missed on his first examination of the place.

Two or three times he repeated to himself crossly:

'Back to square one!'

He had more or less made up his mind to return to Meaux, even Paris, and retrace step by step the route followed by the *Southern Cross*.

There were all kinds of odds and ends lying around: old halters, bits of harness, the end of a candle, a broken pipe . . .

From a distance he noticed something white poking out of a pile of hay. He went over not expecting anything much. The next moment he was holding an American sailor's forage cap just like the one worn by Vladimir.

The material was spattered with mud and horse droppings and misshapen as though it had been stretched in all directions.

Maigret searched all around but failed to come up with anything else.

Fresh straw had been put down over the spot where the body had been found to make it seem less sinister.

'Am I under arrest?'

As he walked towards the stable door, he could not have said why the colonel's question should suddenly surface in his memory. He also saw Sir Walter, as boorish as he was aristocratic, his eyes permanently watering, the drunkenness always just beneath the surface and his amazing composure.

He thought back to the brief talk he had had with the supercilious magistrate in the bar of the café, with its tables covered in brown oilcloth, which, through a sprinkling of polite voices and refined manners, had been magically transformed for a short time into a sophisticated drawing room.

He kept turning the cap round and round in his hands, suspicious, with a calculating look in his eye.

'Tread carefully,' Monsieur de Clairfontaine de Lagny had told him as he took Maigret's hand lightly.

The goose, still furious, followed the horse, screeching abuse at it.

The horse, letting its large head hang down, snuffled among the rubbish littering the yard.

On each side of the door was an old milestone. The inspector sat down on one of them, still holding the cap and his pipe, which had gone out.

Directly ahead of him was a large dung heap, then a hedge with occasional gaps in it, and beyond were fields in which nothing was yet growing and hills streaked with black and white on which a cloud with a dark centre seemed to have rested its full weight.

From behind one edge of it sprang an oblique shaft of sunlight which created sparkles of light on the dung heap.

'*An enchanting woman*,' the colonel had said of Mary Lampson.

'*Nothing if not a gentleman!*' Willy had said of the colonel.

Only Vladimir had said nothing. He had just kept busy, buying supplies, petrol, filling up the tanks of drinking water, baling out the dinghy and helping his employer to dress.

A group of Flemings passed along the road, talking in loud voices. Suddenly, Maigret bent down. The yard was paved with irregular flagstones. Two metres in front of him, in the crack between two of them, something had just been caught by the sun and glinted.

It was a cufflink, gold with a platinum hatching. Maigret had seen a pair just like it the day before, on Willy's wrists, when he was lying on his bed blowing cigarette smoke at the ceiling and talking so unconcernedly.

He took no more interest in the horse or the goose or any of his surroundings. Moments later, he was turning the handle that cranked the phone.

'Épernay . . . Yes, the mortuary! . . . This is the police!'

One of the Flemings was just coming out of the café. He stopped and stared at the inspector, who was extraordinarily agitated.

'Hello? . . . Inspector Maigret here, Police Judiciaire . . . You've just had a body brought in . . . No, not the car accident, this is about the man drowned at Dizy . . . That's right . . . Find the custody officer . . . Go through his effects, you'll find a cufflink . . . I want you to describe it to me . . . Yes, I'll hang on.'

Three minutes later, he replaced the receiver. He had the information. He was still holding the forage cap and the cufflink.

'Your lunch is ready.'

He didn't bother to answer the girl with red hair, though she had spoken as politely as she could. He went out feeling that perhaps he was now holding one end of the thread but also fearing he would drop it.

'The cap in the stables . . . The cufflink in the yard . . . And the YCF badge near the stone bridge . . .'

It was that way he now started walking, very fast. Ideas formed and faded in turns in his mind.

He had not gone a kilometre when he was astonished by what he saw dead ahead.

The *Southern Cross*, which had set off in a great haste a good hour before, was now moored on the right-hand side of the bridge, among the reeds. He couldn't see anyone on board.

But when the inspector was less than a hundred metres short of it, a car coming from the direction of Épernay pulled up on the opposite bank. It stopped near the yacht. Vladimir, still wearing sailor's clothes, was sitting next to the driver. He got out and ran to the boat. Before he reached it, the hatch opened, and the colonel came out on deck, holding his hand out to someone inside.

Maigret made no attempt to hide. He couldn't tell whether the colonel had seen him or not.

Then things happened fast. The inspector could not hear what was said, but the way the people were behaving gave him a clear enough idea of what was happening.

It was Madame Negretti who was being handed out of the cabin by Sir Walter. Maigret noted that this was the first time he had seen her wearing town clothes. Even from a distance it was obvious that she was very angry.

Vladimir picked up the two suitcases which stood ready and carried them to the car.

The colonel held out one hand to help her negotiate the gangplank, but she refused it and stepped forward so suddenly that she almost fell head first into the reeds.

She walked on without waiting for him. He followed several paces behind, showing no reaction. She jumped into the car still in the same furious temper, thrust her head angrily out of the window and shouted something which must have been either an insult or a threat.

However, just as the car was setting off, Sir Walter bowed courteously, watched her drive off and then went back to his boat with Vladimir.

Maigret had not moved. He had a very strong feeling that a change had come over the Englishman.

He did not smile. He remained his usual imperturbable self. But, for example, just as he reached the wheelhouse in the middle of saying something, he put one friendly, even affectionate, hand on Vladimir's shoulder.

Their cast-off was brilliantly executed. There were just the two men on board now. The Russian pulled in the gangplank and with one smooth action yanked the mooring ring free.

The prow of the *Southern Cross* was fast in the reeds. A barge coming up astern hooted.

Lampson turned round. There was no way now he could not have seen Maigret but he gave no sign of it. With one hand, he let in the clutch. With the other, he gave the brass wheel two full turns, and the yacht reversed just far enough to free herself, avoided the bow of the barge, stopped just in time and then moved forward, leaving a wake of churning foam.

It had not gone a hundred metres when it sounded its hooter three times to let the lock at Ay know that its arrival was imminent.

'Don't waste time . . . Just drive . . . Catch up with that car if you can.'

Maigret had flagged down a baker's van, which was heading in the direction of Épernay. About a kilometre ahead they could see the car carrying Madame Negretti. It was moving slowly: the road was wet and greasy.

When the inspector had stated his rank, the van driver had looked at him with amused curiosity.

'Hop in. It won't take me five minutes to catch them up.'

'No, not too fast.'

Then it was Maigret's turn to smile when he saw that his driver was crouching over the steering wheel just like American cops do in car chases in Hollywood crime films.

There was no need to risk life and limb, nor any kind of complication. The car stopped briefly in the first street it came to, probably to allow the passenger to confer with the driver. Then it drove off again and halted three minutes later outside what clearly was a rather expensive hotel.

Maigret got out of the van a hundred metres behind it, thanked the baker, who refused a tip and, having decided he wanted to see more, parked a little nearer the hotel.

A porter carried both bags in. Gloria Negretti walked briskly across the pavement.

Ten minutes later, Maigret was talking to the manager.

'The lady who has just checked in?'

'Room 9. I thought there was something not quite right about her. I never saw anybody more on edge. She talked fast and used lots of foreign words. As far as I could tell, she didn't want to be disturbed and asked for cigarettes and a bottle of kümmel to be taken up to her room. I hope at least there's not going to be any scandal . . . ?'

'None at all!' said Maigret. 'Just some questions I need to ask her.'

He could not help smiling as he neared the door with the number 9 on it, for there was lots of noise coming from inside. The young woman's high heels clacked on the wooden floor in a haphazard way.

She was walking to and fro, up and down, in all directions. She could be heard closing a window, tipping out a suitcase, running a tap, throwing herself on to the bed, getting up and kicking off a shoe to the other end of the room.

Maigret knocked.

'Come in!'

Her voice was shaking with anger and impatience. Madame Negretti had not been there ten minutes and yet she had found time to change her clothes, to muss up her hair and, in a word, to revert to the way she had looked on board the *Southern Cross*, but to an even messier degree.

When she saw who it was, a flash of rage appeared in her brown eyes.

'What do you want with me? What are you doing here? This is my room! I'm paying for it and . . .'

She continued in a foreign language, probably Spanish, unscrewed the top off a bottle of eau de Cologne and poured most of the contents over her hands before dabbing her fevered brow with it.

'May I ask you a question?'

'I told them I didn't want to see anybody. Get out! Do you hear?'

She was walking around in her silk stockings. She was most

likely not wearing garters, for they began to slide down her legs. One had already uncovered a podgy, very white knee.

'Why don't you go and put your questions to people who can give you the answers? But you don't dare, do you? Because he's a colonel. Because he's *Sir* Walter! Don't you just love the *Sir*! Ha ha! If I told you only half of what I know . . .

'Look at this!'

She rummaged feverishly in her handbag and produced five crumpled 1,000-franc notes.

'This is what he just gave me! For what? For two years, for the two years that I've been living with him! That . . .'

She threw the notes on the carpet then, changing her mind, picked them up again and put them back in her bag.

'Of course, he promised he'd send me a cheque. But everybody knows what his promises are worth. A cheque! He won't even have enough money to get him to Porquerolles . . . though that won't stop him getting drunk on whisky every day!'

She wasn't crying, but there were tears in her voice. There was something unnerving about the distress exhibited by this woman who, when Maigret had seen her previously, had always seemed steeped in blissful sloth, supine in a hothouse atmosphere.

'And his precious Vladimir's just the same! He tried to kiss my hand and had the cheek to say: "It's adieu, madame, not au revoir."

'By God, they've got a nerve . . . But when the colonel wasn't around, Vladimir . . .

'But it's none of your business! Why are you still here? What are you waiting for? Are you hoping I'm going to tell you something?'

'Not at all!'

'But you can't deny that I'd be perfectly within my rights if I did . . .'

She was still walking up and down agitatedly, taking things out of her case, putting them down somewhere then a moment later picking them up again and putting them somewhere else.

'Leaving me at Épernay! In that disgusting hole, where it never stops raining! I begged him at least to take me to Nice, where I have friends. It was on his account that I left them.

'Still, I should be glad they didn't kill me.

'I won't talk! Got that? Why don't you clear off! Policemen make me sick! As sick as the English! If you're man enough, why don't you go and arrest him?

'But you wouldn't dare! I know all about how these things work . . .

'Poor Mary! She'll be called all sorts now. Of course, she had her bad side and she'd have done anything for Willy. Me, I couldn't stand him.

'But to finish up dead like that . . .

'Have they gone? . . . So who are you going to arrest, then? Maybe me?

'Well, you just listen. I'll tell you something. Just one thing and you can make of it whatever you like. This morning, when he was getting dressed to appear before that magistrate – because he's forever trying to impress people and flashing his badges and medals – when he was dressing, Walter told Vladimir, in Russian, because he thinks I don't understand Russian . . .'

She was now speaking so quickly that she ran out of breath, stumbled over her words and reverted to throwing in snatches of Spanish.

'He told him to try and find out where the *Providence* was. Are you with me? It's the barge that was tied up near us at Meaux.

'They want to catch up with it and they're afraid of me.

'I pretended I hadn't understood.

'But I know you'd never ever dare to . . .'

She stared at her disembowelled suitcases and then around the room, which in only a few minutes she had succeeded in turning into a mess and filling with her acrid perfume.

'I don't suppose you've got any cigarettes? What sort of hotel is this? I told them to bring some, and a bottle of kümmel.'

'When you were in Meaux, did you ever see the colonel talking to anybody from the *Providence*?'

'I never saw a thing. I never paid attention to any of that . . . All I heard was what he said this morning. Why otherwise would they be worrying about a barge? Does anybody know how Walter's first wife died in India? The second one divorced him, so she must have had her reasons.'

A waiter knocked at the door with the cigarettes and a bottle. Madame Negretti reached for the packet and then hurled it into the corridor yelling:

'I asked for Abdullahs!'

'But madame . . .'

She clasped her hands together in a gesture which seemed like the prelude to an imminent fit of hysterics and shrieked:

'Ah! . . . Of all the stupid . . . Ah!'

She turned to face Maigret, who was looking at her with interest, and screamed at him:

'What are you still doing here? I'm not saying any more! I don't know anything! I haven't said anything! Got that? I don't want to be bothered any more with this business! . . . It's bad enough knowing that I've wasted two years of my life in . . .'

As the waiter left, he gave the inspector a knowing wink. And while the young woman, now a bundle of frayed nerves, was throwing herself on to the bed, he too took his leave.

The baker was still parked in the street outside.

'Well? Didn't you arrest her?' he asked in a disappointed voice. 'I thought . . .'

Maigret had to walk all the way to the station before he could find a taxi to take him back to the stone bridge.

7. The Bent Pedal

When the inspector overtook the *Southern Cross*, whose wash left the reeds swaying long after it had passed, the colonel was still at the wheel, and Vladimir, in the bow, was coiling a rope.

Maigret waited for the yacht at Aigny lock. The boat entered it smoothly, and, when it was made fast, the Russian got off to take his papers to the lock-keeper and give him his tip.

The inspector approached him and said: 'This cap belongs to you, doesn't it?'

Vladimir examined the cap, which was now dirty and ragged, then looked up at him.

'Thank you,' he said after a moment and took the cap.

'Just a moment! Can you tell me where you lost it?'

The colonel had been watching them carefully, without showing the least trace of emotion.

'I dropped it in the water last night,' Vladimir explained. 'I was leaning over the stern with a boat hook, clearing weeds which had fouled the propeller. There was a barge behind us. The woman was kneeling in their dinghy, doing her washing. She fished out my cap, and I left it on the deck to dry.'

'So it was left out all night on the deck.'

'Yes. This morning I didn't notice it was gone.'

'Was it already as dirty as this yesterday?'

'No! When the woman on the barge fished it out she put it in her wash with the rest.'

The yacht was rising by degrees. The lock-keeper already had both hands on the handle of the upper sluice gate.

'If I remember correctly, the boat behind you was the *Providence*, wasn't it?'

'I think so. I haven't seen it today.'

Maigret turned away with a vague wave of his hand then walked to his bicycle, while the colonel, as inscrutable as ever, engaged the motor and nodded to him as he passed through the lock.

The inspector remained where he was for a while, watching the yacht leave, thinking, puzzled by the astonishing ease and speed with which things happened on board the *Southern Cross*.

The yacht went on its way without paying any attention to him. The most that happened was that the colonel, from the wheel, asked the Russian the occasional question. The Russian returned short answers.

'Has the *Providence* got very far?' asked Maigret.

'She's maybe in the reach above Juvigny, five kilometres from here. She don't go as fast as that beauty there.'

Maigret reached there a few minutes before the *Southern Cross*, and from a distance Vladimir must have seen him talking to the bargee's wife.

The details she gave were clear. The day before, while doing her washing, which she then hung out on a line stretched across the barge, where it could be seen ballooning in the wind, she had indeed rescued the Russian's cap. Later, the man had given her little boy two francs.

It was now four in the afternoon. The inspector got back on his bike, his head filled with a jumble of speculations. The gravel of the towpath crunched under the tyres. His wheels parted the grit into furrows.

When he got to Lock 9, Maigret had a good lead over the Englishman.

'Can you tell me where the *Providence* is at this moment?'

'Not far off Vitry-le-François . . . They're making good time. They've got a good pair of horses and especially a carter who is no slouch.'

'Did they look as if they were in a hurry?'

'No more or less than usual. Oh, everybody's always in a hurry on the canal. You never know what might happen next. You can be held up for hours at a lock or go through in ten minutes. And the faster you travel the more money you earn.'

'Did you hear anything unusual last night?'

'No, nothing. Why? What happened?'

Maigret left without answering and from now on stopped at every lock, every boat.

He'd had no trouble making his mind up about Gloria Negretti. Though she'd done her level best to avoid saying anything damaging about the colonel, she had told everything she knew.

She was incapable of holding back! And equally incapable of lying! Otherwise, she would have made up a much more complicated tale.

So she really had heard Sir Walter ask Vladimir to find out about the *Providence*.

The inspector had also started to take an interest in the barge which had come from Meaux on Sunday evening, just before Mary Lampson was murdered. It was wood-built and treated with pitch and tar. Why did the colonel want to catch up with it? What was the connection between the *Southern Cross* and the heavy barge which could not go faster than the slow pace set by two horses?

As Maigret rode along the canal through monotonous countryside, pushing down harder and harder on the pedals, he came up with a number of hypotheses. But they led to conclusions which were fragmentary or implausible.

But hadn't the matter of the three clues been cleared up by Madame Negretti's furious accusations?

Maigret tried a dozen times to piece together the movements of all concerned during the previous night, about which nothing was known, except for the fact that Willy was dead.

Each time he tried, he was left with a poor fit, a gap. He had the impression that there was a person missing who was not the colonel, nor the dead man, nor Vladimir.

And now the *Southern Cross* was on the trail of someone on board the *Providence*.

Someone obviously who was mixed up in recent events! Could it be assumed that this someone had had a hand in the second crime, that is, in the murder of Willy, as well as in the first?

A lot of ground can be covered quickly at night on a canal towpath, by a bike for example.

'Did you hear anything last night? Did you notice anything unusual on the *Providence* when it passed through?'

It was laborious, discouraging work, especially in the drizzling rain that fell out of the low clouds.

'No, nothing.'

The gap between Maigret and the *Southern Cross*, which lost a minimum of twenty minutes at each lock, grew wider. The inspector kept getting back on his bicycle with growing weariness and, as he pedalled through a deserted reach of the canal, stubbornly picked up the threads of his reasoning.

He had already covered forty kilometres when the lock-keeper at Sarry said, in answer to his question:

'My dog barked. I think something must have happened on the road. A rabbit running past, maybe? I just went back to sleep.'

'Any idea where the *Providence* stopped last night?'

The man did a calculation in his head.

'Hang on a minute. I wouldn't be surprised if she hadn't got as far as Pogny. The skipper wanted to be at Vitry-le-François tonight.'

Another two locks. Result: nothing! Maigret now had to follow the lock-keepers on to their gates, for the further he went the busier the traffic became. At Vésigneul, three boats were waiting their turn. At Pogny, there were five.

'Noises, no,' grumbled the man in charge of the lock there. 'But I'd like to know what swine had the nerve to use my bike!'

The inspector had time to wipe the sweat from his face now that he had a glimpse of what looked like light at the end of the tunnel. He was breathing hard and was hot. He had just ridden fifty kilometres without once stopping for a beer.

'Where is your bike now?'

'Open the sluices, will you, François?' the lock-keeper shouted to a carter.

He led Maigret to his house. The outside door opened straight into the kitchen, where men from the boats were drinking white wine which was being poured by a woman who did not put her baby down.

'You're not going to report us, are you? Selling alcohol isn't allowed. But everybody does it. It's just to do people a good turn. Here we are.'

He pointed to a lean-to made of wooden boards clinging to one side of the house. It had no door.

'Here's the bike. It's the wife's. Can you imagine, the nearest grocer's is four kilometres from here? I'm always telling her to bring the bike in for the night. But she says it makes a mess in the house. But I'll say that whoever used it must be a rum sort. I would never have noticed it myself . . .

'But as a matter of fact, the day before yesterday, my nephew, who's a mechanic at Rheims, was here for the day. The chain was broken. He mended it and at the same time cleaned the bike and oiled it.

'Yesterday no one used it. Oh, and he'd put a new tyre on the back wheel.

'Well, this morning, it was clean, though it had rained all night. And you've seen all that mud on the towpath.

'But the left pedal is bent, and the tyre looks as if it's done at least a hundred kilometres.

'What do you make of it? The bike's been a fair old way, no question. And whoever brought it back took the trouble to clean it.'

'Which boats were moored hereabouts?'

'Let me see . . . The *Madeleine* must have gone to La Chaussée, where the skipper's brother-in-law runs a bistro. The *Miséricorde* was tied up here, under the lock . . .'

'On its way from Dizy?'

'No, she's going downstream. Came from the Saône. I think there was just the *Providence*. She passed through last night around seven. Went on to Omey, two kilometres further along. There's good mooring there.'

'Do you have another bike?'

'No. But this one is still rideable.'

'No it isn't. You're going to have to lock it up somewhere. Hire another one if you need to. Can I count on you?'

The barge men were coming out of the kitchen. One of them called to the lock-keeper.

'Deserting your mates, Désiré?'

'Half a tick, I'm with this gentleman.'

'Where do you think I can catch up with the *Providence*?'

'Lemme see. She'll still be making pretty good time. I'd be surprised if you'd be up with her before Vitry.'

Maigret was about to leave. But he turned, came back, took a spanner from his tool bag and removed both pedals from the lock-keeper's wife's bicycle.

As he set off, the pedals he had pushed into his pockets made two unsightly bulges in his jacket.

The lock-keeper at Dizy had said to him jokingly:

'When it's dry everywhere else, there are at least two places where you can be sure of seeing rain: here and Vitry-le-François.'

Maigret was now getting near Vitry, and it was starting to rain again, a fine, lazy, never-ending drizzle.

The look of the canal was now changing. Factories appeared on both banks, and the inspector rode for some time through a swarm of mill girls emerging from one of them.

There were boats almost everywhere, some being unloaded, while others, which were lying up having their bilges emptied, were waiting.

And here again were the small houses which marked the outskirts of a town, with rabbit hutches made from old packing-cases and pitiful gardens.

Every kilometre there was a cement works or a quarry or a lime kiln. The rain mixed the white powder drifting in the air into the mud of the towpath. The cement dust left a film on everything, on the tiled roofs, the apple trees and the grass.

Maigret had started to weave right to left and left to right the way tired cyclists do. He was thinking thoughts, but not joined-up thoughts. He was putting ideas together in such ways that they could not be linked to make a solid picture.

When he at last saw the lock at Vitry-le-François, the growing dusk was flecked with the white navigation lights of a string of maybe sixty boats lined up in Indian file.

Some were overtaking others, some were hove to broadside on. When barges came from the opposite direction, the crew members exchanged shouts, curses and snippets of news as they passed.

'Ahoy, there, *Simoun*! Your sister-in-law, who was at Chalon-sur-Saône, says she'll catch up with you on the Burgundy canal . . . They'll hold back the christening . . . Pierre says all the best!'

By the lock gates a dozen figures were moving about busily.

And above it all hung a bluish, rain-filled mist, and through it could be seen the shapes of horses which had halted and men going from one boat to another.

Maigret read the names on the sterns of the boats. One voice called to him:

'Hello, inspector!'

It was a moment or two before he recognized the master of the *Éco-III*.

'Got your problem sorted?'

'It was something and nothing! My mate's a dimwit. The mechanic, who came all the way from Rheims, fixed it in five minutes.'

'You haven't seen the *Providence*, have you?'

'She's up ahead. But we'll be through before her. On account of the logjam, they'll be putting boats through the lock all tonight and maybe tomorrow night as well. Fact is there are at least sixty boats here, and more keep coming. As a rule, boats with engines have right of way and go before horse-boats. But this time, the powers that be have decided to let horse barges and motorized boats take turns.'

A friendly kind of man, with an open face, he pointed with one arm.

'There you go! Just opposite that crane. I recognize its white tiller.'

As he rode past the line of barges, he could make out people through open hatches eating by the yellow light of oil-lamps.

Maigret found the master of the *Providence* on the lock-side, arguing with other watermen.

'No way should there be special rules for boats with engines! Take the *Marie*, for example. We can gain a kilometre on her in a five-kilometre stretch. But what happens? With this priority system of theirs, she'll go through before us . . . Well, look who's here . . . it's the inspector!'

And the small man held out his hand, as if greeting a friend.

'Back with us again? The wife's on board. She'll be glad to see you. She said that, for a policeman, you're all right.'

In the dark, the ends of cigarettes glowed red, and the lights on the boats seemed so densely packed together that it was a mystery how they could move at all.

Maigret found the skipper's fat wife straining her soup. She wiped her hand on her apron before she held it out to him.

'Have you found the murderer?'

'Unfortunately no. But I came to ask a few more questions.'

'Sit down. Fancy a drop of something?'

'No thanks.'

'Go on, say yes! Look, in weather like this it can't do any harm. Don't tell me you've come from Dizy on a bike?'

'All the way from Dizy.'

'But it's sixty-eight kilometres!'

'Is your carter here?'

'He's most likely out on the lock, arguing. They want to take our turn. We can't let them push us around, not now. We've lost enough time already.'

'Does he own a bike?'

'Who, Jean? No!'

She laughed and, resuming her work, she explained:

'I can't see him getting on a bike, not with those little legs! My husband's got one. But he hasn't ridden a bike for over a year. Anyway I think the tyres have got punctures.'

'You spent last night at Omey?'

'That's right! We always try to stay in a place where I can buy my groceries. Because if, worse luck, you have to make a stop during the day, there are always boats that will pass you and get ahead.'

'What time did you get there?'

'Around this time of day. We go more by the sun than by clock time, if you follow me. Another little drop? It's gin. We bring some back from Belgium every trip.'

'Did you go to the shop?'

'Yes, while the men went for a drink. It must have been about eight when we went to bed.'

'Was Jean in the stable?'

'Where else would he have been? He's only happy when he's with his horses.'

'Did you hear any noises during the night?'

'Not a thing. At three, as usual, Jean came and made the coffee. It's our routine. Then we set off.'

'Did you notice anything unusual?'

'What sort of thing do you mean? Don't tell me you suspect poor old Jean? I know he can seem a bit, well, funny, when you don't know him. But he's been with us now for eight years, and I tell you, if he went, the *Providence* wouldn't be the same!'

'Does your husband sleep with you?'

She laughed again. And since Maigret was within range, she gave him a sharp dig in the ribs.

'Get away! Do we look as old as that?'

'Could I have a look inside the stable?'

'If you want. Take the lantern. It's on deck. The horses are still out because we're still hoping to go through tonight. Once we get to Vitry, we'll be fine. Most boats go down the Marne canal to the Rhine. It's a lot quieter on the run to the Saône – except for the culvert, which is eight kilometres long and always scares me stiff.'

Maigret made his way by himself towards the middle of the barge, where the stable loomed. Taking the storm lantern, which did service as a navigation light, he slipped quietly into Jean's private domain, which was full of a strong smell of horse manure and leather.

But his search was fruitless, though he squelched around in it for a quarter of an hour, during which time he could hear every word of what the skipper of the *Providence* was discussing on the wharf-side with the other men from the barges.

When a little while later he walked to the lock, where, to make up lost time, all hands were working together amid the screech of rusty crank-handles turning and the roar of roiling water, he spotted the carter at one of the gates, his horse whip coiled round his neck like a necklace, operating a sluice.

He was dressed as he had been at Dizy, in an old suit of ribbed corduroy and a faded slouch hat which had lost its band an age ago. A barge was emerging from the lock chamber, propelled by means of boat hooks because there was no other way of moving forward through the tangle of boats. The voices that called from one barge to another were rough and irritable, and the faces, lit at intervals by a navigation light, were deeply marked by fatigue.

All these people had been on the go since three or four in the morning and now had only one thought: a meal followed by a bed on to which they would at last be able to drop.

But they all wanted to be first through the congested lock so that they would be in the right place to start the next day's haul. The lock-keeper was everywhere, snatching up documents here and there as he passed through the crowd, dashing back to his office to sign and stamp them, and stuffing his tips into his pocket.

'Excuse me!'

Maigret had tapped the carter on the arm. The man turned slowly, stared with eyes that were hardly visible under his thicket of eyebrows.

'Have you got any other boots than the ones you've got on?'

Jean didn't seem to understand the words. His face wrinkled up even more. He stared at his feet in bewilderment.

Eventually he shook his head, removed his pipe from his mouth and muttered:

'Other boots?'

'Have you just got those, the ones you're wearing now?'

A yes, nodded very slowly.

'Can you ride a bike?'

A crowd started to gather, intrigued by their conversation.

'Come with me!' said Maigret. 'I want a word.'

The carter followed him back to the *Providence*, which was moored 200 metres away. As he walked past his horses, which stood, heads hanging, rumps glistening, he patted the nearest one on the neck.

'Come on board.'

The skipper, small and puny, bent double over a boat hook driven into the bottom of the canal, was pushing the vessel closer to the bank to allow a barge going downstream to pass.

He saw the two men step into the stable but had no time to wonder what was happening.

'Did you sleep here last night?'

A grunt that meant yes.

'All night? You didn't borrow a bike from the lock-keeper at Pogny, did you?'

The carter had the unhappy, cowering look of a simpleton who is being tormented or a dog which has always been well treated and then brutally thrashed for no good reason.

He raised one hand and pushed his hat back, scratching his head through his white mop, which grew as coarse as horse hair.

'Take off your boots.'

The man did not budge but looked out at the bank, where the legs of his horses were visible. One of them whinnied, as if it knew the carter was in some sort of trouble.

'Boots! And quick about it!'

And joining the action to the word, Maigret made Jean sit down on the plank which ran along the whole length of one wall of the stable.

Only then did the old man become amenable. Giving his tormentor a look of reproach, he set about removing one of his boots.

He was not wearing socks. Instead, strips of canvas steeped in tallow grease were wound round his feet and ankles, seeming to merge with his flesh.

The lantern shed only a dim light. The skipper, who had completed his manoeuvre, came forward and squatted on the deck so that he could see what was going on inside the stable.

While Jean, grumbling, scowling and bad-tempered, lifted his other leg, Maigret was using a handful of straw to clean the sole of the boot he held in his hand.

He took the left pedal from his pocket and held it against the boot.

A bemused old man staring at his bare feet made a strange sight. His trousers, which either had been made for a man even shorter than he was or had been altered, stopped not quite halfway down his calf.

And the strips of canvas greasy with tallow were blackish and pock-marked with wisps of straw and dirty sweepings.

Maigret stood close to the lantern and held the pedal, from

which some of the metal teeth were missing, against faint marks on the leather.

'Last night, at Pogny, you took the lock-keeper's bike,' he said, making the accusation slowly, without taking his eyes off the two objects in his hands. 'How far did you ride?'

'Ahoy! *Providence*! . . . Move up! . . . The *Étourneau* is giving up its turn and will be spending the night here, in the lower reach.'

Jean turned and looked at the men who were now rushing about outside and then at the inspector.

'You can go and help get the boat through the lock,' said Maigret. 'Here! Put your boots on.'

The skipper was already pushing on his boat hook. His wife appeared:

'Jean! The horses! If we miss out turn . . .'

The carter had thrust his feet into his boots, was now on deck and was crooning in a strange voice:

'Hey! . . . Hey! . . . Hey up!'

The horses snorted and began moving forward. He jumped on to the bank, fell into step with them, treading heavily, his whip still wound round his shoulders.

'Hey! . . . Hey up!'

While her husband was heaving on the boat hook, the bargee's wife leaned on the tiller with all her weight to avoid colliding with a barge which was bearing down on them from the opposite direction, all that was visible of it being its rounded bows and the halo around its stern light.

The voice of the lock-keeper was heard shouting impatiently:

'Come on! . . . Where's the *Providence*? . . . What are you waiting for?'

The barge slid silently over the black water. But it bumped the lock wall three times before squeezing into the chamber and completely filling its width.

8. *Ward* 10

Normally, the four sluices of any lock are opened one after the other, gradually, to avoid creating a surge strong enough to break the boat's mooring ropes.

But sixty barges were waiting. Masters and mates whose turn was coming up helped with the operation, leaving the lock-keeper free to take care of the paperwork.

Maigret was on the side of the lock, holding his bicycle in one hand, watching the shadowy figures as they worked feverishly in the darkness. The two horses had continued on then stopped fifty metres further along from the upper gates, all by themselves. Jean was turning one of the crank handles.

The water rushed in, roaring like a torrent. It was visible, a foaming white presence, in the narrow gaps left vacant by the *Madeleine*.

But just as the cascading water was running most strongly, there was a muffled cry followed by a thud on the bow of the barge, which was followed by an unexplained commotion.

The inspector sensed rather than understood what was happening. The carter was no longer at his post, by the gate. Men were running along the walls. They were all shouting at the same time.

To light the scene there were only two lamps, one in the middle of the lift-bridge at the front of the lock and one on the barge, which was now rising rapidly in the chamber.

'Close the sluices!'

'Open the gates!'

Someone passed across an enormous boat hook, which caught Maigret a solid blow on the cheek.

Men from even distant boats came running. The lock-keeper

came out of his house, shaking at the thought of his responsibilities.

'What's happened?'

'The old man . . .'

On each side of the barge, between its hull and the wall, there was less than a foot of clear water. This water, which came in torrents through the sluices, rushed down into those narrow channels then turned back on itself in a boiling mass.

Mistakes were made: for instance, when someone closed one sluice of the upper gate, which protested noisily and threatened to come off its hinges until the lock-keeper arrived to correct the error.

Only later was the inspector told that the whole lower stretch of canal could have been flooded and fifty barges damaged.

'Can you see him?'

'There's something dark. Down there!'

The barge was still rising, but more slowly now. Three sluices out of four had been closed. But the boat kept swinging, rubbing against the walls of the chamber and maybe crushing the carter.

'How deep is the water?'

'There's at least a metre under the boat.'

It was a horrible sight. In the faint light from the stable lamp, the bargee's wife could be seen running in all directions, holding a lifebuoy.

Visibly distressed, she was shouting:

'I don't think he can swim!'

Maigret heard a sober voice close by him say:

'Just as well! He won't have suffered as much . . .'

This went on for a quarter of an hour. Three times people thought they saw a body rising in the water. But boat hooks were directed to those places in the water, with no result.

The *Madeleine* moved slowly out of the lock, and one old carter muttered:

'I'll bet whatever you fancy that he's got caught under the tiller! I seen it happen once before, at Verdun.'

He was wrong. The barge had hardly come to a stop not fifty metres away before the men who were feeling all round the lower gates with a long pole shouted for help.

In the end, they had to use a dinghy. They could feel something in the water, about a metre down. And just as one man was about to dive in, while his tearful wife tried to stop him, a body suddenly burst on to the surface.

It was hauled out. A dozen hands grabbed for the badly torn corduroy jacket, which had been snagged on one of the gate's projecting bolts.

The rest unfolded like a nightmare. The telephone was heard ringing in the lock-keeper's house. A boy was despatched on a bicycle to fetch a doctor.

But it was no good. The body of the old carter was scarcely laid on the bank, motionless and seemingly lifeless, before a barge hand removed his jacket, knelt over the impressive chest of the drowned man and began applying traction to his tongue.

Someone had brought the lantern. The man's body seemed shorter, more thick-set than ever, and his face, dripping wet and streaked with sludge, had lost all colour.

'He moved! I tell you, he moved!'

There was no pushing or jostling. The silence was so intense that every word resounded as voices do in a cathedral. And underscoring it was the never-ending gush of water escaping through a badly closed sluice.

'How's he doing?' asked the lock-keeper as he returned.

'He moved. But not much.'

'Best get a mirror.'

The master of the *Madeleine* hurried away to get one from his boat. Sweat was pouring off the man applying artificial respiration, so someone else took over, and pulled even harder on the waterlogged man's tongue.

There was news that the doctor had arrived. He had come by car along a side road. By then, everyone could see old Jean's chest slowly rising and falling.

His jacket had been removed. His open shirt revealed a chest as hairy as a wild animal's. Under the right nipple was a long scar, and Maigret thought he could make out a kind of tattoo on his shoulder.

'Next boat!' shouted the lock-keeper, cupping both hands to his mouth. 'Look lively, there's nothing more you can do here.'

One bargee drifted regretfully away, calling to his wife, who had joined some other women a little further off in their commiserations.

'I hope at least that you didn't stop the engine?'

The doctor told the spectators to stand well back and scowled as he felt the man's chest.

'He's alive, isn't he?' said the first life-saver proudly.

'Police Judiciaire!' broke in Maigret. 'Is it serious?'

'Most of his ribs are crushed. He's alive all right, but I'd be surprised if he stays alive for very long! Did he get caught between two boats?'

'Most probably between a boat and the lock.'

'Feel here!'

The doctor made the inspector feel the left arm, which was broken in two places.

'Is there a stretcher?'

The injured man moaned feebly.

'All the same, I'm going to give him an injection. But get that stretcher ready as quick as you can. The hospital is 500 metres away . . .'

There was a stretcher at the lock. It was regulations. But it was in the attic, where the flame of a candle was observed through a skylight moving to and fro.

The mistress of the *Providence* stood sobbing some distance from Maigret. She was staring at him reproachfully.

There were ten men ready to carry the carter, who gave another groan. Then a lantern moved off in the direction of the main road, catching the group in a halo of light. A motorized barge, bright with green and red navigation lights, gave three whistles and moved off on its way to tie up at a berth in the middle of town, so that she would be the first to leave next morning.

Ward 10. It was by chance that Maigret saw the number. There were only two patients in it, one of whom was crying like a baby.

The inspector spent most of the time walking up and down the white-flagged corridor, where nurses ran by him, passing on instruction in hushed voices.

Ward 8, exactly opposite, was full of women who were talking about the new patient and assessing his chances.

'If they're putting him in Ward 10 . . .'

The doctor was plump and wore horn-rimmed glasses. He walked by two or three times in a white coat, without speaking to Maigret.

It was almost eleven when he finally stopped to have a word.

'Do you want to see him?'

It was a disconcerting sight. The inspector hardly recognized old Jean. He had been shaved so that two gashes, one on his cheek and the other on his forehead, could be treated.

He lay there, looking very clean in a white bed in the neutral glare of a frosted-glass lamp.

The doctor lifted the sheet.

'Take a look at this for a carcass! He's built like a bear. I don't think I ever saw a skeletal frame like it. How did he get in this state?'

'He fell off the lock gate just as the sluices were being opened.'

'I see. He must have been caught between the wall and the barge. His chest is literally crushed in. The ribs just gave way.'

'And the rest?'

'My colleagues and I will examine him tomorrow, if he's still alive. We'll have to go carefully. One wrong move would kill him.'

'Has he regained consciousness?'

'No idea. That's perhaps the most surprising thing. A while back, as I was examining his cuts, I had the very clear impression that his eyes were half open and that he was watching me. But when I looked straight at him, he lowered his eyelids . . . He hasn't been delirious. All he does is groan from time to time.'

'His arm?'

'Not serious. The double fracture has already been reduced. But you can't put a whole chest back together the way you can a humerus. Where's he from?'

'I don't know.'

'I ask because he has some very strange tattoos. I've seen African Battalion tattoos, but they aren't like those. I'll show you tomorrow after they've removed the strapping so we can examine him.'

A porter came to say that there were visitors outside who were insisting on seeing the patient. Maigret himself went down to the porter's lodge, where he found the skipper and his wife from the *Providence*. They were in their Sunday best.

'We can see him, can't we, inspector? It's all your fault, you know. You upset him with all your questions. Is he better?'

'He's better. The doctors will tell us more tomorrow.'

'Let me see him. Just a peep round the door. He was such a part of the boat.'

She didn't say 'of the family' but 'of the boat', and was that not perhaps even more touching?

Her husband brought up the rear, keeping out of the way, ill at ease in a blue serge suit, his scrawny neck poking out of a detachable celluloid collar.

'I advise you not to make any noise.'

They both looked in at him, from the corridor. From there all they could see was a vague shape under a sheet, an ivory oval instead of a face, a lock of white hair.

The skipper's wife looked as if she was about to burst in at any moment.

'Listen, if we offered to pay, would he get better treatment?'

She didn't dare open her handbag there and then but she kept fidgeting with it.

'There are hospitals, aren't there, where if you pay? . . . The other patients haven't got anything catching, I hope?'

'Are you staying at Vitry?'

'We're not going home without him that's for sure! Blow the cargo! What time can we come tomorrow morning?'

'Ten o'clock!' broke in the doctor, who had been listening impatiently.

'Is there anything we can bring for him? A bottle of champagne? Spanish grapes?'

'We'll see he gets everything he needs.'

The doctor directed them towards the porter's lodge. When she got there, the skipper's wife, who had a good heart, reached furtively into her handbag and pulled out a ten-franc note and slipped it into the hand of the porter, who looked at her in astonishment.

Maigret got to bed at midnight, after telegraphing Dizy with instructions to forward whatever communications might be sent to him there.

At the last moment, he'd learned that the *Southern Cross*, by overtaking most of the barges, had reached Vitry-le-François and was moored at the end of the queue of waiting boats.

The inspector had found a room at the Hotel de la Marne in town. It was a fair way from the canal. There he was free of the atmosphere he had lived in for the last few days.

A number of guests, all commercial travellers, sat playing cards.

One of them, who had arrived after the others, said:

'Seems like someone got drowned in the lock.'

'Want to make a fourth? Lamperrière's losing hand over fist. The man's dead, is he?'

'Don't know.'

And that was all. The landlady dozed by the till. The waiter scattered sawdust on the floor and, last thing, banked up the stove for the night.

There was a bathroom, just one. The bath had lost areas of its enamel. Even so, next morning at eight, Maigret used it, and then sent the waiter out to buy him a new shirt and collar.

But as the time wore on, he grew impatient. He was anxious to get back to the canal. Hearing a boat hooting, he asked:

'Was that for the lock?'

'No, the lift-bridge. There are three in town.'

The sky was overcast. The wind had got up. He could not find the way back to the hospital and had to ask several people, because all roads invariably led him back to the market square.

The hospital porter recognized him. As he walked out to meet him, he said:

'Who'd have believed it? I ask you!'

'What? Is he alive? Dead?'

'What? You haven't heard? The super's just phoned your hotel . . .'

'Out with it!'

'Gone! Flown the coop! The doctor reckons it's not possible, says he can't have gone a hundred metres in the state he was in . . . Maybe, but the fact is he's not here!'

The inspector heard voices coming from the garden at the rear of the building and hurried off towards the sound.

There he found an old man he had never seen before. It was the hospital superintendent, and he was speaking sternly to the doctor from the previous evening and a nurse with ginger hair.

'I swear! . . .' the doctor said several times. 'You know as well as I do what it's like . . . When I say ten broken ribs that's very likely an underestimate . . . And that's leaving aside the effects of submersion, concussion . . .'

'How did he get out?' asked Maigret.

He was shown a window almost two metres above ground level. In the soil underneath it were the prints of two bare feet and a large scuff mark which suggested that the carter had fallen flat on the ground as he landed.

'There! The nurse, Mademoiselle Berthe, spent all night on the duty desk, as usual. She didn't hear anything. Around three o'clock she had to attend to a patient in Ward 8 and looked in on Ward 10. All the lights were out. It was all quiet. She can't say whether the man was still in his bed.'

'How about the other two patients?'

'There's one who's got to be trepanned. It's urgent. We're waiting now for the surgeon. The other one slept through.'

Maigret's eyes followed the trail, which led to a flower-bed where a small rose bush had been flattened.

'Do the front gates stay open at night?'

'This isn't a prison!' snapped the superintendent. 'How are we supposed to know if a patient is going to jump out of the window? Only the main door to the building was locked, as it always is.'

There was no point in looking for footprints or any other tracks. For the area was paved. In the gap between two houses, the double row of trees lining the canal was visible.

'To be perfectly frank,' added the doctor, 'I was pretty sure we'd find him dead this morning. Once it was clear there was nothing more we could try . . . that's when I decided to put him in Ward 10.'

He was belligerent now, for the criticisms the superintendent had directed at him still rankled.

For a while, Maigret circled the garden, like a circus horse, then suddenly, signalling his departure by tugging the brim of his bowler, he strode away in the direction of the lock.

The *Southern Cross* was just entering the chamber. Vladimir, with the skill of an experienced sailor, looped a mooring rope over a bollard with one throw and stopped the boat dead.

Meanwhile, the colonel, wearing a long oilskin coat and his white cap, stood impassively at the small wheel.

'Ready the gates!' cried the lock-keeper.

There were now no more than twenty boats to be got through.

Maigret pointed to the yacht and asked: 'Is it their turn?'

'It is and it isn't. If you class her as a motorboat, then she has right of way over horse-drawn boats. But as she's a pleasure boat . . . Truth is, so few of them pass this way that we don't go much by the regulations. Still, since they saw the bargees right . . .'

The bargees in question were now operating the sluices.

'And the *Providence*?'

'She was holding everything up. This morning she went and moored a hundred metres further along, at the bend this side of the second bridge. Any news of the old feller? This business could set me back a pretty penny. But I'd like to see you try it! Officially, I'm supposed to lock them all myself. If I did that, there'd be a hundred of them queuing up every day. Four gates! Sixteen sluices! And do you know how much I get paid?'

He was called away briefly when Vladimir came to him with his papers and the tip.

Maigret made the most of the interruption to set off along the canal bank. At the bend he saw the *Providence*, which by now he could have picked out from any distance among a hundred barges.

A few curls of smoke rose from the chimney. There was no one about on deck. All hatches and doors were closed.

He almost walked up the aft plank which gave access to the crew's quarters.

But he changed his mind and instead went on board by the wide gangway which was used for taking the horses on and off.

One of the wooden panels over the stable had been slid open. The head of one of the horses showed above it, sniffing the wind.

Maigret looked down through it and made out a dark shape lying on straw. And close by, the skipper's wife was crouching with a bowl of coffee in one hand.

Her manner was motherly and oddly gentle. She murmured:

'Come on, Jean! Drink it up while it's hot. It'll do you good, silly old fool! Want me to raise your head up?'

But the man lying by her side did not move. He was looking up at the sky.

And against the sky Maigret's head stood out. The man must have seen him.

The inspector had the impression that on that face latticed with strips of sticking plaster there lurked a contented, ironic, even pugnacious smile.

The old carter tried to raise one hand to push away the cup which the woman was holding close to his lips. But it fell back again weakly, gnarled, calloused, spotted with small blue dots which must have been the vestiges of old tattoos.

9. The Doctor

'See? He's come back to his burrow. Dragged himself, like an injured dog.'

Did the skipper's wife realize how seriously ill the man was?

Either way, she did not seem to be unduly concerned. She was as calm as if she were caring for a child with 'flu.

'Coffee won't do him any harm, will it? But he won't take anything. It must have been four in the morning when me and my husband were woken up by a lot of noise on board . . . I got the revolver and told him to follow me with the lantern.

'Believe it or not, it was Jean, more or less the way he is now . . . He must have fallen down in here from the deck . . . It's almost two metres.

'At first, we couldn't see very well. For a moment, I thought he was dead.

'My husband wanted to call the neighbours, to help us carry him and lie him down on a bed. But Jean twigged. He started gripping my hand, and did he squeeze! It was like he was hanging on to me for dear life!

'And I saw he was starting to, well, whimper.

'I knew what he was saying. Because he's been with us for eight years, you know. He can't speak. But I think he understands what I say to him. Isn't that right, Jean? Does it hurt?'

It was difficult to know whether the injured man's eyes were bright with intelligence or fever.

She removed a wisp of straw which was touching the man's ear.

'My life, you know, is my home, my pots and pans, my sticks of furniture. I think that if they gave me a palace to live in, I'd be as miserable as sin living in it.

'Jean's life is his stable . . . and his horses! Of course, there's always days, you know, when we don't move because we're unloading. Jean don't have any part in that. So he could go off to some bar.

'But no! He comes back and lies down, just here. He makes sure that the sun can get in . . .'

In his mind, Maigret imagined himself stretched out where the carter was lying, saw the pitch-covered wall on his right, the whip hanging from one twisted nail, the tin cup on another, a patch of sky through the hatch overhead and, to the right, the well-muscled hindquarters of the horses.

The whole place exuded animal warmth, a dense, many-layered vitality which caught the throat like the sharp-tasting wines produced by certain slopes.

'Will it be all right to leave him here, do you think?'

She motioned the inspector to join her outside. The lock was working at the same rate as the evening before. All around were the streets of the town, which were filled with a bustle that was alien to the canal.

'He's going to die, though, isn't he? What's he done? You can tell me. I couldn't say anything before, could I? For a start I don't know anything. Once, just once, my husband saw him with his shirt off when he wasn't looking. He saw the tattoos. They weren't like the ones some sailors have done. We thought the same thing as you would have . . .

'I think it made me even fonder of him for it. I told myself he couldn't be what he seemed, that he was on the run . . .

'I wouldn't have asked him about it for all the money in the world. You surely don't think it was him that killed that woman? If you do, listen: if he did do it, I'd say she asked for it!

'Jean is . . .'

She searched for the word that expressed her thought. It did not come.

'Right! I can hear my husband getting up. I packed him off back to bed. He's always had a weak chest. Do you think that if I made him some strong broth . . .'

'The doctors will be on their way. Meanwhile, maybe it would be best to . . .'

'Do they really have to come? They'll hurt him and spoil his last moments, which . . .'

'It cannot be avoided.'

'But he's so comfortable here with us! Can I leave you here for a minute? You won't bother him again, will you?'

Maigret gave a reassuring nod of his head, went back inside the stable and from his pocket took a small tin. It contained a pad impregnated with viscous black ink.

He still could not tell if the carter was fully conscious. His eyes were half open. The look in them was blank, calm.

But when the inspector lifted his right hand and pressed each finger one after the other against the pad, he had a split-second impression that the shadow of a smile flickered over his face.

He took the fingerprints on a sheet of paper, watched the dying man for a moment, as though he were expecting something to happen, looked one last time at the wooden walls and the rumps of the horses which were growing restive and impatient, then went outside.

Near the tiller, the bargee and his wife were drinking their morning *café au lait* fortified with dunked bread. They were looking his way. The *Southern Cross* was moored less than five metres from the *Providence.* There was no one on deck.

The previous evening, Maigret had left his bicycle at the lock. It was still there. Ten minutes later he was at the police station. He despatched an officer on a motorcycle to Épernay with instructions to transmit the fingerprints to Paris by belinograph.

When he was back on board the *Providence*, he had with him two doctors from the hospital with whom he had a difference of opinion.

The medics wanted their patient back. The skipper's wife was alarmed and looked pleadingly at Maigret.

'Do you think you can pull him through?'

'No. His chest has been crushed. One rib has pierced his right lung.'

'How long will he live for?'

'Most people would be dead already! An hour, maybe five . . .'

'Then let him be!'

The old man had not moved, had not even winced. As Maigret passed in front of the wife of the skipper, she touched his hand, shyly, her way of showing her gratitude.

The doctors walked down the gangplank, looking very unhappy.

'Leaving him to die in a stable!' grumbled one.

'Yes, but they also let him live in one . . .'

Even so, the inspector posted a uniformed officer near the barge and the yacht, with orders to inform him if anything happened.

From the lock he phoned the Café de la Marine at Dizy, where he was told that Inspector Lucas had just passed through and that he had hired a car at Épernay to drive him to Vitry-le-François.

Then there was a good hour when nothing happened. The master of the *Providence* used the time to apply a coat of tar to the dinghy he towed behind the barge. Vladimir polished the brasses on the *Southern Cross*.

Meanwhile the skipper's wife was constantly on deck, toing and froing between the galley and the stable. Once, she was observed carrying a dazzlingly white pillow. Another time it was a bowl of steaming liquid, doubtless the broth which she had insisted on making.

Around eleven, Lucas arrived at the Hotel de la Marne, where Maigret was waiting for him.

'How's things, Lucas?'

'Good. You look tired, sir.'

'What did you find out?'

'Not a lot. At Meaux, I learned nothing except that the yacht caused a bit of a rumpus. The barge men couldn't sleep for all the music and singing and they were talking of smashing the yacht up.'

'Was the *Providence* there?'

'It loaded not twenty metres from the *Southern Cross*. But nobody noticed anything unusual.'

'And in Paris?'

'I saw the two girls again. They admitted it wasn't Mary Lampson who gave them the necklace but Willy Marco. I had it confirmed in the hotel, where they recognized his photo, but no one had seen Mary Lampson. I'm not sure but I think Lia Lauwenstein was closer to Willy than she's letting on and that she'd already been helping him in Nice.'

'And Moulins?'

'Not a thing. I went to see the baker's wife. She really is the only Marie Dupin in the whole area. A nice woman, straight as a die. She doesn't understand what's been happening and is worried that this business is not going to do her any good. The copy of the birth certificate was issued eight years ago. There's been a new clerk in the registry for the last three years, and the previous one died last year. They trawled through the archives but didn't come up with anything involving this particular document.'

After a silence, Lucas asked:

'How about you?'

'I don't know yet. Maybe nothing, maybe the jackpot. It could go one way or the other at any time. What are they saying at Dizy?'

'They reckon that if the *Southern Cross* hadn't been a yacht it wouldn't have been allowed to leave. There's also talk that the colonel has been married before.'

Saying nothing, Maigret led Lucas through the streets of the small town to the telegraph office.

'Give me Criminal Records in Paris.'

The belinogram with the carter's fingerprints should have reached the Prefecture two hours ago. After that, it was a matter of luck. Among 80,000 other sets, a match might be found straightaway, or it might take many hours.

'Listen with the earpiece, Lucas . . . Hello? . . . Who is this? . . . Is that you, Benoît? . . . Maigret here . . . Did you get the telephotograph I sent? . . . What's that? . . . You did the search yourself? . . . Just a moment.'

He left the call-booth and went up to the Post Office counter.

'I may need to stay on the line for quite some time. So please make absolutely sure I'm not cut off.'

When he picked up the receiver again, there was a gleam in his eye.

'Sit down, Benoît. You're going to give me everything in the files. Lucas is standing here next to me. He'll take notes. Go ahead . . .'

In his mind's eye, he could see his informant as clearly as if he had been standing next to him, for he was familiar with the offices located high in the attics of the Palais de Justice, where metal cabinets hold files on all the convicted felons in France and a good number of foreign-born gangsters.

'First, what's his name?'

'Jean-Évariste Darchambaux, born Boulogne, now aged fifty-five.'

Automatically Maigret tried to recall a case featuring the name, but already Benoît, pronouncing every syllable distinctly, had resumed, and Lucas was busy scribbling.

'Doctor of medicine. Married a Céline Mornet, at Étampes. Moved to Toulouse, where he'd been a student. Then he moved around a lot . . . Still there, inspector?'

'Still here. Carry on . . .'

'I've got the complete file, for the record card doesn't say much . . . The couple are soon up to their eyes in debt. Two years after he married, at twenty-seven, Darchambaux is accused of poisoning his aunt, Julia Darchambaux, who had come to live with them in Toulouse and disapproved of the kind of life he led. The aunt was pretty well off. The Darchambaux were her sole heirs.

'Inquiries lasted eight months, for no formal proof of guilt was ever found. Or at least the accused claimed – and some experts agreed with him – that the drugs prescribed for the old woman were not themselves harmful and that their use was an ambitious if extreme form of treatment.

'There was a lot of controversy . . . You don't want me to read out the reports, do you?

'The trial was stormy, and the judge had to clear the court several times. Most people thought he should be acquitted, especially after the doctor's wife had given evidence. She stood up and swore that her husband was innocent and that if he was sent to a penal settlement in the colonies, she would follow him there.'

'Was he found guilty?'

'Sentenced to fifteen years' hard labour . . . Now, don't hang up! That's everything in our files. But I sent an officer on a bike round to the Ministry of the Interior . . . He's just got back.'

He could be heard speaking to someone standing behind him, and then there was a sound of papers being shuffled.

'Here we are! But it doesn't amount to much. The governor of Saint-Laurent-du-Maroni in French Guiana wanted to give Darchambaux a job in one of the hospitals in the colony . . . He turned it down . . . good record . . . "docile" prisoner . . . just one attempt to escape with fifteen others who had talked him into it.

'Five years later, a new governor undertook what he called the "rehabilitation" of Darchambaux. But almost immediately he noted in the margin of his report that there was nothing about the man he had interviewed to connect him with the professional man he once had been nor even to a man with a certain level of education.

'Right! Has that got your attention?

'He was given a job as an orderly at Saint-Laurent but he applied to be sent back to the colony.

'He was quiet, stubborn and spoke little. One of the medical staff took an interest in his case. He examined him from a mental health point of view but was unable to come up with a diagnosis.

'"There is," he wrote, underlining the words in red ink, "a kind of progressive loss of intellectual function proceeding in parallel with a hypertrophy of physical capacity."

'Darchambaux stole twice. Both times he stole food. On the second occasion he stole from another prisoner on the chain gang, who stabbed him in the chest with a sharpened flint.

'Journalists passing through advised him to apply for a pardon, but he never did.

'When his fifteen years were up, he stayed in the place to which he had been transported and found a manual job in a saw mill, where he looked after the horses.

'He was forty-five and had done his time. Thereafter, there is no trace of him.'

'Is that everything?'

'I can send you the file. I've only given you a summary.'

'Anything on his wife? You said she was born at Étampes, didn't you? Anyway, thanks for all that, Benoît. No need to send the details. What you've told me is enough.'

When, followed by Lucas, he stepped out of the phone box, he was perspiring profusely.

'I want you to phone the town hall at Étampes. If Céline Mornet is dead, you'll know, or at least you will if she died under that name. Also check with Moulins if Marie Dupin had any family living at Étampes.'

He walked through the town, looking neither to left nor right, hands deep in his pockets. He had to wait for five minutes at the canal because the lift-bridge was up, and a heavily laden barge was barely moving, its flat hull scouring the mud on the canal bed which rose to the surface in a mass of bubbles.

When he reached the *Providence*, he had a word with the uniformed man he had posted on the towpath.

'You can stand down . . .'

He saw the colonel pacing up and down on the deck of his yacht.

The skipper's wife hurried towards him looking more agitated than she had been earlier that morning. There were damp streaks on her cheeks.

'Oh, inspector, it's terrible!'

Maigret went pale, and his face turned grim.

'Is he dead?' he asked.

'No! Don't say such things! Just now I was with him, by myself. Because I should explain that though he liked my husband, he liked me better.

'I'm a lot younger than him. But despite that, he thought of me sort of as a mother.

'We'd go weeks without speaking. All the same . . . I'll give you an example. Most of the time my husband forgets my birthday, Saint Hortense's Day. Well, for the last eight years, Jean never went once without giving me flowers. Sometimes, we'd be travelling through the middle of open fields, and I'd wonder where he'd managed to get hold of flowers there.

'And on those days he'd always put rosettes on the horses' blinkers.

'Anyhow, I was sat by him, thinking it was probably his last hours. My husband wanted to let the horses out. They're not used to being cooped up for so long.

'I said no. Because I was sure it meant a lot to Jean to have them there too.

'I held his big hand.'

She was weeping now. But not sobbing. She went on talking through the large tears which rolled down her mottled cheeks.

'I don't know how things came to be like that . . . I never had children myself. Though we'd always said we'd adopt when we reached the legal age.

'I told him it was nothing, that he'd get better, that we'd try to get a load for Alsace, where the countryside's a picture in summer.

'I felt his fingers squeezing mine. I couldn't tell him he was hurting me.

'It was then he started to talk.

'Can you understand it? A man like that who only yesterday was as strong as his horses. He opened his mouth, straining so much that the veins on the sides of his head went all purple and swelled up.

'I heard this growly sound, like an animal's cry it was.

'I told him to stay quiet. But he wouldn't listen. He sat up on the straw, how I'll never know. And he still kept opening his mouth.

'Blood came out of it and dribbled down his chin.

'I wanted to call my husband, but Jean was still holding me tight. He was frightening me.

'You can't imagine what it was like. I tried to understand. I asked: "You want something to drink? No? Want me to fetch somebody?"

'He was so frustrated that he couldn't say anything! I should have guessed what he meant. I did try.

'What do you reckon? What was he trying to ask me? And then it was as if something in his throat had burst, though it's no good asking me what. But he had a haemorrhage. In the end he lay down again, his mouth closed now, and on his broken arm too. It must have hurt like the very devil, but you wouldn't have thought he could feel anything.

'He just stared straight in front of him.

'I'd give anything to know what would make him happy before . . . before it's too late.'

Maigret walked to the stable in silence. He looked in through the open panel.

It was a sight as arresting, as unforgiving as watching the death of an animal with which there is no means of communicating.

The carter had curled up. He had partly torn away the strapping which the night doctor had placed around his torso.

Maigret could hear the faint, infrequent whispers of his breathing.

One of the horses had caught a hoof in its tether, but it stood absolutely still, as if it sensed that something grave was happening.

Maigret also hesitated. He thought of the dead woman buried

under the straw of the stable at Dizy, then of Willy's corpse floating in the canal and the men, in the cold of early morning, trying to haul him in with a boat hook.

One hand played with the Yacht Club de France badge in his pocket.

He also recalled the way the colonel had bowed to the examining magistrate and requested permission to go on his way in a toneless, cool voice.

In the mortuary at Épernay, in an icy room lined with metal drawers, like the vaults of a bank, two bodies lay waiting, each in a numbered box.

And in Paris, two young women with badly applied make-up wandered from bar to bar, dogged by their gnawing fears.

Then Lucas appeared.

'Well?' cried Maigret, when he was still some way off.

'There has been no sign of life from Céline Mornet at Étampes since the day she requested the papers she needed for her marriage to Darchambaux.'

The inspector gave Lucas an odd look.

'What's up?' said Lucas.

'Sh!'

Lucas looked all round him. He saw no one, nothing that might give cause for alarm.

Then Maigret led him to the open stable hatch and pointed to the prone figure on the straw.

The skipper's wife wondered what they were going to do. From a motorized vessel chugging past, a cheerful voice shouted:

'Everything all right? Broken down?'

She started crying again, though she couldn't have said why. Her husband clambered back on board, carrying the tar bucket in one hand and a brush in the other, and called from the stern:

'There's something burning on the stove!'

She went back to the galley in a daze. Maigret said to Lucas, almost reluctantly:

'Let's go in.'

One of the horses snickered quietly. The carter did not move.

The inspector had taken the photo of the dead woman from his wallet, but he did not look at it.

10. *The Two Husbands*

'Listen, Darchambaux.'

Maigret was standing over the carter of the *Providence* when he spoke the words, his eyes never leaving the man's face. His mind elsewhere, he had taken his pipe out of his pocket but made no attempt to fill it.

Had he got the reaction he had expected? Whether it was or not, he sat down heavily on the bench fixed to the stable wall, leaned forward, cupped his chin in both hands and went on in a different voice.

'Listen. No need to get upset. I know you can't talk.'

A shadow appearing unexpectedly on the straw made him look up. He saw the colonel standing on the deck of the barge, by the open hatch.

The Englishman did not move. He went on watching what was happening from above, his feet higher than the heads of all three men below.

Lucas stood to one side in so far as he could, given the restricted size of the stable. Maigret, more on edge now, went on:

'Nobody's going to take you away from here. Have you got that, Darchambaux? In a few moments, I shall leave. Madame Hortense will be here instead.'

It was a painful moment, though no one could have said exactly why. Without intending to, Maigret was speaking almost as gently as the skipper's wife.

'But first you have to answer a few questions. You can answer by blinking. Several people might be charged and arrested at any time now. That's not what you want, is it? So I need you to confirm the facts.'

While he spoke, the inspector did not take his eyes off the man, wondering who it was he had before him, the erstwhile doctor, the dour convict, the slow-witted carter or the brutal murderer of Mary Lampson.

The cast of face was rough, and the features coarse. But wasn't there a new expression in those eyes which excluded any hint of irony?

A look of infinite sadness.

Twice Jean tried to speak. And twice there was a sound like an animal moan and beads of pink saliva appeared on the dying man's lips.

Maigret could still see the shadow of the colonel's legs.

'When you were sent out to the penal settlement, all that time ago, you believed your wife would keep her promise and follow you there . . . It was her you killed at Dizy!'

Not a flicker! Nothing! The face acquired a greyish tinge.

'She didn't come . . . and you lost heart. You tried to forget everything, even who and what you were!'

Maigret was speaking more quickly now, driven by his impatience. He wanted it to be over. And above all he was afraid of seeing Jean slip away from him before this sickening interview was finished.

'You came across her by chance. By then you had become someone else. It happened at Meaux. Didn't it?'

He had to wait a good few moments before the carter, unresisting now, said yes by closing his eyes.

The shadow of the legs shifted. The whole barge rocked gently as a motor vessel passed by.

'And she hadn't changed, had she? Pretty, a flirt, liked a good time! They were dancing on the deck of the yacht. At first you didn't think about killing her. Otherwise, you wouldn't have needed to move her to Dizy.'

Was it certain the dying man could still hear? Since he was lying on his back, he must surely be able to see the colonel just above his head? But there was no expression in his eyes. Or at least nothing anyone could make sense of.

'She had sworn she would follow you anywhere. You'd seen the inside of a penal settlement. You were living in a stable. And then you suddenly had the idea of taking her back, just as she was, with her jewels, her painted face and her pale-coloured dress, and making her share your straw mattress. That's how it was, Darchambaux, wasn't it?'

His eyes did not blink. But his chest heaved. There was another moan. In his corner, Lucas, who was finding it unbearable, changed position.

'That's it! I can feel it!' said Maigret, the words now coming faster, as if he was being rushed along by them. Face to face with the woman who had been his wife, Jean the carter, who had virtually forgotten Doctor Darchambaux, had begun to remember, and mists of the past rose to meet him. And a strange plan had started to take shape. Was it vengeance? Not really. More an obscure desire to bring down to his level the woman who had promised to be his for the rest of their lives.

'So Mary Lampson lived for three days, hidden on this horse-boat, almost of her own free will.

'Because she was afraid. Afraid of this spectre from her past, who she felt was capable of anything, who told her she had to go with him!

'And even more scared because she was aware of how badly she had behaved.

'So she came of her own volition. And you, Jean, you brought her corned beef and cheap red wine. You went to her two nights in a row, after two interminable days of driving the boat along the Marne.

'When you got to Dizy . . .'

Again the dying man tried to stir. But his strength was gone, and he fell back, limp, drained.

'. . . she must have rebelled. She could not endure that kind of life any more. In a moment of madness, you strangled her rather than allow her to let you down a second time. You dumped her body in the stable. Is that what happened?'

He had to repeat the question five times until finally the eyelids flickered.

'Yes,' they said with indifference.

There was a faint scuffle on deck. It was the colonel holding back the skipper's wife, who was trying to get closer. She did not resist, for she was cowed by his solemn manner.

'So it was back to the towpath, back again to your life on the canal. But you were worried. You were scared. For you were afraid of dying, Jean. Afraid of being transported again. Afraid of being sent back to the colonies. Afraid, unbearably afraid of having to leave your horses, the stable, the straw, the one small corner which had become your entire universe. So one night, you took the lock-keeper's bike. I asked you about it. You guessed I had my suspicions.

'You rode back to Dizy intending to do something, anything, that would put me off the scent.

'Is that right?'

Jean was now so absolutely still that he might well have been dead. The expression on his face was a complete blank. But his eyelids closed once again.

'When you got there, there were no lights on the *Southern Cross*. You could safely assume that everyone on board was asleep. On deck an American cap was drying. You took it. You went into the stable, to hide it under the straw. It was the best way of changing the whole course of the investigation and switching the focus to the people on the yacht.

'You weren't to know that Willy Marco was outside, alone. He saw you take the cap and followed you. He was waiting for you by the stable door, where he lost a cufflink.

'He was curious. So he followed you when you started back to the stone bridge, where you had left the bike.

'Did he say something? Or did you hear a noise behind you?

'There was a fight. You killed him with those strong hands, the same hands that strangled Mary Lampson. You dragged the body to the canal . . .

'Then you must have walked on, head down. On the towpath, you saw something shining, the YCF badge. You thought that since the badge belonged to someone you'd seen around, maybe you'd noticed it on the colonel's lapel, you left it at the spot where the fight had taken place. Answer me, Darchambaux. That was how it happened, wasn't it?'

'Ahoy, *Providence*! Got a problem?' called another barge captain, whose boat passed so close that his head could be seen gliding past level with the hatch.

But then something strange and troubling happened. Jean's eyes filled with tears. Then he blinked, very fast, as though he was confessing to everything, to get it over and done with once and for all. He heard the skipper's wife answering from the stern, where she was waiting:

'It's Jean! He's hurt himself!'

As Maigret got to his feet, he said:

'Last night, when I examined your boots, you knew that I would sooner or later get to the truth. You tried to kill yourself by jumping into the lock.'

But the carter was now so far gone and his breathing so laborious that the inspector did not even wait for a response. He nodded to Lucas and cast one last look around him.

A diagonal shaft of sunlight entered the stable, striking the carter's left ear and the hoof of one of the horses.

Just as the two men were leaving, not finding anything else to say, Jean tried again to speak, urgently, disregarding the pain. Wild-eyed, he half sat up on his straw.

Maigret paid no attention to the colonel, not immediately. He crooked one finger and beckoned the woman, who was watching him from the stern.

'Well? How is he?' she asked.

'Stay by him.'

'Can I? And no one will come and . . .'

She did not dare finish. She had gone rigid when she heard the muffled cries uttered by Jean, who seemed frightened that he would be left to die alone.

Suddenly, she ran to the stable.

Vladimir sat on the yacht's capstan, a cigarette between his lips, wearing his white cap slantwise, splicing two rope ends.

A policeman in uniform was standing on the canal bank. From the barge Maigret called:

'What is it?'

'We've had the reply from Moulins.'

He handed over an envelope with a brief note which said:

> Marie Dupin, wife of the baker, has confirmed that she had a distant cousin at Étampes named Céline Mornet.

Maigret stared hard at the colonel, sizing him up. He was wearing his white yachting cap with the large crest. His eyes were just starting to acquire the faintest blue-green tinge, which doubtless meant that he had consumed a relatively small quantity of whisky.

'You had suspicions about the *Providence*?' Maigret asked him point blank.

It was so obvious! Wouldn't Maigret also have concentrated on the barge if his suspicions had not been diverted momentarily to the people on the yacht?

'Why didn't you say anything?'

The reply was well up to the standard of Sir Walter's interview with the examining magistrate at Dizy.

'Because I wanted to take care of the matter myself.'

It was more than enough to express the contempt the colonel felt for the police.

'And my wife?' he added almost immediately.

'As you said yourself, and as Willy Marco also said, she was a charming lady.'

Maigret spoke without irony. But in fact he was more interested in the sounds coming from the stable than in this conversation.

Just audible was the faint murmur of a single voice. It belonged to the skipper's wife, who sounded as if she were comforting a sick child.

'When she married Darchambaux, she already had a taste for the finer things of life. It seems very likely that it was on her account that the struggling doctor he then was did away with his aunt. I'm not saying she aided and abetted him. I'm saying that he did it for her. And she knew it, which explains why she stood up in court and swore that she would follow him and be with him.

'A charming lady. Though that's not the same thing as saying she was a heroine.

'She loved life too much. I'm sure you can understand that, colonel.'

The mixture of sun, wind and threatening clouds suggested a shower could break out at any moment. The light was shifting constantly.

'Not many people return from those penal settlements. She was pretty. All of life's pleasures were hers for the taking. There was only her name to hold her back. So when she got to the Côte d'Azur and met someone, her first admirer, who was ready to marry her, she got the idea of sending to Moulins for the birth certificate of a distant cousin she remembered.

'It's so easy to do! So easy that there's talk now of taking the fingerprints of newborn babies and adding them to the official registers of births.

'She got a divorce and then became your wife.

'A charming lady. No real harm in her, I'm sure. But she liked a good time, didn't she? She was in love with youth and love and the good things in life.

'And maybe sometimes the embers would be fanned and she'd feel the unaccountable need to go off and cut loose . . .

'Know what I think? I believe she went off with Jean not so much because of his threats but because she needed to be forgiven.

'The first day, hiding in the stable on board this boat, among the horsey smells, she must have derived some sort of satisfaction from the thought that she was atoning.

'It was the same thing as the time she vowed to the jury she would follow her husband to Guiana.

'Such charming creatures! Their first impulses are generous, if theatrical. They are so full of good intentions.

'It's just that life, with its betrayals, compromises and its over-riding demands, is stronger.'

Maigret had spoken rather bitterly but had not stopped listening for sounds coming from the stable while simultaneously keeping a constant eye on the movement of boats entering and leaving the lock.

The colonel had been standing in front of him with his head bowed. When he looked up now it was with obviously warmer sentiments, even a touch of muted affection.

'Do you want a drink?' he said and pointed to his yacht.

Lucas had been standing slightly to one side.

'You'll keep me informed?' said the inspector, turning to him.

Between them, there was no need for explanations. Lucas had understood and began to prowl silently round the stable.

The *Southern Cross* was as ship-shape as if nothing had happened. There was not a speck of dust on the mahogany walls of the cabin.

In the middle of the table was a bottle of whisky, a siphon and glasses.

'Stay outside, Vladimir!'

Maigret looked round him with new eyes. He was not there now pursuing some fine sliver of truth. He was more relaxed, less curt.

And the colonel treated him as he had treated Monsieur Clairfontaine de Lagny.

'He's going to die, isn't he?'

'He could go at any time. He's known since yesterday.'

The sparkling soda water spurted from the siphon. Sir Walter said sombrely:

'Your good health!'

Maigret drank as greedily as his host.

'Why did he run away from the hospital?'

The rhythm of their conversation had slowed. Before answering, the inspector looked round him carefully, taking in every detail of the cabin.

'Because . . .'

As he felt for his words his host was already refilling their glasses.

'. . . a man with no ties, a man who has severed all links with his past, with the kind of man he used to be . . . a man like that has to have something to cling to! He had his stable . . . the smell of it . . . the horses . . . the coffee he drank scalding hot at three in the morning ahead of a day spent slogging along the towpath until it was evening . . . It was his burrow, if you like, his very own corner, a place filled with animal warmth.'

Maigret looked the colonel in the eye. He saw him turn his head away. Reaching for his glass he added:

'There are all kinds of bolt-holes. Some have the smell of whisky, eau de Cologne, a woman and the sounds of gramophone records . . .'

He stopped and drank. When he looked up again, his host had had time to empty a third glass.

Sir Walter watched him with his large, bleary eyes and held out the bottle.

'No thanks,' protested Maigret.

'Yes for me! I need it.'

Was there not a hint of affection in the look he gave the inspector?

'My wife . . . Willy . . .'

At that moment, a thought sharp as an arrow struck the inspector.

Was not Sir Walter as alone, just as lost, as Jean, who was busy dying in his stable?

And at least the carter had his horses by him and his motherly Madame Hortense.

'Drink up! That's right! I'd like to ask . . . You're a gentleman . . .'

He spoke almost pleadingly. He held out his bottle rather shamefacedly. Vladimir could be heard moving about up on deck.

Maigret held out his glass. But there was a knock at the door. Through it came Lucas's voice:

'Inspector?'

And through the crack in the door he added:

'It's over.'

The colonel did not move. He watched grimly as the two policemen walked away.

When Maigret turned round, he saw him drink the glass he had just filled for his guest in one swallow. Then he heard him sing out:

'Vladimir!'

A number of people had gathered by the *Providence* because from the bank they had heard the sound of sobbing.

It was Hortense Canelle, the wife of the master, on her knees by Jean's side. She was talking to him even though he had been dead for several minutes.

Her husband was on deck, waiting for the inspector to come. He hurried towards him with little skipping steps, thin as a wraith, visibly flustered, and said in a desperate voice:

'What shall I do? He's dead! My wife . . .'

An image which Maigret would never forget: the stable, seen from above, the two horses almost filling it, a body curled up with half its head buried in straw. And the fair hair of the skipper's wife catching all the sun's rays while she gently moaned and at intervals repeated:

'Oh Jean! Poor Jean!'

Exactly as if Jean had been a child and not this granite-hard old man, with a carcass like a gorilla, who had cheated all the doctors!

11. *Right of Way*

No one noticed, except Maigret.

Two hours after Jean died, while the body was being stretchered to a waiting vehicle, the colonel, his eyes bloodshot but as dignified as ever, asked:

'Do you think now they can issue the burial permit?'

'You'll get it tomorrow.'

Five minutes later, Vladimir, with his customary neat movements, cast off.

Two boats making towards Dizy were waiting to descend through the Vitry lock.

The first was already being poled towards the chamber when the yacht skimmed past it, skirted its rounded bow, and slipped ahead of it into the open lock.

There were shouts of protest. The skipper yelled to the lock-keeper, telling him it was his turn, that he'd be making a complaint and much more of the same.

But the colonel, wearing his white cap and officer's uniform, did not even turn round.

He was standing at the brass wheel, expressionless, looking dead ahead.

When the lock gates were closed, Vladimir jumped on to the lock-side, showed his papers and offered the traditional tip.

'For God's sake!' grumbled a carter. 'These yachts get away with anything. All it takes is ten francs at every lock . . .'

The stretch of canal below the Vitry-le-François lock was congested. It hardly seemed possible that anything could pole a way through all the boats waiting for their turn.

But the gates had barely opened when the water started

churning around the propeller, and the colonel, with a perfunctory movement of his hand, let in the clutch.

The *Southern Cross* got up to full speed in a twinkling and flitted past the heavily laden barges despite the shouts and protests but did not so much as graze any of them.

Two minutes later, it vanished round the bend, and Maigret turned to Lucas, who was walking at his side:

'They're both dead drunk.'

No one had guessed. The colonel was a respectable gentleman with a large gold insignia on the front of his cap.

Vladimir, in his striped jersey, with his forage cap perched on his head, had not made one clumsy movement.

But if Sir Walter's apoplectic neck showed reddish-purple, his face was sickly pale, there were large bags under his eyes and his lips had no colour.

The smallest jolt would have knocked the Russian off balance, for he was asleep standing up.

On board the *Providence* everything was shut up, silent. Both horses were tethered to a tree a hundred metres from the barge.

The skipper and his wife had gone into town, to buy clothes for the funeral.

The Grand Banks Café

Translated by DAVID COWARD

LEGRAND

AU RENDEZ-VOUS DES TERRE-NEUVAS

ROMAN

PAR

GEORGES SIMENON

A. FAYARD & Cie - PARIS

PRIX : 6 FR.

1. *The Glass Eater*

. . . that he's the finest young man around here there ever was, and that all this could well be the death of his mother. He's all she's got. I am absolutely sure that he's innocent: everybody here is. But the sailors I've talked to reckon he'll be found guilty because civilian courts never understand anything to do with the sea.

Do everything you can, old friend, just as if you were doing it for me. I see from the papers that you've become something very important in the Police Judiciaire, and . . .

It was a June morning. The windows of the flat on Boulevard Richard-Lenoir were wide open. Madame Maigret was finishing packing large wicker trunks, and Maigret, who was not wearing a collar, was reading aloud.

'Who's it from?'

'Jorissen. We were at school together. He's a primary-school teacher now in Quimper. Listen, are you still set on passing our week's holiday in Alsace?'

She stared at him, not understanding. The question was so unexpected. For the past twenty years they'd always spent their holidays with family, and always in the same village in eastern France.

'What if we went to stay by the sea instead?'

He read out parts of the letter again, in a half whisper:

. . . you are better placed than I am to get accurate information. Very briefly, Pierre Le Clinche, aged twenty, a former pupil of mine, sailed three months ago on the *Océan*, a Fécamp trawler which was going fishing for cod off Newfoundland. The boat docked back in port yesterday. Hours later, the body of the captain was found floating in the harbour, and all the signs point to foul play. Pierre Le Clinche is the man who's been arrested.

'We'll be able to take it just as easy at Fécamp as anywhere else!' said Maigret, holding out no great hopes.

Objections were raised. In Alsace, Madame Maigret was with her family and helped with making jam and plum brandy. The thought of staying in a hotel by the seaside with a lot of other people from Paris filled her with dread.

'What would I do all day?'

In the end, she packed her sewing and her crocheting.

'Just don't expect me to go swimming! I thought I'd better warn you in advance.'

They had arrived at the Hôtel de la Plage at five. Once there, Madame Maigret had set about rearranging the room to her liking. Then they'd had dinner.

Later, Maigret, now alone, pushed open the frosted-glass door of a harbour-front café, the Grand Banks Café.

It was located opposite the berth where the trawler the *Océan* was tied up, just by a line of railway trucks. Acetylene lamps hung from the rigging, and in their raw light a number of figures were busily unloading cod, which they passed from hand to hand and piled into the trucks after the fish had been weighed.

There were ten of them at work, men and women, dirty, their clothes torn and stiff with salt. By the weighing scales stood a well-turned-out young man, with a boater over one ear and a notebook in his hand, in which he recorded the weighed catch.

A rank, stomach-churning smell, which distance did nothing to lessen, seeped into the bar, where the heat made it even more oppressive.

Maigret sat down in a free corner, on the bench seat. He was surrounded by noise and activity. There were men standing, men sitting, glasses on the marble-topped tables. All were sailors.

'What'll it be?'

'A beer.'

The serving girl went off. The landlord came up to him:

'I've got another room next door, you know. For tourists. This lot make such a din in here!' He winked. 'Well, after three months at sea, it's understandable.'

'Are these the crew of the *Océan*?'

'Most of them. The other boats aren't back yet. You mustn't pay any attention. Some of them have been drunk for three days. Are you staying put? . . . I bet you're a painter, right? We get them in now and again. They do sketches. There, see? Over the counter? One of them drew me, head and shoulders.'

But the inspector offered so little encouragement to his chatter that the landlord gave up and went away.

'A copper two-*sou* bit! Who's got a copper two-*sou* bit?' shouted a sailor no taller than a sixteen-year-old youth and as thin.

His head was old, his face was lopsided, and he was missing a few teeth. Drink made his eyes bright, and a three-day stubble had spread over his jaws.

Someone tossed him a coin. He bent it almost double with his fingers, then put it between his teeth and snapped it in two.

'Who wants to have a go next?'

He strutted around. He sensed that everyone was looking at him and was ready to do anything to remain the centre of attention.

As a puffy-faced mechanic produced a coin, he stepped in:

'Half a mo'. This is what you got to do as well.'

He picked up an empty glass, took a large bite out of it and chewed the broken pieces with a show of relish worthy of a gourmet.

'Ha ha!' he smirked. 'You're all welcome to give it a try . . . Fill me up again, Léon!'

He looked round the bar boastfully until his eyes came to rest on Maigret. His eyebrows came together in a deep frown.

For a moment he seemed nonplussed. Then he started to move forwards. He had to lean on a table to steady himself because he was so drunk.

'You here for me?' he blustered.

'Take it easy, Louis boy!'

'Still on about that business with the wallet? Listen, boys. You didn't believe me just now when I told you about my run-ins with the Rue de Lappe boys. Well, here's a top-notch cop who's come out of his way to see yours truly . . . Will it be all right if I have another little drink?'

All eyes were now on Maigret.

'Sit yourself down here, Louis boy, and stop playing the fool!'

Louis guffawed:

'You paying? No, that would be the day! . . . Is it all right with you, boys, if the chief inspector buys me a drink? . . . Make it brandy, Léon, a large one!'

'Were you on the *Océan*?'

The change in Louis was instant. His face darkened so much that it seemed as if he had suddenly sobered up. He shifted his position on the bench seat, backing off suspiciously.

'What if I was?'

'Nothing . . . Cheers . . . Been drunk long?'

'We been celebrating for three days. Ever since we landed. I gave my pay to Léon. Nine hundred francs, give or take. Here until it runs out . . . How much have I got left, Léon, you old crook?'

'Well, not enough for you to go on buying rounds until tomorrow! About fifty francs. Isn't it a stupid shame, inspector! Tomorrow he'll be skint and he'll have to sign as a stoker on the first boat that'll have him. It's the same story every time. Mark you, I don't encourage them to drink! The very opposite!'

'Shut your mouth!'

The others had lost their high spirits. They talked in whispers and kept looking round at the table where the inspector was sitting.

'Are all these men from the *Océan*?'

'All save the big fellow in the cap, who's a pilot, and the one with ginger hair. He's a ship's carpenter.'

'Tell me what happened.'

'I got nothing to say.'

'Watch your step, Louis! Don't forget the wallet business, which ended up with you doing your glass-eating number behind bars.'

'All I'd get is three months, and anyway I could do with a rest. But if you want, why not just lock me up right now?'

'Were you working in the engine room?'

'Sure! As usual! I was second fireman.'

'Did you see much of the captain?'

'Maybe twice in all.'

'And the wireless operator?'

'Dunno.'

'Léon! Same again.'

Louis gave a contemptuous laugh.

'I could be drunk as a lord and still I wouldn't tell you anything I didn't want to say. But since you're here, you could offer to buy the boys a round. After the lousy trip like the one we just been on!'

A sailor, not yet twenty, approached shiftily and tugged Louis' sleeve. They both started talking in Breton.

'What did he say?'

'He said it's time I went to bed.'

'A friend of yours?'

Louis shrugged, and just as the young sailor was about to take his glass off him, he downed it in one defiant gulp.

The Breton had thick eyebrows and wavy hair.

'Sit down with us,' said Maigret.

But without replying the sailor moved to another table, where he sat staring unblinkingly at both of them.

The atmosphere was heavy and sour. The sounds of tourists playing dominoes came from the next room, which was lighter and cleaner.

'Catch much cod?' asked Maigret who pursued his line of thought with the single-mindedness of a mechanical drill.

'It was no good. When we landed, it was half rotten!'

'How come?'

'Not enough salt! . . . Or too much! . . . It was off! There'll not be a third of the crew who'll go out on her again next week.'

'Is the *Océan* going out again?'

'By God, yes! Otherwise what's the point of boats with engines? Sailboats go out the once, from February to October. But these trawlers can fit in two trips to the Grand Banks.'

'Are you going back on her?'

Louis spat on the floor and gave a weary shrug.

'I'd just as well be banged up at Fresnes . . . You must be joking!'

'And the captain?'

'I got nothing to say!'

He had lit the stump of a cigar he'd found lying about. Suddenly he retched, made a rush for the door and could be seen throwing up on the kerb, where the Breton joined him.

'It's a crying shame,' sighed the landlord. 'The day before yesterday, he had nearly a thousand francs in his pocket. Today, it's touch and go if he doesn't end up owing me money! Oysters and lobster! And that's not reckoning all the drinks he stood everybody, as if he didn't know what to do with his money.'

'Did you know the wireless operator on the *Océan*?'

'He had a room here. As a matter of fact, he'd eat his dinners off this very table and then he'd go off to write in the room next door because it was quieter there.'

'Write to who?'

'Not just letters . . . Looked like poetry or novels. A kid with an education, well brought up. Now that I know you're police, I can tell you that it was a mistake when your lot . . .'

'Even though the captain had been killed?'

A shrug for an answer. The landlord sat down facing Maigret. Louis came back in, made straight for the counter and ordered another drink. His companion, still talking Breton, continued to tell him to stay calm.

'Pay no attention . . . Once they're back on dry land, they're like that: they booze, they shout, they fight, they break windows. On board they work like the devil. Even Louis! The chief mechanic on the *Océan* was telling me only yesterday that he does the work of two men . . . When they were at sea, a steam joint split. Repairing it was dangerous . . . No one wanted to do it . . . But Louis stepped up to the mark . . . If you keep him away from the bottle . . .'

Léon lowered his voice and ran his eyes over his customers suspiciously.

'Maybe this time they've got different reasons for going on the bottle. They won't tell you anything, not you! Because you're not a seafaring man. But I overhear them talking. I used to be a pilot. There are things . . .'

'What things?'

'It's hard to explain . . . You know that there aren't enough men in Fécamp to crew all the trawlers. So they bring them in from Brittany. Those boys have their own way of looking at things, they're a superstitious lot . . .'

He lowered his voice even further, until he was barely audible.

'It seems that this time they had the evil eye. It started in port, even before they sailed. There was this sailor who'd climbed the derrick to wave to his wife . . . He was hanging on to a rope, which broke, and the next moment he's lying on deck with his leg in a hell of a mess! They had to ferry him ashore in a dory. And then there was the ship's boy who didn't want to go to sea, he was bawling and yelling! Then three days later, they telegraphed saying he'd been washed overboard by a wave! A kid of fifteen! A small lad with fair hair, skinny he was, with a girlish name: Jean-Marie. And that wasn't all . . . Julie, bring us a couple of glasses of calvados . . . The right-hand bottle . . . No, not that one . . . The one with the glass stopper . . .'

'So the evil eye went on?'

'I don't know exactly. It's as if they're all too scared to talk about it. Even so, if the wireless operator has been arrested, it's because the police must have got to hear that during the whole time they were at sea he and the captain never said a word to each other . . . They were like oil and vinegar.'

'And?'

'Things happened . . . Things that don't make any sense. Like for instance when the skipper made them move the boat to a position where no one ever heard of cod being caught! And he went berserk when the head fisherman refused to do what he was told! He got his revolver out. It was like they were off their heads! For a whole month they didn't even net a ton of fish! And then all of a sudden, the fishing was good. But even then, the cod had to be sold at half price because it hadn't been kept right. And on it went. Even when they were coming into the harbour, they lost control twice and sank a rowing boat. It was like there was a curse on the boat. Then the skipper sent all hands ashore without leaving anyone on watch and stayed on board that evening all by himself.

'It was around nine o'clock. They were all in here getting drunk. The wireless operator went up to his room. Then he went out. He was seen heading in the direction of the boat.

'It was then that it happened. A fisherman down in the harbour who was getting ready to leave heard a noise like something falling in the water.

'He ran to see, with a customs man he'd met on the way. They lit lanterns . . . There was a body in the water. It had caught in the *Océan*'s anchor chain.

'It was the skipper! He was dead when they fished him out. They tried artificial respiration. They couldn't understand it. He hadn't been in the water ten minutes.

'The doctor explained the reason. Seems as how somebody had strangled him *before* . . . Do you follow me? And they found the wireless operator on board in his cabin, which is just astern of the funnel. You can see it from here.

'The police came here and searched his room. They found some burned papers . . .

'What do you make of it? . . . Ho! Julie, two calvados! . . . Your very good health!'

Louis, getting more and more carried away, had gripped a chair with his teeth and, in the middle of a circle of sailors, was holding it horizontally while staring defiantly at Maigret.

'Was the captain from around here?' asked the inspector.

'That he was. A curious sort. Not much taller or wider than Louis. But always polite, always friendly. And always nattily turned out. I don't think he went much to cafés. He wasn't married. He had digs in Rue d'Étretat, with a widow whose husband had worked for customs. There was talk that they'd get wed in the end. He'd been fishing off Newfoundland these fifteen years. Always for the same owners: the French Cod Company. Captain Fallut, to give him his full name. They're in a fix now if they want to send the *Océan* out to the Grand Banks. No captain! And half the crew not wanting to sign on for another tour!'

'Why is that?'

'Don't try to understand! The evil eye, like I told you. There's talk of laying the boat up until next year. On top of which the police have told the crew they have to stay available.'

'And the wireless operator is behind bars?'

'Yes. They took him away the same evening, in handcuffs he was . . . I was standing in the doorway. I tell you God's truth, the wife cried . . . and so did I. But he wasn't a special customer. I used to knock a bit off when I sold him supplies. He wasn't much of a drinker himself.'

They were interrupted by a sudden uproar. Louis had thrown himself at the Breton, presumably because the Breton had insisted on trying to stop him drinking. Both were rolling around on the floor. The others got out of their way.

It was Maigret who separated them, picking them up one in each hand.

'That's enough! You want to argue?'

The scuffle was over quickly. The Breton, whose hands were free, pulled a knife from his pocket. The inspector saw it just in time and with a swift back heel sent it spinning two metres away.

The shoe caught the Breton on the chin, which started to bleed. Louis, still in a daze and still drunk, rushed to his friend and started crying and saying he was sorry.

Léon came up to Maigret. He had his watch in his hand.

'Time I closed up! If I don't we'll have the police on the doorstep. Every evening it's the same story! I just can't kick them out!'

'Do they sleep on board the *Océan*?'

'Yes. Unless, that is, and it happened to two of them yesterday, they sleep where they fall, in the gutter. I found them this morning when I opened the shutters.'

The serving girl went round gathering glasses off the tables. The men drifted off in groups of two or three. Only Louis and the Breton didn't budge.

'Need a room?' Léon asked Maigret.

'No thanks. I'm booked into the Hôtel de la Plage.'

'Can I say something?'

'What?'

'It isn't that I want to give you advice. It's none of my business. But if anyone was feeling sorry for the wireless operator, maybe it wouldn't be a bad idea to *chercher la femme*, as they say in books. I've heard a few whispers along those lines . . .'

'Did Pierre Le Clinche have a girlfriend?'

'What, him? No fear! He'd got himself engaged wherever it was he came from. Every day he'd write home, letters six pages long.'

'Who do you mean, then?'

'I dunno. Maybe it's more complicated than people think. Besides . . .'

'Besides what?'

'Nothing. Behave yourself, Louis! Go home to bed!'

But Louis was far too drunk for that. He was tearful, he had his arms around his friend, whose chin was still bleeding, and he kept saying sorry.

Maigret left the bar, hands thrust deep in his pockets and with his collar turned up, for the air was cool.

In the vestibule of the Hôtel de la Plage, he saw a young woman sitting in a wicker chair. A man got up from another chair and smiled. There was a slight awkwardness in his smile.

It was Jorissen, the primary-school teacher from Quimper. Maigret had not seen him for fifteen years, and Jorissen was not sure whether he should treat him with their old easy familiarity.

'Look, I'm sorry . . . I . . . that is we, Mademoiselle Léonnec and I, have only just got here . . . I did the rounds of the hotels . . . They said you . . . they said you'd be back . . . She's Pierre Le Clinche's fiancée . . . She insisted . . .'

She was tall, rather pale, rather shy. But when Maigret shook her hand, he sensed that behind the façade of small-town, unsophisticated coyness there was a strong will.

She didn't speak. She felt out of her depth. As did Jorissen, who was still just a primary-school teacher who was now meeting up again with his old friend, who now held one of the highest ranks in the Police Judiciare.

'They pointed out Madame Maigret in the lounge just now, but I didn't like to . . .'

Maigret took a closer look at the girl, who was neither pretty nor plain, but there was something touching about her natural simplicity.

'You do know that he's innocent, don't you?' she said finally, looking at no one in particular.

The porter was waiting to get back to his bed. He had already unbuttoned his jacket.

'We'll see about that tomorrow . . . Have you got a room somewhere?'

'I've got the room next to you . . . to yours,' stammered the teacher from Quimper, still unsure of himself. 'And Mademoiselle Léonnec is on the floor above . . . I've got to get back tomorrow, there are exams on . . . Do you think . . . ?'

'Tomorrow! We'll see then,' Maigret said again.

And as he was getting ready for bed, his wife, already half asleep, murmured:

'Don't forget to turn the light out.'

2. *The Tan-Coloured Shoes*

Side by side, not looking at each other, they walked together first along the beach, which was deserted at that time of day, and then along the quays by the harbour.

Gradually, the silences grew fewer until Marie Léonnec was speaking in a more or less natural tone of voice.

'You'll see! You'll like him straight away! He couldn't be anything but likeable! And then you'll understand that . . .'

Maigret kept shooting curious, admiring glances at her. Jorissen had gone back to Quimper, very early that morning, leaving the girl by herself in Fécamp.

'I can't make her come with me,' he had said. 'She's far too independent for that.'

The previous evening, she was as unforthcoming as a young woman raised in the peace and quiet of a small town can be. Now, it wasn't an hour since she and Maigret had walked out of the Hôtel de la Plage together.

The inspector was behaving in his most crusty manner.

But to no effect. She refused to let herself be intimidated. She was not taken in by him, and she smiled confidently.

'His only fault,' she went on, 'is that he is so very sensitive. But it's hardly surprising. His father was just a poor fisherman, and for years his mother mended nets to raise him. Now he keeps her. He's educated. He's got a bright future before him.'

'Are your parents well off?' Maigret asked bluntly.

'They are the biggest makers of ropes and metal cables in Quimper. That's why Pierre wouldn't even speak to my father about us. For a whole year, we saw each other in secret.'

'You were both over eighteen?'

'Just. I was the one who told my parents. Pierre swore that he wouldn't marry me until he was earning at least two thousand francs a month. So you see . . .'

'Has he written to you since he was arrested?'

'Just one letter. It was very short. And that from someone who used to send me a letter pages and pages long every day! He said it would be best for me and my parents if I told everyone back home that it was all over between us.'

They passed near the *Océan*, which was still being unloaded. It was high tide, and its black hull dominated the wharves. In the foredeck three men stripped to the waist were getting washed. Among them Maigret recognized Louis.

He also noticed a gesture: one of the men nudged the third man with his shoulder and nodded towards Maigret and the girl. Maigret scowled.

'Just shows how considerate he is!' continued the voice at his side. 'He knows how quickly scandal spreads in a small town like Quimper. He wanted to give me back my freedom.'

The morning was clear. The girl, in her grey two-piece suit, looked like a student or a primary-school teacher.

'For my parents to have let me come here, they must obviously trust him too. But my father would prefer me to marry someone in business.'

At the police station Maigret left her in the waiting room, sitting some considerable time in the waiting room. He jotted down a few notes.

Half an hour later, they both walked into the jail.

It was Maigret in his surly mood, hands behind his back, pipe clenched between his teeth, shoulders bent, who now stood in one corner of the cell. He had informed the authorities that he was not taking an official interest in the investigation, that he was following its progress out of curiosity.

Several people had described the wireless operator to him, and the picture he had formed corresponded exactly to the young man he was now seeing in the flesh.

He was tall and slim, in a conventional suit, though a little on the shabby side, with the half-solemn, half-timid look about him of a schoolboy who is always top of his class. There were freckles on his cheeks. His hair was cropped short.

He had started when the door was opened. For a moment, he stayed well away from the girl who walked straight up to him. She had had to throw herself into his arms, literally, and cling on hard while he looked around in bewilderment.

'Marie! . . . Who on earth . . . ? How . . . ?'

He was quite disoriented. But he wasn't the sort to get excited. The lenses of his glasses clouded over, that was all. His lips trembled.

'You shouldn't have come.'

He caught sight of Maigret, whom he didn't know, and then stared at the door, which had been left half-open.

He wasn't wearing a collar, and there were no laces in his shoes. He also had a beard, gingerish and several days old. He was still feeling awkward about these things, despite the sudden shock he'd had. He felt his bare neck and his prominent Adam's apple with an embarrassed movement of his hand.

'Is my mother . . . ?'

'She didn't come. But she doesn't think you're guilty any more than I do.'

The girl was no more able than he was to give vent to her feelings. The moment fell flat. Maybe it was the intimidating effect of the surroundings.

They looked at each other and, not knowing what to say, groped for words. Then Mademoiselle Léonnec turned and pointed to Maigret.

'He's a friend of Jorissen's. He's a detective chief inspector in the Police Judiciaire and he's agreed to help us.'

Le Clinche hesitated about offering his hand, then did not dare to.

'Thanks . . . I . . .'

Another moment that failed entirely. The girl knew it and felt like crying. She had been counting on a touching interview which would win Maigret over to their side.

She gave her fiancé a look of resentment, even of muted impatience.

'You must tell him everything that might help your defence.'

Pierre Le Clinche sighed, ill at ease and unsettled.

'I've just a few questions for you,' the inspector broke in. 'All the crew say that throughout the voyage your dealings with the captain were more than cool. And yet, when you sailed, you were on good terms with him. What happened to bring about the change?'

The wireless operator opened his mouth, said nothing, then stared at the floor, looking very sorry for himself.

'Something to do with your duties? For the first two days, you ate with the first mate and the chief mechanic. After that you preferred to eat with the men.'

'Yes . . . I know . . .'

'Why?'

Losing patience, Marie Léonnec said:

'Out with it, Pierre! We're trying to save you! You must tell the truth.'

'I don't know.'

He looked limp, cowed, almost without hope.

'Did you have any differences of opinion with Captain Fallut?'

'No.'

'And yet you lived with him for nearly three months cooped up on the same ship without ever saying a single word to him. Everybody noticed. Some of them talked behind his back, saying that there were times when Fallut gave the impression of being mad.'

'I don't know.'

It was all Marie Léonnec could do to choke back her frustration.

'When the *Océan* returned to port, you went ashore with the others. When you got to your room, you burned a number of papers . . .'

'Yes. Nothing of any importance.'

'You keep a regular journal in which you write down everything you see. Wasn't what you burned your journal of the voyage?'

Le Clinche remained standing, head down, like a schoolboy who hasn't done his homework and keeps his eyes stubbornly on his feet.

'Yes.'

'Why?'

'I don't remember!'

'And you can't remember why you went back on board either? Though not straight away. You were seen crouching behind a truck fifty metres from the boat.'

The girl looked at the inspector, then at her fiancé, then back to the inspector and began to feel out of her depth.

'Yes.'

'The captain walked down the gangplank on to the quay. It was at that moment that he was attacked.'

Pierre Le Clinche still said nothing.

'Talk to me, dammit!'

'Yes, answer him, Pierre! We're trying to save you. I don't understand . . . I . . .'

Her eyes filled with tears.

'Yes.'

'Yes what?'

'I was there!'

'And you saw?'

'Not clearly . . . There were a lot of barrels, trucks . . . Two men fighting, then one running off and a body falling into the water.'

'What was the man who ran away like?'

'I don't know . . .'

'Was he dressed like a sailor?'

'No!'

'So you know how he was dressed?'

'All I noticed was a pair of tan-coloured shoes under a gas lamp as he ran away.'

'What did you do next?'

'I went on board.'

'Why? And why didn't you try to save the captain? Did you know he was already dead?'

A heavy silence. Marie Léonnec clasped both hands together in anguish.

'Speak, Pierre! Speak . . . please!'

'Yes . . . No . . . I swear I don't know!'

Footsteps in the corridor. It was the custody officer coming to say that they were ready for Le Clinche in the examining magistrate's office.

His fiancée stepped forward, intending to kiss him. He hesitated. In the end, he put his arms round her, slowly, deliberately.

So it was not her lips that he kissed but the fine, fair curls at her temples.

'Pierre!'

'You shouldn't have come!' he told her, his brow furrowed, as he wearily followed the custody officer out.

Maigret and Marie Léonnec returned to the exit without speaking. Outside she sighed unhappily:

'I don't understand . . . I . . .'

Then, holding her head high:

'But he's innocent, I know he is! We don't understand because we've never been in a predicament like his. For three days he's been behind bars, and everybody thinks he's guilty! . . . He's a very shy person . . .'

Maigret was moved, for she was doing her level best to make her words sound positive and convincing, though inside she was utterly devastated.

'You will do something to help despite everything, won't you?'

'On condition that you go back home, to Quimper.'

'No! . . . I won't! . . . Look . . . Let me . . .'

'In that case, take yourself off to the beach. Go and sit by my wife and try to find something to do. She's bound to have something you can sew.'

'What are you going to do? Do you think the tan-coloured shoes are a clue? . . .'

People turned and stared at them, for Marie Léonnec was waving her arms about, and it looked as if they were having an argument.

'Let me say it again: I'll do everything in my power . . . Look, this street leads straight to the Hôtel de la Plage. Tell my wife that I might be back late for lunch.'

He turned on his heel and walked as far as the quays. His surly manner had disappeared. He was almost smiling. He'd been afraid there might have been a stormy scene in the cell, heated protests, tears, kisses. But it had passed off very differently, in a way that was more straightforward, more harrowing and more significant.

He had liked the boy, more precisely the part of him that was distant, withdrawn.

As he passed a shop, he ran into Louis, who was holding a pair of gumboots in his hand.

'And where are you off to?'

'To sell these. Do you want to buy them? It's the best thing they make in Canada. I defy you to find anything as good in France. Two hundred francs . . .'

Even so Louis seemed a touch jittery and was only waiting for the nod to be on his way.

'Did you ever get the idea that Captain Fallut was crazy?'

'You don't see much down in a coal bunker, you know.'

'But you do talk. So?'

'There were weird stories going round, of course.'

'What stories?'

'All sorts! . . . Something and nothing! . . . It's hard to put your finger on it. Especially when you're back on dry land again.'

He was still holding the boots in his hand, and the owner of the ship's chandler's shop who had seen him coming, was waiting for him in his doorway.

'Do you need me any more?'

'When did those stories start exactly?'

'Oh, straight away. A ship is in good shape or it's in poor shape. I tell you: the *Océan* was sick as a dog.'

'Handling errors?'

'And how! What can I say? Things that don't make any sense, though they happen right enough! The fact is we had this feeling we'd never see port again . . . Look, is it true that I won't be bothered again over that business with the wallet?'

'We'll see.'

The port was almost empty. In summer, all the boats are at sea off Newfoundland, except the smaller fishing vessels which go out after fresh fish in coastal waters. There was only the dark shape of the *Océan* to be seen in the harbour, and it was the *Océan* that filled the air with a strong smell of cod.

Near the trucks was a man in leather gaiters. On his head was a cap with a silk tassel.

'The boat's owner?' Maigret asked a passing customs man.

'Yes. He's head of French Cod.'

The inspector introduced himself. The man looked at him suspiciously but without taking his eyes off the unloading operation.

'What do you make of the murder of your captain?'

'What do I think about it? I think that there's 800 tons of cod that's off, that if this nonsense goes on, the boat won't be going out again for a second voyage, that it's not the police who'll sort out the mess or cover the losses!'

'I assume you had every confidence in Captain Fallut?'

'Yes. And?'

'Do you think the wireless operator . . . ?'

'The wireless operator is neither here nor there: it's a whole year down the chute! And that's not counting the nets they came back with! Those nets cost two million francs, you know! Full of holes, as if someone has been having fun fishing up rocks! On top of which, the crew's been going on about the evil eye! . . . Hoy, you there! What do you think you're playing at? . . . God give me strength! Did I or did I not tell you to finish loading that truck first?'

And he started running alongside the boat, swearing at all the hands.

Maigret stayed a few moments more, watching the boat being unloaded. Then he moved off in the direction of the jetty, where there were groups of fishermen in pink canvas jerkins.

He'd been there only a moment when a voice behind him said:

'Hoy! Inspector!'

It was Léon, the landlord of the Grand Banks Café, who was trying to catch him up by pumping his short legs as fast as he could.

'Come and have a drink in the bar.'

He was behaving mysteriously. It seemed promising. As they walked, he explained:

'It's all calmed down now. The boys who haven't gone home to Brittany or the villages round about have just about spent all their money. I've only had a few mackerel men in all morning.'

They walked across the quays and went into the café, which was empty except for the girl from behind the bar, who was wiping tables.

'Half a mo'. What'll you have? Aperitif? . . . It's almost time for one . . . Not that, as I told you yesterday, I encourage the boys to drink too much . . . The opposite! . . . I mean, when they've had a drop or three, they start smashing the place up, and that costs me more than I make out of them . . . Julie! Pop into the kitchen and see if I'm there!'

He gave the inspector a knowing wink.

'Your very good health! . . . I saw you in the distance and since I had something to tell you . . .'

He crossed the room to make sure the girl was not listening behind the door. And then, looking even more mysterious and pleased with himself, he took something out of his pocket, a piece of card about the size of a photo.

'There! What do you make of that!'

It was indeed a photo, a picture of a woman. But the face was completely hidden, scribbled all over in red ink. Someone had tried to obliterate the head, someone very angry. The pen had bitten into the paper. There were so many criss-crossed lines that not a single square millimetre had been left visible.

On the other hand, below the head, the torso had not been touched. A pair of large breasts. A light-coloured silk dress, very tight and very low cut.

'Where did you get this?'

More knowing winks.

'Since there's just the two of us, I can tell you . . . Le Clinche's sea-chest doesn't fasten properly, so he'd got into the habit of sliding his girlfriend's letters under the cloth on his table.'

'And you used to read them?'

'They were of no interest to me . . . No, it was luck . . . When the place was searched, nobody thought of looking under the tablecloth. It came to me last night, and that's what I found. Of course, you can't see the face. But it's obviously not the girlfriend, she isn't stacked like that! Anyway, I've seen a photo of her. So there's another woman lurking in the background.'

Maigret stared at the photo. The line of the shoulders was inviting. The woman was probably younger than Marie Léonnec. And there was something extremely sensual about those breasts.

But also something vulgar too. The dress looked shop-bought. Seduction on the cheap.

'Is there any red ink in the house?'

'No! Just green.'

'Did Le Clinche never use red ink?'

'No. He had his own ink, on account of having a fountain pen. Special ink. Blue-black.'

Maigret stood up and made for the door.

'Do you mind excusing . . . ?'

Moments later he was on board the *Océan*, searching first the wireless operator's cabin and then the captain's, which was dirty and full of clutter.

There was no red ink anywhere on the trawler. None of the fishermen had ever seen any there.

When he left the boat, Maigret came in for sour looks from the man in gaiters, who was still bawling at his men.

'Do you use red ink in any of your offices?'

'Red ink? What for? We're not running a school . . .'

But suddenly, as if he'd just remembered something:

'Fallut was the only one who ever wrote in red ink, when he was working at home, in Rue d'Étretat. But what's all this about now? . . . You down there, watch out for that truck! All we need now is an accident! . . . So what are you after now with your red ink?'

'Nothing . . . Much obliged.'

Louis reappeared bootless and a few sheets to the wind, with a roughneck's cap on his head and a pair of scuffed shoes on his feet.

3. The Headless Photograph

. . . and that no one could tell me to my face and that I've got savings, which are at least the equivalent of a captain's pay.

Maigret left Madame Bernard standing on the doorstep of her small house in Rue d'Étretat. She was about fifty, very well preserved, and she had just spoken for a full half-hour about her first husband, about being a widow, about the captain, whom she had taken as her lodger, about the rumours which had circulated about their relationship and, finally, about an unnamed female who was beyond a shadow of a doubt a 'loose woman'.

The inspector had looked round the whole house, which was well kept but full of objects in rather bad taste. Captain Fallut's room was still as it had been arranged in readiness for his return.

Few personal possessions: some clothes in a trunk, a handful of books, mostly adventure yarns, and pictures of boats.

All redolent of an uneventful, unremarkable life.

'. . . It was understood though not finally settled, but we both knew that we would eventually get married. I would bring the house, furniture and bed linen. Nothing would have changed, and we would have been comfortably off, especially in three or four years' time, after he got his pension.'

Visible through the windows were the grocer's opposite, the road that ran down the hill and the pavement, where children were playing.

'And then this last winter he met that woman, and everything was turned upside down. At his age! How can a man lose his head over a creature like that? And he kept it all very secret. He must have been going to see her in Le Havre or somewhere, for no one here ever saw them together. I had a feeling that something was going on. He started buying more expensive underwear. And once, even a pair of silk socks! As there wasn't anything definite between us, it was none of my business, and I didn't want to look as if I was trying to defend my interests.'

The interview with Madame Bernard cast light on one whole area of the dead man's life. The small, middle-aged man who returned to port after a long tour on a trawler and spent his winters living like an upstanding citizen, with Madame Bernard, who looked after him and expected to marry him.

He ate with her, in her dining room, under a portrait of her first husband, who sported a blond moustache. Afterwards, he would go to his room and settle down with an exciting book.

And then that peace was shattered. Another woman burst on to the scene. Captain Fallut went to Le Havre frequently, took more care of his appearance, shaved more closely, even bought silk socks and hid it all from his landlady.

Still, he wasn't married, he had made no promises. He was free and yet he had never appeared once in public in Fécamp with his unknown woman.

Was it the grand passion, his belated big adventure? Or just a sordid affair?

Maigret reached the beach, saw his wife sitting in a red-striped deckchair and, just by her, Marie Léonnec, who was sewing.

There were a few bathers on the shingle, which gleamed white in the sun. A drowsy sea. And further on, on the other side of the jetty, the *Océan* at her berth, and the cargo of cod that was still being unloaded, and the resentful sailors exchanging veiled comments.

He kissed Madame Maigret on the forehead. He nodded politely to the girl and replied to her questioning look:

'Nothing special.'

His wife said in a level voice:

'Mademoiselle Léonnec has been telling me her story. Do you think that her young man is capable of doing such a thing?'

They walked slowly towards the hotel. Maigret carried both deckchairs. They were about to sit down to lunch when a uniformed policeman arrived, looking for the inspector.

'I was told to show you this, sir. It came an hour ago.'

And he held out a brown envelope, which had been already opened. There was no address on it. Inside was a sheet of paper. On it, in a tiny, thin, cramped hand, was written:

> No one should be accused of bringing about my death, and no attempt should be made to understand my action.
>
> These are my last wishes. I leave all my worldly goods to Madame Bernard, who has always been kind to me, on the condition that she sends my gold chronometer to my nephew, who is known to her, and that she sees to it that I am buried in Fécamp cemetery, near my mother.

Maigret opened his eyes wide.

'It's signed Octave Fallut!' he said in a whisper. 'How did this letter get to the police station?'

'Nobody knows, sir. It was in the letterbox. It seems that it's his handwriting right enough. The chief inspector informed the public prosecutor's department immediately.'

'Despite the fact that he was strangled! And that it is impossible to strangle yourself!' muttered Maigret.

Close by, guests who had ordered the set menu were complaining loudly about some pink radishes in a hors d'oeuvres dish.

'Wait a moment while I copy this letter. I imagine you have to take it back with you?'

'I wasn't given any special instructions but I suppose so.'

'Quite right. It must be put in the file.'

A moment or two later, Maigret, holding the copy in his hand, looked impatiently round the dining room, where he was about to waste an hour waiting for each course to arrive. All this time, Marie Léonnec had not taken her eyes off him but had not dared interrupt his grim reflections. Only Madame Maigret reacted, with a sigh, at the sight of pale cutlets.

'We'd have been better off going to Alsace.'

Maigret stood up before the dessert arrived and wiped his mouth, eager to get back to the trawler, the harbour, the fishermen. All the way there, he kept muttering:

'Fallut knew he was going to die! But did he know he would be killed? Was he trying in advance to save his killer's neck? Or was it just that he intended to commit suicide? Then again, who dropped the brown envelope in the station's postbox? There was no stamp on it, no address.'

The news had already got out, for when Maigret had nearly reached the trawler, the head of French Cod called out to him with aggressive sarcasm:

'So, it seems Fallut strangled himself! Who came up with that bright idea?'

'If you've got something to say, you can tell me which of the *Océan*'s officers are still on board.'

'None of them. The first mate has gone on the spree to Paris. The chief mechanic is at home, at Yport and won't be back until they've finished unloading.'

Maigret again looked round the captain's quarters. A narrow cabin. A bed with a dirty quilt over it. A clothes press built into the bulkhead. A blue enamel coffee-pot on an oilcloth-covered table. In a corner, a pair of boots with wooden soles.

It was dark and clammy and permeated with the same acrid smell which filled the rest of the ship. Blue-striped knitted pullovers were drying on deck. Maigret nearly lost his footing as he walked across the gangway, which was slippery with the remains of fish.

'Find anything?'

The inspector gave a shrug, took yet another gloomy look at the *Océan*, then asked a customs officer how he could get to Yport.

Yport is a village built under the cliffs six kilometres from Fécamp. A handful of fishermen's cottages. The odd farm round about. A few villas, most let furnished during the summer season, and one hotel.

On the beach, another collection of bathing costumes, small children and mothers busily knitting and embroidering.

'Could you tell me where Monsieur Laberge lives?'

'The chief mechanic on the *Océan* or the farmer?'

'The mechanic.'

He was directed to a small house with a small garden round it. As he came up to the front door, which was painted green, he heard the sound of an argument coming from inside. Two voices: a man's and a woman's. But he could not make out what they were saying. He knocked.

It all went quiet. Footsteps approached. The door opened and a tall, rangy man appeared looking suspicious and cross.

'What is it?'

A woman in housekeeping clothes was quickly tidying her dishevelled hair.

'I'm from the Police Judiciaire and I'd like to ask you a few questions.'

'You'd better come in.'

A little boy was crying, and his father pushed him roughly into the adjoining room, in which Maigret caught sight of the foot of a bed.

'You can leave us to it!' Laberge snapped at his wife.

Her eyes were red with crying too. The argument must have started in the middle of their meal, for their plates were still half full.

'What do you want to know?'

'When did you last go to Fécamp?'

'This morning. I went on my bike. It's no fun having to listen to the wife going on all day. You spend months at sea, working your guts out, and when you get back . . .'

He was still angry. However, his breath smelled strongly of alcohol.

'Women! They're all the same! Jealous don't say the half of it! They imagine a man's got nothing else on his mind except running after skirts. Listen to her! That's her giving the kid a hiding, taking it out on him!'

The child could be heard yelling in the next room, and the mother's voice getting louder.

'Stop that row, you hear! . . . Just stop it!'

Judging by the sounds, the words were accompanied by slaps and thumps, for the crying started up again, with interest.

'Ah! What a life!'

'Had Captain Fallut told you he was worried about anything in particular?'

Laberge scowled at Maigret, then moved his chair.

'Who made you think he had?'

'You'd been sailing with him for a long time, hadn't you?'

'Five years.'

'On board you took your meals together.'

'Except this last time! He got the idea that he wanted to eat alone, in his cabin . . . But I'd rather not talk any more about that damned trip!'

'Where were you when the crime was committed?'

'In the café, with the others . . . They must have told you.'

'Do you think the wireless operator had any reason for attacking the captain?'

Suddenly, Laberge lost his temper.

'Where are all these questions leading? What do you want me to say? Look, it wasn't my job to keep everybody in order, was it? I'm fed up to the back teeth, fed up with this business and all the rest of it! So fed up that I'm wondering if I'm going to sign up for the next tour!'

'Obviously the last one wasn't exactly a roaring success.'

Another sharp glance at Maigret.

'What are you getting at?'

'Just that everything went wrong! A ship's boy was killed. There were more accidents than usual. The fishing wasn't good, and when the cod arrived back in Fécamp it was off . . .'

'Was that my fault?'

'I'm not saying that. I merely ask if in the events at which you were present there was anything that might explain the captain's death. He was an easy-going sort, led a quiet life . . .'

The mechanic smiled mockingly but said nothing.

'Do you know anything about him that says otherwise?'

'Look, I told you I don't know anything, that I've had enough of the whole business! Is everybody trying to drive me crazy? . . . What more do you want now?'

He had it in most for his wife. She had just come back into the room and was hurrying to the stove, where a saucepan was giving off a smell of burning.

She was about thirty-five. She wasn't pretty and she wasn't ugly.

'I'll only be a minute,' she said meekly. 'It's the dog's dinner . . .'

'Get on with it, woman! . . . Haven't you finished yet?'

And turning to Maigret:

'Shall I give you a piece of good advice? Let it alone! Fallut is well off where he is! The less said about him, the better it'll be! Now listen: I don't know anything. You can ask me questions all day, and I wouldn't have anything else to say . . . Did you get the train here? If you don't catch the one that leaves in ten minutes, you'll not get another until eight this evening.'

He had opened the door. Sunshine flooded into the room.

When he got to the doorway, the inspector asked quietly: 'Who is your wife jealous of?'

The man gritted his teeth and did not speak.

'Do you know who this is?'

Maigret held out the photo with the head obscured by the red scribble. But he kept his thumb over the face. All that was visible was the cleavage in the silk dress.

Laberge glanced up at him quickly and tried to grab the picture.

'Do you recognize her?'

'Why should I recognize her?'

His hand was still open when Maigret put the photograph back in his pocket.

'Will you be coming to Fécamp tomorrow?'

'I don't know . . . Will you be needing me?'

'No. I was just asking. Thanks for the information you gave me.'

'But I didn't tell you anything!'

Maigret had not gone ten paces from the door when it was kicked shut and voices were raised inside the house, where the argument would now start up again, even more acrimoniously.

The chief mechanic was right: there were no trains to Fécamp until eight in the evening, and Maigret, having time on his hands, was inevitably drawn to the beach, where he sat down on the terrace of a hotel.

There was the usual holiday atmosphere: red sun umbrellas, white dresses, white trousers and a group of sightseers clustered around a fishing boat that was being winched up on to the pebble beach with a capstan.

To right and left, light-coloured cliffs. Straight ahead, the sea, pale green with white combers, and the regular murmur of wavelets lapping the shoreline.

'A beer!'

The sun was hot. A family were eating ice-creams on the next table. A young man was taking photos with a Kodak, and somewhere there were the shrill voices of little girls.

Maigret allowed his eyes to wander over the view. His thoughts grew hazy, and his brain sluggishly started weaving a daydream around Captain Fallut, who became increasingly insubstantial.

'Thanks a million!'

The words went round and round in his head, not on account

of their meaning, but because they had been pronounced curtly, with biting sarcasm, by a woman somewhere behind the inspector.

'But Adèle, I told you . . .'

'Shut up!'

'You're not going to start all that again . . .'

'I'll do exactly as I please!'

It was obviously a good day for arguments. First thing that morning, Maigret had encountered a man who bristled: the head man from French Cod.

At Yport, there had been that domestic scene between the Laberges. And now on the hotel terrace an unknown couple were exchanging heated words.

'Why don't you stop and think!'

'Get lost!'

'Do you think it's clever to talk like that?'

'Damn and blast you! Haven't you got the message yet? . . . Waiter, this lemonade is warm. Get me another!'

The accent was common, and the woman was speaking more loudly than was necessary.

'But you must make up your mind!' the man said.

'Just go by yourself! I told you! And leave me alone.'

'You know, what you're doing is pretty shabby.'

'So are you!'

'Me? You dare . . . Listen, if we weren't here, I don't think I'd be able to keep control of myself!'

She laughed. Much too loudly.

'You tell a girl the nicest things!'

'Be quiet! Please!'

'Why should I?'

'Because!'

'Now that really is a clever answer, I must say!'

'Are you going to shut up?'

'If I feel like it.'

'Adèle, I'm warning you I'll . . .'

'You'll what? Kick up a fuss in front of everybody? And where would that get you? People are already listening.'

'If only you'd stop and think for a moment, you'd understand.'

She sprang to her feet like someone who has had enough. Maigret had his back turned to her but saw her shadow grow bigger on the tiled floor of the terrace.

Then he saw her, from the back, as she walked off in the direction of the sea.

From behind, she was just a silhouette against the sky, which was now turning red. All Maigret could make out was that she was quite well-dressed, but not for the beach, not with silk stockings and high heels.

It was an outfit which made it difficult for her to walk elegantly over the pebble beach. At any moment she could twist an ankle, but she was furiously, stubbornly determined to forge ahead.

'Waiter, what do I owe you?'

'But I haven't brought the lemonade which the lady . . .'

'Forget it! What's the damage?'

'Nine francs fifty . . . Won't you be having dinner here?'

'No idea.'

Maigret turned round to get a sight of the man, who was looking very awkward because he was well aware that everyone nearby had heard everything.

He was tall and flashily elegant. His eyes looked tired, and his utter frustration was written all over his face.

When he stood up, he hesitated about which way to go and in the end, trying to look as if he didn't give a damn about anything, he set off in the direction of the young woman, who was now walking along the winding edge of the sea.

'Another pair that aren't married, for sure!' said a voice at a table where three women were busy doing crochet work.

'Why couldn't they wash their dirty linen somewhere else? It's not setting the children a very good example.'

The two silhouettes joined at the water's edge. Their words

were no longer audible. But the way they stood and moved made it easy to guess what was going on.

The man pleaded and threatened. The woman refused to give an inch. At one point he grabbed her by the wrist, and it seemed as if they would come to blows.

Instead, he turned his back on her and walked away quickly towards a street nearby, where he started the engine of a small grey car.

'Waiter! Another beer!'

Then Maigret noticed that the young woman had left her handbag on the table. Imitation crocodile-skin, full to bursting, brand new.

Then a shadow coming towards him on the ground. He looked up and got a front view of the owner of the handbag, who was coming back to the terrace.

The inspector gave a start. His nostrils flared slightly.

He could be wrong, of course. It was more an impression than a certainty. But he could have sworn he was looking at the person in the headless photo.

Cautiously, he took the photo out of his pocket. The woman had sat down again.

'Well, waiter? Where's my lemonade?'

'I thought . . . The gentleman said . . .'

'I ordered lemonade!'

It was the same slightly fleshy line of the neck, the same full but firm breasts, the same voluptuous buoyancy . . .

And the same style of dressing, the same taste for very glossy silk in loud colours.

Maigret dropped the photo in such a way that the woman at the next table could not fail to see it.

And see it she did. She stared at the inspector as though she were trawling through her memories. But if she was disconcerted, her feelings did not show in her face.

Five minutes, ten minutes went by. Then there was the distant thrum of an engine. It grew louder. It was the grey car heading back to the terrace. It stopped, then set off again, as though the driver could not make up his mind to drive away and not come back.

'Gaston!'

She was on her feet. She waved to the man. This time she grasped her bag firmly and the next moment she was getting into the car.

The three women at the next table followed her with their eyes and a disapproving air. The young man with the Kodak turned round.

The grey car was already vanishing in a roar of acceleration.

'Waiter! Where can I get hold of a car?'

'I don't think you'll find one in Yport . . . There is one which sometimes takes people to Fécamp or Étretat, but now that I think I saw it drive off this morning with some English people in it.'

The inspector's thick fingers drummed rapidly on the tabletop.

'Bring me a road map. And get me the chief inspector of Fécamp police on the phone . . . Have you ever seen those two before?'

'The couple who were arguing? Almost every day this week. Yesterday they had lunch here. I think they're from Le Havre.'

There were now only families left on the beach, which exuded all the warmth of a summer evening. A black ship moved imperceptibly across the line of the horizon, entered the sun and emerged on the other side, as if it had jumped through a paper hoop.

4. The Mark of Rage

'Speaking for myself,' said the chief inspector of Fécamp's police department as he sharpened a blue pencil, 'I'll admit I have few illusions left. It's so rarely that we manage to clear up any of these cases involving sailors. And that's being optimistic! Just you try getting to the bottom of one of those mindless brawls that happen every day of the week down by the harbour. When my men get there, they're all beating seven bells out of each other. Then they spot uniforms and they close ranks and go on the offensive. Question them and they all lie, contradict each other and muddy the waters to the point that in the end we give up.'

There were four of them smoking in the office, which was already filled with tobacco fumes. It was evening. The divisional head of Le Havre's flying squad, who was officially in charge of the investigation, had a young inspector with him.

Maigret was there in a private capacity. He sat at a table in a corner. He hadn't yet spoken.

'It looks straightforward enough to me,' ventured the young inspector, who was hoping to earn the approval of his chief. 'Theft wasn't the motive for the crime. So it was an act of revenge. On which member of the crew did Captain Fallut come down hardest when they were away at sea?'

But the chief inspector from Le Havre gave a shrug, and the junior inspector turned red and fell silent.

'Still . . .'

'No, no! It's something else. And top of the list is this woman you unearthed for us, Maigret. Did you give the boys in uniform all the information they need to find her? Dammit, I can't for the life of me work out what part she played in all this. The boat was at sea for three months. She wasn't there when it docked, because no one has reported seeing her get off it. The wireless operator is engaged to be married. By all accounts, Captain Fallut didn't seem the kind of man who'd do anything silly. And yet he wrote his will just before he got himself murdered.

'It would also be interesting to know who exactly went to the trouble of delivering the will here,' sighed Maigret. 'There's also a reporter – he's the one who wears a beige raincoat – who claims in *L'Éclair de Rouen* that the owners of the *Océan* had sent it to sea to do something other than fish for cod.'

'They always say that, every time,' muttered the Fécamp chief inspector.

The conversation languished. There was a long silence during which the spittle in Maigret's pipe could be heard sizzling. He got stiffly to his feet.

'If anyone asked me what the distinctive feature of this case is,' he said, 'I'd say that it has the mark of rage on it. Everything to do with the trawler is acrimonious, tense, overheated. The crew get drunk and fight in the Grand Banks Café. I bring the wireless operator's fiancée to see him, and he could barely conceal his irritation and gave her a pretty cool reception. He almost as good as told her to mind her own business! At Yport, the chief mechanic calls his wife all sorts and treats me like some dog he can kick. And then I come across two people who seem to have the same mark on them: the girl called Adèle, and her boyfriend. They make scenes on the beach, and no sooner do they settle their differences than they disappear together . . .'

'And what do you make of it all?' asked the chief inspector from Le Havre.

'Me? I don't make anything of it. I merely remark that I feel as if I'm going round in circles surrounded by a lot of mad people . . . Anyway, I'll say good night. I'm just an observer here. Besides, my wife is expecting me back at the hotel. You'll let me know, chief inspector, if you locate the Yport woman and the man in the grey car?'

'Of course! Good night!'

Instead of walking through the town, Maigret went via the harbour, hands in pocket, pipe between his teeth. The empty port was a large black rectangle where the only lights that showed were those of the *Océan*, which was still being unloaded.

'. . . the mark of rage!' he muttered to himself.

No one paid attention when he climbed on board. He walked along the deck, with no obvious purpose, he saw a light in a foredeck hatchway. He leaned over it. Warm air blew up into his face, a combined smell of doss-house, canteen and fish market.

He went down the iron ladder and found himself face to face with three men who were eating from mess tins balanced on their knees. For light, there was an oil lamp hung on gimbals. In the middle of their quarters was a cast-iron stove caked with grease.

Along the walls were four tiers of bunks, some still full of straw, the others empty. And boots. And sou'westers hanging on pegs.

Of the three, only Louis had stood up. The other two were the Breton and a black sailor with bare feet.

'Enjoying your dinner?' growled Maigret.

He was answered with grunts.

'Where are your mates?'

'Gone home, haven't they,' said Louis. 'You gotta have nowhere to go and be broke to hang about here when you're not at sea.'

Maigret had to get used to the semi-darkness and especially the smell. He tried to imagine the same space when it was filled by forty men who could not move a muscle without bumping into somebody.

Forty men dropping on to their bunks without taking their boots off, snoring, chewing tobacco, smoking . . .

'Did the captain ever come down here?'

'Never.'

And all the while the throb of the screw, the smell of coal smoke, of soot, of burning hot metal, the pounding of the sea . . .

'Come with me, Louis.'

Out of the corner of his eye, Maigret caught the sailor, full of bravado, making signs to the others behind his back.

But once aloft, on the deck now flooded with shadow, his swagger evaporated.

'What's up?'

'Nothing . . . Listen . . . Suppose the captain died at sea, on the way home. Was there someone who could have got the boat safely back to port?'

'Maybe not. Because the first mate doesn't know how to take a bearing. Still they say that, using the wireless, the wireless operator could always find the ship's position.'

'Did you see much of the wireless operator?'

'Never saw him at all! Don't imagine we walk around like we're doing now. There are general quarters for some, others have separate quarters of their own. You can go for days without budging from your small corner.'

'How about the chief mechanic?'

'Him? Yes. I saw him more or less every day.'

'How did he seem?'

Louis turned evasive.

'How the devil should I know? Look, what are you driving at? I'd like to see how you make out when everything's going wrong, a lad goes overboard, a steam valve blows, the captain's mind is set on anchoring the trawler in a station where there's no fish, a man gets gangrene and the rest of it . . . You'd be effing and blinding nineteen to the dozen! And for the smallest thing you'd take a swing at someone! And to cap it all, when you're told the captain on the bridge is off his rocker . . .'

'Was he?'

'I never asked him. Anyway . . .'

'Anyway what?'

'At the end of the day, what difference will it make? There'll always be someone who'll tell you. Look, it seems there were three of them up top who never went anywhere without their revolvers. Three of them spying on each other, all afraid of each other. The captain hardly ever came out of his cabin, where he'd ordered the charts, compass, sextant and the rest to be brought.'

'And it went on like that for three months?'

'Yes. Anything else you want to ask me?'

'No, that's it. You can go . . .'

Louis walked away almost regretfully. He stopped for a moment by the hatch, watching the inspector, who was puffing gently at his pipe.

Cod was still being extracted from the gaping hold in the glare of the acetylene lamps. But Maigret had had enough of trucks, dockers, the quays, the jetties and the lighthouse.

He was standing on a world of plated steel and, half-closing his eyes, he imagined being out on the open sea, in a field of surging swells through which the bows ploughed an endless furrow, hour after hour, day after day, week after week.

'Don't imagine we walk around like we're doing now . . .'

Men below serving the engines. Men in the forward crew quarters. And on the after deck, a handful of God's creatures: the captain, his first mate, the chief mechanic and the wireless operator.

A small binnacle light to see the compass by. Charts spread out.

Three months!

When they'd got back, Captain Fallut had written his will, in which he stated his intention to put an end to his life.

An hour after they'd berthed, he'd been strangled and dumped in the harbour.

And Madame Bernard, his landlady, was left grieving because now there would be no marriage of two ideally suited people. The chief mechanic shouted at his wife. The girl called Adèle defied an unknown man, but ran off with him the moment Maigret held a picture of herself scribbled on in red ink under her nose.

And in his prison cell the wireless operator Le Clinche in a foul temper.

The boat hardly moved. Just a gentle motion, like a chest breathing. One of the three men he'd seen in the foredeck was playing the accordion.

As he turned his head, Maigret made out the shapes of two women on the quayside. Suddenly galvanized, he hurried down the gangway.

'What are you doing here?'

He felt his face burn because he had sounded gruff, but especially because he was aware that he too was being infected by the frenzy which filled all those involved in the case.

'We wanted to see the boat,' said Madame Maigret with disarming self-effacement.

'It's my fault,' said Marie Léonnec. 'I was the one who insisted on . . .'

'All right! That's fine! Have you eaten?'

'It's ten o'clock . . . Have you?'

'Yes, thanks.'

The windows of the Grand Banks Café were more or less the only ones still lit. A few shadowy figures could be made out on the jetty: tourists dutifully out for their evening stroll.

'Have you found out anything?' asked Le Clinche's fiancée.

'Not yet. Or rather, not much.'

'I don't dare ask you a favour.'

'You can always ask.'

'I'd like to see Pierre's cabin. Could I?'

He shrugged and took her there. Madame Maigret refused to walk over the gangway.

Literally a metal box. Wireless equipment. A steel table, a seat and a bunk. Hanging on a wall, a picture of Marie Léonnec in Breton costume. Old shoes on the floor and a pair of trousers on the bed.

The girl inhaled the atmosphere with a mixture of curiosity and delight.

'Yes! But it isn't at all how I'd imagined. His shoes have never been cleaned . . . Oh look! He kept drinking from the same glass without ever washing it . . .'

A strange girl! An amalgam of shyness, delicacy and a good upbringing on the one hand and dynamism and fearlessness on the other. She hesitated.

'And the captain's cabin?'

Maigret smiled faintly, for he realized that deep down she was hoping to make a discovery. He led the way. He even fetched a lantern he found on deck.

'How can they live with this smell?' she sighed.

She looked carefully around her. He saw her become flustered and shy as she said:

'Why has the bed been raised up?'

Maigret stopped drawing on his pipe. She was right. All the crew slept in berths which were more or less part of the architectural structure of the boat. Only the captain had a metal bed.

Under each of its legs a wooden block had been placed.

'You don't think that's strange? It's as if . . .'

'Go on.'

All trace of ill-humour had gone. Maigret saw the girl's pale face lighten as her mind worked and her elation grew.

'It's as if . . . but you'll only laugh at me . . . as if the bed's been propped up so that someone could hide underneath . . . Without those pieces of wood, the bedstead would be much too low, but the way it is now . . .'

And before he could stop her, she lay down flat on the floor regardless of the dirt on the floor and slid under the bed.

'There's enough room!' she said.

'Right. You can come out now.'

'Just a minute, if you don't mind. Pass me that lamp for a minute, inspector.'

She went quiet. He couldn't work out what she was doing. He lost patience.

'Well?'

She reappeared suddenly, her grey suit covered with dust and eyes shining.

'Pull the bed out . . . You'll see.'

Her voice broke. Her hands shook. Maigret yanked the bed away from the wall and looked at the floor.

'I can't see anything . . .'

When she didn't answer he turned and saw that she was crying.

'What did you see? Why are you crying?'

'There . . . Read it.'

He had to bend down and place the lamp against the wall. Then he could make out words scratched on the wood with a sharp object, a pin or a nail.

Gaston – Octave – Pierre – Hen . . .

The last word was unfinished. And yet it did not look as if it had been done in a hurry. Some of the letters must have taken an hour to inscribe. There were flourishes, little strokes, the sort of doodling that's done in an idle moment.

A comic note was struck by two stag's antlers above the name 'Octave'.

The girl was sitting on the edge of the bed, which had been pulled into the middle of the cabin. She was still crying, in silence.

'Very curious!' muttered Maigret. 'I'd like to know if . . .'

At this point, she stood up and said excitedly:

'Of course! That's it! There was a woman here! She was hiding! . . . All the same, men would come looking for her . . . Wasn't Captain Fallut called Octave?'

The inspector had rarely been so taken off guard.

'Don't go jumping to conclusions!' he said, though there was no conviction in his words.

'But it's all written down! . . . The whole story is there! Four men who . . .'

What could he say to calm her down?

'Look, I've a lot of experience, so take it from me. In police matters, you must always wait before making judgements . . . Only yesterday, you were telling me that Le Clinche is incapable of killing.'

'Yes,' she sobbed. 'Yes, and I still believe it! Isn't it . . .'

She still clung desperately to her hopes.

'His name is Pierre . . .'

'I know. So what? One sailor in ten is called Pierre, and there were fifty men on board . . . There's also a Gaston . . . And a Henry . . .'

'So what do you think?'

'Nothing.'

'Are you going to tell the examining magistrate about this? And to think it was me who . . .'

'Calm down! We haven't found out anything, except that the bed was raised for one reason or another and that someone has written names on a wall.'

'There was a woman there.'

'Why a woman?'

'But . . .'

'Come on. Madame Maigret is waiting for us on the quay.'

'You're right.'

She wiped her tears, meek now, and sniffled.

'I shouldn't have come . . . But I thought . . . But it's not possible that Pierre . . . Listen! I must see him as soon as I can! I'll talk to him, alone . . . You can arrange it, can't you?'

Before starting down the gangway, she looked back with eyes full of hate at the dark ship, which was no longer the same to her now that she knew that a woman had been hiding on board.

Madame Maigret watched her, intrigued.

'Come! You mustn't cry! You know everything will all turn out all right.'

'No, it won't,' she said with a despairing shake of her head.

She couldn't speak. She could hardly breathe. She tried to look at the boat one more time. Madame Maigret, who did not understand what was going on, looked inquiringly at her husband.

'Take her back to the hotel. Try and calm her down.'

'Did something happen?'

'Nothing specific. I expect I'll be back quite late.'

He watched them walk away. Marie Léonnec turned round a dozen times, and Madame Maigret had to drag her away like a child.

Maigret thought about going back on board. But he was thirsty. There were still lights on in the Grand Banks Café.

Four sailors were playing cards at a table. Near the counter, a young cadet had his arm round the waist of the serving girl, who giggled from time to time.

The landlord was watching the card game and was offering suggestions.

He greeted Maigret with: 'Hello! You back again?'

He did not look overjoyed to see him. The very opposite. He seemed rather put out.

'Look sharp, Julie! Serve the inspector! Whatever's your poison. It's on me.'

'Thanks. But if it's all the same to you, I'll order like any other customer.'

'I didn't want to get on the wrong side of you . . . I . . .'

Was the day going to end with the mark of rage still on it? One of the sailors muttered something in his Norman dialect which Maigret translated roughly as:

'Watch out, I smell more trouble.'

The inspector looked him in the eye. The man reddened then stammered:

'Clubs trumps!'

'You should have played a spade,' declared Louis for something to say.

5. *Adèle and Friend*

The phone rang. Léon snatched the receiver, then called Maigret. It was for him.

'Hello?' said a bored voice on the other end of the line. 'Detective Chief Inspector Maigret? It's the duty desk officer at Fécamp police station. I've just phoned your hotel. I was told you might be at the Grand Banks Café. I'm sorry to disturb you, sir. I've been glued to the phone for half an hour. I can't get hold of the chief anywhere. As for the head of the Flying Squad, I'm wondering if he's still actually here in Fécamp . . . Thing is, I've got a couple of odd customers who've just turned up saying they want to make statements, all very urgent, apparently. A man and a woman . . .'

'Did they come in a grey car?'

'Yes, sir. Are they the pair you're looking for?'

Ten minutes later, Maigret was at the police station. All the offices were closed except for the inquiries area, a room divided in two by a counter. Behind it the duty officer was writing. He smoked as he wrote. A man was waiting. He was sitting on a bench, elbows on knees, chin in his hands.

And a woman was walking up and down, beating a tattoo on the floorboards with her high heels

The moment the inspector appeared, she walked right up to him, and the man got to his feet with a sigh of relief and growled between gritted teeth:

'And not a minute too soon!'

It was indeed the couple from Yport, both a little crosser than during the domestic shouting-match Maigret had sat through.

'Come next door with me.'

Maigret showed them into the office of the chief inspector, sat down in his chair and filled a pipe while he took a good look at the pair.

'Take a seat.'

'No thanks,' said the woman, who was clearly the more highly strung of the two. 'What I've got to say won't take long.'

He now had a frontal view of her, lit by a strong electric light. He did not need to look too hard to situate her type. Her picture with the head removed had been enough.

A good-looking girl, in the popular sense of the expression. A girl with alluring curves, good teeth, an inviting smile and a permanent come-hither look in her eye.

More accurately, a real bitch, a tease, on the make, always ready to create a scandal or burst into gales of loud, vulgar laughter.

Her blouse was pink silk. To it was pinned a large gold brooch as big as a 100-*sou* coin.

'First off, I want to say . . .'

'Excuse me,' interrupted Maigret. 'Please sit down as I've already asked. You will answer my questions.'

She scowled. Her mouth turned ugly.

'Look here! You're forgetting I'm here because I'm prepared to . . .'

Her companion scowled, irritated by her behaviour. They were made for each other. He was every inch the kind who is always seen with girls like her. His appearance was not exactly sinister. He was respectably dressed, though in bad taste. He wore large rings on his fingers and a pearl pin in his tie. Even so, the effect was disturbing. Perhaps because he gave off a sense of existing outside the established social norms.

He was the type to be found at all times of day in bars and brasseries, drinking cheap champagne with working girls and living in third-class hotels.

'You first. Name, address, occupation . . .'

He started to get to his feet.

'Sit down.'

'I just want to say . . .'

'Just say nothing. Name?'

'Gaston Buzier. At present, I'm in the business of selling and renting out houses. I'm based mainly in Le Havre, in the Silver Ring Hotel.'

'Are you a registered property agent?'

'No, but . . .'

'Do you work for an agency?'

'Not exactly . . .'

'That's enough. In a word you dabble . . . What did you do before?'

'I was a commercial traveller for a make of bicycle. I also sold sewing machines out in the sticks.'

'Convictions?'

'Don't tell him, Gaston!' the woman broke in. 'You've got a nerve! It was us who came here to . . .'

'Be quiet! Two convictions. One suspended for passing a dud cheque. For the other I got two months for not handing over to the owner an instalment I'd received on a house. Small-time stuff, as you see.'

Even so, he gave the impression that he was used to having to deal with policemen. He stayed relaxed, with something in his eye that suggested he could turn nasty.

'You next,' said Maigret, turning to the woman.

'Adèle Noirhomme. Born in Belleville.'

'On the Vice Squad register?'

'I was put on it five years ago in Strasbourg because some rich cow had it in for me on account of me having snatched her husband off her . . . But ever since . . .'

'. . . you've never been bothered by the police! . . . Fine! . . . Now tell me in what capacity you signed on for a cruise on the *Océan*.'

'First we'd better explain,' the man replied, 'because if we're here, it means we've got nothing to be ashamed of. At Yport, Adèle told me you had a picture of her. She was sure you were going to arrest her. Our first thought was to hop it so we wouldn't get into trouble. Because we both know the score. When we got to Étretat, I saw policemen stopping cars up ahead and I knew they'd go on looking for us. So I decided to come in voluntarily.'

'Now you, lady! I asked what you were doing on board the trawler.'

'Dead simple! I was following my boyfriend.'

'Captain Fallut?'

'Yes, the captain. I'd been with him, so to say, since last November. We met in Le Havre, in a bar. He fell for me. He used to come back to see me two or three times a week. Though from the start I thought he was a bit odd, because he never asked me to do anything. It's true! He was ever so prissy, everything had to be just so! He set me up in a room in a nice little hotel, and I started thinking that if I played my cards right he'd end up marrying me. Sailors don't get rich, but it's steady money, and there's a pension.'

'Did you ever come to Fécamp with him?'

'No. He wouldn't have that. It was him who came to me. He was jealous. He was a decent enough sort who can't have been around much because he was fifty and was as shy with women as a schoolboy. That plus the fact that he'd got me under his skin . . .'

'Just a moment. Were you already the mistress of Gaston Buzier?'

'Sure! But I'd introduced Gaston to Fallut. Said he was my brother.'

'I see. So in short you were both being subsidized by the captain.'

'I was working!' protested Buzier.

'I can see you now, hard at it every Saturday afternoon. And which of you came up with the scheme for sending you to sea on the boat?'

'Fallut. He couldn't bear the thought of leaving me by myself while he was away playing sailors. But he was also scared witless, because the rules about that sort of thing are strict, and he was a stickler for rules. He held out until the very last minute. Then he came and fetched me. The night before he was to set sail, he took me to his cabin. I quite fancied the idea because it made a change. But if I'd known what it was going to be like, I'd have been off like a shot!'

'Buzier didn't try to stop you?'

'He couldn't make up his mind. Do you understand? We couldn't go against what the old fool wanted. He'd promised me he'd retire as soon as he got back after that trip and marry me. But the whole set-up was nothing to write home about! It was no fun being cooped up all day in a cabin that stank of fish! And on top of that, every time anybody came in, I had to hide under the bed! We'd been at sea no time when Fallut starts regretting he'd taken me along. I never saw a man have the jitters like him! A dozen times a day he'd check to see if he'd locked the door. If I spoke, he shut me up in case anyone overheard. He was grumpy, on pins . . . Sometimes he'd stare at me for minutes on end as if he was tempted to get rid of me by throwing me overboard.'

Her voice was shrill, and she was waving her arms about.

'Not to mention the fact that he got more and more jealous! He asked me about my past . . . he tried to find out . . . then he'd go three days without talking to me, spying on me like I was his enemy. Then all of a sudden, he'd be madly in love with me again. There were times when I was really scared of him!'

'Which members of the crew saw you when you were on board?'

'It was the fourth night. I felt like a breath of air out on deck. I'd had enough of being locked up. Fallut went outside and checked to make sure there was no one about. It was as much as he could do to let me walk five steps up and down. He must have gone up on the bridge for a moment, and it was then that the wireless operator showed up and spoke to me . . . He was shy but got worked up. Next day he managed to get into my cabin.'

'Did Fallut see him?'

'I don't think so . . . He didn't mention anything.'

'Did you sleep with Le Clinche?'

She did not answer. Gaston Buzier sneered.

'Admit it!' he barked in a voice full of spite.

'I'm free to do as I please! Especially seeing as how you didn't exactly abstain from female company while I was away! Don't deny it! Are you forgetting the girl from the Villa des Fleurs? And what about that photo I found in your pocket?'

Maigret sat as solemn and impassive as the oracle.

'I asked if you slept with the wireless operator.'

'And I'm telling you to go to blazes!'

She smiled provocatively. Her lips were moist. She knew men desired her. She was counting on the promise of her pouting mouth, her sensuous body.

'The chief mechanic saw you too.'

'What's he been telling you?'

'Nothing. I'll recap. The captain kept you hidden in his cabin. Pierre Le Clinche and the chief mechanic would come to you there, on the quiet. Was Fallut aware of this?'

'No.'

'Although he had his suspicions and prowled round you and never left you alone except when he absolutely had to.'

'How do you know?'

'Did he still talk about marrying you?'

'I don't know.'

In his mind's eye, Maigret saw the trawler, the firemen down in the bunkers, the crew crammed into the foredeck, the wireless room, the captain's cabin aft, with the raised bed.

And the voyage had lasted three months!

All that time three men had prowled round the cabin where this woman was shut away.

'I've done some pretty stupid things, but that . . . !' she exclaimed. 'Hand on heart, if I had to do it again . . . A girl should always be on her guard against shy men who talk about marriage!'

'If you'd listened to me,' said Gaston Buzier.

'You shut your trap! If I'd listened to you, I know what kind of accommodation I'd be in now! I don't want to speak ill of Fallut, because he's dead. But all the same he was cracked. He had peculiar ideas. He'd have thought he'd done something wrong just because he'd broken some rules. And it went from bad to worse. After a week, he never opened his mouth except to go on at me or ask if anybody had been in the cabin. Le Clinche was the one he was most jealous of. He'd say:

'"You'd like that, wouldn't you! A younger man! Say it! Admit that if he came in when I wasn't here you wouldn't turn him away!"

'And he'd laugh so nastily that it hurt.'

'How many times did Le Clinche come to see you?' Maigret asked slowly.

'Oh, all right, the hell with it. Once. On the fourth day. I couldn't even tell you how it happened. After that, it wasn't on the cards, because Fallut kept such a close eye on me.'

'And the mechanic?'

'Never! But he tried! He'd come and look at me through the porthole. When he did that, he looked as white as a sheet . . . What sort of life do you think that was? I was like an animal in a cage. When the sea was rough I was sick, and Fallut didn't even try to look after me. He went for weeks without touching me. Then the urge would come back. He'd kiss me as if he wanted to bite me and held me so tight I thought he was trying to suffocate me.'

Gaston Buzier had lit a cigarette and was now smoking it with a sarcastic expression on his face.

'Please note, inspector, all this had nothing to do with me. While it was going on, I was working.'

'Oh give it a rest, will you?' she said, losing patience.

'What happened when you got back? Did Fallut tell you that he was intending to kill himself?'

'What, him? He didn't say anything. When we got back to port, he hadn't said a single word to me for two weeks. To tell the truth, I don't think he spoke to anyone. He'd stay put for hours with his eyes just staring in front of him. Meantime I'd made up my mind to leave him. I was fed up with it all, wasn't I? I'd have sooner starved to death: I'd never give up my freedom . . . I heard somebody walking along the quayside. Then he came in the cabin and said just a few words:

'"Wait here until I come to fetch you."'

'Spoken like a captain. Didn't he ever speak more . . . fondly?'

'At the finish, no!'

'Go on.'

'I don't know anything else. Or rather, the rest I learned from Gaston. He was there, down at the harbour.'

'Talk!' Maigret ordered the man.

'Like she said, I was down by the harbour. I saw the crew go into the bar. I waited for Adèle. It was dark. Then after a while, the captain came on shore by himself. There were trucks parked nearby. He started walking, and as he did a man jumped him. I don't know exactly what happened but there was a noise like a body falling into the water.'

'Would you recognize the man?'

'No. It was dark, and the trucks stopped me seeing much.'

'Which way did he go when he left?'

'I think he walked along the quay.'

'And you didn't see the wireless operator?'

'I don't know . . . I've no idea what he looks like.'

'And you,' said Maigret, turning to the woman, 'how did you get off the boat?'

'Somebody unlocked the door of the cabin where I was shut in. It was Le Clinche. He said:

'"Go quickly!"'

'Was that all?'

'I tried to ask him what was happening. I heard people running along the quayside and a boat with a lantern being rowed across the harbour.

'"Get going!" he repeated.

'He pushed me on to the gangway. Everybody was looking the

other way. No one paid any attention to me. I had the feeling that something horrible was going on but I preferred to make myself scarce. Gaston was waiting for me a little further along.'

'And what did the two of you do after that?'

'Gaston was as white as a sheet. We went into bars and drank rum. We spent the night at the Railway Inn. The next day all the papers were full of the death of Fallut. So first we took ourselves off to Le Havre, just in case. We didn't want to get mixed up in that business.'

'But that didn't stop her wanting to come back and nose around here,' snapped Gaston. 'I don't know whether it was on account of the wireless operator or . . .'

'Just shut up! That's enough! Of course I was curious about what had happened. So we came back here to Fécamp three times. So that we wouldn't attract attention, we stayed at Yport.'

'And you never saw the chief mechanic again?'

'How do you know about that? One day, in Yport . . . I was scared by the way he looked at me . . . He followed me quite a long way.'

'Why were you arguing earlier this afternoon with Gaston?'

She gave a shrug.

'Because! Look, haven't you got it yet? He thinks I'm in love with Le Clinche, that the wireless operator killed because of me and I don't know what else. He keeps going on and on until I'm sick to death of it. I had my fill of scenes on that damned boat . . .'

'But when I showed you that photo of you, on the hotel terrace . . .'

'Oh very clever! Of course I knew straight off that you were police. I told myself Le Clinche must have talked. I got scared and told Gaston to get us out of there. Only on the way, we thought there was no point because in the end they'd collar us round the next corner. Not to mention the fact that we'd only got two hundred francs between us. What are you going to do with me? . . . You can't send me to jail!'

'Do you think the wireless operator is the killer?'

'How should I know?'

'Do you own a pair of tan-coloured shoes?' Maigret suddenly asked Gaston Buzier.

'I . . . Yes. Why?'

'Oh, nothing. Just asking. Are you absolutely sure you wouldn't be able to recognize the man who killed the captain?'

'All I saw was a man's outline in the dark.'

'Well now, Pierre Le Clinche, who was also there, hidden by the trucks, reckons the murderer was wearing tan shoes.'

Gaston was on his feet like a shot. His eyes were hard, and his lips curled in a snarl.

'He said that? You're sure he said that?'

His anger almost choked him, reduced him to a stammer. He was no longer the same man. He banged the desk with his fist.

'I'm not having this! Take me to him! . . . Where is he? By God! We'll soon see who's lying! Tan-coloured shoes! And that makes me the killer, right? . . . He's the one who took my girl! He's the one who let her off the boat! And he has the nerve to say . . .'

'Calm down.'

He could scarcely breathe. He gasped:

'Did you hear that, Adèle? . . . That's just like all your lover-boys!'

Tears of rage filled both eyes. His teeth chattered.

'This is too much! . . . It wasn't me who . . . ha ha ha . . . this takes the biscuit! It's better than the films! . . . And the minute it comes out that I've got two convictions, he's the one who is believed! So I killed Captain Fallut! . . . Because I was jealous of him, is that it? . . . What else? . . . Oh yes, didn't I kill the wireless operator too?'

He ran one hand feverishly though his hair, which left it in a mess. It also made him look thinner. His eyes had darker rings under them, his complexion was duller.

'If you're going to arrest me, what are you waiting for?'

'Shut up!' snapped Adèle.

But she too had started to panic, though this did not stop her giving Gaston sceptical looks.

Did she have her suspicions? Or was this some sort of play-acting game?

'If you're going to arrest me, do it now . . . But I demand to confront the man . . . Then we'll see!'

Maigret had pressed an electric bell. The station duty officer showed his face warily round the door.

'I want you to keep the gentleman and the lady here until tomorrow, until we get a ruling from the examining magistrate.'

'You rat!' Adèle yelled at him and she spat on the floor. 'You want to lock me up for telling the truth! . . . Right then, listen to me: every word of what I just told you was made up! . . . I'm not going to sign any statement! . . . That'll put the tin lid on your little scheme! . . . So this is the way . . .'

And turning to Gaston:

'Never mind! . . . They can't touch us! You'll see, when it comes to it it's us who'll have the last laugh . . . Only thing is, a woman who's been on the Vice Squad's books, well, all she's good for is for banging up in the cells . . . Oh by the way, just asking, was it me who killed the captain? . . .'

Maigret left the room without listening to the rest. Outside, he filled his lungs with sea air and knocked the ash out of his pipe. He hadn't gone ten metres when he heard Adèle from inside the police station regaling officers with the choicest items of her vocabulary.

It was now two in the morning. The night was unnaturally calm. It was high tide, and the masts of the fishing boats swayed to and fro above the roofs of the houses.

And over everything the regular murmur, wave after wave, of sea on shingle.

Harsh lights surrounded the *Océan*. It was still being unloaded round the clock, and the dock-hands strained to push the trucks as they filled with cod.

The Grand Banks Café was closed. At the Hôtel de la Plage, the porter, wearing a pair of trousers over his night-shirt, opened the door for the inspector.

The lobby was lit by a single lamp. It was why it took a moment before Maigret made out the figure of a woman in a rattan chair.

It was Marie Léonnec. She was asleep with her head resting on one shoulder.

'I think she's waiting for you,' whispered the porter.

She was pale. And possibly anaemic. There was no colour in her lips, and the dark shadows under her eyes showed just how exhausted she was. She slept with her mouth open, as if she was not getting enough air.

Maigret touched her gently on the shoulder. She gave a start, sat up, looked at him in a daze.

'I must have dropped off . . . Aah!'

'Why aren't you in bed? Didn't my wife see you to your room?'

'Yes. But I came down again. I was very quiet. I wanted to know . . . Tell me . . .'

She was not as pretty as usual because sleep had made her skin clammy. A mosquito bite had left a red spot in the middle of her forehead.

Her dress, which she had probably made herself from hard-wearing serge, was creased.

'Have you found out anything new? No? Listen, I've been thinking a lot. I don't know how to say this . . . Before I see Pierre tomorrow, I want you to talk to him. I want you to say that I know all about that woman, that I don't hate him for it. I'm certain, you see, that he didn't do it. But if I speak to him first, he'll feel awkward. You saw him this morning. He's all on edge. If there was a woman on board, isn't it only natural if he . . .'

But it was too much for her. She burst into tears. She could not stop crying.

'And most of all, nothing must get into the papers. My parents mustn't know. They wouldn't understand. They . . .'

She hiccupped.

'You've got to find the murderer! I think if I could question people . . . I'm sorry, I don't know what I'm saying. You know better than me. Only you don't know Pierre. I'm two years older than him. He's like a little boy really, especially if you accuse him of anything, he is likely to clam up – it's pride – and not say anything. He is very sensitive. He has been humiliated too often.'

Maigret put his hand on her shoulder, slowly, holding back a deep sigh.

Adèle's voice was still going round and round in his head. He saw her again, seductive, desirable in the full bloom of her animal presence, magnificent in her sensuality.

And here was this well-brought-up anaemic girl, who was trying to hold back her tears and smile brightly.

'When you really know him . . .'

But what she would never really know was the dark cabin around which three men had circled for days, for weeks on end, far away, in the middle of the ocean, while other crewmen in the engine room and in the foredeck dimly sensed that a tragedy was unfolding, kept watch on the sea, discussed changes of course, felt increasingly uneasy and talked of the evil eye and madness.

'I'll talk to Le Clinche tomorrow.'

'Can I too?'

'Perhaps. Probably. But now you must get some rest.'

A little later, Madame Maigret, still half-asleep, murmured:

'She's very sweet! Did you know she's already got her trousseau together? All hand-embroidered . . . Find out anything new? You smell of perfume . . .'

No doubt lingering traces of Adèle's overpowering scent which had clung to him. A scent as common as cheap wine in cheap bistros which had, on board the trawler and for months on end, mingled with the rank smell of cod while men prowled round a cabin, as determined and pugnacious as dogs.

'Sleep well!' he said, pulling the blanket up to his chin.

The kiss he placed on the forehead of his drowsy wife was solemn and sincere.

6. *The Three Innocents*

The staging was basic: the setting was the same as for most confrontations of witnesses and accused. This one was taking place in a small office in the jail. Chief Inspector Girard, of the Le Havre police, who was in charge of the investigation, sat in the only chair. Maigret stood with his elbows leaning on the mantelpiece of the black granite fireplace. On the wall were graphs, official notices and a lithograph of the President of the French Republic.

Standing in the full glare of the lamp was Gaston Buzier. He was wearing his tan-coloured shoes.

'Let's have the wireless operator in.'

The door opened. Pierre Le Clinche, who had been given no warning, walked in, brow furrowed, like a man in pain who is expecting to get more of the same treatment. He saw Buzier. But he paid him not the slightest attention and looked all round him, wondering which man he should face.

On the other hand, Adèle's lover looked him up and down, a supercilious smile hanging on his lips.

Le Clinche had a crumpled air. His flesh was grey. He did not try to bluster or conceal his dejection. He was as lost as a sick animal.

'Do you recognize this man here?'

He stared at Buzier, as if searching through his memory.

'No. Who is he?'

'Take a good look at him, from head to foot . . .'

Le Clinche obeyed, and the minute his eyes reached the shoes, he straightened up.

'Well?'

'Yes.'

'Yes what?'

'I understand what you're getting at. The tan shoes . . .'

'So that's it!' Gaston Buzier suddenly burst out. He had not said a word until then but his face was now dark with anger. 'Why don't you tell them again that I'm the one who did your captain in? Go on!'

All eyes were on the wireless operator, who looked at the floor and gestured vaguely with one hand.

'Say it!'

'Perhaps those weren't the shoes.'

'Oh yes!' Gaston crowed, already claiming victory. 'So you're backing down . . .'

'You don't recognize the man who murdered Fallut?'

'I don't know . . . No.'

'You are probably aware that this man is the lover of a certain Adèle, who you most certainly do know. He has already admitted that he was near the trawler at the moment the crime was committed. Also that he was wearing tan-coloured shoes.'

All this time, Buzier was facing him down, bristling with impatience and fury.

'That's right! Make him talk! But he'd better be telling the truth or else I swear I'll . . .'

'Hold your tongue! Well, Le Clinche?'

The young man passed his hand over his brow and winced, literally, with pain.

'I don't know! He can go hang for all I care!'

'But you did see a man wearing tan shoes attack Fallut.'

'I forget.'

'That's what you said when you were first interviewed. That wasn't very long ago. Are you sticking to what you said then?'

'No, that is . . . Look, I saw a man wearing tan shoes. That's all I saw, I don't know if he was the murderer.'

The longer the interview went on, the more confident Gaston Buzier, who also looked rather seedy after a night in the cells, became. He was now shifting his weight from one leg to the other, with one hand in his trouser pocket.

'See? He's backing down! He doesn't dare repeat the lies he told you.'

'Answer me this, Le Clinche. Thus far, we know for certain that there were two men near the trawler at the time when the captain was murdered: you were one, and Buzier the other. You say you didn't kill anybody. Now, after pointing the finger at this man, you seem to be withdrawing the accusation. So was there a third person there? If so, then it is impossible you could not have seen him. So who was it?'

Silence. Pierre Le Clinche continued to stare at the ground.

Maigret, still leaning with elbows propped up on the fireplace, had taken no part in the interrogation, happy to leave it to his colleague and content just to observe the two men.

'I repeat the question: was there a third person on the quay?'

'I don't know,' said the prisoner in a crushed voice.

'Is that a yes?'

A shrug of the shoulder which meant: 'As you wish.'

'Who was it?'

'It was dark.'

'In that case tell me why you said the murderer was wearing tan shoes . . . Wasn't it a way of drawing attention away from the real murderer who was someone you knew?'

The young man clutched his head in both hands.

'I can't take any more!' he groaned.

'Answer me!'

'No! You can do what you like . . .'

'Bring in the next witness.'

The moment the door was open, Adèle walked through it with an exaggerated swagger. She swept the room with one glance to get a sense of what had been going on. Her eye lingered in particular on the wireless operator, whom she seemed shocked to see looking so defeated.

'I assume, Le Clinche, that you recognize this woman, whom Captain Fallut hid in his cabin throughout the entire voyage and with whom you were intimate.'

He looked at her coldly. Yet already Adèle's lips were parting and preparing to frame a captivating smile.

'That's her.'

'To cut a long story short, there were three of you on board, who, in plain language, were sniffing around her: the captain, the chief mechanic and you. You went to bed with her at least once. The chief mechanic got nowhere. Was the captain aware that you had deceived him?'

'He never spoke to me about it.'

'He was very jealous, wasn't he? And it was because he was so jealous that he didn't speak to you for three months?'

'No.'

'No? Was there some other reason?'

Now he was red-faced, not knowing which way to look, talking too fast:

'Well it could have been that. I don't know . . .'

'What else was there between you that might have created hatred or suspicion?'

'I . . . There wasn't anything . . . You're right, he was jealous.'

'What feelings did you have that led you to become Adèle's lover?'

A silence.

'Were you in love with her?'

'No,' he sighed in a small dry voice.

But the woman screeched:

'Thanks a million! Always the gentleman, eh? But that didn't stop you hanging round me until the very last day! Isn't that the truth? And it's also true that you probably had another girl waiting for you on shore!'

Gaston Buzier pretended to be whistling under his breath, with his fingers hooked in the arm-holes of his waistcoat.

'Tell me again, Le Clinche, if, when you went on board after witnessing the death of the captain, Adèle was still locked inside her cabin.'

'Locked in, yes!'

'So she couldn't have killed anyone.'

'No! It wasn't her, I swear!'

Le Clinche was getting ruffled. But Chief Inspector Girard went on remorselessly:

'Buzier states that he didn't kill anybody. But, after accusing him, you withdraw the accusation . . . Another way of looking at it is that the pair of you were in it together.'

'Oh very nice, I must say!' cried Buzier in a burst of brutal contempt. 'When I take up crime, it won't be with a . . . a . . .'

'All right! Both of you could have killed because you were jealous. Both of you had been sleeping with Adèle.'

Buzier said with a sneer:

'Me jealous! Jealous of what?'

'Have any of you anything further to add? You first, Le Clinche.'

'No.'

'Buzier?'

'I wish to state that I am innocent and demand to be released immediately.'

'And you?'

Adèle was putting on fresh lipstick.

'Me . . .' – a thick stroke of lipstick – '. . . I . . .' – a look in her mirror – '. . . I've nothing to say, not a thing . . . All men are skunks! You heard that boy there, the one I'm supposed to have been prepared to do silly things for . . . It's no good looking at me like that, Gaston. Now if you want my opinion, there's things we know nothing about in this business with the boat. The minute you found out a woman had been on board, you thought it explained everything . . . But what if there was something else?'

'Such as?'

'How should I know? I'm not a detective . . .'

She crammed her hair under her red straw toque. Maigret saw Pierre Le Clinche look away.

'The two chief inspectors exchanged glances. Girard said:

'Le Clinche will be returned to his cell. You two will stay in the waiting room . . . I'll let you know whether you are free to go or not in a quarter of an hour.'

The two detectives were left alone. Both looked worried.

'Are you going to ask the magistrate to let them go?' asked Maigret.

'Yes. I think it's the best thing. They may be mixed up in the killing, but there are other things we may be missing . . .'

'Right.'

'Hello, operator? Get me the law courts at Le Havre . . . Hello? . . . Yes, public prosecutor's office please . . .'

A few moments later, while Chief Inspector Girard was talking to the magistrate, there was the sound of a disturbance outside. Maigret ran to see what was happening and saw Le Clinche on the ground, struggling with three uniformed officers.

He was terrifyingly out of control. His eyes were bloodshot and looked wild and staring. Spittle drooled from his mouth. But he was being held down now and couldn't move.

'What happened?'

'We hadn't 'cuffed him, seeing as how he was always so quiet . . . Anyway, as we were moving him down the corridor, he made a grab for the gun in my belt . . . He got it . . . was going to use it to kill himself . . . I stopped him firing it.'

Le Clinche lay on the floor, staring at the ceiling. His teeth were digging into the flesh of his lips, reddening his saliva with blood.

But most disturbing were the tears which streamed down his leaden cheeks.

'Maybe get the doctor . . . ?'

'No! Let him go!' barked Maigret.

When the prisoner was alone on his back on the stone floor:

'On your feet! . . . Look sharp now! . . . Get a move on! . . . And no antics . . . otherwise you'll feel the back of my hand across your face, you miserable little brat!'

The wireless operator did what he was told, unresistingly, fearfully. His whole body trembled with the aftershock. In falling he had dirtied his clothes.

'How does your girlfriend fit into that little display?'

Chief Inspector Girard appeared:

'He agreed,' he said. 'All three are free to go, but they mustn't leave Fécamp . . . What happened here?'

'This moron tried to kill himself! If it's all right with you, I'll look after him.'

The two of them were walking along the quays together. Le Clinche had splashed water over his face. It had not washed the crimson blotches away. His eyes were bright, feverish and his lips too red.

He was wearing an off-the-peg suit with three buttons which he'd done up anyhow, not caring about what he looked like. His tie was badly knotted.

Maigret, hands in pockets, walked grimly and kept muttering as if for his own benefit:

'You've got to understand that I haven't got time to tell you what you should and should not do, except for this: your fiancée is here. She's a good kid, got a lot of grit. She dropped everything and came here all the way from Quimper. She's moving heaven and earth . . . Maybe it wouldn't be such a good idea to dash her hopes . . .'

'Does she know?'

'There's no point in talking to her about that woman.'

Maigret never stopped watching him. They reached the quays. The brightly coloured fishing boats were picked out by the sunshine. The streets nearby were busy.

There were a few moments when Le Clinche seemed to be rediscovering his zest for life, and he looked hopefully at his surroundings with optimism. At others, his eyes hardened, and he glared angrily at people and things.

They had to pass close by the *Océan*, now in the final day of unloading. There were still three trucks parked opposite the trawler.

The inspector spoke casually as he gestured to various points in space.

'You were there . . . Gaston Buzier was here . . . And it was on that spot that the third man strangled the captain.'

Le Clinche breathed deeply, then looked away.

'Only it was dark, and none of you knew who the others were. Anyway, the third man wasn't the chief mechanic or the first mate. They were both with the crew in the Grand Banks Café.'

The Breton, who was outside on deck, spotted the wireless operator, went over to the hatch and leaned his head in. Three sailors came out and looked at Le Clinche.

'Come on,' said Maigret. 'Marie Léonnec is waiting for us.'

'I can't . . .'

'What can't you?'

'Go there! . . . Please, leave me alone! . . . What's it to you if I do kill myself? . . . Anyway, it would be best for all concerned!'

'Is the secret so heavy to bear, Le Clinche?'

No answer.

'And you really can't say anything, is that it? Of course you can. One thing: do you still want Adèle?'

'I hate her!'

'That's not what I asked. I said want, the way you wanted her all the time you were at sea. Just between us men: had you had lots of girls before you met Marie Léonnec?'

'No. Leastways nothing serious.'

'And never deep urges? Wanting a woman so much you could weep?'

'Never!' he sighed and looked away.

'So it started when you were on board ship. There was only

one woman, the setting was uncouth, monotonous . . . Fragrant flesh in a trawler that stank of fish . . . You were about to say something?'

'It's nothing.'

'You forgot all about the girl you were engaged to?'

'That's not the same thing . . .'

Maigret looked him in the eye and was astounded by the change that had just come over it. Suddenly the young man had acquired a determined tilt to his head, his gaze was steady, and his mouth bitter. And yet, for all that, there were traces of nostalgia and fond hopes in his expression.

'Marie Léonnec is a pretty girl,' Maigret went on in pursuit of his line of thought.

'Yes.'

'And much more refined than Adèle. Moreover, she loves you. She is ready to make any sacrifice for . . .'

'Why don't you leave it alone!' said the wireless operator angrily. 'You know very well . . . that . . .'

'. . . that it's something else! That Marie Léonnec is a good, well-brought-up girl, that she will make a model wife and a caring mother but . . . but there'll always be something missing? Isn't that so? Something more elemental, something you discovered on board shut away inside the captain's cabin, when fear caught you by the throat, in the arms of Adèle. Something vulgar, brutal . . . The spirit of adventure! . . . And the desire to bite, to burn your bridges, to kill or die . . .'

Le Clinche stared at him in amazement.

'How did you . . .'

'How do I know? Because everyone has had a sight of the same adventure come his way at least once in his life! . . . We cry hot tears, we shout, we rage! Then, a couple of weeks later, you look at Marie Léonnec and you wonder how on earth you could have fallen for someone like Adèle.'

As he walked, the young man had been keeping his eyes firmly on the glinting water of the harbour. In it were reflected the reds, whites and greens that decorated the taffrails of boats.

'The voyage is over. Adèle has gone. Marie Léonnec is here.'

There was a moment of calm. Maigret went on:

'The ending was dramatic. A man is dead because there was passion on that boat and . . .'

But Le Clinche was again in the grip of wild ideas.

'Stop it! Stop it!' he repeated in a brittle voice. 'No! Surely you can see it's not possible . . .'

He was haggard-eyed. He turned to see the trawler, which, almost empty now, sat high in the water, looming over them.

Then his fears took hold of him once more.

'I swear . . . You've got to let me alone . . .'

'And on board, throughout the entire voyage, the captain was also stretched to breaking point, wasn't he?'

'What do you mean?'

'And the chief mechanic too?'

'No.'

'It wasn't just the two of you. It was fear, Le Clinche, wasn't it?'

'I don't know . . . Please leave me alone!'

'Adèle was in the cabin. Three men were on the prowl. Yet the captain would not give in to his urges and refused to speak to his woman for days on end. And you, you looked in through the portholes but after just one encounter you never touched her again . . .'

'Stop it!'

'The men down in the bunkers, the crew in the foredeck, they were all talking about the evil eye. The voyage went from bad to worse, lurching from navigational errors to accidents. A ship's boy lost overboard, two men injured, the cod going bad and the mess they made of entering the harbour . . .'

They turned at the end of the quay, and the beach stretched out before them, with its neat breakwater, the hotels, beach-huts and multicoloured chairs dotted over the shingle.

Madame Maigret in a deckchair was picked out by a patch of sunshine. Marie Léonnec, wearing a white hat, was sitting next to her.

Le Clinche followed the direction of Maigret's eyes and stopped suddenly. His temples looked damp.

The inspector went on:

'But it took more than a woman . . . Come on! Your fiancée has seen you.'

And so she had. She stood up, remained motionless for a moment, as if her feelings were too much for her. And then she was running along the breakwater while Madame Maigret put down her needlework and waited.

7. *Like a Family*

It was one of those situations which crop up spontaneously from which it is difficult to get free. Marie Léonnec, alone in Fécamp, had been placed under the wing of the Maigrets by a friend and had been taking her meals with them.

But now her fiancé was there. All four of them were together on the beach when the hotel bell announced that it was time for lunch.

Pierre Le Clinche hesitated for a moment and looked at the others in embarrassment.

'Come on!' said Maigret, 'we'll get them to lay another place.'

He took his wife's arm as they crossed the breakwater. The young couple followed, not speaking. Or rather, only Marie spoke and did so in a firm voice.

'Any idea what she's telling him?' the inspector asked his wife.

'Yes. She told me a dozen times this morning, to see if I thought it was all right. She's telling him she's not cross with him about anything, *whatever it was that happened*. You see? She's not going to say anything about a woman. She's pretending she doesn't know, but she did say she'd be stressing the words *whatever it was that happened*. Poor girl! She'd go to the ends of the earth for him!'

'Alas!' sighed Maigret.

'What do you mean?'

'Nothing . . . Is this our table?'

Lunch passed off quietly, too quietly. The tables were set very closely together so that speaking in a normal voice was not really possible.

Maigret avoided watching Le Clinche, to put him at his ease, but the wireless operator's attitude gave him cause for concern, and it also worried Marie Léonnec, whose face had a pinched look to it.

Her young man looked grim and depressed. He ate. He drank. He spoke when spoken to. But his thoughts were elsewhere. And more than once, hearing footsteps behind him, he jumped as if he sensed danger.

The bay windows of the dining room were wide open, and through them could be seen the sun-flecked sea. It was hot. Le Clinche had his back to the view and from time to time, with a jerk of the head, would turn round quickly and scour the horizon.

It was left to Madame Maigret to keep the conversation going, mainly by talking to the young woman about nothing in particular, to keep the silence at bay.

Here they were far removed from unpleasant events. The setting was a family hotel. A reassuring clatter of plates and glasses. A half-bottle of Bordeaux on the table next to a bottle of mineral water.

But then the manager made a mistake. He came up as they were finishing dessert and asked:

'Would you like a room to be made up for this gentleman?'

He was looking at Le Clinche: he had spotted a fiancé. And no doubt he took the Maigrets for the girl's parents.

Two or three times the wireless operator made the same gesture as he had that morning during the confrontation. A rapid movement of his hand across his forehead, a very boneless, weary gesture.

'What shall we do now?'

The other guests were getting up and leaving. The group of four were standing on the terrace.

'Shall we sit down for a while?' suggested Madame Maigret.

Their folding chairs were waiting for them, on the shingle. The Maigrets sat down. The two young people remained standing for a moment, uncertain of what they should do.

'I think we'll go for a little walk, shall we?' Marie Léonnec finally brought herself to say with a vague smile meant for Madame Maigret.

The inspector lit his pipe and, once he was alone with his wife, he muttered:

'Tell me: do I really look like the father-in-law!'

'They don't know what to do. Their position is very delicate,' remarked his wife as she watched them go. 'Look at them. They're so awkward. I may be wrong but I think Marie has more backbone than her fiancé.'

He certainly made a sorry sight as he strolled listlessly along, a slight figure who paid no attention to the girl at his side and, you would have sworn even from a distance, did not say anything.

But the girl gave the impression that she was doing her level best, that she was talking as a way of distracting him, that she was even trying to appear as if she was having a good time.

There were other groups of people on the beach. But Le Clinche was the only man not wearing white trousers. He was wearing a dark suit, which made him look even more pitiful.

'How old is he?' asked Madame Maigret.

Her husband, lying back in his deckchair with eyes half-closed, said:

'Nineteen. Just a boy. I'm very afraid that he'll be easy meat for anybody now.'

'Why? Isn't he innocent?'

'He probably never killed anybody. No. I'd stake my life on it. But all the same, I'm afraid he's had it . . . Just look at him! And look at her!'

'Nonsense. Leave the pair of them alone for a moment and they'll be kissing.'

'Perhaps.'

Maigret was pessimistic.

'She isn't much older than him. She really loves him. She is quite ready to become a model little wife.'

'Why do you think . . .'

'That it won't ever happen? Just an impression. Have you ever looked at photos of people who died young? I've always been struck by the fact that those pictures, which were taken when the subjects were fit and healthy, always have something of the graveyard about them. It's as if those who are doomed to be the victims of some awful experience already have a death sentence written on their faces.'

'And do you think that boy . . .'

'He's a sad case. Always was! He was born poor. He suffered from being poor. He worked like a slave, put his head down, like a man swimming upstream. Then he managed to persuade a nice girl from a higher social class than his to say yes . . . But I don't believe it'll happen. Just look at them. They're groping in the dark. They're trying to believe in happy endings. They want to believe in their star . . .'

Maigret spoke quietly, in a half-whisper, as he stared at the two outlines, which stood out against the sparkling sea.

'Who is officially in charge of the investigation?'

'Girard, a chief inspector at Le Havre. You don't know him. An intelligent man.'

'Does he think he's guilty?'

'No. In any case, he's got nothing solid on him, not even any real circumstantial evidence.'

'What do you think?'

Maigret turned round, as if to get a glimpse of the trawler, though it was hidden from him by a row of houses.

'I think that the voyage was, for two men at least, tragic. Tragic enough that Captain Fallut *couldn't go on living any longer* and the wireless operator *couldn't go back to living his old, normal life.*'

'All because of a woman?'

He did not answer the question directly but went on:

'And the rest of them, the men who had no part in events, all of them including the stokers, were, if they did but know it, deeply marked by it too. They came back angry and scared. For three months, two men and a woman raised the tension around the deck-house in the stern. A few black walls with portholes . . . But it was enough.'

'I've hardly ever seen you get so worked up about a case . . . You said three people were involved. What on earth did they do out there in the middle of the ocean?'

'Yes, what did they do exactly? Something which was serious enough to kill Captain Fallut! And also bad enough to leave those two young people not knowing which way to turn. Look at them out there, trying to find what's left of their dreams in the shingle.'

The young people were coming back, arms swinging, uncertain whether courtesy required them to rejoin the Maigrets or whether it would be more tactful to leave them to themselves.

During their walk, Marie Léonnec had lost much of her vivaciousness. She gave Madame Maigret a dejected look. It was as if all her efforts, all her high spirits had run up against a wall of despair or inertia.

It was Madame Maigret's custom to take some light refreshment of an afternoon. So at around four o'clock, all four of them sat down on the hotel terrace under the striped umbrellas, which exuded the customary festive air.

Hot chocolate steamed in two cups. Maigret had ordered a beer and Le Clinche a brandy and soda.

They talked about Jorissen, the teacher from Quimper who had written to Maigret on behalf of the wireless operator and had brought Marie Léonnec with him. They said the usual things:

'You won't find a better man anywhere . . .'

They embroidered on this theme, not out of conviction, but because they had to say something. Suddenly, Maigret blinked, then focused on a couple now walking towards them along the breakwater.

It was Adèle and Gaston Buzier. He slouched, hands in pockets, his boater tilted on the back of his head, seemingly unconcerned, while she was as animated and as eye-catching as ever.

'As long as she doesn't spot us . . . !' the inspector thought.

But at that very moment, Adèle's eye caught his. She stopped and said something to her companion, who tried to dissuade her.

Too late! She was already crossing the road. She looked around at all the tables in turn, chose the one nearest to the Maigrets, then sat down so that she was facing Marie Léonnec.

Her boyfriend followed with a shrug, touched the brim of his boater as he passed in front of the inspector and sat astride a chair.

'What are you having?'

'Not hot chocolate, that's for sure. A kümmel.'

What was that if not a declaration of war? When she mentioned chocolate, she was staring at Marie Léonnec's cup. Maigret saw the girl flinch.

She had never seen Adèle. But surely the penny had dropped? She glanced across at Le Clinche, who looked away.

Madame Maigret's foot nudged her husband's twice.

'What say the four of us walk over to the Casino.'

She too had worked it out. But no one answered. Only Adèle at the next table said anything.

'It's so hot!' she sighed. 'Take my jacket, Gaston.'

She removed her suit jacket and was revealed in pink silk, opulently sensual and bare-armed. She did not take her eyes off the girl for an instant.

'Do you like grey? Don't you think they should ban people from wearing miserable colours on the beach?'

It was so obvious. Marie Léonnec was wearing grey. But Adèle was demonstrating her intention to go on the attack, by any means and without wasting any time.

'Waiter! Shift yourself! I can't wait all day.'

Her voice was shrill. And it sounded as if she was deliberately exaggerating its coarseness.

Gaston Buzier scented danger. He knew Adèle of old. He muttered a few words to her. But she replied in a very loud voice:

'So what? They can't stop anyone sitting on this terrace. It's a free country!'

Madame Maigret was the only one with her back to her. Maigret and the wireless operator sat sideways on but Marie Léonnec faced her directly.

'We're all as good as everybody else, isn't that right? Only there's some people who trail round after you when you're too busy to see them and then won't give you the time of day when they're in company.'

And she laughed. Such an unpleasant laugh! She stared at the girl, whose face flushed bright red.

'Waiter! What do I owe you?' asked Buzier, who was anxious to put a stop to this.

'We've got plenty of time! Same again, waiter. And bring me some peanuts.'

'We don't have any.'

'Well go and get some! That's what you're paid for, isn't it?'

There were people at two other tables. They all stared at the new couple, who could not go unnoticed. Maigret began to worry. He wanted of course to put an end to a scene which might turn nasty.

On the other hand, the wireless operator was trapped opposite him: he could see him sit there and sweat.

It was fascinating, like being present at a dissection. Le Clinche did not move a muscle. He was not facing the woman, but he must surely have been able to see her, however vaguely, on his left, at the very least to make out the pink cloud of her blouse.

His eyes, grey and lacklustre, were fixed and staring. One hand lay on the table and was closing slowly, as slowly as the tentacles of some undersea creature.

There was no telling yet how it would all turn out. Would he get up and run away? Would he turn on the woman who talked and talked? Would he . . . ?

No. He did none of those things. What he did was quite different and a hundred times more unnerving. It was not just his hand that was closing, but his whole being. He was shrivelling, shrinking into his shell.

His eyes steadily turned as grey as his face.

He did not move. Was he still breathing? Not a tremor. Not a twitch. But his stillness, which grew more and more complete, was mesmerizing.

'. . . puts me in mind with another of my gentleman friends, married he was, with three kids . . .'

Marie Léonnec, on the other hand, was breathing quickly. She gulped down her chocolate to hide her confusion.

'. . . now he was the most passionate man on the planet. Sometimes, I refused to let him in and he'd stop outside on the landing and sob, until the neighbours worked up a right old head of steam! "Adèle my sweety pie, my pet, my own . . ." All the usual lovey-dovey stuff. Anyway, one Sunday I met him out walking with his wife and kiddies. I heard his wife ask him:

'"Who's that woman?"

'And all pompous, he says to her:

'"Obviously a floozie. You can tell from the ridiculous way she's dressed."'

And she laughed, playing to the crowd. She looked at the faces around her to see what effect her behaviour was having.

'Some people are that slow on the uptake you can't get a rise out of them.'

Again Gaston Buzier said something to her quietly in an attempt to shut her up.

'What's the matter? Not turning chicken are you? I pay for my drinks, don't I? I'm not doing anybody any harm! So nobody's got any right to tell me what to do . . . Waiter, where are those peanuts? And bring another kümmel!'

'Maybe we should leave,' said Madame Maigret.

It was too late. Adèle was on the rampage. It was clear that if they tried to leave, she would do anything to cause a scene, whatever the cost.

Marie Léonnec was staring at the table. Her ears were red, her eyes unnaturally bright, and her mouth hung open in distress.

Le Clinche had shut his eyes. And he went on sitting there, unseeing, with a fixed expression on his face. His hand still lay lifelessly on the table.

Maigret had never had an opportunity like this to scrutinize him. His face was both very young and very old, as is often the case with adolescents who have had difficult childhoods.

Le Clinche was tall, taller than average, but his shoulders were not yet those of a man.

His skin, which he had not looked after, was dotted with freckles. He had not shaved that morning, and there were faint blond shadows around his chin and on his cheeks.

He was not handsome. He could not have laughed very often in his life. On the contrary, he had burned large quantities of midnight oil, reading too much, writing too much, in unheated rooms, in his ocean-tossed cabin, by the light of dim lamps.

'I'll tell you what really makes me sick. It's seeing people putting on airs who're really no better than us.'

Adèle was losing patience. She was ready to try anything to get what she wanted.

'All these proper young ladies, for instance. They pretend to be lily-white hens but they'll run after a man the way no self-respecting trollop would dare to.'

The hotel owner stood by the entrance, surveying his guests as if trying to decide whether or not he should intervene.

Maigret now had eyes only for Le Clinche, in close-up. His head had dropped a little. His eyes had not opened.

But tears squeezed out one by one from under his clamped eyelids, oozed between the eyelashes, hesitated and then snaked down his cheeks.

It wasn't the first time the inspector had seen a man cry. But it was the first time he had been so affected by the sight. Perhaps it was the silence, the stillness of his whole body.

The only signs of life it gave were those rolling, liquid pearls. The rest was dead.

Marie Léonnec had seen nothing of all this. Adèle was still talking.

Then, a split second later, Maigret *knew*. The hand which lay on the table had just imperceptibly opened. The other was out of sight, in a pocket.

The lids rose no more than a millimetre. It was enough to allow an eye-glance to filter through. That glance settled on Marie.

As the inspector was getting to his feet, there was a gunshot. Everyone reacted in a confused pandemonium of screams and overturned chairs.

At first, Le Clinche did not move. Then he started to lean imperceptibly to his left. His mouth opened, and from it came a faint groan.

Marie Léonnec, who had difficulty understanding what had happened, since no one had seen a gun, flung herself on him, grabbed him by the knees and his right hand and turned in panic:

'Inspector! . . . What . . . ?'

Only Maigret had worked out what had happened. Le Clinche had had a revolver in his pocket, a weapon he had found God knows where, for he hadn't had one that morning when he was released from his cell. And he'd fired from his pocket. He'd been gripping the butt all the interminable time Adèle had been talking, while he kept his eyes shut and waited and maybe hesitated.

The bullet had caught him in the abdomen or the side. His jacket was scorched, cut to ribbons at hip level.

'Get a doctor! Ring for the police!' someone somewhere was shouting.

A doctor appeared. He was wearing swimming trunks. He'd been on the beach hardly a hundred metres from the hotel.

Hands had reached out and held Le Clinche up just as he began to fall. He was carried into the hotel dining room. Marie, utterly distraught, followed the stretcher inside.

Maigret had not had time to worry about Adèle or her boyfriend. As he entered the bar, he suddenly saw her. She looked deathly pale and was emptying a large glass, which rattled against her teeth.

She had helped herself. The bottle was still in her hand. She filled the glass a second time.

The inspector paid her no further attention, but retained the image of that white face above the pink blouse and particularly the sound of her teeth chattering against the glass.

He could not see Gaston Buzier anywhere. The dining-room door was about to be closed.

'Move along, please,' the hotel-owner was telling guests. 'Keep calm! The doctor has asked us to keep the noise down.'

Maigret pushed the door open. He found the doctor kneeling and Madame Maigret restraining the frantic Marie, who was trying desperately to rush to the wounded man's side.

'Police!' the inspector muttered to the doctor.

'Can't you get those women out of here? I'm going to have to undress him and . . .'

'Right.'

'I'll need a couple of men to help me. I assume someone has already phoned for an ambulance?'

He was still wearing his trunks.

'Is it serious?'

'I can't tell you anything until I've probed the wound. You do of course understand . . .'

Yes! Maigret understood all too well when he saw the appalling, lacerated mess, a coalescence of flesh and fabric.

The tables had been laid for dinner. Madame Maigret took Marie Léonnec outside. A young man in white trousers asked shyly:

'If you'll allow me, I could help . . . I'm studying pharmacy.'

A burst of fierce red sunlight slanted through a window and was so blindingly bright that Maigret closed the Venetian blind.

'Will you take his legs?'

He recalled the words he had said to his wife that afternoon as he lounged in his folding chair watching the gangling figure move across the beach with the smaller and livelier outline of Marie Léonnec at his side:

'Easy meat.'

Captain Fallut had died as soon as he had docked. Pierre Le Clinche had fought long and hard, perhaps had even still been fighting as he sat eyes closed, one hand on the table, the other in his pocket, while Adèle went on talking, endlessly talking and playing to the gallery.

8. The Drunken Sailor

It was a little before midnight when Maigret left the hospital. He had waited to see the stretcher being wheeled out of the operating theatre. On it lay the prone figure of a tall man swathed in white.

The surgeon was washing his hands. A nurse was putting the instruments away.

'We'll do our best to save him,' he said in reply to the inspector. 'His intestine is perforated in seven places. You could say it's a very, very nasty wound. But we've tidied him up.'

He gestured to receptacles full of blood, cotton-wool and disinfectant.

'Believe me, it took a lot of damned hard work!'

They were all in high good humour, surgeons, assistant-surgeons and theatre nurses. They had been brought a patient as near to death's door as he could be, bloodstained, abdomen not only gaping but scorched too, with scraps of clothing embedded in his flesh.

And now an ultra-clean body had just been carried out on a trolley. And the abdomen had been carefully stitched up.

The rest would be for later. Maybe Le Clinche would regain consciousness, maybe not. The hospital did not even try to find out who he was.

'Does he really have a chance of pulling through?'

'Why not? We used to see worse than that during the War.'

Maigret had phoned the Hôtel de la Plage at once, to set Marie Léonnec's mind at rest. Now he set out to walk back by himself. The doors of the hospital closed behind him with the smooth sound of well-oiled hinges. It was dark. The street of small middle-class houses was deserted.

He had only gone a few metres when a figure stepped away

from the wall and the light of a street lamp illuminated the face of Adèle. In a mean voice she asked:

'Is he dead?'

She must have been waiting for hours. Her features were drawn, and the kiss-curls at her temples had lost their shape.

'Not yet,' replied Maigret in the same tone of voice.

'Will he die?'

'Maybe, maybe not.'

'Do you think I did it on purpose?'

'I don't think anything.'

'Because it's not true!'

The inspector continued on his way. She followed him and to do so she had to walk very quickly.

'Basically, it was his own fault, you must see that.'

Maigret pretended he wasn't even listening. But she was stubborn and persisted:

'You know very well what I mean. On board he nearly got to the point of asking me to marry him. Then once we'd docked . . .'

She would not give up. She seemed driven by an overmastering need to talk.

'If you think I'm a bad woman, it's because you don't know me. Only, there are times . . . Look, inspector, you've got to tell me the truth. I know what a bullet can do, especially in the belly from point-blank range. They performed a laparotomy on him, right?'

She gave the impression that she was no stranger to hospitals, that she had heard how doctors talked and knew people who'd been shot more than once.

'Was the operation a success? . . . I believe it depends on what the patient has been eating before . . .'

Her distress was not acute. More a raw, stubborn refusal to take no for an answer.

'Aren't you going to say? But there, you know, don't you, why I sounded off like that this afternoon. Gaston is a cheap crook. I never loved him. But the other one . . .'

'He may live,' said Maigret carefully, looking the girl straight in the eyes. 'But if what happened on the *Océan* is not cleared up, it won't do him much good.'

He paused, expecting her to say something, to have a reaction. She dropped her eyes.

'Of course, you think that I know everything . . . From the moment both men were my lovers . . . But I swear . . . ! No, you don't know what sort of man Captain Fallut was, so you'll never understand . . . He was in love with me, it's true. He used to come to Le Havre to see me. And falling, I mean really falling, for a woman at his age turned his brain . . . But that did not stop him being pernickety about everything, very controlled, very faddy about wanting everything just so . . . I still can't work out why he ever agreed to let me hide on board . . . But what I do know is the minute we were out on the open sea he regretted it and because he regretted it he began to hate me . . . His character changed just like that.'

'But the wireless operator hadn't spotted you yet?'

'No. That didn't happen until the fourth night, like I told you . . .'

'Are you quite sure that Fallut was already in a strange mood before then?'

'Maybe not quite as strange. But afterwards there were days when it all got weird, and I wondered if he wasn't actually mad.'

'And you had no idea about what the reason for the change might have been?'

'No. I thought about it. Sometimes I told myself there had to be some funny business going on between him and the wireless operator. I even thought they were involved in smuggling . . . Ah, you won't ever get me to go anywhere near a fishing boat again! Can you believe that it went on for three months? And then for it to end like that! One is murdered as soon as he steps ashore and the other who . . . It is true, isn't it, that he's not dead?'

They had reached the quays, and the young woman seemed reluctant to go any further.

'Where is Gaston Buzier?'

'Back at the hotel. He knows it's not the moment to rub me up the wrong way, that I'd dump him if he says one word out of place.'

'Are you going back to him now?'

She gave a shrug, a gesture which signified: 'Why not?'

And then there was a glimpse of her flirtatious self. Just as she was taking her leave of Maigret, she murmured with an awkward smile:

'Thank you so much, inspector. You've been ever so kind . . . I . . .'

But she didn't dare say the rest. It was an invitation. A promise.

'All right, all right!' he growled and walked on.

He pushed open the door of the Grand Banks Café.

Just as he reached for the latch, he clearly heard a hubbub coming from inside the bar, like a dozen men's voices all talking at once. The moment the door opened, complete silence fell with brutal abruptness. Yet there were more than ten men there, in two or three groups, who must have been calling to each other from one table to the next.

The landlord stepped forward to meet Maigret and shook his hand, though not without a certain unease of manner.

'Is it true what they're saying? That Le Clinche shot himself?'

His customers toyed with their drinks in a show of indifference. Present were Louis, the black sailor, the chief mechanic from the trawler and a few others besides whom Maigret had finally got to know by sight.

'Quite true,' he said.

He observed that the chief mechanic, looking suddenly very shifty, kept fidgeting on the oil-cloth of the bench seat.

'Some voyage!' muttered someone in a corner in a pronounced Norman accent.

The words probably were a fair expression of the general

opinion, for many heads dropped, a fist was brought down on a marble tabletop while one voice echoed the sentiment:

'Yes! A voyage of the damned!'

But Léon gave a cough to remind his customers to watch what they said and with a nod to them motioned towards a sailor in a red jerkin, who was drinking alone in a corner.

Maigret sat down near the counter and ordered a brandy and soda.

No one was talking now. Every man there was trying to look calm and unruffled. Léon, a practised master of ceremonies, called out to the group sitting around the largest table:

'Want me to bring the dominoes?'

It was a way of breaking the silence, of occupying hands. The black-backed dominoes were shuffled on the marble tabletop. The landlord sat down next to the inspector.

'I shut them up,' he said quietly, 'because the fellow in the far corner, to your left, by the window, is the father of the boy . . . You know who I mean?'

'What boy?'

'The ship's boy, Jean-Marie, the one who fell overboard on their third day out.'

The man had his head on one side and was listening. If he hadn't heard the words, he had certainly understood that they concerned him. He called to the serving girl to refill his glass and downed it in one, with a shudder of disgust.

He was already drunk. He had bulging light-blue eyes which were now more sea-green. A quid of tobacco raised a lump in his cheek.

'Does he go out on the Grand Banks boats too?'

'He used to. But now that he's got seven kids, he goes out after herring in winter, because the periods away are shorter: a month to start with and then for increasingly shorter spells as the fish go south.'

'And in summer?'

'He fishes for himself, lays dragnets, lobster pots . . .'

The man was sitting on the same bench-seat as Maigret, at the far end of it. But the inspector had a good view of him in a mirror.

He was short, with wide shoulders. He was a typical northern sailor, squat, fleshy, with no neck, pink skin and fair hair. Like most fishermen, his hands were covered with scars of old ulcers.

'Does he usually drink this much?'

'They're all hard drinkers. But he's been really knocking it back since his boy died. Seeing the *Océan* again hit him hard.'

The man was now staring at them, openly insolent.

'What you after, then?' he spluttered at Maigret.

'Nothing at all.'

All the mariners followed the scene without interrupting their game of dominoes.

'Because you'd better out with it . . . A man's not entitled to have a drink, is that it?'

'Not at all!'

'Go on, say it, say I'm not entitled to have a sup or two,' he repeated with the obstinacy of a drunk.

The inspector's eye picked out the black armband he wore on one sleeve of his red jerkin.

'So what you up to, then, sneaking around here, the pair of you, talking about me?'

Léon shook his head, advising Maigret not to reply, and went over to his customer.

'Easy now! Don't go kicking up a fuss, Canut. The inspector's not talking about you but about the lad who shot himself.'

'Serve him right! Is he dead?'

'No. Maybe they can save him.'

'Too bad! I wish they'd all die!'

The words had an immediate impact. All heads turned to stare at Canut, who felt the urge to shout it ever louder:

'That's right! The whole lot of you!'

Léon was worried. He looked imploringly at everyone there, adding a gesture of helplessness in Maigret's direction.

'Go home. Go to bed. Your wife will be waiting up . . .'

'Don't give a damn!'

'In the morning, you won't feel like going out to clear your nets.'

The drunk sniggered. Louis took the opportunity to call to Julie:

'How much does it come to?'

'Both rounds?'

'Yes. Put it on the slate. Tomorrow I'll get my advance pay before I sail.'

He got to his feet. The Breton automatically followed his lead, as if he were his shadow. He tipped his cap. Then he did it again for Maigret's particular benefit.

'Bunch of chicken-hearts!' muttered the drunk as the two men walked past him. 'Cowards, the whole lot of them!'

The Breton clenched his fists and was about to say something. But Louis dragged him away.

'Go home to bed,' Léon repeated. 'Anyway, it's closing time.'

'I'll go when everybody else goes. My money's as good as the next man's, right?'

He looked around for Maigret. It was as if he was ready to start an argument.

'It's like the big fella there . . . What's he trying to ferret out?'

He was referring to the inspector. Léon was on tenterhooks. The last customers lingered, sure that something was about to happen.

'Second thoughts, I think I'd rather go home. What do I owe you?'

He fumbled beneath his jerkin and produced a leather wallet, threw a few greasy notes on the table, stood up, swayed and staggered to the door, which he had difficulty opening.

He kept muttering indistinctly what might have been insults or threats. Once outside, he pressed his face to the window for a last look at Maigret, flattening his nose against the steamed-up glass.

'It hit him real hard,' sighed Léon, returning to his seat. 'He had just the one son. All his other kids are girls. Which is to say they don't count.'

'What are they saying here?' asked Maigret.

'About the wireless operator? They don't know anything. So they make things up. Fanciful tales . . .'

'Such as?'

'Oh, I don't know. They're always on about the *evil eye* . . .'

Maigret sensed that there was a keen eye watching him. It belonged to the chief mechanic, who was sitting at the table opposite.

'Has your wife stopped being jealous?' the inspector asked.

'Given that we sail in the morning, I'd like to see her try to keep me stuck in Yport!'

'Is the *Océan* leaving tomorrow?'

'With the tide, yes. If you think the owners intend to let her fester in the harbour . . .'

'Have they found a new captain?'

'Some retired master or other who hasn't been at sea for eight years. And on top of that, he was then skipper of a three-masted barque! It'll be no fun!'

'And the wireless operator?'

'Some kid they've got straight out of college . . . Some big technical school, they said it was.'

'And is the first mate coming back?'

'They recalled him. Sent him a cable. He'll be here in the morning.'

'And the crew?'

'The usual story. They take whatever's hanging around the docks. It always works, doesn't it?'

'Have they found a ship's boy?'

The chief mechanic looked at him sharply.

'Yes,' he said curtly.

'Glad to be off?'

No reply. The chief mechanic ordered another grog. Léon, keeping his voice low, said:

'We've just had news of the *Pacific*, which was due back this week. She's a sister ship of the *Océan*. She sank in less than three minutes after splitting her seams on a rock. All hands lost. I've got the first mate's wife staying upstairs. She came from Rouen to meet her husband. She spends every day down by the harbour mouth. She doesn't know yet. The Company is waiting for confirmation before breaking the news.'

'It's the design of those boats,' growled the chief mechanic, who had overheard.

The black sailor yawned and rubbed his eyes but was not thinking of leaving just yet. The abandoned dominoes formed a complicated pattern on the grey rectangle of the tabletop.

'So in a word,' Maigret said slowly, 'no one has any idea why the wireless operator tried to kill himself?'

His words met with an obstinate silence. Did all the men there know why? Was this the freemasonry of seamen taken to an extreme, closing ranks against landlubbers who poked their noses into their business?

'What do I owe you, Julie?' asked Maigret.

He stood up, paid, headed wearily to the door. Ten pairs of eyes followed him. He turned but saw only faces that were blank or resentful. Even Léon, for all his bar-keeper's chumminess, stood shoulder to shoulder with his customers.

It was low tide. All that could be seen of the trawler was the funnel and the derricks. The trucks had all gone. The quay was deserted.

A fishing boat, with its white light swinging at the end of its mast, was slowly moving away towards the jetties, and the sound of two men talking could be heard.

Maigret filled one last pipe, looked across the town and the towers of the Palais de la Bénédictine, at the foot of which were walls which were part of the hospital.

The windows of the Grand Banks Café punctuated the quay with two rectangles of light.

The sea was calm. There was a faint murmur of water lapping the shingle and the wooden piles of the jetties.

The inspector stood on the edge of the quay. Thick hawsers, the ones holding the *Océan* fast, were coiled round bronze bollards.

He leaned over. Men were battening down the hatches over the holds in which salt had been stowed earlier that day. One of them was very young, younger than Le Clinche. He was wearing a suit and, leaning against the wireless room, was watching the sailors as they worked.

It could only be the replacement for the wireless operator who not long since had put a bullet in his own belly. He was smoking a cigarette, taking shallow, nervous pulls on it.

He'd come straight from Paris, fresh out of the National Technical School. He was apprehensive. Perhaps he dreamed of adventure.

Maigret could not tear himself away. He was rooted there by a feeling that the mystery was close, within his grasp, that he had to make just one last effort.

Suddenly, he turned, sensing a strange presence behind him. In the dark, he made out a red jerkin and a black armband.

The man had not seen him, or at least was not paying him any attention. He was walking along the lip of the quayside, and it was a miracle that in the state he was in that he did not go over the edge.

The inspector now had only a rear view of him. He had a feeling that the drunk, overcome by dizziness, was about to fall down on to the deck of the trawler.

But no. He was talking to himself. He laughed derisively. He brandished a fist.

Then he spat, once, twice, three times on the boat below. He spat to express his total and utter disgust.

After which, doubtless having relieved his feelings, he wandered off, not in the direction of his house, which was in the fishermen's quarter, but towards the lower end of town, where there was a bar still with its lights on.

9. Two Men on Deck

From the cliff side of the town came a silvery chime: it was the clock of the Palais de la Bénédictine, striking one.

Maigret, his hands clasped behind him, was walking back to the Hôtel de la Plage. But the further he went the slower he walked until he finally came to a complete stop halfway along the quay.

In front of him was his hotel, his room and his bed, a welcoming, comforting combination.

Behind him . . . He turned his head. He saw the trawler's funnel, from which smoke was gently rising, for the boilers had just been lit. Fécamp was asleep. There was a wide splash of moonlight in the middle of the harbour. The wind was rising, blowing in off the sea, raw and almost freezing, like the breath of the ocean itself.

Maigret turned back wearily, reluctantly. Again he stepped over the hawsers coiled round the bollards, then stood on the side of the quay, staring down at the *Océan*.

His eyes were small, his mouth threatening, his hands were bunched into fists deep in his pockets.

Here was Maigret in solitary mood, disgruntled, withdrawn, when he digs his heels in defiantly and is not afraid of making a fool of himself.

It was low tide. The deck of the trawler was four or five metres below the level of the quay. But a plank had been laid between the quayside and the bridge. It was thin and narrow.

The sound of the surf was growing louder. The tide must be on the turn. Pallid waves ate imperceptibly into the shingle of the beach.

Maigret stepped on to the plank, which bent into the arc of a circle when he reached the middle. His soles squealed when he reached the iron bridge. But he did not go any further. He sat down on the seat of the officer of the watch, behind the wheel and the compass, from which dangled Captain Fallut's thick sea mittens.

Maigret settled in the way grim dogs crouch stubbornly by the mouth of a burrow where they have got a scent of something.

Jorissen's letter, his friendship with Le Clinche, all the steps taken by Marie Léonnec were no longer the issue. It was now personal.

He had formed a picture of Captain Fallut. He had met the wireless operator, Adèle and the chief mechanic. He had gone to considerable lengths to get a sense of the whole way of life on board the trawler.

But it was not enough. Something was eluding him. He felt he understood everything except, crucially, what was at the heart of the case.

Fécamp was asleep. On board, the sailors were in their bunks. The inspector slumped heavily in the seat of the officer of the watch, round-shouldered, legs slightly apart, his elbows on his knees.

His eye settled on random details: the gloves, for instance, huge, misshapen, which Fallut would have worn during his spells on the bridge and had left hanging there.

And half turning, he looked back over the afterdeck. Ahead were the full sweep of the deck, the foredeck and, very near, the wireless room.

The sound of water lapping. A barely perceptible surge as the steam began to stir. Now that the furnace had been lit and water filled the boilers, the boat felt more alive than it had in the last few days.

And wasn't Louis asleep below, next to the bunkers full of coal?

To the right was the lighthouse. At the end of one jetty, a green light; a red light at the head of the next.

And the sea: a great black hole emitting a strong, heavy smell.

There was no conscious effort of the mind involved, not in the strict sense. Maigret let his eye roam slowly, sluggishly, seeking to bring his surroundings to life, to acquire a feel for them. Gradually he slipped into something akin to a state of trance.

'It was a night like this, but colder, because spring had scarcely begun . . .'

The trawler, tied up at the same berth. A thin spiral of smoke rising from the funnel.

A few sleeping men.

Pierre Le Clinche, who had dined at Quimper in his fiancée's house. Family atmosphere. Marie Léonnec had doubtless shown him to the door, so that they could kiss unobserved.

And he had travelled all night, third class. He would return in three months. He would see her again. Then another voyage and after that, when it was winter, around Christmas time, they would marry.

He had not slept. His sea-chest was on the rack. It contained provisions made for him by his mother.

At the same time, Captain Fallut was leaving the small house in Rue d'Étretat, where Madame Bernard was asleep.

Captain Fallut was probably uneasy and very troubled, racked in advance by guilt. Was it not tacitly agreed that one day he would marry his landlady?

Yet all winter he had been going to Le Havre, sometimes three times a week, to see a woman. A woman he dared not show his face with in Fécamp. A woman he was keeping as his mistress. A woman who was young, attractive, desirable, but whose vulgarity gave her an aura of danger.

A respectable man, of regular, fastidious habits. A model of probity, held up as an example by his employers, whose sea-logs were masterpieces of detailed record-keeping.

And now he was making his way through the sleeping streets to the station where Adèle was due to arrive.

Perhaps he was still hesitating?

But three months! Would he find her waiting for him when he got back? Wasn't she too alive, too eager for life not to deceive him?

She was a very different kind of woman from Madame Bernard. She did not spend her time keeping her house tidy, polishing brasses and floors, making plans for the future.

Absolutely not! She was a woman, a woman whose image was fixed on his retina in ways that brought a flush to his cheek and quickened his breath.

Then she was there! She laughed with that tantalizing laugh which was almost as sensual as her inviting body. She thought it would be fun to sail away, to be hidden on board, to have a great adventure!

But should he not tell her that the adventure would not be much fun? That being at sea cooped up in a locked cabin would be an ordeal?

He vowed that he would. But he didn't dare. When she was there, when her breasts heaved as she laughed, he was incapable of saying anything sensible.

'Are you going to smuggle me on board tonight?'

They walked on. In the bars and the Grand Banks Café, members of the crew went on the spree with the advance on their wages they'd been paid that afternoon.

And Captain Fallut, short, smartly turned out, grew paler the nearer he got to the harbour, to his boat. Now he could see the funnel. His throat was dry. Perhaps there was still time?

But Adèle was hanging on his arm. He could feel her leaning against him, warm and trembling with excitement.

Maigret, facing the quayside which was now deserted, imagined the two of them.

'Is that your ship? It smells bad. Have we got to go across on this plank?'

They walked over the gangway. Captain Fallut was nervous and told her to not to make a noise.

'Is this the wheel for driving the ship?'

'Sh!'

They went down the iron ladder. They were on the deck. They went into the captain's cabin. The door closed behind them.

'Yes! That's how it was!' muttered Maigret. 'There they are now, the pair of them. It's the first night on board . . .'

He wished he could fling back the curtain of night, reveal the pallid sky of first light and make out the figures of the crew staggering, slowed by alcohol, as they made their way back to the boat.

The chief mechanic arrived from Yport by the first morning train. The first mate was on the way from Paris and Le Clinche from Quimper.

The men tumbled on to the deck, argued in the foredeck about bunks, laughed, changed their clothes and re-emerged stiffly in oilskins.

There was a boy, Jean-Marie, the ship's boy. His father had brought him, leading him by the hand. The sailors jostled him, made fun of his boots, which were too big, and of the tears already welling in his eyes.

The captain was still in his cabin. Finally, he opened the door. He closed it carefully behind him. He was curt, very pale, and his features were drawn.

'Are you the wireless operator? . . . Right. I'll give you your orders in a little while. Meanwhile, take a look round the wireless room.'

Hours passed. Now the boat's owner stood on the quay. Women and mothers were still arriving with parcels for the men who were about to sail.

Fallut shook, fearful for his cabin, whose door was not to be opened at any price, because Adèle, dishevelled, mouth half open, was sprawled sideways, fast asleep, across the bed.

A touch of the early-morning nausea, which was felt not only by Fallut but by all the men who had toured the bars of the town or travelled there overnight by train.

One by one, they drifted away to the Grand Banks Café, where they drank coffee laced with spirits.

'See you soon! . . . if we come back!'

A loud blast of the ship's horn. Then two more. The women and children, after one last hug, rushing towards the end of the breakwater. The ship's owner shaking Fallut's hand.

The hawsers were cast off. The trawler slid forward, moved clear of the quay. Then Jean-Marie, the ship's boy, choking with fright, stamped his feet in desperation and thought of making a bid to get back to dry land.

Fallut had been sitting where Maigret was sitting now.

'Half ahead! . . . One five-oh turns! . . . Full steam ahead!'

Was Adèle still asleep? Would she be woken up by the first swell and be nervous?

Fallut did not move from the seat which had been his for so many years. Ahead of him was the sea, the Atlantic.

His nerves were taut, for he now realized what a stupid thing he had done. It had not seemed so serious when he was ashore.

'Two points port!'

And then there were shouts, and the group on the breakwater rushed forward. A man, who had clambered up the derrick to wave goodbye to his family, had fallen on to the deck!

'Stop engine! . . . Astern engine! . . . Stop engine!'

There was no sign of life from the cabin. Wasn't there still time to put the woman ashore?

Rowing boats approached the vessel, which was now stationary between the jetties. A fishing boat was asking for right of way.

But the man was injured. He would have to be left behind. He was lowered into a dinghy.

The women were demoralized. They were deeply superstitious.

On top of which the ship's boy had to be restrained from jumping into the water because he was so terrified of leaving!

'Ahead steam! . . . Half! . . . Full! . . .'

Le Clinche was settling into his workplace, headphones on head, testing the instruments. And there, in his domain, he was writing:

My Darling Girl,
It's eight in the morning! We're off. Already we can't see the town and . . .

Maigret lit a fresh pipe and got to his feet so that he would have a better view of his surroundings.

He was in full possession of the characters in the case and, in a sense, was now able to move them around like counters on the boat which lay spread out before him.

'First meal in the narrow officers' mess: Fallut, the first mate, the chief mechanic and the wireless operator. The captain announces that henceforth he will be taking all his meals in his cabin, alone.'

They have never heard the like of it! Such an outlandish idea! They all try in vain to come up with a reason for it.

Maigret, clasping his hand to his forehead, muttered:

'It's the ship's boy's job to take the captain his food. The captain opens the door only part of the way or else hides Adèle under the bed, which he has propped up.'

The two of them have to make do with a meal for one. The first time, the woman laughs. And no doubt Fallut leaves nearly all his share to her.

He is too solemn. She makes fun of him. She is nice to him. He unbends. He smiles.

And up in the foredeck are they not already muttering about the evil eye? Aren't they talking about the captain's decision to eat by himself? And moreover, who ever saw a captain walking around with the key to his cabin in his pocket!

The twin screws turn. The trawler has acquired the sense of unease which will continue to fill it for three months.

Below deck, men like Louis shovel coal into the maw of the

furnaces for eight or ten hours a day or keep a drowsy eye on the oil-pressure gauge.

Three days. That's the general view. It has taken just three days to create an atmosphere of anxiety. And it was at that point that the crew began wondering if Fallut was mad.

Why? Was it jealousy? But Adèle stated that she didn't see Le Clinche until about day four.

Until then, he is too busy with his new equipment. He tunes in and listens, for his personal satisfaction. He makes trial transmissions. And with his headphones constantly on his head, he writes page after page as if the postman was standing by to whisk his letters away and deliver them to his fiancée.

Three days. Hardly time to get to know one another. Perhaps the chief mechanic, peering through portholes, has caught sight of the young woman? But he never mentioned it.

The atmosphere on board builds only gradually as the crew are drawn together through shared adventures. But as yet there are no adventures to share. They have not yet even started to fish. For that they must wait until they reach the Grand Banks, yonder, off Newfoundland, on the other side of the Atlantic, where they will not be for another ten days yet, at the earliest.

Maigret was standing on the bridge, and any man waking then and seeing him would have wondered what he was doing there, an imposing, solitary figure calmly surveying his surroundings.

And what was he doing? He was trying to understand! All the characters were in position, each with a particular outlook and all with their own preoccupations.

But after this point, there was no way of guessing the rest. There was a large gap. The inspector had only witnesses to rely upon.

'It was on about the third day out that Captain Fallut and the wireless operator started thinking of each other as enemies. Each had a revolver in his pocket. They seemed afraid of each other.'

Yet Le Clinche was not yet Adèle's lover!

'But from that moment, the captain behaved as if he was mad.'

They are now in the middle of the Atlantic. They have left the regular lanes used by the great liners. Now they hardly ever sight even other trawlers, English or German, as they steam towards their fishing grounds.

Does Adèle start to grumble and complain about being cooped up?

. . . wondered if he wasn't actually mad . . .

Everyone agrees that mad is the right word. And it seems unlikely that Adèle alone is responsible for bringing about such an astonishing change in a well-adjusted man who has always made a religion of order.

She has not deceived him yet! He has allowed her two or three turns around the deck, at night, provided she takes multiple precautions.

So why is he behaving as if he is *actually mad*?

Here the evidence of witnesses begins to mount up:

'He gives the order to anchor the trawler in a position where for as long as anyone can remember no one ever caught a single cod . . .'

He is not an excitable man or a fool, nor does he lose his temper easily! He is a steady, upstanding citizen of careful habits who for a time dreamed of sharing his life with his landlady, Madame Bernard, and of ending his days in the house full of embroidery in Rue d'Étretat.

'There's one accident after another. When we finally get on to the Banks and start catching fish, it gets salted in such a way that it's going bad by the time we get back.'

Fallut is no novice! He's about to retire. Until now, no one has ever had reason to question his competence.

He takes all his meals in his cabin.

'He doesn't talk to me,' Adèle will say. 'He goes for days, weeks sometimes, without saying a word to me. And then suddenly it comes over him again . . .'

A sudden wave of sensuality! She's there! In his cabin! He shares her bed! And for weeks on end he manages to stay at arm's length until the temptation proves too strong!

Would he behave this way if his only grievance was jealousy?

The chief mechanic prowls round the cabin, licking his lips. But he doesn't have the nerve to force the lock.

And finally, the Epilogue. The *Océan* is on the way home to France, laden with badly salted cod.

Is it during the voyage back that the captain draws up what is virtually his will in which he says no one should be accused of causing his death?

If so, he clearly wants to die. He intends to kill himself. No one on board, except him, is capable of taking a ship's bearings, and he has enough of the seafaring spirit to bring his boat back to port first.

Kill himself because he has infringed regulations by taking a woman to sea with him?

Kill himself because insufficient salt was used on the fish, which will sell for a few francs below the market rate?

Kill himself because the crew, bewildered by his odd conduct, believe that he is a lunatic?

The captain, the most cool-headed, the most scrupulously careful master in all Fécamp? The same man whose log books are held up as models?

The man who for so long has been living in the peaceful house of Madame Bernard?

The steam vessel docks. The members of the crew rush on shore and make a bee-line for the Grand Banks Café, where they can at last get a proper drink.

And every man jack of them is stamped with the mark of mystery! On certain questions they all remain silent. They are all on edge.

Is it because a captain has behaved in ways that no one understands?

Fallut goes on shore alone. He will have to wait until the quays are deserted before he can disembark Adèle.

He takes a few steps forwards. Two men are hiding: the wireless operator and Gaston Buzier, the girl's lover.

But the captain is jumped by a third man, who strangles him and drops his body into the harbour.

And all this happened at the very spot where the *Océan* is now gently rocking on the black water. The body had got tangled in the anchor chain.

Maigret was smoking. He scowled.

'Even at the first interview, Le Clinche lies when he talks about a man wearing tan-coloured shoes who killed Fallut. Now the man with the tan-coloured shoes is Buzier. When he is brought face to face with him, Le Clinche retracts his statement.'

Why would he lie about this if not to protect a third person, in other words the murderer? And why wouldn't Le Clinche name him?

He does no such thing. He even lets himself be put behind bars instead of him. He makes little effort to defend himself, even though there is every likelihood that he will go down for murder.

He is grim, like a man riddled with guilt. He does not dare look either his fiancée or Maigret in the eye.

One small detail. Before returning to the trawler, he headed back to the Grand Banks Café. He went up to his room. He burned a number of papers.

When he gets out of jail, he isn't happy, even though Marie Léonnec is there, encouraging him to look on the bright side. And somehow he manages to get hold of a revolver.

He is afraid. He hesitates. For a long time he just sits there, eyes closed, finger on the trigger.

And then he fires.

*

As the night wore on, it turned cooler, and the smell of seaweed and iodine weighed more strongly on the breeze.

The trawler had risen by several metres. The deck was now level with the quayside, and the push and drag of the tide caused the boat to buck sideways and made the gangway creak.

Maigret had forgotten how tired he was. The hardest time was over. It would soon be dawn.

He summarized:

Captain Fallut, who had been retrieved dead from the anchor chain.

Adèle and Gaston Buzier, who argued all the time, reached the stage where they could not stand each other and yet had no one else to turn to.

Le Clinche, who had been wheeled out on a trolley, swathed in white, from the operating theatre.

And Marie Léonnec . . .

Not forgetting the men in the Grand Banks Café, who, even when drunk, seemed haunted by painful memories . . .

'The third day!' Maigret said aloud. 'That's where I need to look!'

Something much worse than jealousy . . . *But something which flowed directly from the presence of Adèle on board the boat.*

The effort took it out of him. The effect of the strain on all his mental faculties. The boat rocked gently. A light came on in the foredeck, where the sailors were about to get up.

'The third day . . .'

His throat contracted. He looked down on the after-deck and then along the quay, where, hours before, a man had leaned over and brandished a fist.

Maybe it was partly the effect of the cold and maybe not. But either way he suddenly shivered.

'The third day . . . The ship's boy, Jean-Marie, who kicked up a fuss because he did not want to go to sea, was swept overboard by a wave, at night . . .'

Maigret's eye ran round the whole deck, as if trying to determine where the accident had happened.

'There were only two witnesses, Captain Fallut and the wireless operator, Pierre Le Clinche. The next day or the day after that, Le Clinche became Adèle's lover!'

It was a turning point! Maigret did not loiter for another second. Someone was stirring in the foredeck. No one saw him stride across the plank connecting the boat to dry land.

With his hands in his pockets, his nose blue with the cold, unsmiling, he returned to the Hôtel de la Plage.

It was not yet light. Yet it was no longer night because, out at sea, the crests of waves were picked out in crude white. And gulls were light flecks against the sky.

A train whistled in the station. An old woman set out for the rocks, a basket on her back and a hook in her hand, to look for crabs.

10. *What Happened on the Third Day*

When Maigret left his room and came downstairs at around eight that morning, his head felt empty and his chest woolly, the way a man feels when he has drunk too much.

'Aren't things going the way you'd like?' asked his wife.

He had given a shrug, and she had not insisted. But there on the terrace of the hotel, facing a frothing, sly-green sea, he found Marie Léonnec. And she was not alone. There was a man sitting at her table. She stood up quickly and stammered to the inspector:

'May I introduce my father? He's just got here.'

The wind was cool, the sky overcast. The gulls skimmed the tops of the water.

'An honour to meet you, sir. Deeply honoured and most happy . . .'

Maigret looked at him without enthusiasm. He was short and would not have been any more ridiculous to look at than the next man but for his nose, which was disproportionately large, being the size of three normal noses and, furthermore, was stippled, like a strawberry.

It wasn't his fault. But it was a physical affliction. And it was all anyone saw. When he spoke it was the only thing people looked at, so that it was impossible to feel any sympathy for him.

'You must join us in a little . . . ?'

'Thank you, no. I've just had breakfast.'

'Perhaps a small glass of something, to warm the cockles?'

'No, really.'

He was insistent. Is it not a form of politeness to make people drink when they don't want to?

Maigret observed him and observed his daughter, who, apart

from that nose, bore him a strong resemblance. By looking at her in this light, he was able to get a picture of what she would be like in a dozen years, when the bloom of youth had faded.

'I'll come straight to the point, inspector. That's my motto, and I've travelled all night to do just that. When Jorissen came to me and said that he would accompany my daughter, I gave him my permission. So I don't think anyone could say that I am at all narrow-minded.'

Unfortunately Maigret was anxious to be elsewhere. Then there was the nose. And also the pompous tone of the middle-class worthy who likes the sound of his own voice.

'Even so, it's my duty as a father to keep myself fully informed, don't you agree? Which is why I'm asking you to tell me, in your heart and conscience, if you think this young man is innocent.'

Marie Léonnec did not know where to look. She must have known deep down that her father's initiative was unlikely to help arrange matters.

As long as she had been by herself, rushing to the aid of her fiancé, she had seemed rather admirable. Or at any rate she made a touching figure.

But now, inside the family, it was another matter. There was more than a whiff here of the shop back in Quimper, the discussions which had preceded her departure, the tittle-tattle of the neighbours.

'Are you asking me if he killed Captain Fallut?'

'Yes. You must understand that it is essential that . . .'

Maigret stared straight in front of him in his most detached manner.

'Well . . .'

He noticed the girl's hands, which were shaking.

'No, he didn't kill him. Now, if you'll excuse me, there's something I really must attend to. I shall doubtless have the pleasure of meeting up with you later . . .'

Then he turned tail! He fled so fast that he knocked over a chair on the terrace. He assumed that father and daughter were startled but did not turn round to find out.

Once on the quay, he followed the paved walkway. The *Océan* was some distance away. Even so, he noticed that a number of men had arrived with their sailor's kitbags slung over their shoulders and were getting their first sight of the boat. A cart was unloading bags of potatoes. The company's man was there with his polished boots and his pencil behind his ear.

There was a great deal of noise coming from the Grand Banks Café. Its doors were open, and Maigret could just make out Louis holding forth in the middle of a circle of the 'new' men.

He did not stop. Though he saw the landlord making a sign to him, he hurried on his way. Five minutes later he was ringing the bell of the hospital.

The registrar was very young. Visible under his white coat were a suit in the latest fashion and an elegant tie.

'The wireless operator? It was I who took his temperature and pulse this morning. He's doing as well as can be expected.'

'Has he come round?'

'Oh yes! He hasn't spoken to me, but his eyes followed me around all the time.'

'Is it all right if I talk to him about important matters?'

The registrar waved a hand vaguely, an indifferent gesture.

'Don't see why not. If the operation has been a success and he hasn't got a temperature, then . . . You want to see him?'

Pierre Le Clinche was by himself in a small room with distempered walls. The air was hot and humid. He watched Maigret coming towards him. His eyes were bright, and there was not a trace of anxiety in them.

'As you see, he's making excellent progress. He'll be on his feet in a week. On the other hand, there's a chance that he'll be left with a limp, for a tendon in his hip was severed. And he'll have to take care. Would you prefer it if I leave you alone with him?'

It was really quite disconcerting. The previous evening, a bleeding, unwholesome mess had been brought which could not possibly, it seemed, have harboured the faintest breath of life.

And now Maigret found a white bed, a face that was slightly drawn and a little pale, which was more tranquil now than he had ever seen it. And there was what looked like serenity in those eyes.

That is perhaps why he hesitated. He paced up and down the room, leaned his head for a moment against the double window, from which he could see the port and the trawler, where men in red jerkins were busily moving about.

'Do you feel strong enough to talk to me?' he growled, firing the question without warning as he turned to face the bed.

Le Clinche assented with a faint nod of his head.

'You are aware that I am not officially involved in this case? My friend Jorissen asked me to prove your innocence. It is done. You are not the killer of Captain Fallut.'

He sighed deeply. Then, to get it over with, he put his head down and charged:

'Tell me the truth about what happened on the third day out, I mean about the death of Jean-Marie.'

He avoided looking directly at the patient. He filled a pipe as a way of appearing casual and when the silence went on and on, he murmured:

'It was evening. There were only Captain Fallut and you on deck. Were you standing together?'

'No!'

'The captain was walking near the afterdeck?'

'Yes. I'd just left my cabin. He didn't see me. I watched him because I felt there was something odd about the way he was behaving.'

'You didn't know at that point that there was a woman on board?'

'No! I thought that if he was being so careful about keeping his door locked, it was because he was storing smuggled goods inside.'

The voice was weary. And yet, it became suddenly more emphatic for he said distinctly:

'It was the most terrible thing I ever saw, inspector! Who talked? Tell me!'

And he closed his eyes, exactly as he had as he sat waiting for the moment when he would fire a bullet through his pocket into his belly.

'Nobody. The captain was strolling on deck, feeling apprehensive no doubt, just as he had ever since he'd left port. Was there anybody at the wheel?'

'A helmsman. He couldn't see us because it was dark.'

'The ship's boy showed up . . .'

Le Clinche interrupted him by heaving himself half up, both hands gripping the rope hanging from the ceiling which enabled him to change his position.

'Where's Marie?'

'At the hotel. Her father has just come.'

'To take her back! Fair enough. He should take her home. But whatever happens, she mustn't come here!'

He was getting worked up. His voice was flatter and its flow more broken.

Maigret could sense that his temperature was climbing. His eyes were becoming unnaturally bright.

'I don't know who has been talking to you. But it's time I told you everything.'

His agitation had reached such a pitch, and was so vehement, that he looked and sounded as if he was almost raving.

'It was awful! You never saw the kid. Skinny's not the word. Wore clothes made from an old cut-down canvas suit of his father's . . . On the first day, he'd been scared and he blubbed. How can I explain . . . Afterwards he got his own back by playing nasty tricks on people. What do you expect at his age? Do you know what *a little brat* is? Well, that was him. Twice I caught him reading the letters I wrote to my fiancée. He'd just look me brazenly in the eye and say:

'"Writing to your bit of fluff?"

'That evening . . . I think the captain was walking up and down because he was too jumpy to sleep. There was quite a swell on. From time to time, a green sea would wash over the foredeck rail and flood across the metal plates of the deck. But it wasn't a storm.

'I was maybe ten metres from them. I only heard a few words but I could see their shapes. The kid was on his high horse, he was laughing. And the captain stood there, his neck sunk in his jerkin and his hands in his pockets . . .

'Jean-Marie had talked about my "bit of fluff" and he must have been taking the same sort of rise out of Fallut. He had a piercing voice. I remember catching a couple of words:

'"And if I ever told everybody how . . ."

'I didn't understand until later . . . He'd found out that the captain was hiding a woman in his cabin. He was full of himself. There was a swagger about him. He wasn't aware of how vindictive he was being.

'Then this is what happened. The captain raised one hand to give him a cuff over the ear. The kid was very nimble and ducked. Then he shouted something, probably another threat about telling what he knew.

'Fallut's hand struck a rigging stay. It must have hurt like the devil. He saw red.

'It was the fable of the lion and the gnat all over again. Forgetting he was a ship's master, he started chasing the kid. At first, the boy ran off laughing. The captain started to panic.

'A chance remark and anyone who heard it would know everything. Fallut was out of his mind with fear.

'I saw him reach out to catch Jean-Marie by the shoulders, but instead of grabbing hold of him he pushed him over, head first . . .

'That's it. Fatalities occur. His head collided with a capstan. I heard the sound, it was awful, a dull thud. *His skull . . .*'

*

He held both hands up to his face. He was deathly pale. Sweat streamed down his forehead.

'A big wave swept over the deck at that moment. So it was a waterlogged body that the captain bent down to examine. At the same time, he caught sight of me. I don't think it crossed my mind to hide. I started walking towards him. I got there just in time to see the boy's body clench and then stiffen in a reflex that I'll never forget.

'Dead! It was so senseless! The two of us looked at each other, not taking it in, unable to understand what an appalling thing had happened.

'No one else had seen or heard anything. Fallut didn't dare touch the boy. It was me who felt his chest, his hands and that crumpled skull. There was no blood. No wound. Just the skull, which had cracked.

'We stayed there for maybe a quarter of an hour, not knowing what to do, grim, shoulders frozen, while at intervals the spray lashed our faces.

'The captain was not the same man. It was as if something inside him had been broken too.

'When he spoke, his voice was sharp, without warmth.

'"The crew mustn't learn the truth! Bad for ship's discipline."

'And while I looked on, he himself picked the boy up. Then just one more effort. Though . . . though I do remember that with his thumb he made the sign of the cross on the boy's forehead.

'The body, which had been snatched by the sea, was swept back twice against the hull. Both of us were still standing in the dark. We did not dare look at each other. We didn't dare speak.'

Maigret had just lit his pipe, clamping his teeth hard on the stem.

A nurse came in. Both men watched her with eyes that seemed so vacant that she was disconcerted and stammered:

'Time to take your temperature.'

'Come back later!'

When the door closed behind her, the inspector asked:

'Was it then that he told you about the woman?'

'From then on, he was never the same again. He probably wasn't certifiably mad. But there was definitely something unhinged about him. He put one hand on my shoulder and murmured:

'"And all because of a woman, young man!"

'I was cold. I was not thinking straight. I couldn't take my eyes off the sea on the side where the body had been carried away.

'Did they tell you about the captain? A short, lean man with a face full of energy. He usually spoke in terse, unfinished phrases.

'That was it! Fifty-five years old. Coming up to retirement. Solid reputation. A little put by in the bank. All over! Finished! In one minute! Less than a minute. On account of a kid who . . . No, on account of a woman . . .

'And then and there, in the darkness, in a quiet, angry voice, he told me the whole story, bit by bit. A woman from Le Havre. A woman who couldn't have been up to much, he was well aware of that. But he couldn't live without her . . .

'He'd brought her with him. And the moment he did, he had a sudden feeling that her presence on board would mean trouble.

'She was there. Asleep.'

The wireless operator began to fidget restlessly.

'I can't remember everything he told me. For he had this need to talk about her, which he did with a mixture of loathing and passion.'

'"A captain is never justified in causing a scandal likely to undermine his authority."

'I can still hear those words. It was my first time out on a boat and I now thought of the sea as a monster which would swallow us all up.

'Fallut quoted examples. In such a year such and such a captain, who had brought his mistress along with him . . . There were so many fights on board that three men never came back.

'The wind was strengthening. The spray kept coming at us.

From time to time, a wave would lick at our feet which kept sliding on the slippery metal deck.

'He wasn't mad, oh no! But he wasn't Fallut any more either.

'"See this trip through and then we'll see!"

'I didn't understand what he meant. He struck me as being both sensible and freakish, a man still clinging to his sense of duty.

'"No one must know! A captain can never be in the wrong!"

'My nerves were so strung out I was ill with it. I couldn't think any more. My thoughts were all jumbled up in my head, and by the finish it felt as if I was living through a waking nightmare.

'That woman in the cabin, the woman a man like the captain could not live without, the woman whose very name made him catch his breath.

'And there was me writing reams and reams to my fiancée, who I wouldn't be seeing again for three months, and I never felt obsessed, possessed like that! And when he said words like her *flesh* or her *body* I felt my cheeks go hot without knowing why.'

Maigret put the question slowly:

'And no one, apart from the two of you, knew the truth about the death of Jean-Marie?'

'No one!'

'And was it the captain who, in the customary way, read out the prayers for the dead?'

'At first light. The weather had got thick. We were steaming through icy grey mist.'

'Didn't the crew say anything?'

'There were funny looks and some whispering. But Fallut was more authoritarian than ever, and his voice had acquired a new cutting edge. He would not tolerate any answering back. He got angry with anyone who looked at him in a way he didn't like. He spied on the men, as if he was trying to detect any suspicions they might be getting.'

'What about you?'

Le Clinche didn't answer. He stretched out one arm for a glass of water on his bedside table and drank from it greedily.

'So you began prowling round the cabin more often, didn't you? You wanted to see this woman who had got so far under the captain's skin? Did you start the following night?'

'Yes. I ran into her, just for a moment. Then the next night . . . I'd noticed that the key to the wireless room was the same as the key of the cabin. It was the captain's watch. I crept in, like a thief.'

'You went to bed with her?'

The wireless operator's face hardened.

'I swear you won't understand, you can't! The whole atmosphere was nothing like anything that happens in the real world. The kid . . . the previous day's ceremony . . . But whenever I thought about it, the same picture kept surfacing in my mind, the image of a woman unlike any other, a woman whose body, whose flesh could turn a man into something that he was not.'

'She led you on?'

'She was in bed, half-dressed . . .'

He turned bright scarlet. He looked away.

'How long did you stay in the cabin?'

'Maybe a couple of hours, I don't remember. When I left with the blood still pounding in my ears, the captain was there, just outside the door. He didn't say a word. He watched me walk past. I almost went down on my knees so I could say it wasn't my fault and that I was sorry. But he remained stony-faced. I walked on. I returned to my post.

'I was scared. After that, I always went around with my loaded revolver in my pocket because I was convinced he was going to kill me.

'He never spoke to me again, except for ship's business. And even then, most of the time he sent me his orders in writing.

'I wish I could explain it better, but I can't. Each day it got worse. I had a feeling that everybody knew about the terrible thing that happened.

'The chief mechanic went sniffing around the cabin too. The captain stayed inside it for hours and hours.

'The men started giving us inquisitive, anxious looks. They guessed that something was going on. How many times did I hear talk of the evil eye?

'But there was only one thing I wanted . . .'

'Of course there was,' grunted Maigret.

There was a silence. Le Clinche stared at the inspector with eyes full of resentment.

'We ran into bad weather, ten days on the trot. I was seasick. But I kept thinking about her. She was . . . fragrant! She . . . I can't explain. It was like a pain. That's it! A desire capable of inflicting pain, of making me weep tears of rage! Especially when I saw the captain go into his cabin. Because now, I could imagine . . . You see, she'd called me her *big boy*! In a special voice, sort of breathy. I kept saying those two words over and over to torture myself. I stopped writing to Marie. I built impossible dreams: I'd run away with that woman the moment we got back to Fécamp.'

'What about the captain?'

'He got even more stony-faced and brusque. Maybe there was a touch of madness about him after all, I don't know. He gave orders that we were to fish at some location or other, and all the old hands claimed no one had ever seen a fish in those waters. He refused to have his orders questioned. He was afraid of me. Did he know I had a gun? He had one too. Whenever we met, he kept his hand near his pocket. I kept trying to see Adèle again. But he was always around, with bags under his eyes and his lips drawn back. And the stink of cod. The men who were salting the fish down in the hold . . . There was one accident after another.

'And the chief mechanic was also on the prowl. It got so that none of us spoke freely any more. We were like three lunatics. There were nights when I believe I could have killed somebody to get to her. Can you understand that? Nights when I tore my handkerchief to shreds with my teeth while I repeated over and over, in the same voice that she had used:

'"*My big boy! That's my big fool!*"

'How long it seemed! Each night was followed by a new day! And then more days! And with nothing but grey water around us, freezing fogs, fish-scales and cod guts everywhere!

'A taste of pickling brine in the back of the throat that made your stomach heave . . .

'Just that once! I believe that if I could have gone to her one more time I'd have been cured! But it was impossible. *He* was there. He was always there, more hollow-eyed all the time.

'The constant pitching and tossing, with nothing as far as the eye could see. And then we saw cliffs!

'Can you grasp the fact that it had been like that for three months? Well, instead of being cured, I was even sicker. It's only now that I'm beginning to realize that it was a sickness.

'I hated the captain who was always in my way. I detested that man who was already old and kept a woman like Adèle under lock and key.

'I was afraid of returning to port. I was afraid of losing her for ever.

'By the finish, I was as scared of him as of the devil himself! Yes, as if he were some kind of evil genie who was keeping the woman all to himself!

'As we got in, there were a few navigation errors. Then the men jumped ashore, relieved to be back, and headed straight for the bars. But I knew the captain was only waiting for the cover of night to get Adèle off the boat.

'I went back to my room over Léon's bar. There were old letters, photos of my fiancée and the like, and I don't know why but I got into a vile temper and I burned the whole lot.

'Then I went back out. I wanted her! I'll say it again: I wanted her! Hadn't she told me that when we got back Fallut would marry her?

'I bumped into a man . . .'

He let himself slump back on to his pillow, and on his tortured features appeared an expression of agonized torment.

'Because you know . . .' he gasped.

'Yes. Jean-Marie's father. The trawler was berthed. Only the captain and Adèle were still on board. He was about to bring her out. And then . . .'

'Please, no more!'

'And then you told the man who had come to look at the boat on which his boy had died that his son had been murdered. True? And you followed him. You were hiding behind a truck when he went up to the captain . . .'

'Stop!'

'The murder happened there, while you watched.'

'Please stop!'

'No! You were there when it happened. Then you went on board and let the woman out.'

'I didn't want her any more!'

From outside came a long blast of a hooter. Le Clinche's lips trembled as he stammered:

'The *Océan* . . .'

'That's right. She sails at high tide.'

Neither of them spoke. They could hear all the sounds made in the hospital, down to the muffled swish of a patient's trolley being wheeled to the operating theatre.

'I didn't want her any more!' the wireless operator repeated wildly.

'But it was too late!'

There was another silence. Then Le Clinche's voice came again:

'And yet . . . now . . . I want so much to . . .'

He did not dare pronounce the word that stuck to his tongue.

'Live?'

Then he went on:

'Don't you understand? I was mad. I don't understand it myself.

It all happened elsewhere, in another world . . . Then we got back here, and I realized what had been happening. Listen. There was that dark cabin and men prowling round, and nothing else existed. I felt as if that was my whole life! I longed to hear those words again, *my big boy!* I couldn't even begin to say how it all happened. I opened the door. She slipped out. There was a man in tan-coloured shoes waiting for her, and they started hugging each other on the side of the quay.

'And I woke up – it's the only word for it. And ever since all I've wanted is not to die. Marie Léonnec came with you to see me. Adèle came too, with that other man.'

'What do you want me to say?'

'It's too late now, isn't it? I was let out of jail. I went on board and got my revolver. Marie was waiting for me by the boat. She didn't know . . .

'And that same afternoon, that woman was there, talking. And the man in the tan-coloured shoes . . .

'Who could possibly make sense of it all? I pulled the trigger. It took me an age to bring myself to do it, on account of Marie Léonnec, who was there!

'And now . . .'

He sobbed. Then he literally screamed:

'All the same, I've got to die! And I don't want to die! I'm afraid of dying! I . . . I . . .'

His body was racked by such spasms that Maigret called a nurse, who quietly and unfussily subdued him with an economical ease born of long professional experience.

The trawler gave a second harrowing summons on its hooter, and the women hurried down to line the jetty.

11. *The* Océan *Sails*

Maigret reached the quay just as the new captain was about to give the order to cast off the hawsers. He caught sight of the chief mechanic, who was saying goodbye to his wife. He went up to him and took him to one side.

'Something I need to know. It was you, wasn't it, who found the captain's will and dropped it into the police station letter-box?'

The man looked worried and hesitated.

'You've nothing to worry about. You suspected Le Clinche. You thought that it was a way of saving his neck. Even though you both had had your eye on the same woman.'

The hooter, peremptory now, barked at the latecomers, and hugging couples on the quayside peeled away from each other.

'Don't bring all that up again, do you mind? Is it true that he's going to die?'

'Unless we can save him. Where was the will?'

'Among the captain's papers.'

'What exactly were you looking for?'

'I was hoping to find a photo,' the man said, lowering his eyes. 'Look, let me go, I've got to . . .'

The hawser fell into the water. The gangway was being raised. The chief mechanic jumped on to the deck, gave his wife a last wave and cast a final look at Maigret.

Then the trawler headed slowly towards the harbour entrance. A sailor lifted the ship's boy, who was barely fifteen, on to his shoulders. The boy had got hold of the man's pipe and was proudly clenching it between his teeth.

On the land, women were weeping.

By walking quickly, they could follow the vessel, which did not pick up speed until it was clear of the jetties. Some voices were shouting out reminders:

'If you come across the *Atlantique*, don't forget to tell Dugodet that his wife . . .'

The sky was still low and threatening. The wind pressed down on the water, ruckling its surface and raising small white-crested waves, which made an angry washing sound.

A Parisian in whites was taking photos of the departing trawler. He had two little girls in white dresses in tow. They were laughing.

Maigret collided with a woman, almost knocking her over. She clutched his arm and asked:

'Well? Is he better?'

It was Adèle, who hadn't powdered her nose since at least that morning, and the skin of her face was shiny.

'Where's Buzier?' asked the inspector.

'He said he'd rather go back to Le Havre. He doesn't want any trouble. Anyway, I said I was finishing with him. But what about that boy, Le Clinche?'

'Don't know.'

'Go on, you can tell me!'

Absolutely not. He turned and left her standing there. He'd picked out a group on the jetty: Marie Léonnec, her father and Madame Maigret. All three were facing in the direction of the trawler which for a moment drew level with them. Marie Léonnec was saying fervently:

'That's *his* boat!'

Maigret slowly walked towards them, in a surly mood. His wife was the first to spot him among the crowd which had gathered to see the trawler set off for the Grand Banks.

'Did he pull through?'

Monsieur Léonnec, looking anxious, turned his misshapen nose in his direction.

'Ah! I'm so glad to see you. Where are you with your inquiries, inspector?'

'Nowhere.'

'Meaning?'

'Nothing . . . I don't know.'

Marie opened her eyes wide.

'But Pierre?'

'The operation was a success. It seems he'll be all right.'

'He's innocent, isn't he? Oh please! Tell my father he didn't do it!'

She put her whole heart into the words. Contemplating her, he saw how she would be in ten years' time, with the same look as her father, a somewhat overbearing manner ideally suited to dealing with customers in the shop.

'He didn't kill the captain.'

Turning to his wife:

'I've just had a telegram calling me back to Paris.'

'So soon? I'd promised to go swimming tomorrow with . . .'

She caught his eye and understood.

'If you'll excuse us.'

'We'll walk back to the hotel with you.'

Maigret saw Jean-Marie's father, dead drunk, still brandishing his fist at the trawler, and looked away.

'Don't put yourselves out, please.'

'Tell me,' said Monsieur Léonnec, 'do you think I could arrange for him to be transferred to Quimper? People are bound to talk.'

Marie looked pleadingly at him. She was very pale. She said in a faltering voice:

'After all, he is innocent,'

'I don't know. You are better placed . . .'

'But at least you must allow me to offer you something? A bottle of champagne?'

'No thanks.'

'Just a glass of something? Benedictine, for example, since we're in the town where . . .'

'A beer, then.'

Upstairs, Madame Maigret was shutting their cases.

'So you share my opinion, then. He's a fine boy who . . .'

She still had that little-girl look about her! The look that pleaded with him to say yes!

'I think he'll make a good husband.'

'And be a good hand at business!' said her father, going one better. 'Because I won't have him sailing the high seas for months on end. When a man's married, he has a responsibility to . . .'

'Goes without saying.'

'Especially since I have no son. Surely you can understand that!'

'Of course.'

Maigret was keeping an eye on the stairs. Eventually, his wife appeared.

'The luggage is all ready. They say there's not a train until . . .'

'Doesn't matter. We'll hire a car.'

It was a getaway!

'If ever you have occasion to be in Quimper . . .'

'Yes, yes . . .'

And the way the girl looked at him! She seemed to have understood that things were not all as straightforward as they seemed, but her eyes pleaded with Maigret not to say any more.

She wanted her fiancé.

The inspector shook hands all round, paid the bill and finished his beer.

'Thank you so much, Detective Chief Inspector Maigret.'

'There really is no need.'

The car which had been hired by phone arrived.

so unless you have come up with something which I have missed,
I shall sign off with a recommendation that the case be closed.

This was a passage from a letter sent by Chief Inspector Grenier, of the Le Havre Police, to Maigret, who replied by telegraph:

> Agreed.

Six months later, he was sent a card through the post, which said:

> Madame Le Clinche has great pleasure in announcing the wedding of her son, Pierre, and Mademoiselle Marie Léonnec, which . . .

And shortly afterwards, when in connection with another inquiry he was looking round a certain kind of establishment in Rue Pasquier, he thought he recognized a young woman who looked quickly away.

Adèle!

And that was all. Or not quite. Five years later, Maigret was on a short visit to Quimper. He saw the proprietor of a chandler's shop, standing in his doorway. He was still a young man, very tall with the beginnings of a paunch.

He walked with a slight limp. He called to a toddler of three, who was playing with his top on the pavement.

'Come in now, Pierrot. Your mother will be cross!'

The man, too preoccupied with his offspring, did not recognize Maigret, who in any case quickened his step, looked away and pulled a wry face.

The Art of Fiction – Georges Simenon

The Paris Review, No. 9
Summer 1955

Interviewer: Carvel Collins

Mr Simenon's study in his rambling white house on the edge of Lakeville, Connecticut, after lunch on a January day of bright sun. The room reflects its owner: cheerful, efficient, hospitable, controlled. On its walls are books of law and medicine, two fields in which he has made himself an expert; the telephone directories from many parts of the world to which he turns in naming his characters; the map of a town where he has just set his forty-ninth Maigret novel; and the calendar on which he has X-ed out in heavy crayon the days spent writing the Maigret – one day to a chapter – and the three days spent revising it, a labour which he has generously interrupted for this interview.

In the adjoining office, having seen that everything is arranged comfortably for her husband and the interviewer, Mme Simenon returns her attention to the business affairs of a writer whose novels appear six a year and whose contracts for books, adaptations and translations are in more than twenty languages.

With great courtesy and in a rich voice, which gives to his statements nuances of meaning much beyond the ordinary range, Mr Simenon continues a discussion begun in the dining room.

GEORGES SIMENON

Just one piece of general advice from a writer has been very useful to me. It was from Colette. I was writing short stories for *Le Matin*, and Colette was literary editor at that time. I remember I gave her two short stories and she returned them and I tried again and tried again. Finally she said, 'Look, it is too literary, always too literary.' So I followed her advice. It's what I do when I write, the main job when I rewrite.

INTERVIEWER

What do you mean by 'too literary'? What do you cut out, certain kinds of words?

SIMENON

Adjectives, adverbs, and every word which is there just to make an effect. Every sentence which is there just for the sentence. You know, you have a beautiful sentence – cut it. Every time I find such a thing in one of my novels it is to be cut.

INTERVIEWER

Is that the nature of most of your revision?

SIMENON

Almost all of it.

INTERVIEWER

It's not revising the plot pattern?

SIMENON

Oh, I never touch anything of that kind. Sometimes I've changed the names while writing: a woman will be Helen in the first chapter and Charlotte in the second, you know; so in revising I straighten this out. And then, cut, cut, cut.

INTERVIEWER

Is there anything else you can say to beginning writers?

SIMENON

Writing is considered a profession, and I don't think it is a profession. I think that everyone who does not *need* to be a writer, who thinks he can do something else, ought to do something else. Writing is not a profession but a vocation of unhappiness. I don't think an artist can ever be happy.

INTERVIEWER

Why?

SIMENON

Because, first, I think that if a man has the urge to be an artist, it is because he needs to find himself. Every writer tries to find himself through his characters, through all his writing.

INTERVIEWER

He is writing for himself?

SIMENON

Yes. Certainly.

INTERVIEWER

Are you conscious there will be readers of the novel?

SIMENON

I know that there are many men who have more or less the same problems I have, with more or less intensity, and who will be happy to read the book to find the answer – if the answer can possibly be found.

INTERVIEWER

Even when the author can't find the answer do the readers profit because the author is meaningfully fumbling for it?

SIMENON

That's it. Certainly. I don't remember whether I have ever spoken to you about the feeling I have had for several years. Because society today is without a very strong religion, without a firm hierarchy of social classes, and people are afraid of the big organization in which they are just a little part, for them reading certain novels is a little like looking through the keyhole to learn what the neighbour is doing and thinking – does he have the same inferiority complex, the same vices, the same temptations? This is what they are looking for in the work of art. I think many more people today are insecure and are in search of themselves.

There are now so few literary works of the kind Anatole France wrote, for example, you know – very quiet and elegant and reassuring. On the contrary, what people today want are the most complex books, trying to go into every corner of human nature. Do you understand what I mean?

INTERVIEWER

I think so. You mean this is not just because today we think we know more about psychology but because more readers need this kind of fiction?

SIMENON

Yes. An ordinary man fifty years ago – there are many problems today which he did not know. Fifty years ago he had the answers. He doesn't have them anymore.

INTERVIEWER

A year or so ago you and I heard a critic ask that the novel today return to the kind of novel written in the nineteenth century.

SIMENON

It is impossible, completely impossible, I think. Because we live in a time when writers do not always have barriers around them, they can try to present characters by the most complete, the most full expression. You may show love in a very nice story, the first ten months of two lovers, as in the literature of a long time ago. Then you have a second kind of story: they begin to be bored; that was the literature of the end of the last century. And then, if you are free to go further, the man is fifty and tries to have another life, the woman gets jealous, and you have children mixed in it; that is the third story. We are the third story now. We don't stop when they marry, we don't stop when they begin to be bored, we go to the end.

INTERVIEWER

In this connection, I often hear people ask about the violence in modern fiction. I'm all for it, but I'd like to ask why you write of it.

SIMENON

We are accustomed to see people driven to their limit.

INTERVIEWER

And violence is associated with this?

SIMENON

More or less. We no longer think of a man from the point of view of some philosophers; for a long time man was always observed from the point of view that there was a God and that man was the king of creation. We don't think any more that man is the king of creation. We see man almost face-to-face. Some readers still would like to read very reassuring novels, novels which give them a comforting view of humanity. It can't be done.

INTERVIEWER

Then if the readers interest you, it is because they want a novel to probe their troubles? Your role is to look into yourself and –

SIMENON

That's it. But it's not only a question of the artist's looking into himself but also of his looking into others with the experience he has of himself. He writes with sympathy because he feels that the other man is like him.

INTERVIEWER

If there were no readers you would still write?

SIMENON

Certainly. When I began to write I didn't have the idea my books would sell. More exactly, when I began to write I did commercial pieces – stories for magazines and things of that kind – to earn my living, but I didn't call it writing. But for myself, every evening, I did some writing without any idea that it would ever be published.

INTERVIEWER

You probably have had as much experience as anybody in the world in doing what you have just called commercial writing. What is the difference between it and non-commercial?

SIMENON

I call 'commercial' every work, not only in literature but in music and painting and sculpture – any art – which is done for such-and-such a public or for a certain kind of publication or for a particular collection. Of course, in commercial writing there are different grades. You may have things which are very cheap and some very good. The books of the month, for example, are commercial writing; but some of them are almost perfectly done, almost works of art. Not completely, but almost. And the same with certain magazine pieces; some of them are wonderful. But very seldom can they be works of art, because a work of art can't be done for the purpose of pleasing a certain group of readers.

INTERVIEWER

How does this change the work? As the author you know whether or not you tailored a novel for a market, but, looking at your work from the outside only, what difference would the reader see?

SIMENON

The big difference would be in the concessions. In writing for any commercial purpose you have always to make concessions.

INTERVIEWER

To the idea that life is orderly and sweet, for example?

SIMENON

And the view of morals. Maybe that is the most important. You can't write anything commercial without accepting some code. There is always a code – like the code in Hollywood, and in television and radio. For example, there is now a very good program on television, it is probably the best for plays. The first two acts are always first-class. You have the impression of something completely new and strong, and then at the end the concession comes. Not always a happy end, but something comes to arrange everything from the point of view of a morality or philosophy – you know. All the characters, who were beautifully done, change completely in the last ten minutes.

INTERVIEWER

In your non-commercial novels you feel no need to make concessions of any sort?

SIMENON

I never do that, never, never, never. Otherwise I wouldn't write. It's too painful to do it if it's not to go to the end.

INTERVIEWER

You have shown me the manila envelopes you use in starting novels. Before you actually begin writing, how much have you been working consciously on the plan of that particular novel?

SIMENON

As you suggest, we have to distinguish here between consciously and unconsciously. Unconsciously I probably always have two or three, not novels, not ideas about novels, but themes in my mind. I never even think that they might serve for a novel; more exactly, they are the things about which I worry. Two days before I start writing a novel I consciously take up one of those ideas. But even before I consciously take it up I first find some atmosphere. Today there is a little sunshine here. I might remember such-and-such a spring, maybe in some small Italian town, or some place in the

French provinces or in Arizona, I don't know, and then, little by little, a small world will come into my mind, with a few characters. Those characters will be taken partly from people I have known and partly from pure imagination – you know, it's a complex of both. And then the idea I had before will come and stick around them. They will have the same problem I have in my mind myself. And the problem – with those people – will give me the novel.

INTERVIEWER

This is a couple of days before?

SIMENON

Yes, a couple of days. Because as soon as I have the beginning I can't bear it very long; so the next day I take my envelope, take my telephone book for names, and take my town map – you know, to see exactly where things happen. And two days later I begin writing. And the beginning will be always the same; it is almost a geometrical problem: I have such a man, such a woman, in such surroundings. What can happen to them to oblige them to go to their limit? That's the question. It will be sometimes a very simple incident, anything which will change their lives. Then I write my novel chapter by chapter.

INTERVIEWER

What has gone on the planning envelope? Not an outline of the action?

SIMENON

No, no. I know nothing about the events when I begin the novel. On the envelope I put only the names of the characters, their ages, their families. I know nothing whatever about the events that will occur later. Otherwise it would not be interesting to me.

INTERVIEWER

When do the incidents begin to form?

SIMENON

On the eve of the first day I know what will happen in the first chapter. Then, day after day, chapter after chapter, I find what comes later. After I have started a novel I write a chapter each day, without ever missing a day. Because it is a strain, I have to keep pace with the novel. If, for example, I am ill for forty-eight hours, I have to throw away the previous chapters. And I never return to that novel.

INTERVIEWER

When you did commercial fiction, was your method at all similar?

SIMENON

No. Not at all. When I did a commercial novel I didn't think about that novel except in the hours of writing it. But when I am doing a novel now I don't see anybody, I don't speak to anybody, I don't take a phone call – I live just like a monk. All the day I am one of my characters. I feel what he feels.

INTERVIEWER

You are the same character all the way through the writing of that novel?

SIMENON

Always, because most of my novels show what happens around one character. The other characters are always seen by him. So it is in this character's skin I have to be. And it's almost unbearable after five or six days. That is one of the reasons my novels are so short; after eleven days I can't – it's impossible. I have to – it's physical. I am too tired.

INTERVIEWER

I should think so. Especially if you drive the main character to his limit.

SIMENON

Yes, yes.

INTERVIEWER

And you are playing this role with him, you are –

SIMENON

Yes. And it's awful. That is why, before I start a novel – this may sound foolish here, but it is the truth – generally a few days before the start of a novel I look to see that I don't have any appointments for eleven days. Then I call the doctor. He takes my blood pressure, he checks everything. And he says, 'Okay.'

INTERVIEWER

Cleared for action.

SIMENON

Exactly. Because I have to be sure that I am good for the eleven days.

INTERVIEWER

Does he come again at the end of the eleven days?

SIMENON

Usually.

INTERVIEWER

His idea or yours?

SIMENON

It's his idea.

INTERVIEWER

What does he find?

SIMENON

The blood pressure is usually down.

INTERVIEWER

What does he think of this? Is it all right?

SIMENON

He thinks it is all right but unhealthy to do it too often.

INTERVIEWER

Does he ration you?

SIMENON

Yes. Sometimes he will say, 'Look, after this novel take two months off.' For example, yesterday he said, 'Okay, but how many novels do you want to do before you go away for the summer?' I said, 'Two.' 'Okay,' he said.

INTERVIEWER

Fine. I'd like to ask now whether you see any pattern in the development of your views as they have worked out in your novels.

SIMENON

I am not the one who discovered it, but some critics in France did. All my life, my literary life, if I may say so, I have taken several problems for my novels, and about every ten years I have taken up the same problems from another point of view. I have the impression that I will never, probably, find the answer. I know of certain problems I have taken more than five times.

INTERVIEWER

And do you know that you will take those up again?

SIMENON

Yes, I will. And then there are a few problems – if I may call them problems – that I know I will never take again, because I have the impression that I went to the end of them. I don't care about them any more.

INTERVIEWER

What are some of the problems you have dealt with often and expect to deal with in future?

SIMENON

One of them, for example, which will probably haunt me more than any other is the problem of communication. I mean communication between two people. The fact that we are I don't know how many millions of people, yet communication, complete communication, is completely impossible between two of those people, is to me one of the biggest tragic themes in the world. When I was a young boy I was afraid of it. I would almost scream because of it. It gave me such a sensation of solitude, of loneliness. That is a theme I have taken I don't know how many times. But I know it will come again. Certainly it will come again.

INTERVIEWER

And another?

SIMENON

Another seems to be the theme of escape. Between two days changing your life completely: without caring at all what has happened before, just go. You know what I mean?

INTERVIEWER

Starting over?

SIMENON

Not even starting over. Going to nothing.

INTERVIEWER

I see. Is either of these themes or another not far in the offing as a subject, do you suppose? Or is it harmful to ask this?

SIMENON

One is not very far away, probably. It is something on the theme of father and child, of two generations, man coming and man going. That's not completely it, but I don't see it neatly enough just yet to speak about it.

INTERVIEWER

This theme could be associated with the theme of lack of communication?

SIMENON

That's it; it is another branch of the same problem.

INTERVIEWER

What themes do you feel rather certain you will not deal with again?

SIMENON

One, I think, is the theme of the disintegration of a unit, and the unit was generally a family.

INTERVIEWER

Have you treated this theme often?

SIMENON

Two or three times, maybe more.

INTERVIEWER

In the novel *Pedigree*?

SIMENON

In *Pedigree* you have it, yes. If I had to choose one of my books to live and not the others, I would never choose *Pedigree*.

INTERVIEWER

What one might you choose?

SIMENON

The next one.

INTERVIEWER

And the next one after that?

SIMENON

That's it. It's always the next one. You see, even technically I have the feeling now that I am very far away from the goal.

INTERVIEWER

Apart from the next ones, would you be willing to nominate a published novel to survive?

SIMENON

Not one. Because when a novel is finished I have always the impression that I have not succeeded. I am not discouraged, but I see – I want to try again. But one thing – I consider my novels about all on the same level, yet there are steps. After a group of five or six novels I have a kind of – I don't like the word 'progress' – but there seems to be a progress. There is a jump in quality, I think. So every five or six novels there is one I prefer to the others.

INTERVIEWER

Of the novels now available, which one would you say was one of these?

SIMENON

The Brothers Rico. The story might be the same if instead of a gangster you had the cashier of one of our banks or a teacher we might know.

INTERVIEWER

A man's position is threatened and he will do anything to keep it?

SIMENON

That's it. A man who always wants to be on top with the small group where he lives. And who will sacrifice anything to stay there. And he may be a very good man, but he made such an effort to be where he is that he will never accept not being there anymore.

INTERVIEWER

I like the simple way that novel does so much.

SIMENON

I tried to do it very simply, simply. And there is not a single 'literary' sentence there, you know? It's written as if by a child.

INTERVIEWER

You spoke earlier about thinking of atmosphere when you first think of a novel.

SIMENON

What I mean by atmosphere might be translated by 'the poetic line'. You understand what I mean?

INTERVIEWER

Is 'mood' close enough?

SIMENON

Yes. And with the mood goes the season, goes the detail – at first it is almost like a musical theme.

INTERVIEWER

And so far in no way geographically located?

SIMENON

Not at all. That's the atmosphere for me, because I try – and I don't think I have done it, for otherwise the critics would have discovered it – I try to do with prose, with the novel, what generally is done with poetry. I mean I try to go beyond the real, and the explainable ideas, and to explore the man – not doing it by the sound of the words as the poetical novels of the beginning of the century tried to do. I can't explain technically but – I try to put in my novels some things which you can't explain, to give some message which does not exist practically. You understand what I mean? I read a few days ago that T. S. Eliot, whom I admire very much, wrote that poetry is necessary in plays having one kind of story and not in plays having another, that it depends on the subject you treat. I don't think so. I think you may have the same secret message to give with any kind of subject. If your vision of the world is of a certain kind you will put poetry in everything, necessarily.

But I am probably the only one who thinks there is something of this kind in my books.

INTERVIEWER

One time you spoke about your wish to write the 'pure' novel. Is this what you were speaking of a while ago – about cutting out the 'literary' words and sentences – or does it also include the poetry you have just spoken of?

SIMENON

The 'pure' novel will do only what the novel can do. I mean that it doesn't have to do any teaching or any work of journalism. In a pure novel you wouldn't take sixty pages to describe the South or Arizona or some country in Europe. Just the drama, with only what is absolutely part of this drama. What I think about novels today is almost a translation of the rules of tragedy into the novel. I think the novel is the tragedy for our day.

INTERVIEWER

Is length important? Is it part of your definition of the pure novel?

SIMENON

Yes. That sounds like a practical question, but I think it is important, for the same reason you can't see a tragedy in more than one sitting. I think that the pure novel is too tense for the reader to stop in the middle and take it up the next day.

INTERVIEWER

Because television and movies and magazines are under the codes you have spoken of, I take it you feel the writer of the pure novel is almost obligated to write freely.

SIMENON

Yes. And there is a second reason why he should be. I think that now, for reasons probably political, propagandists are trying to create a type of man. I think the novelist has to show man as he is and not the man of propaganda. And I do not mean only political propaganda; I mean the man they teach in the third grade of school, a man who has nothing to do with man as he really is.

INTERVIEWER

What is your experience with conversion of your books for movies and radio?

SIMENON

These are very important for the writer today. For they are probably the way the writer may still be independent. You asked me before whether I ever change anything in one of my novels commercially. I said, 'No.' But I would have to do it without the radio, television, and movies.

INTERVIEWER

You once told me Gide made a helpful practical suggestion about one of your novels. Did he influence your work in any more general way?

SIMENON

I don't think so. But with Gide it was funny. In 1935 my publisher said he wanted to give a cocktail party so we could meet, for Gide had said he had read my novels and would like to meet me. So I went, and Gide asked me questions for more than two hours. After that I saw him many times, and he wrote to me almost every month and sometimes oftener until he died – always to ask questions. When I went to visit him I always saw my books with so many notes in the margins that they were almost more Gide than Simenon. I never asked him about them; I was very shy about it. So now I will never know.

INTERVIEWER

Did he ask you any special kinds of questions?

SIMENON

Everything, but especially about the mechanism of my – may I use the word? it seems pretentious – creation. And I think I know why he was interested. I think Gide all his life had the dream of being the creator instead of the moralist, the philosopher. I was exactly his opposite, and I think that is why he was interested.

I had the same experience two years later with Count Keyserling. He wrote to me exactly the same way Gide did. He asked me to visit him at Darmstadt. I went there and he asked me questions for three days and three nights. He came to see me in Paris and asked me more questions and gave me a commentary on each of my books. For the same reason. Keyserling called me an '*imbécile de génie*'.

INTERVIEWER

I remember you once told me that in your commercial novels you would sometimes insert a non-commercial passage or chapter.

SIMENON

Yes, to train myself.

INTERVIEWER

How did that part differ from the rest of the novel?

SIMENON

Instead of writing just the story, in this chapter I tried to give a third dimension, not necessarily to the whole chapter, perhaps to a room, to a chair, to some object. It would be easier to explain it in the terms of painting.

INTERVIEWER

How?

SIMENON

To give the weight. A commercial painter paints flat; you can put your finger through. But a painter – for example, an apple by Cézanne has weight. And it has juice, everything, with just three strokes. I tried to give to my words just the weight that a stroke of Cézanne's gave to an apple. That is why most of the time I use concrete words. I try to avoid abstract words, or poetical words, you know, like 'crepuscule', for example. It is very nice, but it gives nothing. Do you understand? To avoid every stroke which does not give something to this third dimension.

On this point, I think that what the critics call my 'atmosphere' is nothing but the impressionism of the painter adapted to literature. My childhood was spent at the time of the Impressionists and I was always in the museums and exhibitions. That gave me a kind of sense of it. I was haunted by it.

INTERVIEWER

Have you ever dictated fiction, commercial or any other?

SIMENON

No. I am an artisan; I need to work with my hands. I would like to carve my novel in a piece of wood. My characters – I would like to have them heavier, more three-dimensional. And I would like to make a man so that everybody, looking at him, would find his own problems in this man. That's why I spoke about poetry, because this goal looks more like a poet's goal than the goal of a novelist. My characters have a profession, have characteristics; you know their age, their family situation, and everything. But I try to make each one of those characters heavy, like a statue, and to be the brother of everybody in the world. And what makes me happy is the letters I get. They never speak about my beautiful style; they are the letters a man would write to his doctor or his psychoanalyst. They say, 'You are one who understands me. So many times I find myself in your novels.' Then there are pages of their confidences; and they are not crazy people. There are crazy people too, of course; but many are on the contrary people who – even important people. I am surprised.

INTERVIEWER

Early in your life did any particular book or author especially impress you?

SIMENON

Probably the one who impressed me most was Gogol. And certainly Dostoyevsky, but less than Gogol.

INTERVIEWER

Why do you think Gogol interested you?

SIMENON

Maybe because he makes characters who are just like everyday people but at the same time have what I called a few minutes ago the third dimension I am looking for. All of them have this poetic aura. But not the Oscar Wilde kind – a poetry which comes naturally, which is there, the kind Conrad has. Each character has the weight of sculpture, it is so heavy, so dense.

INTERVIEWER

Dostoyevsky said of himself and some of his fellow writers that they came out from Gogol's *The Overcoat*, and now you feel you do too.

SIMENON

Yes. Gogol. And Dostoyevsky.

INTERVIEWER

When you and I were discussing a particular trial while it was going on a year or two ago, you said you often followed such newspaper accounts with interest. Do you ever in following them saying to yourself, 'This is something I might some day work into a novel'?

SIMENON

Yes.

INTERVIEWER

Do you consciously file it away?

SIMENON

No. I just forget I said it might be useful some day, and three or four or ten years later it comes. I don't keep a file.

INTERVIEWER

Speaking of trials, what would you say is the fundamental difference, if there is any, between your detective fiction – such as the Maigret which you finished a few days ago – and your more serious novels?

SIMENON

Exactly the same difference that exists between the painting of a painter and the sketch he will make for his pleasure or for his friends or to study something.

INTERVIEWER

In the Maigrets you look at the character only from the point of view of the detective?

SIMENON

Yes. Maigret can't go inside a character. He will see, explain, and understand; but he does not give the character the weight the character should have in another of my novels.

INTERVIEWER

So in the eleven days spent writing a Maigret novel your blood pressure does not change much?

SIMENON

No. Very little.

INTERVIEWER

You are not driving the detective to the limit of his endurance.

SIMENON

That's it. So I only have the natural fatigue of being so many hours at the typewriter. But otherwise, no.

INTERVIEWER

One more question, if I may. Has published general criticism ever in any way made you consciously change the way you write? From what you say I should imagine not.

SIMENON

Never. I have a very, very strong will about my writing, and I will go my way. For instance, all the critics for twenty years have said the same thing: 'It is time for Simenon to give us a big novel, a novel with twenty or thirty characters.' They do not understand. I will never write a big novel. My big novel is the mosaic of all my small novels. You understand?